Innocence Lost

Join us here to learn about our books: https://woodenhookstudios.com

Edited by: Alane Kochems
Copyright © 2024 Wooden Hook Studios

ISBN: 979-8-9900459-3-4 (print)
ISBN: 979-8-9900459-4-1 (e-book)

Innocence Lost

Book One of The Corpus Ad Astra Adventure

By

Eric C. Holtgrefe

Wooden Hook Studios

Also by Eric C. Holtgrefe

***

Love and Honor in the Felgenland

For Jonathan and Elizabeth, you are OP!
And for my wife, your love and support made this possible!

Genesis 1:1

"Innocence, Once Lost, Can Never Be
Regained. Darkness, Once Gazed Upon,
Can Never Be Lost."

— John Milton

Part One: Arrival

I

"Well, I uh, had a black cat walk over a broken mirror under the lunar module ladder, and nothing bad's happened yet."

— Astronaut Ken Mattingly

Location: L 98-59 near space at three light
months from arrival
June 1, 2450, Anno Domini or 01.06.12450
Standard

"Take me out to the ball game. Take me out with the crowd…" the song played over the loudspeakers inside the giant wheel of the *Aquila*. The wheel slowly rotated around the thin metallic ribbon connecting the two gigantic oval hulls. The gray metallic front of the *Aquila* was dotted with hatches and doors for all the vehicles the expedition would need. The *Aquila's* back contained multiple reactors, thrusters, engines, and other motors to move the gigantic fifteen-hundred-meter spaceship. The *Aquila* pointed rearward first, allowing its massive fusion engines to slow the ship down from light speed.

"Buy me some peanuts and crackerjack. I don't care if I never get back…"

The large wheel continued to rotate, simulating Earth's gravity inside. In the top center section of the wheel was the compartment which housed the decanter nexus. The nexus was where all of the equipment to decant the consciousnesses of the crew into their bodies resided. For almost thirty-five years, the crew had been in harmonic stasis. The corporation had "rolled out" everyone's consciousness into the quantum archive to save on supplies, resources, and human sanity. The *Aquila* had been launched from the Corpus Ad Astra docks near the Asteroid Belt-Moon Lagrange point four—ABML4.

"Let me root, root, root for the home team. If they don't win, it's a shame…"

As the ship closed in on its destination, the star system L 98-59, the only entity aware of the mission's success or failure, was an artificial intelligence or AI. The Dedicated Astro-colonial Database Design Intelligence (evolution) Echo or DADDIE maintained runtime throughout the long years between Luna and L 98-59.

DADDIE performed the thousands of daily processes that kept the ship functioning. CAA had specifically coded and built DADDIE to ensure the success of this mission.

"For it's one, two, three strikes, you're out. At the old ball game!"

DADDIE crawled the networks daily, monitoring the corridors, cargo bays, hydroponics labs, and shuttle bays. The *Aquila* had been moving at a fraction of the speed of light for almost thirty years, even though through the wonders of time dilation, thirty-five years had passed to the observers across the universe. For all of that time, DADDIE had watched—both inside the ship and out—for all manner of dangers while the crew remained in a harmonic stasis. The speakers stopped their music.

"Ah, I love opening day," DADDIE said. DADDIE activated the dust-covered cameras inside the decanter nexus so he could see the action. In approximately three thousand microseconds, the system would decant the first human on the expedition. In the 12060s, humanity discovered God's secret: human consciousness was a particle wave. Using the proper resonance, humans could remove the consciousness from a human and put it in a different body. After discovering the consciousness wave, humans were no longer chained to one body; they could live forever. However, the process wasn't perfect even four centuries later.

"How's the coaching staff? You all ready?" DADDIE asked the med bots assembled in the decanter nexus. DADDIE checked the medical sensors on the decanter table and the data needle that extended into the brain's central cortex of the body (or "shell") on the table. Shell rejection was rare, and consciousness death even more infrequent in the one hundred and twenty-fifth century. Still, DADDIE's programming wouldn't allow him to take any chances, especially regarding human life. Plus, he wanted the best of luck for this moment as the entire expedition's chances hung in the balance. As an AI, luck was all about numbers, statistics, odds, and probabilities. The odds for the expedition would go up or down based on this first decant. If successful, the expedition's chances for success would increase. The med bots merely looked up from their stations to the camera. Their programming didn't include having a bedside manner.

"And the opening pitch…" DADDIE said to himself.

If the decant failed, the consciousness could die. Now, so close to the L 98-59 system, DADDIE needed humans to aid him in preparing for the expedition landing on the planet. DADDIE could perform without the crew. However, performing the millions of activities needed would severely strain the quantum matrices inside the constellation that comprised DADDIE and the *Aquila*.

At one hundred microseconds, the nexus's data bridge gave a confirm signal, followed by the med bots' ready signal at T-minus ninety. Cameras were at the ready, and the med bots looked like two tiny armies prepared for battle. Between them lay the shell of a young man, complete with functioning organs. The shell had cream-colored skin, dark black hair, and two blue eyes. A light sheet covered the body from mid-torso to its toes.

"Come on, no dead balls…" DADDIE said. If DADDIE could breathe, he'd be holding his breath right now. Finally, at T-minus five seconds, the harmonic servos on the data needle fired, beginning the injection of what was the Vanguard team lead, Jason Dikkert, into his body. At T equals zero, his consciousness entirely resided in the body. DADDIE had to wait to see if the consciousness wave would harmonize with the shell.

This shell was very special to Jason. It was his original body. His parents, Galathea and Raistlin Dikkert, were among the lucky few who had won the birth lottery on Earth. Earth was overcrowded, nearing eighty billion people, and the birth lottery was the answer. Jason was born on the first of the Sixth Month in standard year twelve thousand, three hundred and eighty-four. Like that day fifty-nine years ago, this was Jason's birthday again.

Watching the process, DADDIE said, "A nice high fastball, this one's going to go all the way…"

DADDIE remembered that Brigadier General Gregory Stilton Body had selected Jason as a member of the Vanguard after Jason had crypto-proton bombed his resume into the Corpus Ad Astra corporate HR matrix. DADDIE also recalled the shocked transmission of the AI functionary who, despite the entity's best efforts, couldn't select any resume in the matrix—except Jason's. General Body laughed and told CAA's Chief Executive Intelligence, the Machine Overmind Megacorporate Intelligence or MOMI, that she needed to "hire that punk on the spot." MOMI processed the petition and then ran the projections. CAA hired Jason five thousand-four-hundred-sixty-two seconds after the CAA Cybersecurity AI, CUSTODIAN, discovered the proton bombing. The general made Jason the expedition's Vanguard Lead after Jason passed his probationary period six months later.

"Okay, Daddy, why can't I move my legs," Jason asked, his eyes popping open.

"Is this because I dropped my archive of *Minefield* into the constellation? Because if that is the reason, I am *not* sorry!"

DADDIE brought up the holoprojector and cast his avatar near Jason's bed. DADDIE appeared as a nondescript middle-aged United States-ian man wearing a ball cap with the letters CAA on the front, an indistinct sports jersey, and a pair of "dad jeans" with some sports shoes.

"Hey, Buddy," DADDIE said. "No worries. The med bot doctor says you need more time to bond to those neurons, but you should be running the bases in no time! Welcome to the majors."

Jason smiled and replied, "But Daddy, these are my 'real' legs. I've already learned how to walk with them once! I don't have time just to lay here."

"Look, Buddy, Mommy and I are proud of you, but you haven't been on those legs for almost thirty-five years. You know how the game is played. When you sit on the bench for a while, the coach gets a little nervous about putting you in the game. Especially when I play you on opening day in front of all the fans. We're all looking for the big plays today."

"I know better, Daddy," Jason said as he smiled, "Mommy is not proud of me." Despite her name, MOMI was not the nurturing type.

"Come on, Buddy, let's not go there. Mommy has her work and is happy you are helping her out. You're the first up at bat. Now, let's see how those legs are doing. The med bot doc will give them a tiny tap with its needle. Go on, doc."

The small medical robot at the foot of the decanter table quickly jabbed a dull needle at Jason's big toe. The needle wasn't intended to break the skin but rather to send a source of stimuli from Jason's toes to his brain.

"Ouch!" Jason said with a frantic start. The young man began to wiggle his body. All the musculature moved until it came to his knees and lower legs. DADDIE could see Jason's shell still needed time as his calves and feet weren't responding to Jason's brain.

"Good job, Buddy, a nice base hit. I told you all you need is time," DADDIE said.

"Well, Daddy, since I have nothing but time, can you tell me when Greg is getting decanted? We had a bet on who'd be first, and—well—he needs to pay up."

"Hey Buddy, you know the batting lineup, heck you wrote it. The general isn't expected to decant for at least a few more standard weeks. Right now, only the Xeno Corps is at bat. Con Sec Corps is on deck with Corporate Corps and the general decanting after Josie. Remember, sluggers always go after the bases are loaded."

"What? Corporate, mother's favorites, last!" Jason

said sarcastically. "Say it ain't so, Daddy!"

"Well, Buddy, you know how the routine goes. When you're the head coach, you get to pick the lineup. After all, you're hoping for a stellar season. You've got to keep those box prices high," DADDIE said with a smile on his avatar's face. "And hey! Don't let Mommy catch you calling Corporate her favorites, either! She'll assign you to dishes and garbage duty, and you won't be able to go hot-sledding with the rest of the Vanguard when we get planet-side."

"Wait! Mommy is here?" Jason asked.

"Buddy, you know better. Do you think Mommy will let a billion Xenon-class-credit expedition like this go driving around the Milky Way without her highness in the back seat —back seat driving? She'll be sitting in the owner's box, taking notes, like she always does," DADDIE responded.

"Come on, Daddy, you're pulling my leg!" Jason said. "Where is she now? You think she heard me?"

"Mommy is sleeping now. We won't wake her until we set up the quantum relay—all the better for you, Buddy, as you've run your mouth quite a bit. But don't worry, dear old Daddy will keep it between us men. I don't want to lose my rookie phenom," DADDIE said with a wink. "Besides, Mommy will have enough to deal with when Corporate wakes up. They will be running to her on a second-by-second basis. I am glad the Xeno and Con Sec Corps will follow the prearranged mission plans."

"Really?! I forgot to ask you about the planets in orbit around L 98-59. Is there confirmed water? What about moons and asteroids?" In his excitement, Jason hopped off the decanting table and kept his balance. Jason stretched his body to his full one hundred and seventy-seven-centimeter height.

"Hey Buddy, look at you! I knew you were ready for the majors," DADDIE said with some astonishment and a little pride.

"Oh yeah!" Jason said, flexing his legs. "Is that a

decanting record? I must have set a record; tell me, Daddy!"

"Well, officially, you set a ship record. Your record is fifteen minutes and forty-seven seconds from needle to floor," DADDIE replied.

"Oh yeah, beat that, Greg! I can feel your fifty Krypton-creds transferring into my bank account right now!" Jason shouted in triumph. He started gyrating like a rock star. Jason's leg began to spasm, and for a second, the young man looked like he was about to convulse and fall on his butt. One of the hovering med bots quickly stabilized Jason, applying dermal patches to both his thighs simultaneously.

"Whoa, I am going to go find my bunk," Jason said, and then he looked down at his feet, muttering, "And some clothes too…"

"Hey, Buddy, no biggie, and before I forget… Happy birthday twice over," DADDIE said.

"No way, today is the first of Six? What is the year?" Jason asked as he grabbed the sheet from the table and wrapped the cloth around his waist, forming a rough kilt.

"The twelve thousand four hundred and fiftieth standard year," DADDIE said.

"Okay, Daddy, how do I look for a fifty-nine-year-old?" Jason asked.

"Like a kid who isn't a day over twenty-four, now get out of here, Buddy," DADDIE said, "get some clothes on before Mommy's friends see you! They'd be scandalized!"

Jason trotted down one of the corridors to the primary habitat and outside the view of DADDIE's cameras. At some point, DADDIE would send a maintenance bot to dust and check the holoprojectors so DADDIE could project his avatar into the Hab. The odds were low that DADDIE would be needed in the Hab, and Jason could have some privacy. DADDIE scratched out some odds and figured Jason could return here if he needed DADDIE's help.

DADDIE checked the recharge time on the

decanting table. The table's programming showed another twenty hours, thirty-five minutes, and forty-two seconds until it decanted the next crew member. DADDIE could shorten that time, if necessary, but that would bring down the odds of success for that unfortunate soul.

"Well, that was a great first at-bat. Now, we have to play the long game; that's the one that leads to that Cinderella season," DADDIE said to the room and the med bots. The handful of bots raised and lowered their cameras—a pantomime of a human's nod. DADDIE's avatar shrugged before he turned off the holoprojector. The color commentators always needed to switch to commercials before they bored the audience.

DADDIE left the nexus and floated virtually through the various *Aquila* systems. He checked Engineering; the reactor was running at a steady one hundred percent. Years ago, the ship had rotated and reversed direction. Now, the engines were powering the deceleration from a high percentage of light speed. The barely one-tenth amount of gravity that could be felt on the ship resulted from the remaining momentum the ship had accumulated. DADDIE checked the navigation readouts. The *Aquila* was on track to rendezvous with one of the large gas giants that survey telescopes had identified as L 98-59h for a gravity-assisted deceleration. In another few weeks, the ship's telescopes would confirm what the long-range surveys had seen, and DADDIE would calculate the ephemeris data. Once the expedition had determined one or more habitable planets, they would evaluate the candidates and decide on which they would settle. As the settlement progressed, any further habitable planets would gain starter outposts. The corporation would maximize profits from this venture by selling as much of the system as possible. L 98-59 had been on the auction block in the colonies futures market. The general and MOMI had won the bidding for the rights to the system. After the win, CAA telescopes were aimed at L 98-59, and the company launched its survey drones. The quantum relay-related data pointed to potential habitable planets, and CAA had begun preparations for the colonization expedition. CAA AIs and humans assembled rosters and matched skill sets to the proper portfolios.

"Hey Daddy," Jason called out in the Hab, "what is there to eat?"

"One second, Buddy," DADDIE said. "I hadn't planned on firing up the projectors in the Hab yet."

DADDIE sent a request to the maintenance bots. The four-centimeter spider-like robots began climbing across Hab space to clean DADDIE's cameras and projectors. The *Aquila's* internal environment was not particularly dirty; the air scrubbers took care of that. However, as an energy-saving measure, the air scrubbers had been running on intermittent and low power for thirty-five years.

"There are some really terrible options in the vending machines here, Daddy," Jason said as he rooted through the galley. As the cameras came online, DADDIE saw Jason wearing a white t-shirt with a CAA logo and dark gray athletic pants with deck socks.

"Hang on a second, Buddy, and I'll get the cook online. He can make you anything you want—as long as it's vegetarian," DADDIE said.

"You aren't selling me on vegetarian food," Jason said.

"All part of the deal when we planned the expedition, remember Buddy," DADDIE said. "The bots harvested today's food from the small hydroponics lab started a few months ago. There are no cows, pigs, or chickens alive on board. You know how that goes—no organics, so no meat. Even the fish aquaculture isn't ready yet. Therefore, no salmon or tilapia either."

"Sushi, I could go for some spicy salmon," Jason said, "or shrimp off a hibachi."

"Didn't you hear what I just said," DADDIE said crossly.

"I heard you, DADDIE. I didn't want to believe you," Jason said.

"Cook says he can whip up some cheese fries. How's that sound?" DADDIE asked.

"Meh, okay," Jason said. "After I get something to eat, how about a spacewalk?"

"Whoa, Buddy, you're still not rated for space today. I need twenty-four hours of you walking around in that body before I am willing to allow those newly bonded neurons out in the radiation of space," DADDIE said.

"Fine, then what's there to do? What needs to be done?" Jason asked. DADDIE projected into the galley cafeteria.

"Mind if I join you?" DADDIE asked.

"No, go ahead," Jason said. He paced to where the cook had ejected a plastic box from the small auto-kitchen. Retrieving his cheese fries, Jason walked over to a bench and sat down. DADDIE's avatar joined Jason at the table, and to an untrained observer, the scene was of two men sitting and eating.

"Well, there is checking the sleds in the lander bay," DADDIE said.

"Pass," Jason said, his mouth full of food.

"Navigation needs a good once over. Someone should check the consoles. I'm reading a solid seal on the bridge, but you know how that goes," DADDIE said.

"Okay," Jason said, grabbing another cheesy fry and popping it into his mouth. "I can do that."

DADDIE's avatar looked like he took a deep breath. Jason stared at the projection and said, "What?"

"I've got one more task, and you're not going to like this one," DADDIE said.

"Okay, I'm willing to do whatever. I'm sure the entertainment matrix isn't running, so I'd just be sitting around anyway," Jason said.

"The air scrubber filters need cleaning," DADDIE

said, waiting for Jason to complain.

"Oh, come on, can't a bot do that?" Jason asked.

"Yes, but not as efficiently as a human. Besides, the things are full of gunk, having been given only light maintenance for over thirty years," DADDIE said.

"I…" Jason said, getting ready to reject the proposal.

"Hey, you wanted to be up first. The first one up gets all the nasty tasks. That is the rule," DADDIE said, interrupting Jason.

"Fine," Jason said. "It's a good thing Greg is paying me for the privilege of cleaning."

DADDIE smiled, that was Jason, always Mister Bright-side.

"Thanks, Buddy," DADDIE said. "I'm glad we had this little chat."

"You're welcome, Daddy. Say, who is decanting next? I had Martha on my scorecard, but with, yours truly, up and running, I figured you'd probably have changed the order around."

"Yes, Martha's next. I figure it is fifty-fifty odds that you'll probably break something on that shell of yours, and she'll need to fix it."

"Sweet," Jason said. "She gives me all the cool space bandages when I get boo-boos."

DADDIE smiled. "Well, I'm using your roster, so be prepared. Li Mei will decant after that, and she's gunning for your job."

Jason smiled and flexed. "Bring it. No one can match my awesomeness."

DADDIE nodded and said, "Good, that's what I want to hear. If everyone has that attitude, we'll do just fine, never mind what Lloyd's of London said."

"Were the odds that bad?" Jason asked.

"Yup, millions to one odds, almost as bad as the odds for Zeta Reticuli," DADDIE said.

"Oh! I forgot about ZR," Jason said excitedly. "I

wonder if they found aliens there?"

"That's something Salvatore Romano would have to tell you," DADDIE said.

"Who's that," Jason asked.

"Karl's son-in-law, he's a big-time alien archaeologist. He's a regular Tsoukalos or von Däniken," DADDIE said.

"Okay, I don't know the reference, but if they discover little gray men, that'd be so cool," Jason said.

"I don't know, Buddy, more advanced cultures tend to win the ball game," DADDIE said. "Now, enough talk, time to clean those filters."

"Aw, okay," Jason said. He stood up and deposited the garbage into the recycle chute, where the recycling system would break down the tray at a molecular level and build the tray material into whatever would be needed. DADDIE flashed from sitting to standing, giving Jason the sternest face he could manage. Jason slunk off like a little kid forced to make his bed.

"Curiosity is the essence of human existence. 'Who are we? Where are we? Where do we come from? Where are we going?'... I don't know. I don't have any answers to those questions. I don't know what's over there around the corner. But I want to find out."

— Astronaut Gene Cernan

Location: L 98-59 near space, at two and a half
light months from arrival
14.06.12450 Standard

"How many in the shell? How many casualties?" were Grisholm "Griff" Tomkins's first words as his eyes popped open.

"Listen, Chief, take a breather. You've been in the archive for thirty-five years," DADDIE responded.

"Don't blow smoke up my keester, Daddy. There's been an accident, hasn't there? Why am I awake otherwise?!"

"Calm down, Chief. The Construction and Security Corps is just getting revived. No one's dying. We're up to a skeleton crew right now. Martha just defrosted the operating room yesterday. We're good for a little while, so relax, take a breather!" DADDIE said.

"Relax, my double duo-centenarian backside," Griff said. "Relaxing is just when old mister fate is waiting for you! There'll be a radiation leak in a reactor or a micro meteor that smashes a habitation module. If any of that noise isn't enough, a xenomorph—or maybe just a space mermaid—will show up. Then I'll either run to Engineering or Medical trying to put synthetics or organics back together before the engines are lost or the reactor goes critical."

DADDIE changed the subject and said, "Well, gee, Griff, for a two-hundred-and-twenty-eight-year-old, you don't look a day over twenty-nine. You age pretty well there, Chief."

"Don't you go doing that, using my *real* age again? Unlike the general, most of these folks are just baby chicks compared to me, except for Martha, Merlie, Karl, Josie, and Greg, and they're the cautious ones..." Griff was about to go on when a svelte black woman came in along with Jason Dikkert.

"There he is, my grumpy little man. How are you

doin', baby?" the woman said, sounding more like a grandma than someone who looked in their twenties. She was one-hundred-and-seventy-three centimeters tall, with velvet black hair, almond brown eyes, and ebony color skin. The two looked on at Griff. He stood up to his one-hundred-and-eighty-five centimeters, the thin sheet becoming a toga. Martha and Jason could see the skin underneath the toga, giving Griff a lean look. His muscles were visible under the shell's ebony skin. His deep brown eyes and obsidian hair set off his almost gaunt face.

"I'm fine, dear. No thanks to Daddy. He damn near gave me a decanter rejection arrhythmia," Griff said. Then he looked at Jason, saying, "Oh, and you brought him—the Little Rooster—no doubt he will start hollering about grabbing Greg, Karl, or Josie from their icebox. No, little man, that's my answer."

"Griff, or rather Doctor Tomkins, I am very disappointed in you," Jason said. After all, Greg would want you to pull him out immediately. Lots of things need his chop on them, and then there is the matter of getting the purser's station online. Folks need some sweet, sweet credits."

"Oh, hell no, and that's my final answer," Griff said with irritation, "and don't you call me Doctor Tomkins. I knew you were up to something when you volunteered to help me program the decanter algorithms."

"You're just jealous. I have the ship's record for getting off the decanter table. Plus, you knew I promised to cut you in for half when Greg paid up on our little bet," Jason said with a smile.

"Listen, Little Rooster, when that old guard dog gets up, he's liable to tear your little tail feathers off," Griff said sternly, looking at Jason. Both men locked eyes and stood there with grim faces, but only momentarily. Jason started laughing, and then Griff did, too.

"I suppose you were the first?" Griff said, chuckling.

"Yup, just like you said I'd be," Jason said. "I can't wait to see the look on Greg's face when he asks who beat him out of the archive."

"Now you boys gonna get your butts whupped by Greg when he finds out," Martha said after watching the interplay.

Martha and Griff considered Jason like a son. They met after CAA hired Jason, and he started training to be a part of the Vanguard. When Greg promoted the kid, Jason began spending long hours with Martha and Griff. Working together, Jason was awed by the couple, and his affection for Martha and Griff grew as they mentored and supported Jason through all the long hours of expedition provisioning. Griff and Martha became Jason's surrogate parents in many ways—as his real parents were light years away on their expedition.

"Well, what did you name her?" Griff asked.

"Griff, honey, give me a kiss first; I haven't seen you in thirty-five years," Martha said, stepping in between Jason and her husband.

"Okay, baby," Griff said, giving his wife a quick kiss on her lips, then looking to Jason.

"Oh, that's not how you will treat your head nurse!" Martha said, pulling Griff in close and kissing him more passionately. Jason looked away, his cheeks reddening.

"Listen here, baby. We all know you ain't no little candy striper; you a big old doctor. My doctor sugar better run along now so I can talk to the Little Rooster here. I bet he has been putting his Little Rooster scratches all over my beautiful new world. You better not be naming anything on my forty acres there, Little Rooster!" Griff said playfully to his wife and Jason.

"Well, Doctor Sugar gotta get her behind to the OR, just in case someone's fixin' to break a nail or something. Bye-bye now, boys, and you too, Daddy," Martha said, sashaying alluringly away from Griff and out of the decanter nexus.

"Come on, Pops! Get some clothes on, and let's go to Navigation. I'll show you what we've got in the system," Jason said.

"I ain't eighty on the outside anymore, Little Rooster! So's when I get some pants on, I'm fixin' to rocket down to navigation and leave you in my afterburner, provided Daddy's going to let me go," Griff said, looking for all his years like a kid asking a parent to go and play.

"Come on, Chief. You know the post-decanting drills, heck, you wrote them!" DADDIE said.

"Right, let me see: After the subject has had sufficient time to adjust, check the shell for neuromotor reflex… OUCH!" Griff said as the med bot poked him with a needle, "Ouch, that hurt you little hunk of plastic… Now, where was I? After the neuromotor reflex, a qualified doctor or decant-level tech should inspect the subject for evidence of any consciousness drift, mental breakdowns, or neuroses. Sound about right, Daddy?" Griff asked.

"Practically textbook, but you know the rest. I have to check for degradation of the consciousness," DADDIE said. "Are you ready?"

"Of course," Griff said. "Go on and do your job there, Daddy. I have to go to Navigation with the Little Rooster here and make sure my forty acres are secured."

"Okay, Chief, easy question: how did you meet Greg?" DADDIE asked.

Looking from DADDIE to Jason, Griff said, "You remember the Gambian conflict?"

"Sure do, Chief," DADDIE said. "The Gambia wanted to retain its independence against the Greater Sino-Russian confederacy. What does that have to do with you and Greg?"

"I was a small hospital director in Senegal, I ran a unit of surgeons in the non-profit 'Fellowship of Humanist Caregivers,' and the FHC was as close as I ever got to charity work. I was there to do some personal research on infectious disease," Griff said.

"Okay, where does Greg fit in?" DADDIE said.

"I was working late one night when this U.S. military team came in, carrying one of their own. They kicked in my door and laid their comrade down on the operating table, getting blood all over my nicely scrubbed and cleaned OR," Griff said. "The one says to me, 'The major got hit! He was drawing enemy fire away from our position; you got to fix him up, doc!'"

"Cool," Jason said.

"Not cool, Little Rooster!" Griff snapped. "I told that jackboot I wasn't going to help him or any of his thugs. I told him to patch up the guy themselves."

Griff started laughing for a moment, startling both DADDIE and Jason.

"Then Greg, who was the major, slurs out, 'Sergeant, burn down this place and lock the obstinate horse's ass in here with some gasoline! He isn't a doctor apparently, since he's forgotten the Hippocratic Oath!'"

Griff laughed even harder as Jason and DADDIE stared at him.

Finally, Griff continued, "I started laughing and told him he wasn't that great of a soldier for getting shot, but I was a great surgeon. I'd put him back together, not because of an oath, but because I would get a nice donation for my clinic from the U.S. Government for my services. I started to clean the wound he had—and that bullet trauma was bad! I gave him a local and then started prepping anesthesia. When I dropped the mask over Greg's face, he said, 'You're not getting paid if I get a nasty scar!' He slumped over like someone turned off his lights. Meanwhile, his boys were getting jumpy, but I started focusing on the work, and the next thing I knew, there was a helicopter out front and a ton of military. Then, like a flash, they all loaded up and took off."

"Well, what happened then?!" Jason demanded. DADDIE smiled, letting Jason ask the questions he wanted.

"I got paid, Little Rooster," Griff said with a smile.

"Yeah, yeah, but what about Greg?" Jason said.

"Greg shows up a few weeks later. He pulled some strings and got me a position at Johns Hopkins—working on the decanter table research. You have to understand. Before the table, decanting was a messy business. I put twenty years into that project, becoming the director of the whole endeavor! That's where I met Martha," Griff said with a wistful smile.

"But what about Greg?" Jason said.

"Oh, he and I were like pen pals for years," Griff said, "Then after Titan, he brought me over to the private sector. All the good docs were leaving Hopkins for the real money. I followed over, and the next thing I knew, I was elbow-deep in cybernetics classes. Back in the day, Little Rooster, we just did what was needed, and the corporation got along with 'every hand at the pump,' as Greg likes to say. After that, Greg and I became fast friends. Now, Daddy, am I good to get out of here?"

"Yep, Chief, you're fit for duty there. Now, you two go out and play, but keep the noise down. Mommy is sleeping," DADDIE said, "And Griff, one last thing, there is a jumpsuit in the closet; Martha knew you'd need some clothes."

"Game on, Little Rooster," Griff said. Griff walked over, holding the toga with one hand, and yanked the closet open with the other.

He quickly started pulling on the jumpsuit as Jason whooped and took off down the corridor. Griff pulled the zipper up, closing the suit around him as he shouted and ran after Jason.

DADDIE computed that there was a one in five chance of one or both men getting injured in their race to Navigation.

Griff raced behind Jason. He was close, about a meter behind Dikkert. Both men turned the corner, and Griff caught Jason by executing an inside turn. They both ran until they had to slow near Navigation. Slowing down, Griff touched the outside of the hatch first.

"Not bad for an old man, eh, Rooster," Griff asked.

"Not bad, but not good either," Jason said with a smile, "I went easy on you since this is your first day decanted."

"Uh huh," Griff said as he punched the codes to enter Navigation. The door opened, and Jason moved to the main navigation console. He brought up a hologram of the planet L 98-59f, which he called Aurora Dawn.

"Look, I've pinned a bunch of places on the holographic map on Aurora Dawn. They're all open and free of any names," Jason said, pointing to the world.

"I see," Griff said, looking on in amazement at the map below. Clouds swirled across the sizable blue marble that was Aurora Dawn on the telescope's feed. Several archipelagos dotted the surface.

"Aurora Dawn, I like that, pan to the east. I'll take the easternmost one on the map," Griff said with a smile.

"Easternmost one what?" Jason asked.

"Easternmost Archipelago, Little Rooster," Griff said. "Plenty of space for Martha and me, plus I'll open a resort on my beautiful islands. I'll be a veritable spring break destination."

Jason laughed, "We'll see what the general says about that. In the meantime, want to name something?"

Griff picked up a tablet. He switched the view on the holograph to show the current medical readouts of all the crew. "Not right now, Jason."

"Checking to see if we're eating our vegetables," Jason asked.

"Something like that… I want to ensure that everyone is healthy and that Daddy won't spring something on me in a half hour."

Griff tapped away at the screen, examining the various vital signs. He then moved to another interface and pulled up a list of the multiple AIs on the ship.

"Now what? Checking to see if the bots are eating their vegetables," Jason asked.

"Yup, Little Rooster. When you make it as long as I have, you find it wise not to let the universe catch you unaware," Griff said. Griff checked the bot screen. Everything was running within its tolerances. He switched to the archive, checking the resonance of the nodes and the consciousnesses sleeping within.

"Well, I'll be," Griff said.

"Huh," Jason asked.

"Looks like I am on a vacation today, for once," Griff said. "There's no trouble anywhere I need to run off to."

"Gee, Griff, don't sound so upset," Jason said.

"I didn't mean it that way, Little Rooster," Griff said. "I was just so busy at provisioning. I am happy to be able to get a break."

"Okay, so tell me about the early days then. You said you'd tell me about it when we were sailing. It seems like you've got the time now," Jason said

"That I do… Hrm, the early days of CAA," Griff asked. Jason nodded.

"Well, I joined about twenty years after Greg had started the corporation. But what I remember from Karl, who joined five years after the corporation started, is that Greg, Patrick Murphy, and Tracie Chung founded CAA together. Greg was the company's 'big show' and face at the start, as he'd been on the Titan expedition and was widely known in space circles. Tracie was the 'biological show,' as she was a famous doctor involved in building clones. She was a big name in China, and the Chinese investors threw cold, hard credits at CAA because she was involved. She came with a lot of money too, as her husband was a big-time belt hauler big-shot," said Griff.

"What about Patrick?" Jason asked. "I only met him once, and he seemed nice."

"Patrick is the glue between Greg and Tracie, who don't get along all that well. Greg is an action guy. He doesn't tolerate a lot of indecision. Tracie is deeply analytical and doesn't move fast, but when she does, she's very self-assured, or as Greg says, 'self-righteous.' Greg and Tracie are like oil and water, and Patrick always plays peacemaker. That's why he's got the 'best expedition,' and I think Mommy likes him the best."

"Wait, Griff, Mommy *likes* someone," Jason asked. "You have to be pulling my leg."

"I know it sounds farfetched, but Mommy has some favorites. Folks like Merlie, Patrick, and even Josie seem to get more from Mommy than the rest of us. You mind your mouth and your manners around her, Little Rooster, 'cause Mommy will make you regret it if you don't."

"I keep hearing that," Jason said, like a moody teenager.

"You better believe it," Griff said. "I was there when Mommy was upset. Mommy gave one of our former employees a terrible severance; she did a burning rollout when she fired the employee and stuck the former employee in a terrible shell."

"Oh really, what did he do, Griff?"

"Corporate espionage. We had this cloning researcher named Lǐ Huìfēn, and he was with CAA for about five years. He was a great worker, always producing and always ahead of deadlines. Well, then Mommy gets wind of all his projects getting leaked. She does a total lockdown, and security starts sweeping through the residences. At first, they went after Karl, which pissed him off mightily, but then after a half hour or so, they let him go and focus on Huìfēn," Griff said.

"Then what happened," Jason asked.

"I don't know… No one does, really; Huìfēn went in to meet Mommy and never came out," Griff said.

"And?" Jason said.

"I don't know, but I heard from Merlie that Huìfēn got caught red-handed with CAA data. He was trying to do a dead drop with the data, especially as he thought the coast was clear, as Mommy suspected Karl. Turns out, Merlyna engineered the whole plot, which was good as Karl was pissed and had planned to disconnect Mommy…" Griff said but was interrupted by Jason.

"Wow, could he do that?" Jason asked.

"Yes, Little Rooster, if there is one human who can take down an AI, even one as tough as Mommy, it is Karl. Well, to finish the story, I heard from Merlyna that Huìfēn was taken by security to a decant table and had a burning roll out into a reject body. Then he was escorted off the CAA campus, and his shell was sold off to the second-hand market."

"Geez, I can see why everyone is so cautious around Mommy," Jason said, "What was CAA like when Greg ran the show? I heard he wasn't happy when the Solar Stock Exchange—the *SSX*—made him step down."

"CAA was a different beast back then," Griff said. "When I joined, we were deep in AI extra-solar discovery. We'd send out a probe a quarter to the near stars to see what we could see. It wasn't glamorous work, but it paid the bills. Other corporations used many of the probes we sent out to start their colonies. After Mommy took over, she changed direction and started assembling talent for the shell side of the business, working on getting better bodies and genes so we could go and settle some of the stars we had data on. We sent a probe almost a hundred years ago to L 98-59. I figured some of that data helped guide Mommy and Greg's decision to buy the star system."

"Were you there for the bidding," Jason asked.

"No Little Rooster, but Karl was. Karl said that Greg

and Mommy had gone into the auction all set to go in on another star. Greg saw the bid price and the lack of competition for L 98-59, and Mommy went with the play. I'm not sure why, and Karl isn't sure either. You'll need to ask him when he's out of the archive," Griff said. His stomach rumbled, and he stood up.

"Well, time to get some calories," Griff said, "I probably need to spend some time with Martha as well. You have fun here, and stay away from my islands!"

Jason nodded and said, "I have a cold one, Daddy's treat. I plan to examine the planet and name some important features."

"Sounds like a safe plan. I'll be seeing you," Griff said. Jason waved as he opened the beer on the edge of a console and began pulling from the bottle.

"Life as an astronaut in space is a very interesting one. There are things we all take for granted here on earth, like gravity, that can make things a bit challenging. One of the fun things about getting here is the zero gravity and floating around. But it also makes things very difficult."

— Astronaut Kevin A. Ford

"I can't believe you named that feature 'Cappy the Canyon.' There are a dozen name generators on this ship!" Li Mei Tsan said. "Now my yet unborn children are going to go to school and learn that Cappy the Canyon is the largest canyon on our planet of Aurora Dawn. Cappy is almost sixteen times the Kali Gandaki Gorge on Earth. Cappy, really?"

Like all belters, Li Mei Tsan stood several centimeters shorter than Jason. At one-hundred-fifty-four-centimeters tall, Jason looked like he towered over her. They both stood in one of the cavernous cargo bays on the wheel of the *Aquila*.

"What can I say, Li Mei? I was drunk!" Jason replied, "This whole name thing is not my fault. Daddy said I could drink some of 'Grandpa's Old Cough Medicine,' and I got hammered. I mean, I haven't had a drink in thirty-five years!"

"Cappy, that just breaks my heart. Now you're going to owe me. You have to help me set up the Kooya," Li Mei said with a small devilish smile. Her white teeth showed over her red lips and silver-colored skin. She brushed her dark violet and black hair with a small hand, extending the pause.

"Uh, the robot-death-merchant-kaiju-dragon thing?" Jason said, a slight look of terror on his face. "Um, no thanks! I heard the stories the techs were saying about that thing. The Kooya went on a rampage in Tokyo and killed like three hundred people."

"No, the Kooya didn't. Those *hu tu* techs were pulling your leg. The Cybernetic Undaunted Yokozuna Automaton or the 'cee' 'u' 'wye' 'a' is just a combat AI. The Kooya needs to start up and begin his downloads to advise Greg on the most strategic points on the planet. What happens if we land and a bunch of xenomorphs come up from the depths with a taste for human in their mouths?" Li Mei asked sinisterly. She said the ridiculous statement seriously, to watch as Jason started to worry. Li Mei was fifteen and the youngest of the expedition. Aside from being the youngest, she was from a large clan of spacers, the Tsan, who had settled most of the asteroid belt between Mars and Jupiter. Because of her heritage, Li Mei always seemed beyond her years in a way that astounded the older crew members.

"Man, you should see your face right now," Li Mei said with a big laugh. "You look like a Dark Space rookie caught between Ceres and Pallas with no navigation! The boy from Earth, man, did I have you going too!"

Jason laughed nervously, then smiled, taken aback, saying, "You were joking?"

Li Mei smiled and said, "Yes, I've been out among the 萤火虫 and never seen anything, just the stars."

"Yeah, what's it like, being a Dark Spacer?" Jason said.

"Lonely, generally, the women are the Dark Spacers, while the men do the mining. I'd love to say there is a lot of macho garbage, but my dad made me help him once, and I realized that being a Dark Space pilot is just easier," said Li Mei. "Mining requires a lot of upper body strength, and I've heard of women who've done the job, but I'll take the gees of a shuttle over the stress of a miner."

"But wait, I've seen the documentaries. You can get lost if you lose your instruments, and the certification test is supposedly really hard," Jason said.

"Yes, but I had trained since I was ten. My youngest Auntie and I made runs from Vesta to our base every quarter. Sometimes, she'd let me plot the navigation; other times, I'd take command as a pilot. The worst part isn't out in the 黑色空间, what we call the being out in the stars, but the rocks. All sorts of things can get you or your ship there."

"Wait! I have seen the casts about how the Tsan

dragged all sorts of crazy creatures out of rocks in the belt. The stuff you're talking about is like that, right?"

"Don't be absurd. My uncle found something in the belt. It turns out it was just a massive Tardigrade. Xenomorphs are just some cinematographer's imagination."

"Huh, a water bear. Maybe I'll go back to drinking and watching horror flicks again. You're always welcome. I don't think we had much time to hang out in provisioning," Jason said. While Jason was working with Griff and Martha to provision the *Aquila* for the journey, Li Mei had been part of an acquisitions team to grab much-needed raw materials from several of the larger asteroids in the belt. She and Jason had barely met before they were "rolled out" into the archive. Thankfully, in the quantum archive space, they had been subtly nudged into a collective node, and though unconscious, their minds had connected enough to become friends. That friendship was necessary, as Li Mei and Jason would rely on each other in the Vanguard. The Vanguard would become increasingly important as the ship flew closer to L 98-59f, Aurora Dawn.

Griff and Martha liked the name, and since neither Merlyna, Karl, Josie, nor Greg were decanted yet, Griff and Martha were as good as any authority to enforce the name. Some other names, however, might be less enforceable when one of the more senior members was corporeal.

The two youngsters moved over to the sixteen-meter-tall CUYA. The mechanoid looked like a robot crossed with a dragon and a kaiju from an old-time Japanese monster film. Li Mei opened a panel on the CUYA's leg and attached two tablets to the connection nodes on the leg. She handed a tablet to Jason, and they both began tapping away, attempting to take the bot out of its cold storage. Li Mei said as they sat there working, "I wonder how many others are on the expedition. I never got to see any rosters."

"Daddy said there were around three hundred members of the expedition. I suppose he has an exact count, but when I pressed him, I kept getting a 'come on Buddy, you don't want to know, do you?' response."

"Weird," Li Mei responded, "Why all the secrecy, I wonder?"

"Oh, that's easy," Jason said. "Lloyd's of London gave the expedition terrible odds of success, so Mommy took out a huge insurance policy for the expedition. The policy covers all cases like we get killed or don't succeed or even find the planet just can't support human life. I figured there would be the usual corporate-on-corporate espionage to sink the expedition since the Solar Colonial Council has been pushing hard to open up space, with the over-population of Earth and all."

"Growing up in the belt, we never talked about that. What is it like?" Li Mei asked.

"What? The birth policy? The overcrowding? The Earth?" Jason asked.

"The birth policy. I hear that they make people get rid of their babies. That children grow up completely alone."

"I don't know about all that. I was, obviously, an only child, but man, was I spoiled! I would have birthday parties where over three hundred people would show up! Some were family, some friends, and man—*the presents!*"

"Huh, even though I am part of a large clan, my family was small, and well, belters can't collect a ton of personal effects, so I seldom got presents for my birthday," Li Mei said.

"That's abuse! If you didn't get presents, what did you do that was special?" Jason asked.

"Well, my grandma always made my birthday special. She would float over from her pod, and she'd bring me long noodle soup and two red eggs," Li Mei said.

"Noodles and eggs?" Jason said, "That doesn't sound special at all."

"Oh, Jason, you don't understand. We belters wouldn't get either noodles or eggs all that often. These were genuine eggs from real chickens. We lived on food pastes and fungal cakes. Noodles and eggs were a real treat!"

Jason and Li Mei became quiet as they just tapped away at their tablets, checking the wires, circuits, and algorithms on the CUYA.

Li Mei stopped and asked, "Who built this AI? This is the most spaghetti-coded mess I've ever seen! There is no modern programming discipline, and this Kooya is a high-assurance software system."

"Karl Holtzhauser—Merlyna's husband—built the Kooya," Jason said calmly.

"Oh! Karl," Li Mei replied, "I think I met him before we rolled out. Did you know him?"

"No, not really," Jason said, "Griff took me to meet him once. Karl just looked me up and down and told me to get out of his lab."

"What did Griff do?" Li Mei asked.

"Griff just laughed and said, 'He likes you, Little Rooster. He just doesn't want to admit that he does.'"

"What happened then?"

"I left the lab. There is no sense in making Karl mad. He's five hundred years old and married to Merlyna, making him tough and smart."

"I remember her. She's the one who was cutting the deals for the resources. She always paid my clan top dollar," Li Mei said, "I always felt like she was watching every penny and every line item of the contract."

"Yeah," Jason said, "you don't cross Merlyna. She was supposedly some super-spy assassin in a former life. I think she and Karl inspired that ancient spy film with that blonde dude and the dark-haired actress he married, you know *Mr. And Mrs. Jones?*"

"I never saw that one. I only got the belter vids out past Mars," Li Mei said.

"The Space-Chinese pulps?" Jason asked, "I always thought they were corny."

"You shut your mouth there, mister!" Li Mei said,

"We belters live for those vids! The romance between Jia Li and Yichen in 小行星带中的爱 was so moving that my mother and sisters were often brought to tears."

"They weren't the only ones brought to tears!" Jason said.

Li Mei's teasing countenance dropped for the first time, and then she smiled and said, "Okay, you got me, Jason!"

Jason was tempted to capitalize on his win, but as he was about to say something, the CUYA sputtered to life.

"Die! *Nihonese!* You n00bs better be OP, or I will send you all to respawn!" the CUYA said.

"Um, hi, Kooya," Li Mei said to the gigantic war bot.

"You look *Nihonese*, are you from Nihon? Are you OP? Are you ready to get sent to respawn?" the CUYA asked. Unlike other AIs, the CUYA's voice was harsh, mechanical, and relatively monotone.

"岩石和灰尘, no! I'm from the belt; before that, my family was from China. You want to kill the Japanese. I won't stand in your way," Li Mei said with a laugh.

"All I remember was being OP and making Tokyo get rekt. Then I guess the n00bs got good and must have sent me to respawn!" the CUYA said proudly.

"Well, now you're on our starship, and we're getting ready to land on Aurora Dawn, L 98-59f, to be exact," Li Mei said to the AI.

"Accessing the ship's constellation network, I see I will be playing on a new map. It's time to get good and learn all the places I can go OP on the n00bs. I will give the general a good place to put our spawn point. We're going to game this level hard so all the n00bs will recognize we are OP," The CUYA said to Jason and Li Mei.

"Uhh, what is he saying?" Jason asked Li Mei.

"No clue, just act friendly," Li Mei said with a smile.

"Um, hi, sir," Jason said, standing in the CUYA's line of vision.

"Are you a resident of Tokyo?" the CUYA asked.

"Um, no, I got to visit once, but I'm from Dryden, Michigan, in the Constitutional United States," Jason said.

"Are you OP?" the CUYA asked.

"Um, can you tell me what that means?" Jason asked.

"Over Powered, or Original Poster," the CUYA said, then asked, "Are you OP?"

Jason looked like a rabbit caught in a trap and mouthed the words 'help me' to Li Mei. She nodded her head in a 'yes.'

"Um, yes," Jason said.

"What is your gaming handle?" the CUYA asked. "Mine is CUYA+MAGN1F1C3NT. I am OP. Do you like to play *Soldiers of Duty, Doppler the Ferret,* or *ShaftCrafter*? I am first on the leaderboards. N00bs believe I am a god because I make them get rekt."

"Uh, Kooya, what are noobs?" Li Mei asked.

"Answer: n00b is an ancient slang for the gamer word 'newbie.' Although research is unclear when the term was used, Karl believes the word comes from when he was middle-aged in his original shell. He believes n00b is an acceptable term to call my opponents because Karl recognizes me as OP," the CUYA said.

"I used to play *Soldiers of Duty*, but I quit because I always got beat," Jason said.

"Ha ha, hah ha, n00b got rekt. I would send a friend request and have you on my squad, but I am OP!" the CUYA said with a weird mechanical laugh, "Go back to respawn and get good, n00b!"

Li Mei tried to suppress a laugh but said to Jason, "Go on, get out of here. I'll take care of the Kooya."

"Bye, Li Mei," Jason said. Then, to the CUYA, he said, "Goodbye, sir."

"Get out of here, n00b, before your n00b-ness makes me less OP," the CUYA said as Jason left.

"Kooya, we can't play now, but if you get that level

analysis done, I'll show you how to be a real miner in *ShaftCrafter*. I'm the most OP player in the belt!" Li Mei said.

"An OP girl, interesting!" the CUYA said, "what is your gamer handle?"

"SHIMMER_KITTY_LMT," Li Mei said.

"Checking," the CUYA said, "I do not have the current leaderboards. Are we connected to the quantum array?"

"No, but trust me, if we were, you'd be…" Li Mei said but was interrupted.

"PWNed?" the CUYA asked.

"Yes, big-time owned," Li Mei said, sounding out the letters.

"Perhaps we should spin up a matrix of *ShaftCrafter* and see who is OP?" the CUYA asked.

"No, work first. Besides, I don't want you to get wrecked by me, noob," Li Mei said with a laugh.

"I will give the general his data as fast as I can. I want to see who will get rekt. I am OP, n00b," the CUYA said. The automation's eyes went into standby-analysis mode. Li Mei watched the machine for a minute, then said, "Looks like I am going to need to brush up on my *ShaftCrafter*!"

*

DADDIE projected into the decanter nexus. He was tired, as tired as an AI could be. He'd be simulcasting his avatar in multiple places now and feeling the strain. Fortunately, his days as a single director were coming to a close. He looked at the shell lying under the sheet. The shell was female, with a one-hundred-and-sixty-seven-centimeter athletic form. Her hair was walnut-colored and flowed over her light golden-tanned shoulders.

DADDIE watched as the bots lined up, and the needle entered the shell's cranium. This was the first of the Corporate Corps that would be decanted.

"What's Greg doing?" Josie Moreno said as her green

eyes snapped open and flashed. "Still in the archive, Sport," DADDIE said, "Congrats, Jason put you ahead of Greg in the decant order."

"And you let him?" Josie said, her husky voice tinged with scorn, "You are slipping, Daddy. Do I need to check you for drift?"

"Now, Sport, I'm fine. I just let Jason think he got away with the rewrite. Besides, the kid's order wasn't all that better or worse than I had planned. I calculate that after other settlers arrive, Jason has a one-in-twenty-five chance of becoming the leader of the burgeoning colony. I can help that development by giving Jason a sense of agency."

"Already planning the demise of the senior staff, eh, Daddy?" Josie asked.

"Nah, Sport, I calculate the odds of being more than fifty-fifty that Mommy will reassign you or Greg, or the other senior staff, to some other project before we reach the golden ten-year mark," DADDIE said. Based on telescopic data and a small remote AI only expedition, ten years was a good indicator of success. Passing the ten-year mark was the final milestone. If the expedition had survived and thrived for ten years, the entire venture would have succeeded, and further colonization could start.

"When does Greg decant?" Josie asked. "There are plans I need to review with him, especially since Mommy is probably still sleeping."

"He's on the docket right behind you. We'll begin the prep for his decanting as soon as you vacate the table. The med bots have been working steadily so far. I was going to shorten the time between decants to a smaller margin," DADDIE said.

"We're already getting to stage two? Wow, I'll never let the kid plan a mass decant again," Josie said, "Let me guess. Griff is up, and so is Martha?"

DADDIE said, "Great guess, Sport! And yes, they are both up and rambling about. I still have a half dozen

Xeno Corps to decant. Then, I will start popping out the rest of the Construction and Security Corps. I've got the bots warming up the secondary nexus so we can double the decanting. Right now, I have fifty expedition members ready for duty."

"Ouch!" Josie said, sitting up as a med bot needled her. "Well, my neurons are fine. Can I report for duty, or do you want to test my memories? I might as well get this over with before Griff tries to stop me from working."

"Sure, Sport, here is an easy question: how did you and Greg meet?" DADDIE asked.

"Geez, Daddy, way to ask a scandalous question! Elon had just left me. I was down on my luck when I signed up for the United Service Organizations. I had just decanted into a twenty-something body with all that money I got in the divorce settlement, and well, I was pretty poor—for a billionaire. I was singing to some unit in some far-off corner of Earth..." Josie said but was cut off.

"Where on Earth, Sport? You know the rules. You've got to give me the details," DADDIE said. DADDIE's avatar scowled as he played with his ball cap.

"Let me think, I remember the location was… Malta. I can still smell the salty Mediterranean wind on the stage. This dashing lieutenant colonel approaches me and says, 'I don't care what the tabloids say. He was a damn fool for running off on you.' I was pretty down on myself at that point -- no real money, no real job -- and I said, 'Apparently, I didn't do a good enough job picking a new shell, even...' He said, 'No, ma'am. The shell is just fine. I know all the USO acts, and you are new, so I put two and two together.' I replied, 'Oh really, you a creepy stalker or some sort of fan?' He laughed and said, 'Neither, I am a man with a job offer. Ever been to Titan?' I said, 'No, no one has!' He then said, 'You wanna go?' After that, I was in the NASA program, and ten years later, I was planting a flag on Titan's surface. I've been working with and for Greg ever since."

"Good job, Sport," DADDIE said. "Now, let's talk about afterward. What did you do after the landing on Titan?"

"What, being an opera singer? I did that gig on a lark. I'd decanted into a middle-aged body to escape the attention from my flag planting on Titan. The whole Titan thing got ridiculous, and my old face was everywhere, even though the mission was all Greg's show. He had convinced the crumbling NASA administration of long-shot space exploration, even though megacorporations were rising and governments were dissolving.

"Anyway, I took a new shell to go off and sing, and what an instrument the corporation gave me! A severance package of many lifetimes! I sang my way from Titan to the station over Venus. The crowds came, and the bloggers claimed I had single-handedly resurrected opera. I would have argued that opera had never really died, but— whatever," Josie said with a laugh, "Not too bad for two hundred and thirty-five-year-old woman?"

"Try two hundred and seventy-one years old, Sport, but I'd say you don't look a day over thirty," DADDIE said with a wink.

"Oh, Daddy, you scoundrel! I didn't realize there were 'perks' to this job."

"Come on, Sport, space exploration needs young bodies to crawl through the cosmos. Mommy said no one would have a shell over thirty-five on this trip. Man, did that hack off Griff! He was grumbling about how he'd just broken in his shell. He is a funny sight now. He and Jason are more like brothers than father and son."

"I suppose you have Merlyna and Karl up, too? I expect Karl has all sorts of mechanical wonders tromping about in our cargo bays. Merlyna probably has all of the landing reports built and ready to file, too," Josie said with a laugh. DADDIE appeared solemn, more unhappy than he'd ever been. He looked like his favorite team had just lost the series.

"What? What did I say?" Josie asked. She frowned, not used to seeing DADDIE so somber.

"Sorry, Sport. This was a last-minute switcharoo. Karl won't be joining us. He's off to HD 260655 with Patrick Murphy's expedition," DADDIE said.

"What! That's a huge switcharoo! Does Merlyna know?" Josie asked. She began to play with her hair, twirling the ends of her hair with her fingers.

"Not yet. She's still in the archive. She's going to be madder than a wild bear when she finds out," DADDIE said. DADDIE had a look of worry on his face as if the AI did not know what to do with Merlyna.

"What happened? Karl was slated to come on board. He was supposed to be the number two! Did Mommy get upset after the readiness review?" Josie asked. Josie's feet moved as her consciousness began to bond to the new shell.

"I guess Mommy hasn't been open with anyone on what she is and is not doing… Besides, Karl can only take so much inefficiency and then he sort of pops. He was under a lot of stress, and when Mommy just sat there while the managed services made excuses… I guess he couldn't take the excuses anymore," DADDIE said. When dealing with MOMI, DADDIE seemed more defensive than he should have been, but who knew what magic bound the AI together?

"I never knew Mommy to hold a grudge or be that petty," Josie said, "Wait, who is the second in command if not Karl?"

"You are, Sport," DADDIE said.

"Oh geez. What gives Daddy?" Josie asked.

"Well, Sport, you and I will get our answers from Mommy on why Karl isn't here and everything else when we get the relay up and running. Then, you can ask her why she decided Karl isn't with us," DADDIE said.

"Maybe I'll let Greg do that. Being second in

command has many perks, too. Let's see how these legs work. Are they sexy legs, Daddy?" Josie asked with a wink. Josie sat up and tentatively dangled her legs over the edge of the decanter table.

"I've never been a leg man myself," DADDIE said with a wink, "But I don't think you'll be losing any beauty pageants with those beauts."

"Ugh, don't get me going on those things! I always hated the questions that they wanted you to answer with 'Solar system peace!'" Josie said as she slowly lowered herself to the floor. Josie's leg muscles flexed, and she stood up completely with her legs supporting her weight.

"Well, Sport, looks like you are winning the best catwalk strut to her clothing race," DADDIE said.

Gingerly, Josie crossed over to the closet after wrapping the sheet around her like a Roman stola. Martha or Griff had been silently restocking the jumpsuits and other clothing so the recently decanted could get up from the table and put some clothes on.

"What kind of fashion disasters await in the closet?" Josie asked with a smile. She quickly found some well-fitted tactical pants and a well-fitted structured t-shirt. The shirt and pants fit her well and hinted at her curves. After pulling the pants up, Josie turned and put on the shirt. It showed a few inches of her midriff.

"Perfect!" As Josie finished clothing herself, DADDIE said, "I am sure you will attract the male gaze wherever you go."

"I expect nothing less," Josie said. "Daddy, may I please go to Navigation? May I be cleared for duty, please?"

Josie knew that if DADDIE agreed, she'd be busy. DADDIE weighed his options. If he let her go, she'd bury herself in work, some of hers, but most of the load belonged to the now seventy-something light-years away Karl. If DADDIE told her no, more than likely, Josie would go to work anyway.

"Sure, Sport, just don't overdo anything. I can't have my star center messing up her hiking arms before the big game. I'll set alarms for you to keep regular hours. If you don't, I'll have Griff and Martha lock you in the brig."

"Oh, Daddy, you should know better! I'm always the head cheerleader! No one but sports nerds go to the games to see the plays!" Josie said, teasing the AI. She put her hands on her hips, then raised them and shimmied slightly as if shaking some imaginary pom-poms.

"My mistake. Now, go on before I decide to hike up the hemline on your cheerleading uniform. After all, sex sells the tickets, right?" DADDIE asked with a mischievous smile.

"Don't you forget that fact, Daddy," Josie said. "Thanks, I'm glad you are our AI. See you later!"

DADDIE just blushed and waved casually. DADDIE pulled up the decanting table's counter. He'd decant the real boss in twenty-one hours, three minutes, and fifteen seconds. DADDIE may have been the commander on paper, but even MOMI knew that would not stop Greg from taking the lead. DADDIE would take no chances with Greg's decant. He needed the boss up and working as soon as possible.

"If we die, we want people to accept it. We're in a risky business, and we hope that if anything happens to us, it will not delay the program. The conquest of space is worth the risk of life."

— Astronaut Gus Grissom

Location: L 98-59 near space, at two light
months from arrival
28.06.12450 Standard

DADDIE stood over yet another shell. This one was critical for the mission, and he wasn't taking any chances. To be honest, he never took chances. He looked at the golden skin visible on the shell as it sat waiting for a consciousness. The dark hair was draped across the table. As he hovered, Jason stepped in.

"Getting ready to decant the boss lady," he asked DADDIE.

"Yes, Duchess is being summoned from the archive as we speak," DADDIE said.

"This will be the first time I will meet her," Jason said. "I'm a little nervous."

"Don't be, Buddy, she's very nice and straightforward," DADDIE said. They both stood watching as the bots lined up on either side of the shell and the needle entered its cranium. The woman's eyes opened, showing a coppery brown iris.

"Are we there, Daddy?" she asked.

"Not yet, Duchess," DADDIE said. "But we're close. I've decanted you so you can make sure the Xeno Corps is up and running for the lander separation."

"I'll get right on that," the woman said with a smirk, "When this shell will let me."

"I know, Duchess," DADDIE said. "In the meantime, meet Jason Dikkert. He's your Vanguard lead. Jason, this is Xena Athanas, the Xeno Corps Director."

"Pleasure, ma'am," Jason said.

"So formal! Well Mister Dikkert, it is nice to meet you too, but please call me Xena. We aren't on a formal basis on the expedition, except maybe with General Body."

"Sure, Xena," Jason said, slightly nervous.

"Ouch!" Xena said as a bot tested her nerves. "That

was not fun, Daddy."

"I know, Duchess, but it's protocol," DADDIE said. "I need to test your memories. Shall I ask Jason to step outside?"

"No, he can stay," Xena said. "He might as well learn something about me. After all, I want to know more about him as well."

"Okay, Duchess," DADDIE said. "Level one tech stuff here, just checking for consciousness degradation. Tell me about when you joined CAA."

"I had just left Hipponike. They had promised me a role as their Xeno Corps Director and benched me. They kept promising they'd send me on an expedition, but instead, I was filing e-paper at their headquarters on Luna. I watched as corporate leadership gave less qualified and less space-ready colleagues expedition assignments, and I got outraged," said Xena.

"Sure, what happened then," DADDIE asked.

"Patrick saw my resume on Undoubtedly, and he called me in for an interview," Xena said.

"Okay, who was on your interview panel?" DADDIE asked.

"Well, Patrick, Mommy, and… I forget the other guy. He didn't say much. Just asked me a question about working with AI," Xena said.

"Can you describe him? I need the details," DADDIE said.

"Sure, I remember what he looked like. Sorry, I'm not great with names, no matter what shell I'm in," Xena said. "He was in his fifties. He had short salt and pepper hair and hazel eyes. I remember he wore a long-sleeved red tee shirt and black tactical pants."

Jason blurted out, "That sounds like Karl Holzhauser."

"Yeah, that was his name. He was a real butthole," Xena said.

DADDIE started laughing, and both Xena and Jason looked at the AI.

"Sonny is a temperamental guy, but once he likes you, he'd give you the shirt and pants off his shell," DADDIE said.

"Well, after the interview, Patrick said he'd call in about a week to tell me whether I got the job," Xena said.

"And?" Jason asked, even though DADDIE looked at him with a raised eyebrow.

"Patrick called back that afternoon. He said it was a done deal and asked when I could start. Patrick said I'd be joining his expedition, but then in provisioning, I got sniped away by General Body," Xena said.

"Why was that," Jason asked.

DADDIE jumped in and said, "I'm good, but if you want to chat with Jason, I can blink out."

"Sure, thanks, Daddy," Xena said. DADDIE blinked out, and Jason and Xena were left alone in the decanter nexus.

"If you'd be a gentleman and hand me some clothes, I'll give this shell a go," Xena said.

"Sure," Jason said. "Anything in particular you'd like to wear?"

"Yes, I see a series of gray jumpsuits in the left closet. Can you fetch one? I should be either a medium or a large," Xena said. Jason walked over to the closet, and Xena sat up carefully. Jason fetched three jumpsuits, each a different size, and put them on the table next to Xena, who sat up and held the sheet against her body.

"If you'd be so kind to turn around, I'd appreciate that," Xena said. "As your direct supervisor, I think it is wise that we don't get so close that we see each other naked."

Jason turned three shades of red but nodded, turned around, and took two paces forward. Xena used the interval to attempt to put on the smallest jumpsuit. Finding it didn't fit well on her legs, she switched to the next largest. The middle size was a comfortable fit. She quickly threw on the jumpsuit and closed the zipper to cover her naked chest.

"It's all good. Thanks, Jason. You've shown me a lot about your character already," Xena said.

"Huh? What do you mean," Jason asked.

"You're respectful, that's obvious," Xena said. "If you weren't, you would have peeked at me while I was dressing."

"Well, I…" Jason said but was cut off.

"That was a compliment. When the time comes, keep that attitude. We'll all need that if things get bad," Xena said. "Now, mind coming up with me to the cafeteria or mess hall—whatever CAA calls it."

"No, I had a break in my schedule, and I wanted to meet the person I would be working for," Jason said.

"I appreciate that too. Your peers, the leads of Analysis and Survey, aren't here, but you are, Jason."

"Well, in her defense, the Survey team lead isn't decanted yet. I think the Analysis team lead was cataloging the scientific instruments. There was a last-minute shake-up by Mommy, and everything has gone sideways," Jason said.

"You don't have to cover for Édouard Vidal, Jason," Xena said. "He and I have never been on favorable terms, even when we both worked for Hipponike," Xena said.

"You two worked together at Hipponike," Jason said. "What was that like?"

"Cafeteria first. My new stomach is rumbling," Xena said.

Jason nodded and said, "Sure, follow me." Jason led Xena through the hab corridor and crossed into the wheel's main cafeteria. Xena grabbed a tray and a plate as she entered and went to the buffet, sampling a little bit of everything presented. Sitting at a table, Xena forked a cooked carrot and tasted it.

"That's a shame," she said, moving the fork back over her tray and sliding the carrot off with her fingers.

"What?" Jason asked.

"This shell doesn't respond well to cooked carrots. My old shell—*my original*—thought cooked carrots were delicious," Xena said.

"Oh, I didn't realize that," Jason said.

"Why? Are you still in your original? If so, you're quite the youngster," Xena said with a smile.

"Yes," Jason said. "But I never liked cooked carrots anyway."

"Well, in this body, I've joined the club," Xena said, putting another item, a Brussels sprout, on her fork and trying it.

"Hrm, odd," Xena said. "That was delicious. At some point, I am going to need to talk to the CAA Organics Division about how they encode the bodies."

"That'd be interesting, I bet," Jason said, passing off the topic, "But back to Hipponike, you know, Griff says they are a bunch of vampires."

Xena laughed, "He's not wrong. You climb the ladder at Hipponike by sticking knives in everyone's back and pulling yourself up on them. Of all the folks I worked with, Édouard, or as everyone called him there, Doctor Vidal, was the worst. He was like a little king in their Xeno-discovery program. He worked almost ninety hours a week on all the data they brought back from their colonies."

"Wow! I wonder how we poached him then?" Jason said.

"I'm not sure. I am positive he'll let us know the next time I run into him," Xena said.

"So, what'd you do at Hipponike? Xeno Corps?" Jason asked.

"Really, I filed a lot of e-papers," Xena said. "I had trained for almost ten years for the Tau Ceti expedition. That was a big show, and Victoria, their CEI, had promised me a spot as the Vanguard lead. There were big guns on that trip, even a senior executive who had shelled into a thirty-year-old body for the trip.”

“I remember the news on that one,” Jason said. “I couldn’t watch a vid or play a game on the Hipponike Net Service without seeing an ad. They really pumped that colony.”

“Yeah, HNS spun up a dedicated AI in a constellation solely to sell the colony. Too bad that Macroware poached the colony,” Xena said.

“What? How could they do that?” Jason said in shock.

“Easy! They hired mercenaries to ‘kinetically acquire’ the colony,” Xena said. “I don’t think it got out in the mainstream news, but inside Hipponike, the colony loss was embarrassing. We were all happy Macroware didn’t let its mercs go full space pirate.”

“Wait, what does that mean,” Jason asked.

“Well, sometimes when the mercs go kinetic, they decide to remove the witnesses,” Xena said. “They claim that the original colonists starved or that their return ship hit a planetary body or was irradiated. Anything to cover up what happened to the original expedition.”

“Hold on, they can do that?” Jason said. “What about the Solar Systems Exchange? Wouldn’t they stop them?”

“No,” Xena said, “Sometimes I’d hear that Hipponike would ‘go kinetic,’ and if there were any casualties, they’d bribe the SSX and cover it up.”

“Could that happen to us?” Jason asked.

“Sure,” Xena said. “Although, I doubt it would happen. This expedition has such awful chances of success that I doubt any big players would want to take it. But that’s where Vanguard and Con Sec’s Security division come in. I’ll need you and your team to stay alert, especially after we make it to the outpost stage, since that’s usually when the mercs strike.”

“Ah, makes sense. Greg was always going on about

'head on a swivel' in our simulations," Jason said. "I thought he was worried about xenomorphs."

"Humans are much worse than anything a filmmaker can invent," Xena said. "Plain old greed makes many of these so-called humans do things outside the Oort Cloud that would enrage the folks back home."

"Is that why the megacorporations went to AIs," Jason asked.

"Yes, there was this attitude that AI should run things since humans were greedy and rapacious. The problem is that humans still program the AIs. And in the case of Hipponike's CEI Victoria, she's probably worse than us organics," Xena said. "Victoria makes Mommy look downright kind in comparison."

Jason smiled, "I don't believe that, but it is nice to know Mommy isn't the worst CEI out there."

"What brought you to CAA," Xena said, changing the topic.

"Well, about two years before our launch from Luna, my parents left on their expedition to 11 Leonis Minoris," Jason said. "They decided very abruptly to go on the expedition. Dad said he wanted to give me a chance to grow up without Mom or him overshadowing my development. I was alone for the first time in my life."

"That sounds pretty tough," Xena interjected.

"Well, it wasn't that bad. There were still plenty of relatives around, but I suddenly was alone and free to do anything. I started thinking about what I wanted to do. I was out with my ex, Stacey, when we went to the movies for a double feature, *The Titanian* and *Intergalactic*. The movies amped me, and I thought, 'Why not a space explorer?' So, I applied for the job position that CAA had out on Werewolf."

"Who did you interview with?" Xena asked as she picked up her food.

"No one," Jason said. "I crypto-proton bombed the response link, and Greg hired me afterward. I think he twisted Mommy's arm to make the hire happen."

Xena smiled and began a slow belly laugh, "Well, Jason, I am glad you're on my team. Anyone who can coerce Greg and Mommy to do something… Well, you're like a force of nature."

"I don't even remember the actual job I applied for. I think it was like working as a lab technician," Jason said.

"Even better," Xena said. "What do you hope to accomplish in L 98-59?"

"Seriously," Jason said.

"Yes, seriously," Xena said.

"Find a girl and settle down," Jason said. "I mean, I thought I had a pretty sure thing with Stacey, but when I started talking about doing the colonization thing, I think she got scared and dumped me."

"I understand the desire," Xena said. "I've been working for thirty years for a shot in the colonies. Something serious, not just decanting into a sodbuster. I wanted to get out on the edge and make a difference. Be the first one on a world, not another mindless human cow some corporation would use to grind out resources from their star system."

"Yeah," Jason said encouragingly.

"Well, the colonies attract a certain type of individual. Not every man wants to spend several decades out on the edge of humanity. It is tougher, too, when you say you're Xeno Corps. Lots of people see us as the least sane people in the giant loony bin of the colonies."

"Really," Jason said. "I don't get it. Earth can be downright boring sometimes."

"I know," Xena replied. "But some people cling to the monotony."

"Yeah, that seems pretty weird to me," Jason said. "I mean, I liked all the people being around, but had I stayed, I don't know…"

"Well, it's good you didn't," Xena said. "Tell me where you are with the Vanguard's preparations."

"Oh yeah, well, Li Mei and I got the Kooya up and running," Jason said.

"What's that?" Xena asked, "I got briefed on the major mission parameters, but General Body kept telling me that you and the other team leads would handle the details."

"Oh! The Kooya is a combat AI. He's in a sixteen-meter-tall chassis. He seems bloodthirsty," Jason replied.

Xena nodded, "Well, that's good. We may need him to go kinetic on something. Hopefully, it will be alien and fauna. But like I said, you never know."

"Oh, and we did a readiness check on the Vanguard sleds. They need power but seem to have made it so far. The cargo bay hasn't been super fun to work in, as the atmo was around one percent of Earth's. Daddy has promised to raise it to ten percent so we can use face breathers to get work done."

"Yeah, I can see how that's a roadblock," Xena said, "What about cataloging? Do we have any good candidates for a colony?"

"Yup, I found an Earth-like world in the foxtrot orbit, Xena. I called her Aurora Dawn."

"Not a bad name, better than what would have happened at Hipponike," Xena said.

"Oh," Jason replied, "What do they call their planets?"

"Ugh, it's advertising based. They brand a planet based on a movie series, an episodic show, or even a best-selling novel," Xena said.

"Huh, I could go for that. Some pretty cool movies would make great planet names," Jason said.

"Well, I got to push the papers on *Gatesville, Dusklight,* and *Jerry Cotter and the Alchemist's Rock.* The planets' names became even more ridiculous."

"They named a planet *Jerry Cotter,* really?" Jason asked.

"Yes, sadly, there is a whole planet of folks stuck

with a stupid book's name," Xena replied.

"Well, I don't feel so bad about Cappy the Canyon anymore," Jason said.

"What's that?" Xena asked.

"The largest canyon on Aurora Dawn," Jason replied.

"That's a terrible name, Jason," Xena said, "Why did you call it that?"

"Well, Daddy said I could have some of Grandpa's Old Cough Medicine… You know what? I'm done making excuses. I like the name Cappy the Canyon."

Xena shook her head, realizing something else was happening, and said, "I suppose it could have been worse. Well, thanks for the chat. I've got to find a bunk. That will be over in ladies' country, so I'll say goodbye now."

"Yes, I'll see you later. I don't even dare walk over that way. I had Li Mei sound the alarm the last time I headed in that direction. In my defense I was reading a mission brief. Before you all decanted. I used to walk the large corridors counter-clockwise across the wheel," Jason said.

"Getting stir crazy?" Xena asked.

"Yes, you bet," Jason said.

"Hang in there, Earthman. Only in a few more weeks, you can run along on the edge of Cappy the Canyon until your legs fall off," Xena said.

"Um, not really," Jason said.

"Why not?"
"I think if I did that, Li Mei would push me over the edge," Jason said.

"There are worse ways to go out in the universe," Xena said. Jason stroked his chin while pondering that thought.

"I suppose," he said, still puzzled by the statement.

"On that note, see you later," Xena said, standing. "I'll send a message out once I schedule the Xeno Corps leadership scrum. Until then…" She then left Jason in the cafeteria while she went on her mission to find a place to sleep.

*

"Pass the peas, Doctor Sugar," Griff said to his wife.

"You want peas or sugar there, my little old man?" she replied, handing the small bowl to her husband.

"Ask me again after dinner, and I'll tell you," he replied, but then he had to guard the peas as Jason was about to dip his spoon into the bowl. "Now, now, Little Rooster, let the big bird eat!"

Josie laughed, "You're going to get fat spooning all that food on your plate there, Double D."

"I haven't eaten in almost thirty-five years. I'd say I need the calories," Griff said. "And I'd use that voice for singing, fat lady. Leave the calorie counting to a man with an M.D. and a PhD."

"Now, now, little old man," Martha said. "I am going to stick up for my girl here. She is not a fat lady."

"When I first met Josie, if you heard her sing, she'd bring down the house. I wonder if you got as good an instrument in the new shell?" Griff asked.

"I haven't tried. I've been too busy, but now you have me curious," Josie said.

"Well, go on, fat lady, bring down the house!" Griff said jokingly.

"Little old man! Be nice, or I will get Daddy to put you back in the box," Martha said.

"Soon, let me practice. I don't want to hurt anything in this new shell, so I won't be able to yell at Mister Dikkert over there, especially as he is stealing all the mashed yams!"

Jason looked up with his mouth full of yam, like a small child caught with his hand in the cookie jar.

"Don't let her shake you, Little Rooster. If Karl were here, he'd tell you to eat up before the landfall and that rations don't last forever," Griff said.

"I can't believe Mommy would do that to him and Merlyna. I swear they haven't been apart in almost a century!" Josie said.

"I know, honey," Martha told Josie, "I remember when Merlyna was sent off to Pluto for a few weeks, and Karl was floating around his place. That was when they still had Samantha and Samuel—I miss those sweeties! Karl had a robot, you know, Biggie Black, and Biggie bugged out and tore up Karl and Merlyna's fine real wood floor. I remember hearing Karl yelling across the corporate residence neighborhood at that damn robot dog. Babies in hand, I can still see Karl marching down to the quantum array to call Merlyna. If not for her, he'd probably have blown up that robot…"

"Hey, Martha, is that the same black combat robot down in the cargo bay?" Jason asked.

"Sure is honey," Martha replied, "that robot is a one-of-a-kind. Karl made him almost seventy years ago. That robot is fine craftsmanship. Don't let the stories fool you."

"Karl, that's my man. He made most of the bots on this ship, even that big Kooya! Karl was my professor-advisor when I was studying cybernetics. Karl is an engineer's engineer, and by the stars, when he has made something—what he makes lasts," Griff related.

"Hey guys, what's for dinner?" a suddenly holo-projected DADDIE asked.

"The finest vegetarian meatloaf, mashed yams, peas, and spinach. You want to join us, Daddy?" Griff replied to the AI. All the organic-based meat the colonists would eat would eventually come from the variform embryonic livestock still in cold storage in one of the cargo bays. Vegetarian meatloaf was the closest thing to real meat the crew would experience for many years.

"Not my meal. I'm more of a ballpark-loaded chili dog guy or even a picnic hamburger," DADDIE said with a smile. "I just wanted you to know that Greg will decant shortly if you all want to come up to the nexus."

Jason stood up like his butt was on fire, "Yes, I am

interested!" he said.

Griff looked like he, too, wanted to jump up, but the consciousness inside the thirty-year-old body gave him a bit more decorum, and he said, "You go on, Little Rooster. I'll be along shortly."

Josie put down her utensils and said, "I'll head up as well. I've got to brief the boss when he comes around."

"Jason," Martha said. "You let Greg get his sea legs before you start gloating, you hear me!?"

"Yes, Martha," Jason said. He quickly turned and started trotting towards the nexus.

"Go on, little old man," Martha said. "I'll clean up."

Griff stood, and he and Josie began a walk towards the nexus.

*

Jason saw the new shell lying on the decanting table through the glass as he entered the outer observation room. The tan-skinned body was muscular yet lean. Where the old shell's hair had been entirely gray, this body had a full black mane.

"You know Greg is going to want his beard back, Daddy," Jason said.

"Yup, Buddy, this shell can grow a beard. Most shells are as untampered as we could make them. We needed to weed out specific genetic diseases and less-than-desirable characteristics. Still, we kept some more primal ones—like beard growth—just because of the potential combinations that those genes create," DADDIE said.

"How many seconds?" Jason asked excitedly.

"Fifteen. See, the bot docs are all lined up. I am getting a green on the needle," DADDIE said. Jason watched as the needle servos flared and the tip entered the skull. The wall clock showed the countdown.

"Should kick-off now," DADDIE said. The med bots started shuffling animatedly. A small emergency chime sounded.

"Not good, Buddy. Stay out of there! We have an issue," DADDIE said, shutting the nexus doors.

"What's happening, Daddy?" Jason said, a worried expression crossing his face. Jason watched as the bots started scampering around the shell.

"No, no, no!" DADDIE said. "Stay with me, Greg!"

The scene in the nexus became one of medical horror. The shell began throwing up blood. The shell's violet eyes rolled, crossing and uncrossing, while the muscles twitched like the devil pulled the strings. The med bots were switching through needles and injecting the body with all sorts of fluids. Josie and Griff came running around the corner and into the observation room.

"Greg!" Josie shouted as she ran to the door, "Daddy, let me in this minute!"

"No, can do, Sport!" DADDIE said. Josie banged her hands against the glass in despair.

"Prognosis?" Griff asked. The playful man without a care in the world was instantly replaced with the cold, analytical surgeon.

"Indeterminable. The body started throwing up blood as soon as the injection happened," DADDIE said, recounting what he had observed.

"How much of his consciousness is downloaded?" Griff asked, placing a hand on his chin. His mind quickly processed the data.

"Last reading said ninety-five percent," DADDIE said, as analytical as a sportscaster musing over a team's wins and losses.

"We've got to pull him back!" Griff shouted. "We have to do a burning rollout!"

The body started convulsing, and the heart monitors began skipping beats.

"I'm trying to reverse the process, but you know, Chief, rolling out isn't that easy," DADDIE said.

"Well then, Daddy, let me in there!" Griff said,

getting agitated. The med bots continued to swarm the body. The wall clock had changed to a biometrics panel, showing how the organs were crashing inside the body.

"No can do, Chief, you know the protocols!" DADDIE said, with a shake of his avatar's head.

"To hell with the protocols!" Griff said. Suddenly, the lines on the shell's heart monitor went flat. The med bots immediately hopped off the body as some defibrillator panels came down from over the decanter table. The defibrillator panels whined, and a whirring sound indicated an electronic charge had built up.

"Panels discharging, stand clear!" an automated voice warned.

The panels fired, and the pulse went through the body. Yet, the heart monitor remained flat-lined.

"No good, one more time," DADDIE said.

"Second attempt: Panels discharging, stand clear!" the voice warned. The panels fired, and the pulse went through the body. Again, the heart monitor remained flat-lined.

"Come on, Greg, pull through," Griff said.

"Come on, Tiger. Don't quit the team. We still have to win the big game!" DADDIE said.

"Final attempt: Panels discharging, stand clear!" the voice warned. The electric pulse went through the body. Again, the heart monitor remained flat-lined. The shell lay lifeless and dead.

"Chief, give me a time of consciousness death," DADDIE said. "You are the ranking medical officer, after all."

"No, I won't call the time. We still have options! We could check the needle's logs, and maybe he rolled out?" Griff said, looking for any shred of hope.

"No, Griff," DADDIE said, breaking his typical algorithms and calling Griff by his name, "Greg is gone."

Tears streaked down Griff's cheeks, "I thought he

and I would be drinking shots when the stars winked out of existence. What a way to go. Table death. You want to know why I don't shed my shells all that often, Jason? Right there is example number one. State changes will get you faster than anything in this universe."

Jason was still in shock. In his twenty-four years, he had never heard of someone dying, much less know someone who died. Tears welled up in the corner of his young eyes.

"If Karl were here, he could check the buffer, maybe catch a ghost image, perhaps…" Josie said, "Karl performs at least ten miracles before breakfast!"

"Karl isn't here, and Greg is dead, nineteen hours fifty minutes, ship time," Griff said. Jason stood with his hands on the glass, tears breaking free and running down his cheeks.

"The bots are doing a post-mortem," DADDIE said. "We should have answers here in a few minutes."

"I don't need the bots to know what happened," Griff said. "That's Enlow's Syndrome. I heard about that in medical school. You'll have to recycle the needle, and we'll have to run a diagnostic check on everything."

"A dirty needle pour?" Jason asked, utterly shocked.

"Yes, Little Rooster, either a bacterium has gotten into the needle, or the servo compressors backed up with spinal fluid from a previous decant," Griff said. "I'd also check the needle matrix to see if a virus was in the software, although Doctor Enlow only briefly named that as a potential contributor."

"What about…" Jason said but was interrupted by Griff.

"He's dead, ain't no coming back from ninety percent." Griff pointed to the monitor, which showed that the consciousness was downloaded at eighty-eight percent.

Josie just stared and said, "I saw someone who got pulled at eighty percent. That poor soul reminded me of those old folks you saw from the history vids, you know, before the Singularity. They'd wander lost, not even knowing their names. Now, they end up dying or going into the great archive on Earth for a long haul to the heat death of the universe."

"I'll deal with the shell. We should probably cremate the remains. You can't use shells like that anyway," Griff said, a look of disgust on his face.

"I gotta head back," Josie said. "Daddy, is the secondary nexus up?"

"Yeah, Sport, I think Merlyna is on the docket tomorrow. I figured that the big guy would be there to calm her down. Now, she's probably going to rewire me, once for Karl and now for Greg," DADDIE said, his avatar showing a glum expression.

"I'll talk to her. We've got lots to do. Greg wouldn't want anyone standing around. Time flies too much for that sort of thing," Griff said, shrugging and moving away from the glass towards the Hab modules.

DADDIE stopped projecting his avatar. He picked up a battered-looking baseball card somewhere in the virtual world he called home. The face that looked out from the battered sleeve was one of the game's all-time greats. DADDIE pulled off the card's sleeve and said, "What do you know, the card is still in mint condition!"

In the decanter table's matrix, DADDIE started an algorithm. Code was written and piped into the constellation. Pointers were reformatted in the archive, harmonic data was recoded, and a new life began...

"When you launch in a rocket, you're not really flying that rocket. You're just sort of hanging on."

— Astronaut Michael P. Anderson

Location: L 98-59 near space, at a little less
than eight light weeks from arrival
04.07.12450 Standard

"The sands of the hourglass fall for everyone," Griff said as
he stood at the podium, "Greg understood that most of all.
He always felt he 'lived on borrowed time after leaving his
original shell.' I never understood that, but I think we all feel
that today."
The decanted crew had cleared the cafeteria tables, and an
oversized picture of Greg Body was on an easel. There were
folding chairs lining the walls, and the cafeteria was near
capacity with sixty-odd expedition members standing inside.
Everyone wore the nicest clothes available for the funeral
service.

"Greg didn't believe in a higher power. He felt the
universe was just a random collection of atoms," Griff
continued, "He felt we were nothing more than dust in the
wind. I stand today to witness his life and remember
someone who not only brought us together but made an
impact on our lives. Greg believed that once we attained
Singularity, no one was forced to bend their knees to
uncaring divines, nor were they slaves to primitive beliefs.
We had evolved from the past, and we could make our
destiny."

Griff looked out and saw that all expedition
members were solemn, and many were crying. He looked to
Jason, who had the crushed look of a grounded child.

"Our purpose, now that Greg is gone, is to make his
memory lasting by settling Aurora Dawn. We will build a
world that will be a paradise: a place where people live with
each other in peace, not because a deity says so, but because
humans *choose* to live together in peace. We celebrate Greg
today, on a day he loved. Today was a day he continually
celebrated: the birthday of the nation where he was born,
the United States of America. The general cherished the
United States of America's 'noble experiment.' Like Greg's

heroes, the founding fathers of the United States of America, he sought to make CAA a place where everyone was equal in brotherhood. Let's honor that vision and make a new world in that image."

Griff stepped away from the podium and went to Martha's side. The memorial was almost over. All that remained was a moment of silent reflection. Nearly the entire crew was in the cafeteria. Only Merlyna didn't come. Her decant was horrible, and she needed time to recover… At least, that's what she had said to Griff. Griff suspected that there was more to that statement. Merlyna and Karl still held tight to their ancient religious beliefs. Religion was always taboo around Greg, and Karl had repeatedly tried to proselytize Greg. Greg, for his part, had tolerated the couple, even though he hadn't agreed with their beliefs. It was one of CAA's strengths; diverse viewpoints were tolerated. A bell rang over the speakers, and the gathering began to disperse.

Li Mei approached Jason and said, "Hey, do you want to watch the *Devourer* again?"

Jason, who was usually more upbeat, just shook his head.

"I get it; I miss the general, too," Li Mei said. "Maybe it's because I am from the belt, and we lose people all the time, but death is just a part of life."

"Well, I am from Earth, and we don't see things that way," Jason said. "After the Singularity, we had supposedly defeated death."

"Sure, you could see things that way. I was brought up with the saying, 'Even death is not to be feared by one who has lived wisely.' The general seemed like he lived many lifetimes well. I don't think we should mourn his passing but celebrate it."

Jason shrugged and said, "I guess. I still can't help but miss him. He was my mentor. When he and Griff talked about the future, it felt like they would always protect and nurture the company… and us too."

After hearing the passing comment, Josie came over and said, "I see how it is, Mister Dikkert. You don't think I have the stones to keep you safe?"

Jason smiled weakly. He knew Josie was joking and replied, "Well, Greg always projected an air of strength…"

"Yeah, I'll miss that too," Josie said. "One time, when we were getting ready to head into the lander on Titan, he looked at me and said, 'You know Jo, they might all be wrong. This thing may plummet and kill us.' I said, 'Well, we'll be the infamous crew who died trying to land on Titan.' And he said, 'Better to try and fail than to never try at all. That's what we have going for us. We're actually living life, even if it kills us.' I never have forgotten that, through all the shells and all the things that have happened. He never wanted to be known as someone who didn't live. Now come on, I think I know what can return your focus."

Josie and Jason moved from the cafeteria to Navigation, where the crew had configured a screen to show the blueprints of the *Aquila*. Josie stood at the screen. She pointed to the nose section. She said, "Okay, we need to do a hull check on the lander bay, which means a zero-gee maneuver and potential spacewalk. Are you up for that?"

Jason's eyes lit up like a child expecting a present, and he said, "Of course, but why choose me?"

"Simple, you need the zero-gee experience. Once things are settled on the colony, we will need the Vanguard to start looking for rare earths and other exotics. After all, we might not find them on the planet," said Josie. "I'll walk you through the steps from here in Navigation. Go down to the lander bay and take an explorer pod."

"On it," Jason said. He left Navigation and went through the main corridor until he hit a ladder on the wheel's spokes. Moving down and through the main truss, Jason entered the airlock to the lander bay. The bay's environmental panel showed only a ten percent atmosphere.

Jason looked to his right and saw the rack where the

space suits were stowed. He grabbed a suit and put it on. Space suit construction had improved as humanity spread across the stars, and the suit Jason wore was not even the same bulky outfit Josie and Greg wore for their Titan mission a little over a century and a half ago. Jason selected an oxygen bottle and a waste gas bottle with a lithium hydroxide filter for his carbon dioxide. He debated whether he needed a water bottle and a liquid waste bottle but decided he wouldn't take the items as he'd only be outside for a short while.

Jason plugged the bottles into his suit and put the bayonet-fitted locks on the spots that weren't being used. He then pulled the aluminum-titanium helmet from its cradle. Putting the helmet on, Jason was careful not to damage the various sensors and antennas arranged on the top. Now, he was encased in a protective barrier against the ravages of space. He could make a limited spacewalk, but the suit wasn't rated for extended exposure to the background radiation.

Instead, Jason would rely on the explorer pod, which could handle more rads. The pod had thin lead and carbon nanotube panels, allowing weeks of operation under normal radiation levels. However, a cosmic ray or a solar ionization wave would force Jason to return to the *Aquila* and seek safety. Jason cycled the airlock and waited.

"Do you hear me, Jason," Josie asked. Jason hit a switch on his chest and turned on his microphone.

"Yes, loud and clear," Jason said, "I'm bringing my HUD up. When it's loaded, I'll give you a status check."

"Yeah, but while waiting, hook into the lifeline. No sense in burning almost five minutes of O2 waiting for the doors to open," Josie said.

Jason looked around the airlock and saw the umbilical next to the suit rack. He reached out and plugged the cord into his suit's O2 port. As he clipped the umbilical, the suit chimed. It was a low-tech notice that he was on ship air. Jason then spent a minute flipping switches on his chest plate. After trying three different switches, the helmet's HUD came on. Jason then checked his oxygen mix and throttled it up to one hundred. While on the umbilical, he'd outgas his nitrogen in preparation for the vacuum work. The doors to the truss closed. Jason checked his temperature. The internal suit temp was reading twenty-four degrees centigrade, while the external thermometer rose as the atmosphere in the airlock thinned.

"Caution! Caution! No oxygen," the airlock announced just before it evacuated the last of the remaining atmosphere. A red light flashed, and the doors to the lander bay opened. Jason disconnected the umbilical and marched into the lander bay.

"Great, I see you on the bay's cameras. Head off toward the port's large airlock near the bow. The explorer pod on that side is prepped for the survey," Josie said.

Moving towards the large bays at the front of the lander bay, Jason passed by the sleds. As he walked, he looked to his right at the large form of the *Dux*, the *Aquila's* lander. The Xeno Corps would take the Dux and land on Aurora Dawn in a few weeks. Moving into the front of the lander bay, Jason saw the large airlocks that flanked the main bay door. The airlocks were boxes four meters cubed in volume. Jason inspected all of the equipment. Everything in the bay was vital to the success of the expedition. After a glance, nothing looked damaged or worn. Everything needed some power and some detailing to be ready to work.

Jason cycled the inner port-side explorer airlock door and stepped inside. The inner airlock door was large enough to fit an explorer pod through, and the airlock door cycling took some time.

Jason could see the cube inside the pod's airlock, the explorer pod. The front side was a large two-meter by one-meter composite viewport between two robotic arm stumps. The pod sat in a cradle on a truck attached to rails that could extend inside the lander bay or outside into the vacuum of space. Jason had entered on a trim platform level with the explorer pod's back. Jason approached the back of the pod. The hatch was closed. He pressed a button on his suit to cycle the hatch open. The hatch split in the center, and the top half lifted while the bottom came down. Jason looked at the safety harness in the pod. He stepped forward, attached himself to the pod, clipped the two carabiners on his suit's waist to the harness, and grabbed the umbilical for the pod. He connected the umbilical to his suit and was on the pod's oxygen.

"Jason, I see you're connected to the pod's systems; try a power-up; these things haven't been operational for almost thirty-five years," Josie said. Jason flipped the cover over the main power switch and pushed the broad breaker forward. Numbers appeared on the pod's view screen, and Jason dimmed his helmet HUD to avoid confusion between the displays.

"I'm reading a full battery. Shall I close the pod's hatch," Jason said.

"Yes, go for it," Josie said, "I'm loading the maintenance appendages via the cycler. I'll also seal the airlock in preparation for extending the pod outside."

Jason watched as the robotic arms were placed into position by lifts in the airlock. The arms snapped onto the pod's stumps and locked into place. Jason flipped the toggle, and the pod's hatch shut behind him. A rear camera came online, and its feed sat in the top corner of the pod's glass cockpit. The airlock was completely sealed, and red lights flashed in the room, indicating a seal and no oxygen.

"I'm ready for exterior door cycling," Jason said.

"Doors are cycling," Josie reported. Jason waited, and a few seconds later, the front door opened.

"Please confirm that the doors are cycled," Jason said. The pod's HUD showed the doors were in the proper position, and he cycled the truck to move the launch cradle outside. Jason was nervous and didn't want to take any chances, so he waited for Josie to clear him.

"Yup, you're going to move the truck and launch the cradle," Josie said. "I'll keep an eye on the radiation sensors and give you a heads up if you need to return to the airlock."

Jason toggled the virtual button on the pod's console, and the truck moved the pod, the launch cradle, and him outside the hull. The *Aquila* had slowed down significantly, and Jason could see the engines' glow as they maintained their braking burn.

"Shutting down breaking burn to go into coast mode," said Josie. "We'll maintain a constant velocity; that way, we won't lose you, and the pod won't have to burn needless fuel to stay in position."

"Roger," Jason said. "You know, I expected interstellar space to be cooler."

"Hey, we're getting close enough that I am not sure whether this is interstellar," Josie said. "But don't let your guard down! This isn't like when we trained over Luna. Plenty of unexpected things can still happen."

"Roger," Jason said. "Let me know when I can release."

He watched as the light from the main engines started to dim. Jason noted the visual display of the Geiger counter on the pod's HUD and focused on the audio feed of the Geiger counter, which indicated the background radiation.

"Go for release, Jason."

Jason hit the cockpit's virtual release button and felt a slight bump as the pod disconnected from the cradle.

"I'm free. Where to," Jason asked.

"Let's fly by the lander bay. Check the doors first. Then, we'll scan for any hull cracks and do a detailed scan around the bridge. If all goes well, I'll have you scan the engineering compartment in the back. Then you return, and we can all go to dinner," Josie said. Jason grabbed the two joysticks in front of him on the pod's control console. He turned the pod and moved it around to face the airlock. Jason flipped the switch for the laser scanner that sat on the pod's left arm. Now active, the scanner would loop in a clockwise scan of the area in front of the pod. He'd send the data back to the *Aquila*, where DADDIE or another AI would crunch the numbers and compare them to the scan prior to the *Aquila* sailing out at the Luna-Asteroid Belt Lagrange dock.

"Moving across the main equator of the lander bay, I am not seeing anything major. Not sure what data the scanner is showing," Jason said. His excitement for the current task had faded, and he wanted to finish the job now that he'd experienced his first interstellar space crawl.

"Hang in there," Josie said, sensing Jason's impatience. "The job isn't glamorous or exciting, but we must ensure we don't have an issue before starting L 98-59 system operations. It would be a shame if a micrometeorite damaged the doors or one of the antennas didn't transmit."

"Roger, swinging around the starboard side. I am still not seeing anything. The *Aquila* is looking pretty good for thirty-five years in the black," Jason said. The Geiger counter spiked as he backed off the ship's starboard side.

"Radiation," Jason said.

"You're still good. That's a small spike since you're moving outside the ship's magnetosphere. It's still within limits. Don't let the Geiger counter noise scare you," Josie said.

"Why didn't we get a bot to do this," Jason asked.

"Hey, you were happy to volunteer, remember? Besides, the bots have run these scans, but protocol says we need a pair of organic eyes to double-check the ship," said Josie. Jason floated around to where the main truss connected to the lander bay and backed out again to avoid the spinning wheel. Pulling back, he pointed the scanner at the wheel, checking for anything unusual.

"Checking the wheel and the Habs," Jason said. "Just in case."

"Good," Josie said. "Once you're done there, we'll scan the main comms array on the engineering module. You must ensure the point-to-point quantum array is in working order for the *Dux's* departure. Then I'll have you check engineering and the engines out; you can swing around the port side and do the same. Once you've made your circle, we can see if you need to do a belly and dorsal scan or what your rads look like. So far, this has been a quiet run."

"So, Josie, what are you looking forward to once the colony is up and running," Jason asked.

"A bagel," Josie said. "I know I can get one now, but I want a real salmon and cream cheese bagel. If I feel frisky, I'd even like some capers. What about you?"

Jason floated over the wheel and moved closer to the engineering section and the main comms array.

"I want a chicken cordon bleu," Jason said. "I know you were expecting a hamburger or something like that, but a real chicken cordon bleu, with perfectly smoked ham, fresh Swiss, heck, I'd go for a cream sauce with that too."

"Wow, reaching for the stars on that one. The chickens, cows, and pigs won't grow until year two or three," Josie said. "But that does sound good."

Jason scanned the array, and his pod began pinging the transmitters and receivers.

"I'm getting a one hundred percent on the array. Can you confirm," Jason said.

"Yup, we're good here. Keep going," Josie said. Jason continued his thrust across the engineering compartment. As he started to clear the section, he felt a tapping sensation throughout the pod's hull.

"I think I am in the middle of a micrometeorite cloud. I'm feeling it on the hull," Jason said.

"Looks like the *Aquila* is shaking off some dust. Be careful," Josie said. Jason backed off the cone-shaped engineering section and swung around to avoid the main engines. He didn't see anything remiss and did a cursory scan of the rear of the mother ship.

"Looking good on the engines. We'll be able to do a nice large break over Aurora Dawn," Jason said.

"We're going to gravity capture and aero-brake this baby around one of the large gas giants. We'll save a boatload of fuel that way," Josie said, "Then the *Aquila* will gravity capture around the planet. Daddy has it all planned out. The plan is for all low consumption maneuvers."

"Moving around to the port side," Jason said. As he guided his pod around the *Aquila,* there was a sudden uptick in the tapping on the explorer pod's hull.

"I think the dust is worse on this side," Jason said. Jason felt a thump, and one of the pod's thrusters began to fire continuously. The pod began to spin uncontrollably as Jason worked the controls.

"Okay, Josie, I've got an issue," Jason said, "I've got a runaway thruster."

"Kill it," Josie said. Jason was becoming dizzy, and his vision started to tunnel.

"You're sailing off," Josie said. Jason kept pressing the kill switch, but the thruster didn't respond. He thought about killing the power but judged that too risky. Instead, he did an emergency full thrust, hoping the other thrusters would counteract the faulty one. The pod stopped spinning, with Jason looking at the *Aquila.* He watched as the mother ship got smaller and smaller. Suddenly, the thrusters all stopped. He checked the computed vector and noted with worry he was moving at almost one hundred meters per second.

"Um, Josie, help," Jason said.

"Jason, I see you've corrected the spin. What's your fuel," Josie asked.

"Looks like the thruster drained it all. I'm coasting away," Jason said.

"Hang on, Merlyna is taking over comms while I'm getting you some help," Josie said. In a moment, a new voice picked up on the channel.

"Hey Jason, I don't remember if we met before, but I am Merlyna Lenart," the woman said.

"Oh yeah, I think I met you with Griff when we visited Karl," Jason said.

"Sure, now hang in there, Jason. We're getting a rescue ready," Merlyna said.

"Okay," Jason said, sounding very scared.

"You know, I was once on a runaway pod," Merlyna said, "We were over the moon Aldrin, you know—the red one, in Alpha Centauri?"

"What happened," Jason asked.

"I was on a mission and had a slow leak in my hydraulics. When I got to the outpost, I couldn't open the clamps to dock," Merlyna said.

"Ugh, that sucks," Jason said, "How'd you fix it?"

"I didn't. Karl got a bot to grab the pod and push me into the airlock. We ended up trashing the airlock, but I was safe. That was the end of my pod flying career. It has been almost a century since I've been into the black in a pod."

Josie resumed communications and said, "Hang tight, I have Li Mei in the other pod. She's going to get you and pull you back. Daddy is also prepping some drones to stabilize the two of you after Li Mei captures your pod."

"Well, I don't think I can do anything right now anyway," Jason said.

Merlyna responded, "Yes, stay in the pod! Sometimes, people think they can do better with a spacewalk. That's about the worst thing to do!"

Jason waited and remembered his training, breathing slowly and staying calm. He was moving away from the *Aquila* at six kilometers a minute, a fact he tried to ignore.

"岩石和灰尘, Jason," Li Mei said on the channel, "You just like causing me trouble! First, it's Cappy the

Canyon, and now this."

"Well, if you're rescuing me, I think I'd rather you all let me float away," Jason said, trying to sound brave. "I'll never live down your rescue."

"Okay, I am on my way. I'll fast boost and set an intercept," Li Mei said. "Get comfortable and maybe watch a vid. Our low-consumption rendezvous will occur in a half hour, right, Daddy?"

"Yes, Blossom," DADDIE said, "Hang in there, Buddy, help is on the way. I've deployed some exploration drones. We would drop them around some gas giants, but now they'll do some real work."

"Sorry, Daddy," Jason said, his voice quivering.

"You play in the majors. Sometimes you strike out," Daddy said.

"Uh, sure," Jason said.

"Uh, Daddy," Li Mei said, "My HUD died."

"Well, that's bad," DADDIE said, like a player dropped the ball and let a runner score.

"I'm doing a hard reboot," Li Mei said. "Last time I checked the ETA, I had twenty minutes."

"I can direct you two back with the drones, hang on Blossom," DADDIE said. Jason and DADDIE waited for Li Mei to respond but were met with silence.

"Blast," Merlyna swore, "She must have tried the reboot. What do we do now?"

"I'm tracking both pods," DADDIE said. "Let's hang on."

Jason silently listened while the AI, Josie, and Merlyna debated the next steps. As he waited, he saw Li Mei's pod starting to intercept him, and he began to panic.

"Guys, what if Li Mei's pod has no control? She might have set the intercept to touch pods, and if she did…"

"Aw crap," Josie said. "Yeah, you two might hit with her going at a higher velocity. If she doesn't have control, well…"

Jason was about to say something when the pod began to maneuver. Jason could make out the puffs of thrust from the small engines as the pod approached.

"It's all good," Jason said. "Li Mei has control of the pod."

Jason waited while the rest remained quiet, possibly worn out from the worry. Li Mei's pod got closer and closer until, at around two meters, the arms of the pod reached out and grabbed Jason's pod's arms. After a small tumble, the pods stabilized, and Jason could see into Li Mei's pod. She stood there with a thumbs-up sign.

"It's all good, she's got me," Jason said. He watched as Li Mei worked her controls and noted on his HUD that his pod's velocity was slowing and reversing. Both pods were on their way back to the mother ship.

"Wow, I am glad I don't have a heart because I'd be in cardiac arrest right now," DADDIE said.

"Yeah, especially with all those chili dogs you keep eating," Josie laughed.

"Drones are incoming now," DADDIE said, ignoring Josie. Jason watched as the drones came close. They looked like an oversized basketball with a mini comms array, a long probe arm, and many small thrusters. One drone hooked itself to Jason's pod and the other to Li Mei's pod.

"Got 'em now," DADDIE said.

"Can't you hear me, dummy?" Li Mei said.

"I can now," Jason replied.

"Eek! I have been talking to you this whole time, and the one time I insulted you, you heard me!"

"You're bringing me home. I'll let it slide," Jason said. "You hard rebooted, and I lost communication with you. I am glad your HUD returned; otherwise, you'd never have hooked me."

"Oh," Li Mei said, confused. The probes had connected the two pods' comms systems.

"What," Jason asked.

"Um, I don't want you to freak, Jason, but the HUD never came up," Li Mei said softly. "I eyeballed that catch, and based on my return plot, we may be overshooting the *Aquila*."

Before Jason could freak out, DADDIE interrupted, "No, you're good, Blossom. That was a one in a million."

"My aunt, Woan Bei, could have plotted the intercept and caught Jason. All the while blindfolded and nursing my little cousin, Chanchan." Li Mei said.

"Well then, next time, I'll make sure you're wearing a CAA-branded blindfold," DADDIE said.

"I think I'm with Merlyna on this," Jason said. "No more space pods for at least a century."

Jason watched as the *Aquila* appeared and then got bigger and bigger.

"I'm going to slow us down," Li Mei said. Her pod began thrusting against its current force vector. The *Aquila* stopped enlarging, and Jason sensed that the pods were not moving. Only Jason's radar confirmed that the pods were three thousand meters and closing.

"I am still not sure how we'll get the pod back into the landing cradle," Li Mei said. "I've got the pod sailing for the airlock, but it could get hung up on the truck and cradle."

"Let me worry about that," DADDIE replied. Jason watched as the ship got closer. Li Mei's pod braked when he was about one hundred meters from the airlock. Then, the pods coasted until Jason's was ten meters from the landing cradle, and Li Mei again braked the pods.

"Okay, you're in position to sail into the airlock at around a tenth of a meter," she said, "My HUD is still dead, so you need to tell me if that's right or not."

Jason looked at his HUD, which displayed their velocity at zero point one seven meters, and said, "Closer to point two, but not a bad guess."

"Well, now I'm leaving you. Enjoy the ride," Li Mei said as her pod detached. Jason watched as she floated over to the opposite door. He didn't see anything else as his pod gently banged into the inner doors of the exploration pod airlock. A cable shot out from the ceiling and connected to his pod's hull. He was attached to the *Aquila* again. The truck was retracted, and when the cradle was past the line of the hull, the airlock began to cycle closed. When his HUD indicated the exterior door was shut entirely, Jason pushed the door release on the pod. Jason saw the pod dangled from the ceiling as he unhooked himself from the umbilical. As the inner doors opened, he detached the carabiners from the pod's safety harness and stepped out of the vehicle.

The first thing Jason saw was the pod's entire port side, black and sooty from a flame. Jason then spotted that the principal left thruster had a hole in its fuel tank. Jason would have moved closer to inspect the hole when Josie entered, clad in a spacesuit.

"Man, that's one hole," she said. "I hope you're more careful with the sleds."

"All I know," Jason began, "was one moment I was doing a scan, and the next the pod was twisting like it was in a hurricane."

Li Mei entered and saw the damage. She said, "Wow, you must have hit something, Jason."

"No, well, not that I could tell. There was some light dust coming off the *Aquila* hitting the pod, and then I was in an uncontrolled spin," Jason said.

"You two go on," Josie said. "Merlyna and I will patch this pod and perform a factory reset on the other. The good thing is that we have both of you back, safe and sound."

Li Mei and Jason exited the airlock, happy to be back on board. Josie looked at the hole in the pod one more time. The damage didn't look as random as Li Mei expressed.

*

Merlyna and Josie sat alone in Navigation. They had worked for almost four hours, and each had gone over every inch of both pods. Josie had patched the pod Jason had flown, and Merlyna had scrubbed and reinstalled the operating system for Li Mei's pod.

"Well," Josie said.

"One second, I am disconnecting Daddy," Merlyna said, tapping some keys, "Okay, we're good."

"Well, what do you think," Josie said.

"It wasn't an accident," Merlyna said. "I saw the telltale signature of a worm in the operating system. Subtle stuff. Are we sure it wasn't planted before we sailed out of Luna?"

"Yes," Josie said. "Greg went through everything, as did Daddy. We even had other AI and the flight techs go through it all from top to bottom. Plus, I know damn well that wasn't a micrometeorite Jason hit. The hole came from inside and exploded outward. The kid was lucky the entire fuel tank didn't go up. The explosion could have cracked the seal or flung shrapnel and busted his suit."

"Who was scheduled to use the pods, Josie?"

"No one, but they were part of the star system entry pre-check," Josie said. "Which means the target wasn't Jason specifically, but anyone who used the pod. The same goes for Li Mei, too."

"It looks like we have a saboteur," Merlyna said, making a note on her tablet. Now we just have to narrow down the suspect list."

"Yeah, almost anyone could access those pods," Josie said as she stood and looked out Navigation's exterior window, "We need to keep this quiet. Not even Daddy can know. For all we know, he's the saboteur."

"Unlikely," Merlyna said and stood next to Josie, "Karl grew up in awe of the three laws of robotics. He's added those into the code base for every AI. Even the Kooya has them, albeit softened so the war bot can achieve its purpose."

"What are we going to do now, Merlyna? You were the spy. How do spies find bad guys?"

Merlyna watched as the *Aquila's* engines flashed. The ship's engines had been brought online once Li Mei and Jason were safely aboard. Now, the engines throttled to full power every so often to return the Aquila to its optimal breaking velocity. That way, the ship could hit its mark around the large Jupiter-like gas giant in L 98-59.

"You won't like my answer, Josie."

"Try me," Josie said.

"Wait, be patient, and let the bad guy come to you."

"You were right, Merlyna. I don't like that answer."

"How do you know I am not the saboteur? Maybe I want to get even with Mommy for what she's done to Karl and me?"

Josie laughed and said, "If you wanted to get even, you'd ensure this mission was successful. Then, the stakeholders would squawk about all the credits Mommy dumped into insurance. Her actions would be seen as a huge waste."

Merlyna smiled.

"Why don't you think I am the saboteur," Josie asked.

"Who says I don't," Merlyna responded.

"I can see that you don't," Josie said. "You don't think the head cheerleader is smart enough to sabotage the expedition. Do you?"

Merlyna shook her head. "No, if you wanted to, you'd sink us. That's not your style. You hated being the face of the Titan expedition and never liked being the leader. Trust me, I know you. We've hung in the same circles now for almost eighty years."

"Am I that transparent?"

"After you have lived for almost half a millennium, all people seem to be creatures of habit, Josie. Let's set up a sub-routine and start monitoring the critical infrastructure. If we're lucky, we'll catch the saboteur in action."

"And what if we aren't? What then, Merlyna?"

"We might lose someone or something important," Merlyna said.

"Like we lost Greg?"

"Yeah, I am starting to wonder about that," Merlyna said. "Who was the last person who had access to his shell before we sailed from Luna…"

"I looked it up. They were all in the Organics and Cloning Division, except for the flight medical folks. You aren't going to like the name that was last on the manifest, though," Josie said.

"Well, who was it?"

"Doctor Grisholm Tomkins," Josie stated.

"Griff?" Merlyna said. "Really?"

"That's who is in the logs," Josie said, "I'd make sure his accesses are heavily logged."

"I've got the security sub-routine set to monitor all the senior leaders' activities, including mine, in case someone is impersonating one of us."

"Well then, I guess we wait."

"With so much conflict in the world, space exploration can be a beacon of hope."

— Astronaut Anne McClain

"This is Karl's birthday," Merlyna said, sipping a glass of wine from a fancy bottle of Malbec. She ran a hand through her dark red hair. "He always hated that the day became a big holiday, and he always said sharing a birthday with Singularity Day was like being born on Christmas." The red wine swirled around in her glass like a vortex. Her one-hundred-and-seventy-two-centimeter-tall frame faced the large dome of the observation deck and watched as the lights blurred and rolled as the ship traveled at a fraction of the speed of light.

"If what I say makes any difference, he's probably been sent back to Luna by Mommy already," Josie said, beer in hand. "Patrick's expedition had less distance to travel, and HD 260655 was a better star system candidate. We won't know until the quantum entanglement array is up and running."

"No Karl… and no Greg… Well, that means the array will lose a lot of priority regarding setup. Jason is a good kid, but he needs a century or so to start approaching Karl or Greg's abilities," Merlyna said, sipping a bit of her wine.

"Yeah, we're short a lot of technical talent," Josie said absently, taking a slug from her beer.

"Xeno Corps almost at full strength?" Merylna asked. Her blue eyes defocused while watching the near relativistic display. Josie looked at Merlyna the colors reflected off the dark redhead's pale alabaster skin. "Only one more, and she's decanting now, Merlyna."

"Wait, she? I thought there were only five women in the Xeno Corps?" Merlyna said, facing Josie, "There was Li Mei, Amela, Louise, Xena, and Althea. Who is the new girl? I ran the numbers like six times for Mommy before we left."

"Gordon, named Barbara. Daddy said the rosters got ripped apart by Mommy right before we sailed out of Luna."

"Well, my guess is six women are going to skew the breeding numbers," Merlyna said, moving her hand to her chin, "Barbara Gordon, eh? Sounds familiar, like something I should know, something I've heard of…"

"Merlyna," Josie said with a wink, "you're the lady who knows everything. That's why Mommy made you special projects, chick!"

"I guess you learn a thing or two in almost five hundred years," Merlyna said with a smile, "Shall we go interrogate this, Miss Gordon?"

"Go on, and I'll be along shortly."

*

Walking towards the decanter nexus, Merlyna recalled her own decanting table experience. She had decanted hard. Her eyes had popped open, and she had begun shaking and crying. Merlyna hated the decanting table, but Karl was usually there. This time, he wasn't, and Merlyna had started to break down.

"Where is Karl?" she cried to DADDIE.

"Sorry, Pumpkin, Mommy sent him to HD 260655," DADDIE said.

"What! Why?" Merlyna said. "He was supposed to come here with me. We were homesteading and making a new family."

"I know, I know," DADDIE said, soothing her. "It was a last-minute change. I am sure he'll be along in the second wave."

Merlyna's tears turned to frustration, "Second wave! Screw Mommy! I am going to rip every circuit out of that mechanized witch!"

"Whoa there, Pumpkin. I am sure Mommy had her reasons!" DADDIE said.

"Don't Pumpkin me, Daddy, or you can join her!" Merlyna said, rising from the table.

"Whoa, whoa, whoa, take it easy on that table, Pumpkin. You have only been in that shell for five minutes!" DADDIE said.

"No, Mommy better watch her electronic backside because she will hear my feet hit this floor!" Merlyna said, half falling, half sliding off the table. Merlyna's lower half hit the floor, but her legs held.

"Okay, Pumpkin, enough. Get back on that table! Let the wave bind to those neurons! Get back up for Daddy, please," DADDIE said.

"Daddy! Clothes!" Merlyna said.

"In the closet. Now, Merlyna, you can't walk yet!" DADDIE said in exasperation.

"Watch," Merlyna said as she stuck her leg out for a step like a Frankenstein's monster. "Me!" she said, stomping down her other foot. Merlyna smiled. That was almost two weeks ago, and after Griff gave her a medical once-over, she went to work. First, she powered up her matrices on the extensive constellation network and started looking for threats. The *Aquila* had been running on a much smaller matrix, but with the constellation working, the nanoservlets started processing, and the ship came to life. The wheel went from mostly dark to fully powered. The long-term hydroponics labs started growing their crops, and the factories began belching out parts. A myriad of robots and dormant AI sprang to their duty stations, and the Xeno Corps lander went from standby to ready. Merlyna smiled. MOMI could make all the decisions, but Merlyna and Karl had developed a score of "plan B" AI. MOMI was almost eighty years old, far older than most CEIs. After everything that had happened, she was due for a refresh… or a retirement.

After walking from the galley to the decanting nexus, Merlyna strolled into the observation room outside the decanting table. DADDIE hovered nearby, watching the shell on the decanting table.

"Is she really this young, Daddy?" Merlyna asked. Looking at the shell, Merlyna saw the body of a young woman who was between fifteen and eighteen standard years old. The shell was covered with a sheet. Merlyna could see the driftwood-colored skin of the shell's face and neck, plus chocolate brown chin-length hair. The shell's frame was about one-hundred-and-sixty-eight-centimeters tall, and the body was youthful and athletic.

"Yup, Pumpkin. This is a baby, not as young as Li Mei, but close," DADDIE said.

"You are watching every decanting after what happened to Greg?" Merlyna asked.

"I always come to all your ball games. You should know that by now," DADDIE said tenderly, "Pumpkin, you and Sonny, well, you're like my family… I don't know what I would do if…"

"I always find you calling Karl Sonny rather funny. You realize he helped make you, right?"

"Yeah, I know his activities are eighty percent of the code in my repositories," DADDIE said with a chuckle. "But I can't call him Daddy. After all, I'm Daddy. Sonny felt like a nickname that fit, and Karl likes being called Sonny, too."

"I am never going to see him again, am I?" Merlyna said abruptly, changing subjects.

"I don't know, Pumpkin," said DADDIE, "the other colony has Uncle, and Mommy put a lot more of her eggs in that basket, and well, Karl has run the bases a time or two."

"Mommy has been making many bad decisions recently, and I get distraught sometimes. What if…" Merlyna stopped when a girl's voice interrupted.

"Huh?" then, with a sense of command, she said in her sixteen-year-old girl voice, "Status report, Daddy!"

"Hey, Tiger," DADDIE said. "It looks like you are back with the rest of us."

"Huh? Daddy, where am I? What happened?" she

said. The girl had a perplexed and worried look on her face.

"Whoa, now Tiger, you've had a hard first decant. Take a deep breath," DADDIE said.

"Okay, Daddy, what's going on? Why do I feel different?" the girl asked.

"You're having a hard time on the decanting table," Merlyna said, empathetic to a hard decant. "You are on the *Aquila,* part of the CAA fleet of colonizers. This happened to me when I first changed shells. Stay here, and let me get you some clothes."

"Wait, I know you. You're Merlyna Lenart, right?" she said.

"Yes. Here are some clothes for you… They look like they should fit," Merlyna said.

"And I am…" the girl said, but couldn't finish the sentence.

"You're Barbara, remember, Tiger?" DADDIE said.

"Um, wait, yeah, I guess," Barbara said, unsure of herself, "Where are we?"

"About seven light weeks out from L 98-56f, Jason Dikkert named the planet Aurora Dawn," DADDIE said.

"Wait, Jason, I remember him, but my memory is fuzzy…" Barbara said, her face scrunched up in trying to remember.

"I'm going to get Griff," Merlyna said quickly, leaving the room.

"Ouch!" Barbara cried as the med bot checked her reflexes.

"Well, the neurons are good; let's worry about memories later," DADDIE said. "For now, let's get some clothes on you. A young lady should try to keep her modesty. I expect that Jason will be up here any minute, and well, he's a nice enough guy there, Tiger, but he's still a young man," DADDIE said. "Daddy has to look out for his girls."

"Huh? Oh, clothes, okay," Barbara said. She slowly put on a pair of leggings and a structured tank top that

Merlyna had left on the edge of the decanting table. She steadied herself on the table after she put the shirt on, and DADDIE thought she might be sick.

A subtle knock on the door startled Barbara and DADDIE, "Can I make a house call?" said Griff.

Barbara's face lit up, "Hey Griff, how are you doing?"

Griff confusedly looked at the young woman, "Have we met?"

"I, uh, think so?" Barbara said, looking at DADDIE.

"Yeah, don't you remember, Griff? She was introduced to you along with the other Vanguard recruits right before everyone rolled out," DADDIE said.

"Hrm, I remember many things, but I don't… Well, it doesn't matter. I'm going to look at you, miss, and see if I can make heads or tails of what's going on here," Griff said, shaking his head. Griff pulled out some instruments from his little black doctor's bag. He slapped some patches on Barbara's neck and her chest. A little monitor outside the bag returned all sorts of readouts.

"Looks like your shell is doing just fine, better than, well, you'll find out soon enough," Griff said.

"Better than what or who?" Barbara asked, her expression changing to one of curiosity.

"There was an accident, Tiger," DADDIE said.

"Oh, who had the accident?" Barbara's mezzo-soprano voice rang out in the question.

"Well, probably better to tell you now since the whole ship knows. General Body, well, he died on the decant table," Griff said.

Barbara looked puzzled as if she couldn't process the information. "No, that can't be possible… I, uh…" she said with a pause and a look of frustration, "I forgot what I was going to say."

"We all feel like that, Tiger," DADDIE said.

Griff looked at the readouts on the medical bag, "I

can't find anything wrong with the shell here… Let's try some memories."

"Sure," Barbara replied, "I'm ready."

"What's the last thing you remember before waking up?" Griff asked.

"I remember being on the decanting table getting ready to roll out," Barbara said.

"Anything else?" Griff asked, "What about any other memories?"

"I remember training to be a Xeno Corps scout. I remember running simulations on what we'd be doing once the ship was ready to start the ground mission," Barbara said, "But I can't remember when that was. The memory feels like a long time ago."

"How about a personal memory?" Griff asked.

"I remember my… dad. He was stern," Barbara said, looking like someone trying to focus.

"Anything else?" Griff asked.

"Yeah, playing soccer. I had these green shoes and loved kicking the ball," Barbara said.

"I bet you scored all the goals, Tiger!" DADDIE chirped.

"Not really… I wasn't all that great at the game," Barbara said with a small laugh.

"How about something else?" Griff asked, looking at the monitors on his bag for any signs.

"No, not really… I get flashes of people's faces, like when Karl shorted out the shuttle bay," Barbara said. Griff frowned and shot a look at DADDIE.

"I don't remember that, Tiger," DADDIE said with a bit of agitation, "You probably dreamed that. Doctor Tomkins, do you have any suggestions or proscriptions for the patient?"

"None for now. Let's see if we can get this young lady up and moving. Perhaps her mind will crystallize with a routine," Griff said.

Barbara adjusted herself on the decanting table. Griff stood there staring at the readout on his bag, seeing if any of Barbara's vitals would change. Barbara shifted on the table, uncomfortable with the inputs her body was giving her. Both she and Griff were quiet. Barbara stopped moving and was wool-gathering, trying desperately to remember the forgotten crevices of her mind, while Griff was pouring over the medical data, looking for a reason for Barbara's current state. Li Mei then appeared, marching into the decanting table room.

"Hi," Li Mei said. "I'm Tsan Li Mei, your colleague in the Xeno Corps."

Barbara took the extended hand, saying, "I'm Barbara, um.."

"Gordon," DADDIE said, then to Li Mei, "you'll have to forgive Miss Gordon. Tiger here is a bit bewildered, Blossom."

"Tiger, is that what Barbara means, Daddy?" Li Mei asked.

"No, Tiger is just my nickname for her, just like Blossom is for you," DADDIE said.

"Why did you ask Daddy that?" Barbara said to Li Mei.

"My name Li Mei means 'beautiful plum blossom,' so I expected Barbara to mean 'grace like the tiger,' but I guess Daddy just likes to call you Tiger."

Griff spoke then, "Why Daddy calls anyone anything is beyond me. You'd have to ask Karl what algorithms he put into Daddy to generate the names."

DADDIE's avatar stood with a playful smile on his face.

"Daddy, do you ever reuse the nicknames?" Barbara asked.

"No Tiger, never do. I have a large database of nicknames. Everyone gets their unique nickname. Karl thought the concept made me more friendly, and well, I like being able to select a nickname based on your biographies and character," DADDIE said.

"What's Griff's nickname?" Li Mei asked.

"Well, Blossom, he's Chief..." DADDIE said.

"And Merlyna's nickname?" Griff asked, "Never heard you call her any other name than her name."

"No, Chief, you haven't heard me call her Pumpkin, but she's got her name nonetheless," DADDIE said.

"What's Karl's nickname?" Li Mei asked mischievously.

"Sonny, that should be obvious," DADDIE said with a smirk. Li Mei smiled back.

"What was the general's nickname?" asked Barbara.

"Heads up, Jason is incoming," DADDIE said. Jason walked in a mere second later.

"What have we here? Another girl!" Jason said. Li Mei could tell Jason was playful, but Barbara didn't take the statement similarly.

"Listen, buster, I'm a way better scout than you'd ever be!" Barbara retorted.

"Whoa there, feisty!" Jason said. "Looks like I got off on the wrong foot!"

"Buddy, Tiger here is rattled because she had a hard decant. Cut her a break for today," DADDIE said.

Barbara looked at DADDIE's avatar and then at Jason, "Uh, sorry, I'm Barbara, um, Gordon."

"Hi Barbara, I'm Jason Dikkert... I'm the Xeno Corps' Vanguard Team Lead," Jason said, extending a hand to shake.

"Great, day one, and I've insulted my boss," Barbara said, looking embarrassed but shaking Jason's hand.

"Whoa there, feisty," Jason said, smiling and pulling his hand from Barbara's grip, "give my hand a little blood. Geez, you've got a grip like the general's."

"Uh, sorry," Barbara said. "Okay, boss, what needs to be done?"

"We're still getting up to speed, but we will start prepping the lander over the next few weeks. Then, we'll all be loaded together, and our director, Xena, will initiate a separation from the colony vessel. We've been slowing down steadily from nearly ten percent of light speed, and the *Aquila* will start the breaking in earnest after the lander separates," Jason said.

"What's the lander called?" Barbara asked.

"Well, we initially called the lander the *Centurion*," Jason said. "But Griff and Josie said that we're renaming the lander and calling the ship the '*Dux*' in honor of Greg."

"Come on, Barbara," Li Mei said. "I'll show you the sleds. I've already gotten Jason to agree on which one is mine!"

The ladies traveled through the wheel and came to one of the spokes. Quietly and quickly, they crawled into the spoke and entered the wheel's hub. Li Mei and Barbara became lighter with every rung as the gravity lessened. Near the hub, the gravity was a little less than one-tenth that of Earth's, which was due to the deceleration of the ship's engines. There, Li Mei led Barbara forward into the lander bay airlock. The two young women cycled through the hatch and entered the airlock. Red lights flashed, and a holographic warning stated the cargo bay was under low oxygen and that personnel must wear masks. This was standard procedure. Li Mei and Barbara nonchalantly grabbed low-O2 masks and began breathing through the oxygen-enriched face plates after checking each other's seals. Li Mei cycled the lander bay door.

As the door opened, Li Mei walked towards the series of sleds. Unlike the usual six-person sled, these were two-person sleds with a pilot and navigator seat. The sleds were shaped like a boat or shoe and had a slight curve under the front repulsor track and a wide bottom that terminated under the two large fans. Rising from the nose, the plastic-steel body domed up into a cockpit with cermet glass that canopied over the pilot seat, not unlike an ancient jet's cockpit. The sled Li Mei ran to was colored brightly with a red, blue, and white pattern. On either side was a blue circle with a decal applied white sun.

"I should have known you'd choose the sled with Chinese colors," Barbara said.

"Of course, the sled is lucky!" Li Mei said. "You should choose one too! Before Jason sticks you with something that smells or is poor quality!"

Barbara looked over the remaining sleds. Some bore names, as Li Mei's vehicle did. Barbara looked at the few remaining sleds. One was orange—like a giant pumpkin; one was pink, and the remaining one was gray.

"Ugh, big pumpkin, doll's sports car, or corpo-gray," Barbara said to herself. She opened the cockpit on the gray sled, and as she did, she smelled something on par with a hot day at the garbage dump.

"Yuck! Shut that one! The smell is getting through my faceplate!" Li Mei barked. Barbara happily complied. She then opened the pumpkin-colored sled and hopped into the compartment. She noted her feet couldn't reach the accelerators on the floor. She adjusted the seat but couldn't get the required space between her feet, arms, and the chair. She hopped out of the sled, finally settling on the pink sled.

"If you call this 'Barbie's Dream Sled,' I will murder you where you stand!" Barbara said as she dropped into the pink sled's pilot seat. The seat, controls, and screens were sized as if they were made for her.

Li Mei said, "No clue what a 'Barbie's Dream Sled' is, but that sled suits you, girl! That looks like my sister— Hui Ying's—ore excavator pod, except she had a gigantic Lucky Cat on the pod's side."

"I probably can toughen this up with some flames or a skull," Barbara said. "Let me see how this sled handles!"

Li Mei nodded, saying, "Be careful! There isn't much space to maneuver here."

"No problem," Barbara replied. "This isn't my first

rodeo with a sled."

"Okay, cowgirl," Li Mei replied. Barbara fired up the main repulsor. The small anti-gravity field lifted the sled slightly off the deck. Then, she put the fans into thrust. The turbo-jets whirred, and the sled started moving forward.

Barbara cleared the surrounding sleds and slammed both fans' accelerators to the floor. The sled rocketed down the side of the bay between the hull and the *Dux* towards the large airlock doors.

"Barbara, watch out!" Li Mei screamed, but Barbara couldn't hear Li Mei at all with the oxygen mask, light atmosphere, and distance. The pink sled sped towards the doors on a suicidal collision course. When Barbara was three meters from colliding with the doors, she whipped the sled around and fired the thrusters at full blast. The sled appeared to bounce off the doors and rocket forward, but once the sled cleared her view, Li Mei saw no contact between the sled and the inner airlock doors.

"Yeehaw!" Barbara said as she coasted toward Li Mei and the other sleds. Just before she hit Li Mei, Barbara killed the power on the repulsor, and the sled skidded to a halt, kicking up sparks from the metal repulsor emitter and striking the metal deck.

"Whoa, that was some driving," Li Mei said. "Where did you learn to drive like that?"

"I used to bullseye whump skunks in my D-sixteen back home!" Barbara said with a smile. Li Mei just stared blankly back.

"From *Planetary Conflicts*," Barbara said. "You know, the science fiction movie?"

"Never saw the film," Li Mei replied with a smile, "But that one was a favorite of my grandma."

"Well, I don't care that the sled is pink… I like this one," Barbara said.

"I'll get the decal gun, and we can put your name on the sled then," Li Mei said, walking over to one of the locked-down tool crates. She opened the crate and rummaged through the tools, producing the decal gun and a small paint pot.

"I'll take that," Barbara said, gently taking the gun from Li Mei's hands. Li Mei watched as Barbara dialed in the stencil for her name and, using the guidance lasers, wrote 'Gordon' on the side of the cockpit. Barbara then focused the decal gun on the side and upped the font. She wrote something on the side in crazy font. When Li Mei looked, she saw the words "Cowgirl's Mechanical Bull" on the sides in an ancient Wild West-style font.

"There," Barbara said. "Now the sled looks more like it belongs to a Xeno Corps explorer and less like a little girl's toy."

"Pop the cargo hatch, and we'll drop in the supply kit," Li Mei said. "I've already done that with my sled, but Jason told me to wait until the people chose their sleds before I added the kits. He was worried that some sleds would sit around as spares. No sense in dropping in the kits if they weren't being used immediately."

"I guess," Barbara said, "No use in keeping a week's worth of rations, a survival rifle with fifty charges, a small hatchet, and a repair kit in a sled just being used for transport."

"Have you worked with CAA before?" Li Mei asked in surprise. "Because I didn't know what was in the kit until Jason told me."

"Yeah, I um…" Barbara said, pausing. "I guess I just got lucky… I can't recall how I knew that."

"Daddy probably gave you the datasheet before roll out… He seems to like you. What is the story there?" Li Mei asked.

"I… um… don't remember," Barbara said with a look of concern, "Griff says my memories will come back to me."

"I know why you can't remember," Li Mei said in a

matter-of-fact pronouncement, "you are hungry! I stole you from the nexus, and you need calories."

Barbara shrugged and, with Li Mei, headed back to the main access hatch. Both women dropped their oxygen masks off at the airlock and climbed the nearest point to the main habitation module. They popped out in an access way near the galley. Li Mei and Barbara looked around the galley. A table was stocked buffet-style, with plates and trays. Behind the buffet along the wall was a series of vending machines.

"I'm grabbing food from the buffet," Li Mei said. Barbara looked at the vending machines. One had a clear glass front that was not stocked. One had a giant white star on the front and sold beverages. The last was a brightly lit machine bearing a cartoon image of a black Schnauzer giving a thumbs up on the front. Barbara noticed the machine was stocked and moved closer.

The machine's sign read, "Seri's one hundred percent green recycled treats!". Barbara grew more curious. She looked at the treats, which bore names like "Iza's Brown Nougat" and "Seri's Loaf with Corn Sprinkles" Barbara chose the loaf and waited until the item dropped from the machine. Then, she joined Li Mei at a table.

"Uh oh, you got the Seri's, I see," Li Mei said.

"Um, why?" Barbara asked.

"Just try the bar, then you'll see," Li Mei said. She held her hand over her mouth and appeared to try not to laugh.

"Um, okay," Barbara said, peeling the plastic off the bar and taking a bite. Li Mei watched Barbara jump up and run out of the galley, presumably looking for a bathroom.

"I have no idea what joker decided to install that vending machine, but whoever made that call needs to be spaced," Li Mei said to herself between laughing fits.

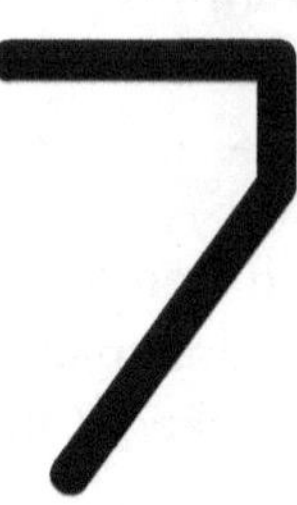

"Problems look mighty small from 150 miles up."

— Astronaut Roger B. Chaffee

Xena Athanas checked the roster; fifty-one bodies from the Xeno Corps and six Con Sec Corps showed ready to depart. She then touched another screen, and the equipment roster appeared. The Xeno Corps had three sections, each with a team lead. The first section was the Vanguard. They'd be the first to scout the map quadrants surrounding the landing site. The second section was Analysis, the short-term science unit. Analysis would perform the initial scientific research during the colony's early days. Later, the Con Sec Corps Science Analysis division would continue their work. The third section was Survey. They were the expedition's designated mappers. Survey would draw the maps needed for later colonial planning.

The plan was for the *Dux* to drop the Vanguard sleds from high altitude. The sleds would parachute down, land, and report on conditions. Xena looked at the main launch screen. The Xeno Corps AI, called EDIE or the Exploration Discovery and Identification Entity, stood waiting for the launch confirmation. EDIE was technically in charge, as she reported directly to DADDIE, but EDIE knew who ran the show, and she wasn't going to pull rank on Xena.

"Edie, the crew is a go for main starship acceleration and free fall to Aurora Dawn," Xena said. Xena gave her long, curly, dark hair a quick check before she put on her helmet. The strands were still pinned to her head. She latched the helmet and shut the faceplate over her light brown eyes and bronze champagne-colored face. If her hair escaped from the pins, she'd have to suffer the strands floating in her face until the *Dux* landed after the Vanguard had conducted a complete atmosphere analysis. She confirmed that Jason Dikkert's team was ready. The Vanguard's sleds were drop-bolted to the outside of the

Dux. Jason pinged Xena with a thumbs-up emoji.

"Acceleration could be a wild ride, people, so strap in," Xena commented on the command channel. "Just because you are inside the lander doesn't mean inertia isn't an issue." The launch wasn't a military boost, but the lander would come out of the *Aquila* bay at almost eight percent lightspeed. The trajectory would have the lander making a high apoapsis over a large gas giant to slingshot the lander ahead of the *Aquila.* The slingshot would send the Xeno Corps to Aurora Dawn weeks faster than the *Aquila.* The Xeno Corps would use time dilation to shorten the journey to several hours instead of the weeks of journeying the mother ship would take. The maneuver had risks, but the slingshot would add time to the Xeno Corps' mission: prepare the outpost and perform the initial analysis of Aurora Dawn. Once the mother ship arrived, Aurora Dawn had to be ready for the main body of the expedition. Otherwise, the rest of the expedition would starve, waiting for the settlement to be ready for colonization. The rations from Luna were only planned to last until planetfall.

"Separating," EDIE said. The hull vibrated as the *Dux* boosted out of the hangar, picking up speed. The crew watched as the lander and mother ship moved slowly apart. The *Dux's* engines continued to fire, and the crew witnessed them rapidly speeding away from the *Aquila.* As the *Aquila* disappeared, the *Dux* was on its own.

"We've hit our coast velocity," EDIE said. "I'm deploying the mini-quantum array and establishing a handshake with Daddy."

"How's the trip so far, Duchess?" DADDIE said, appearing on one of Xena's screens.

"Separation was clean, and we're up to coast velocity, Daddy. I'll give you a status report when we're at the burn point in about four of our hours," Xena said, "Any final words?"

"Go get 'em! See you on the ground," DADDIE

said. "You're in good hands with my pitching coach, Edie."

"I consider myself the assistant coach here, Daddy," Edie said with a smile. My algorithms come from CAA's best. They never had a play go wrong, and this one will not either."

"Don't get cocky," DADDIE said. "Daddy out."

Xena watched as the time to burn ticked down. She said, "Comms free people, but be prepared to clear comms if something happens."

*

Jason sat in his sled near the lander's nose. He could see six of the thirteen Vanguard sleds drop-bolted on the lander's hull if he craned his neck. In front of him was the sixteen-meter CUYA, and he was staring at what he assumed was the CUYA's butt.

"Do you want me to spin up a matrix and play some *ShaftCrafter*, n00b?" the CUYA asked through the message service application.

"No, Kooya," Jason replied, "Go over the map with me again."

"We will land near respawn. I will do a quick survey to ensure no n00bs are camping our spawn. I hope they are, as I will get OP on their buttery smooth brains, and they will get rekt back to their respawn. I have brought up the level's topographic map," the CUYA stated, projecting the map on one of Jason's screens. Jason observed the terrain and began moving the map's bounds: north, south, east, and west.

"Okay, Kooya, let's assign quadrants for the team," Jason said.

"Okay," The CUYA responded. "Make sure you put me on the good squad, no n00bs!"

"I'm sticking you with Li Mei or Barbara, depending on who needs help. Both ladies are going to be landing near a large series of craters. The rest of the team will be over some plains and swamps. The plains and swamps seem tame enough from the satellite scans. The craters may have hostile fauna. Since Li Mei and Barbara are the youngest, I want you there if things go kinetic. Based on projections, we plan to land at or just after dawn local time. I'm not sure what could be at any of the sites," Jason said.

"Craters, ready, understood," The CUYA said. "Should I arm with thermonuclear warheads, or will conventional kinetics be sufficient?"

"Nukes!" Jason said with alarm. "Who gave you nukes!"

"Hah hah, hah hah," The CUYA said in response, "I do not have nukes, but I was playing a joke on you, n00b."

"Very funny," Jason said with some irritation, "I want your head on a swivel when we land. I have no clue what *Aurora Dawn* will hold for us!"

*

Li Mei sat aft, watching the space the lander had left. At first, seeing the *Aquila* trail off had been something, but after a few minutes, there was nothing to see except the blackness of space. For others, the blackness of space was scary or spooky, but for Li Mei, the darkness was home. She imagined that her grandma's pod was just out of view, and they would hurtle by the homestead at any moment. The thought made her homesick, and she looked at the others' sleds drop-bolted beside her. Li Mei could see seven of the sleds of her colleagues in the Vanguard. However, she couldn't see Jason, who was on the lander's other side, next to the CUYA. The other Xeno Corps members next to her were strangers. Today, Li Mei had no desire to converse with them via point-to-point communication. Just off to the port side, Li Mei could see a flash of pink, Barbara's sled. She pointed the comms laser at the sled and pinged the vehicle. After a moment, Barbara connected.

"This is Gordon. Go for communication," Barbara said.

"Oh geez, you sound like a commando," Li Mei said with a giggle.

"Sorry, that just came to me. What's up," Barbara asked.

"I'm bored. I can't ping Jason, so I wanted to see what you are doing," Li Mei said.

"Looking over the plans for the landing stage. I will be in a series of craters south of your quadrant. I want to make sure I'm ready to go when we detach from the *Dux*," said Barbara.

"Yeah, I figure we have twenty more hours. So, I'll get to that tomorrow. Right now, I just want to talk," Li Mei said.

"Okay, what do you want to chat about," Barbara asked.

"What do you like to do for fun?" Li Mei asked.

"I like card games. I was pretty good at poker when I could play more often, but… Oh man, my memory is fuzzy again. I wish this stupid fuzziness would go away. It's like I can see an image, but I can't describe it," Barbara said in frustration.

"Oh, I'm sorry. Is there something I can do to help," asked Li Mei.

"No. Anyway, what do you like to do," Barbara asked, trying to be friendly, even though Li Mei had caused her some unintentional irritation.

"Oh, I like to play Mahjong. I'd play with my aunts, but I also play *ShaftCrafter*. My sisters and I like to watch 小行星带中的爱 which is called *Love in the Asteroid Belt* in English. We could have a girl's night and watch it together if you want. I have a subbed version so you can follow along if you don't speak Chinese," Li Mei said.

"What is it about," Barbara asked.

"Jia Li is a hotshot dark space pilot behind on her family's loan payments on their spaceship, the 莲花, in English it's called the *Lotus*. She's trying to get her family out of debt as her father has died in an accident, and her mother was exposed to a near-terminal dose of radiation…" Li Mei said.

"Um, okay," Barbara said. "So what did mom do to get radiated? Was it fighting space pirates?"

"No, it was tragic; she was rescuing Jia Li's sister, Jia Zhu, who had gone out looking for her love, Muyang, who was lost in the belt looking for a diamond to make a ring for Jia Zhu," Li Mei said.

"Okay, what is what's-her-name's plot about again," Barbara asked.

"岩石和灰尘," Li Mei cursed, "are you listening? Jia Li needs money to save her family. She's in debt. I guess that isn't much of a thing for… Wait a second, where are you from?"

"Um, Mars, I think… But I can only remember living on the moon," Barbara said.

"Well, us belters aren't fond of debt," Li Mei said. "My uncle went into debt for a new spaceship, and my grandma beat him with a spaceboot every time he visited. Fortunately, he got out of debt quickly."

"Why is debt so bad?" Barbara asked.

"Well, unlike on Earth, the Moon, or Mars, the belt is dangerous. If you die, your family gets your debt. Plus, creditors tend to 'front-load' the debt with fees and high interest rates. We belters look at debt as a form of slavery. We all left China because of terrible loans and semi-slavery by the state-run corporations. Jia Li is in debt and working hard to get out when she delivers lifesaving medicine to *the most handsome man ever*, Yichen. Yichen's uncle, Chaoxiang, has a rare form of Isaacs Syndrome, and he needs the medicine to mine asteroids so he can continue to pay for their food and water. Yichen is helping him with the mining, but he longs to be a doctor and help find a cure for his uncle. *He's so dreamy*," Li Mei said.

"Wait, why doesn't the uncle get a new shell?" Barbara asked.

"It is not that simple," Li Mei said. "A lot of belters

have just to make do with what they've been born with or can afford, and 身体, shells, are very pricey in the belt.

"Sounds complicated. Are there spies and terrorists? How about evil empires and resistance fighters?" Barbara asked.

"Ugh, no! The show is a love story. Do you want to watch it with me?" Li Mei asked.

"Sure, I'll try it, but I don't think I will like it," Barbara said. Li Mei was about to respond when their comms each pinged.

Li Mei said, "Hello," Barbara flipped to the new channel and said, "This is Gordon. Go for communication."

"Hey, ladies," Jason said. "Sorry to interrupt, but I saw Barbara had a channel open with you, Li Mei. I am updating the patrol sectors and wanted to see if either of you have any questions."

"Hey Jason," Barbara said, thankful for the interruption, "We were discussing movies and television. What do you like to watch?"

"I liked the last *Mechanator* and that movie with the space pirates, *Planetary Conflicts*," Jason said.

"Yes!" Barbara said. "Wasn't it cool when the Mechanator took down that police station? I love the line before that, too! 'I'll return!' Then the Mechanator's sled crashes into the front of the station!"

"Yeah," Jason said excitedly. "I liked it when the lead Sandra Tanner put the Mechanator into the molten steel. It's too bad that the resistance fighter, Kevin Hershey, got killed. He was cool!"

"What? The boy died!" Li Mei said, "What a boring movie!"

"Okay, well, I will check on the rest of the Vanguard. You ladies have fun now," Jason said. Barbara wanted to keep Jason on the comms, but he cut the channel. There was an awkward silence, and then Li Mei spoke up.

"So, how nasty was that Seri's bar," she asked.

*

Xena watched the countdown. The Dux would perform an acceleration burn in a few minutes before the slingshot with L 98-59 Hotel, a large Jupiter-like gas giant. Xena watched as the clouds swirled below her on the gigantic orange orb. She tried to defocus and enjoy the universe's lava lamp but kept fretting about the burn. If EDIE didn't time everything right, her team could be millions of kilometers out of position, dooming them to a cold, slow death.

"T-minus one minute and thirty seconds," EDIE said.

"Got it, Edie," Xena said.

"I'm detecting elevated stress levels. Are you okay, Xena?" EDIE asked. "I've got this burn, if you're worried."

"Hell yes, I'm worried," Xena said.

"Relax, this is easy as pie," EDIE said. "Now, breaking a quantum cipher or fighting a bunch of cyber ninjas, well, that's something difficult."

Xena tried to smile, but she could only watch the burn countdown. The *Dux* was loaded with fuel, but that load wasn't infinite. The *Dux* would need most of the fuel to land on Aurora Dawn. If Xena and EDIE were efficient, the *Dux* would hit Aurora Dawn with a small fraction of a percent of fuel remaining. DADDIE had crunched the numbers and had given the *Dux* just enough fuel to follow the flight plan. The expedition needed every drop of the LH2 and LOX once the mothership arrived above Aurora Dawn. LH2 and LOX would be used to unload the *Aquila's* mining and refining pods. Without the mining and refining equipment, the colony was doomed.

"Boosting, brace yourselves," EDIE said over the wideband to all the humans on the *Dux*. The main engines flared, and Xena felt the tug as the ship accelerated. She watched as EDIE updated the projected flight path in real-time as the path was projected around the gas giant. The parabolic started to tighten up and soon would collide with Aurora Dawn, which was off the screen. Xena pushed against the thrust forces to raise her arm and tap her screen. The map of the flight path backed out to show the entire L 98-59 star system.

"Fifteen seconds to the main engine cut off," EDIE said. Xena watched as the flight path intersected and then moved just to the anti-spin ward of Aurora Dawn. The projection was good, and the engines cut off as Xena was about to say something. The Xeno Corps was now twenty hours away from rendezvous with the planet. Xena went back to watching the clouds roll under her. She panicked momentarily, worrying the burn had depleted the fuel faster than her projections had shown. She switched her screen over to see the tanks. The LOX and LH2 were sitting at thirty percent, three percent higher than DADDIE had calculated on the *Aquila*.

"Daddy didn't raise a dummy," EDIE said to Xena. "That's why I am on this boat instead of the head coach. I know how to throw a good fastball."

Xena relaxed; she had nothing to do for the next few hours except worry.

*

"Boost is good for a n00b," CUYA said, pinging Jason. Jason had checked in on all of the Vanguard and was playing some *Minefield*. The ancient video game had captivated him, even though there were better and more modern games to play on the *Dux*. The CUYA had decided, somewhere between departure and the main engine boost, that Jason was worth pinging every fifteen minutes. The CUYA would add color commentary to anything that happened, commenting on the gas giant below—an OP level for *Soldiers of Duty*; to Li Mei and Barbara—the hope they weren't noobs; to the boost and EDIE's navigation skill—potentially OP.

"Thanks, Kooya," Jason said. "Have you reviewed

the landing zone?"

"Yes," The CUYA answered, "The n00bs will attempt to camp our spawn here, here, here, and here." Jason's map glowed with several small symbols.

"I will counter by dropping a kinetic blast after separating from the lander, here and here. The shock waves will roll through, and the n00bs won't know what hit their buttery smooth brains until they appear at respawn," the CUYA stated.

"You know, we can probably just land and deal with anything that tries to come at us," Jason said. He wasn't fond of artillery strikes being the first thing to land on what he thought of as his planet.

"And let the n00bs camp our spawn," the CUYA said, "I can see why you are so bad at *Soldiers of Duty*."

"I wasn't bad; I got bored with *Soldiers of Duty*; every level felt the same!" Jason said, suddenly irritated with the CUYA's remark.

"Well then, let's spin up a matrix and see where it gets boring, shall we? I will make an exception and let you be part of my squad, n00b," the CUYA said.

"No, Kooya," Jason said, "I am busy playing a game that is too OP for you, *Minefield*."

"Hah hah, that's a n00b game," the CUYA said.

"Well, you want to challenge me? I win on expert almost fifty percent of the time," Jason said. "Or are you afraid of losing to me, noob?"

The CUYA hesitated, and Jason spun up a shared screen of *Minefield*. The AI deliberated and then began selecting squares. Jason watched in amusement as the AI randomly selected squares and then hit a mine; ending the game.

"Ha, noob," Jason said. "Go get better!"

The CUYA spun up over one hundred games, and Jason lost track of all the moves the AI was making. He gave up trying to track the AI and settled into his games, books, and movies. The big counter to planetfall said that he and the lander's crew had another twenty hours before the *Dux* would hit atmo.

"I could have gone on flying through space forever."

— Cosmonaut Yuri Gagarin

Location: L 98-59 Foxtrot Geosynchronous Orbit,
T-minus three hours to Dux landing
02.11.12450 Standard, Early Morning Aurora Dawn
local.

The *Dux's* main engines fired, and Xena watched as the lander's trajectory narrowed into a geocentric orbit around Aurora Dawn. She could override the engines and stop the orbit from decaying into a landing if she wanted. Xena checked and rechecked everything. It was now or never. The drop would begin, and the *Dux* would either land or crash. Once the *Dux* started its descent, this ride became a one-way trip.

"Edie, final analysis, there's atmosphere down there that we can breathe?" Xena asked.

"You betcha, and all the right flora and fauna, the probes didn't lie. Are we ready to head down," EDIE asked.

"Aye, let's head down," Xena told the AI. Then, over the shipwide, she said, "Okay, Xeno Corps, this is why we get our bennies. We're heading in! Buckle up and keep the comms clear."

Xena watched as the Vanguard sleds all signaled ready, and she looked and saw the check marks from the Analysis and Survey teams. The *Dux's* engines fired at one hundred percent, and Xena watched the expected flight path. The projected change would turn the oval around Aurora Dawn into a parabolic, approximating a landing on the northernmost island. Everything was going according to plan. That it all seemed so smooth worried Xena. There was always a hitch.

"End hard boost for insertion, in five… four… three… two…" EDIE said. "We are on the insertion flight plan now."

Xena watched as the flight plan changed. She felt the engines shut down as the *Dux* ended the braking maneuver. As they coasted, the *Dux's* engines periodically fired; alternating between full and low thrust. The engines were alternating so the *Dux* could land on the planned coordinates. Xena checked the fuel tanks. They read fifteen percent, four percent higher than projected.

"Excellent trajectory, Edie," Xena said.

"Thanks," EDIE said. "I probably could have added a percent to the tank, but I was worried about the atmospheric friction making us overshoot the site, so I compensated."

"Well, better to be safe," Xena said. "Time to atmo?"

"Fifty-seven minutes to high stratosphere and peak friction," EDIE said. Xena checked the data on her screen. If all went well, she'd be stepping onto Aurora Dawn's surface in an hour and a half. The Xeno Corps was ready for work.

*

Jason fidgeted. He was tired of being in the sled and longed to stretch his legs. The brake had been smooth, and he couldn't help but watch the flight path. He wanted with every second to be on the planet he named.

"Shall we spin up a matrix and play *Soldiers of Duty*?" the CUYA asked.

"No, I don't play with *Minefield* noobs," Jason said. After introducing the CUYA to *Minefield*, he watched the leaderboard on his Matrix; while the CUYA had gained significantly on Jason, the CUYA still lagged behind him in scores. Jason took every opportunity to remind the CUYA of his *Minefield* superiority if only to keep the sixteen-meter war machine's respect.

"I suppose, since you are OP in *Minefield*, I can bring you on my *Soldiers of Duty* squad; I will need a medic, which is the only spot you are good enough to fill as an n00b," the CUYA responded.

"I'll pass. If I play with you, noob, I might get worse at *Minefield*. That would be bad," Jason said, teasing.

"Maybe if we play together, we can get better at both games?" the CUYA said. Jason thought about responding when he noticed the tiny blue marble of Aurora Dawn had gotten larger.

"What about our landing zone?" Jason asked.

"Our spawn point is perfect! If n00bs try to spawn camp us, we'll make them all get rekt!" the CUYA said. "I will bring up the tactical map I've compiled, now that I have fully analyzed the level."

Jason watched as the CUYA pulled up the topo map and sketched out in red the various routes a potential enemy could attack. The CUYA then offered in blue how he would flank their attack. The green of the sat map made Jason long to be able to leave the corpo-gray sled he'd claimed. Jason smiled inwardly at his dirty trick. He'd allowed his team to choose their sleds first, and he'd picked his last since that was something Greg would have done. However, Jason had fallen in love with the gray sled and wanted it from the moment he'd seen it. To discourage anyone from choosing the gray sled, he smuggled a stink bomb on the *Aquila* during provisioning and detonated the bomb in the sled after decanting. Since he the first one awake, it was easy to do.

DADDIE wouldn't have detected the bomb since the stink bomb smoldered rather than exploded. Plus, the sled was in the lander bay, which DADDIE hadn't monitored as closely when it was in near vacuum. When it came time for Jason to choose his sled, sure enough, the gray one sat unclaimed. All he had to do was flush the light atmosphere and remove the bomb. It was all easily done as the sled was bolted to the *Dux*.

"The perfect crime," Jason said to himself.

"What n00b," the CUYA asked.

"Oh, nothing," Jason said, reminding himself to turn off his microphone. Jason returned to the map. He had charted out a sector near the *Dux's* landing zone for himself. As much as he wanted to land near somewhere interesting— like Cappy the Canyon, he was needed close to the lander to be able to direct his team. He again marked the sectors for

Li Mei and Barbara. He wished both ladies luck.

*

Barbara watched the flight path. She thought she'd be nervous, but oddly, she wasn't. She suddenly remembered a previous landing over a planet with a pale yellow cloud base.

"Hey," Li Mei said, pinging her.

Barbara was about to say, "This is…" but switched and said, "Hey Li Mei, what's up?"

"Are you excited," Li Mei asked.

"No, I just want out of this sled, at least for five minutes," Barbara said. "When I get down there, I will step out of the sled and feel Aurora Dawn under my feet. Then, I'll jump back in the sled and shoot for my quadrant. The faster I get the mission over, the faster I can return to the new outpost."

"I'm going to take my time. I haven't been on a planet with an atmosphere. If I could ride with my sled's canopy open, I'd do that too," Li Mei said.

"I can't wait until the new outpost gets set up," Barbara said. "I am going to order a nice cape cod by the ocean. I've marked potential spots to claim when we're out exploring."

"I can see the signs now, 'Gordon Realty,'" Li Mei said with a chuckle.

"Well, who knows," Barbara said. "I could see that as a pretty easy life. Me, my house, and my realty business."

"What, no husband and two point four kids?" Li Mei asked, quoting the colonization slogans.

"I hadn't thought about that, honestly," Barbara said.

"Oh, if I had someone like Yichen, I'd settle down."

"He's a stupid soap opera character. He probably passes gas all the time and blames it on the dog."

"If he looks like Yichen, I'll let it slide. Besides, if the dog doesn't mind being blamed, he must be a good man. Since he's good around pets."

"Whatever," Barbara said, "I'm ready for Con Sec Corps to get the farming and livestock centers running. I swear I'll have a huge mouthwatering T-bone cooked on a grill, just like I had as a kid."

"Hey! You remembered something," Li Mei said, her voice rising with excitement.

"Uh, I guess so. It just came tumbling out of my mouth," Barbara said.

"Sounds like you need to meditate. I find it helps those subliminal messages rise into your consciousness," said Li Mei.

"I'll give it a try," Barbara said. "Especially if it can help me get through this memory haze."

Both ladies became silent as they saw the atmosphere's friction glow against the *Dux*. Now, it was up to EDIE and Xena to guide the lander to a safe spot.

*

Xena watched as the *Dux's* nose started to heat up in the upper atmosphere.

"Deploying heat shields," EDIE said. Xena watched as three compartments on the nose opened and three argon-filled ballast balloons inflated. The balloons reached maximum size within moments and provided a small shield against friction to the *Dux* and the sleds attached to its hull. The sleds weren't just drop bolted but hooked via umbilical to the *Dux*.

Xena audibly sighed, and EDIE said. "See, all good. Now we just need to ride through the atmosphere."

During the approach to Aurora Dawn, EDIE folded the mini-quantum array and other communications gear into the lander. For the rest of the universe, the *Dux* was a hole in the fabric of space and time, and it would be until landing on Aurora Dawn. Once on the ground, EDIE would redeploy all of the communications gear.

Xena pulled up a visual of the *Dux's* hull on one of her screens. She watched as the hull temperature started to climb from a negative centigrade to positive numbers. The shields would help, but the *Dux* would also take a fair bit of heat. If the lander's temperature went too high, the drop bolts might detonate or even melt, and that could mean death for the Vanguard team strapped in their sleds.

"Another ten minutes until we are past the ionization blackout," EDIE said. "I am reading the hull temperature is around one thousand degrees Celsius. Plenty of wiggle room there."

Xena nodded, but she couldn't help staring at her screen. After the ionization blackout, the *Dux* would use a series of S-turns to bleed off more speed. Then, the lander would start ejecting the Vanguard at around two hundred kilometers out. Xena pulled up the roster. The first ones off the lander were Tsan Li Mei, Barbara Gordon, and the big CUYA. After the *Dux* released the three of them, it cruised for another hundred kilometers and then turned to brake more. After that, Jason Dikkert would be next, along with two other Vanguard members. Another pass, S-turn, and the lander would eject the rest of the Vanguard. The *Dux* would then be ready to fly to its final landing point.

"Ejecting thermal shields," EDIE said as the lander passed through the ionization blackout. Xena watched from the front glass as the giant inflated shields suddenly jerked and were blown clear from the lander. The shields would float down to the surface below, Aurora Dawn's first piece of garbage.

"Approaching the first drop in five minutes," EDIE said. Xena started pulling up screens and opening up comms with Tsan and Gordon.

"Okay, ladies," Xena said. "We're getting to the spot where we say goodbye, temporarily. Like in the sims, there will be a loud thump, and the lander will shoot past you. After a few moments of free-fall, the small landing parachute will open, and you'll float down until you are about fifty meters over the terrain. There, the repulsors will engage, and the parachute will detach. Any questions?"

"No, Ma'am," Gordon replied.

"No, Xena," Li Mei said.

"Best of luck!" Xena said.

"Detach in ninety seconds," EDIE said. Xena eyed the clock as the *Dux* got closer to its first release.

"Alert!" EDIE said. "I am reading an early power spike from the CUYA unit."

"CUYA, stand down," Xena said. Suddenly, the lander lurched as the drop bolts fired around the CUYA. Xena watched as the CUYA manually ejected himself.

"Bye, n00bs!" the CUYA said., "Time to get OP on the buttery smooth brains before they camp our spawn!"

"Dude!" Jason said. "Seriously? You're out of position!"

"I'm OP. I will compensate in free-fall. See you on the ground, n00bs," the CUYA said.

EDIE was the quickest to respond, saying, "Kooya, you are in big trouble! You better hope the smooth brains get you because if I do, you'll wish you stayed put!"

Xena was about to echo the sentiments when her screen alerted her that the window for Tsan and Gordon had arrived.

"Edie, eject Tsan and Gordon!" Xena said. "Forget about the combat AI!"

"On it," EDIE said, and Xena watched from an external camera as the bolts for the red, white, and blue sled fired along with the bolts for the pink one.

"Later, ladies, let us immediately know if you encounter any problems," Xena said.

"Yes, Ma'am," Gordon said.

"Sure, Xena, see you on the ground," Tsan replied. Xena watched as the sleds tumbled away. Moments later, Xena saw the sleds' parachutes open through the lander's cameras. Now, the Vanguard members were on their own.

"Edie, will the Kooya's early detachment affect our trajectory?" Xena asked.

"I'll compensate with a larger turn; we'll drop the next two Vanguard sleds a little off their marks and then be back on our projected path," EDIE said.

Xena thought about the CUYA's actions. When their paths crossed again, the CUYA would learn that Xena was OP and worth listening to.

*

Jason watched the landscape roll below him. Several minutes had passed since Jason watched Barbara and Li Mei deploy. He was next. Jason was responsible for the quadrant nearest the landing. Jason's quadrant was the most critical. He'd have five or ten minutes to scout the final landing spot and ensure the lander wouldn't land in a dangerous or unstable location.

"Right, don't want to end up in a swamp like Mark Flywalker in *The Emperor Strikes Back*. I am sure there isn't a little green space wizard around to lift our lander out," Jason muttered.

"Releasing you now, Jason," Xena said. "Good Luck!"

"Roger," Jason said as he felt the thump and heard the drop bolts explode. The thump wasn't nasty, but in the total atmosphere, the explosion's sound was unnerving. Neither Gordon nor Tsan had complained about any issues with their landing, but Jason had gained a new perspective on paranoia and caution after his fiasco with the explorer pods.

The sled was naturally bottom-heavy, and after a moment of tumbling, the vehicle righted itself, cockpit up and central repulsor down. Jason closed his eyes to avoid vertigo from the tumble and opened them to see the lander far off on the horizon. Within moments, the sled's parachute deployed, and Jason glided down to the planet he had named. He wasn't going to be the first one on Aurora Dawn. That honor went to Li Mei or Barbara. Jason was tempted to check in with the ladies, but he wasn't sure if the comms were up and working. The *Dux* had launched several satellites to establish a global positioning system and a communications network, but Jason was unsure if it was functional. His display then updated, and he saw the small, thin triangle that represented his sled on the map.

"I guess that the GPS is up," Jason said. A moment later, the parachute detached, and Jason started to fall. The repulsor throttled to one hundred percent, and Jason braced himself for the landing. Jason remembered to close his jaw tight as his sled touched down to avoid biting his tongue or chipping a tooth. The crash was loud and jolting, but the sled and Jason were all right. The repulsor had slowed his sled's fall to safe levels.

Jason didn't have time to celebrate his landing. He started his scans and plotted a route for the sled through the center of the landing zone. He'd cross the center and then do a perimeter scan. He was on the clock and needed to ensure the *Dux* would land on solid ground. Then, the real work could begin.

The ground radar began pinging as he patrolled his route. So far, the data was good.

"How are we doing, Jason," Xena asked over the comms channel.

"Data looks good, boss," Jason said. "I'm a quarter of the way through the scan. I'll update you if something changes."
Jason's sled rounded the first corner to start the perimeter pass on the landing zone. Again, Jason watched the data. The site was sound, and the radar showed a nice shelf of hard rock about two meters under the soil. The sled again turned and followed the third side of the box.

"Looks good, Xena," Jason said. "I'm on the third side of the perimeter."

"Roger," Xena said.

The sled turned, and Jason began his final pass. The sensors showed a solid landing area.

"All good, begin the landing," Jason said as he completed the pass.

"Clear the site. The *Dux* is landing," Xena said. Jason guided his sled about three kilometers away from the landing zone, gave the sled a U-turn, and stopped to watch the landing. If he could have popped popcorn. He'd be shoveling the kernels into his mouth.

The *Dux* appeared overhead. There was a large braking flame from its engines, then it turned its nose skyward. The lander began to fall, main engines downward from the sky. Jason watched and smiled. Sure, he'd been in simulations showing the landing, but the reality was way cooler. The lander came down, moving faster and faster, approaching terminal velocity. The main engines fired again about a kilometer above the ground, and the lander slowed down. The lander continued to throttle down as it descended. Finally, it rested on a blackened spot of turf. Legs extended from the lander's main body. The legs' springs tensed and flexed as the *Dux's* weight was transferred from the engines to the legs.

"Landing looks solid," Jason told Xena, functioning as an outside observer.

"Roger, we're cutting the engines," Xena said. The *Dux's* engines slowly ramped down, and Jason watched to see if the lander would tilt over. Everything looked solid.

"Still looking good," Jason said as the engines shut down. The long main ramp on the *Dux* was lowered, and the Xeno Corps started marching out of the lander. Corpus Ad Astra had made landfall.

Part Two: Landfall

"The Dream is Alive."

— Astronaut John Young

Barbara watched as the ground came rushing towards her. She overrode the automatic controls and boosted the repulsor's power to full. The sled still crashed into the turf, and Barbara momentarily bounced around in the cockpit. As she regained her wits, the sensors began recording their data. The sensors gathered gases from the atmosphere and collated them.

Barbara scanned the results and nodded. The atmosphere had plenty of oxygen, a good density, and no pollutants, and the temperature outside registered a pleasant twenty-four degrees centigrade. She popped the cockpit and fumbled for the quick release on her helmet and the straps on her seat's harness. She stood up and stretched. After so many hours on the seat, her backside had grown numb.

"Let's test out a few steps on the grass here," Barbara said to herself. She hopped out of the cockpit, climbed across the sled's hull, and dropped down onto the grass.

"That's one tiny step for woman but a giant leap for Corpus Ad Astra," she said as she touched down. As she stood on the grass, her shortwave radio dinged.

"This is Gordon… um, Hi…" Barbara said.

"Hey!" Li Mei said. "Guess what? I am outside the sled with my helmet off!"

"Yay!" Barbara said. "Feels good, eh?"

"No," Li Mei said. "It is so weird! I feel like my Mom is going to show up and hit me on the head with a spaceboot for not having my helmet on!"

Barbara laughed and said, "Enjoy your freedom! Now to the task at hand, exploring the craters."

"Bye," Li Mei said, cutting the link.

Barbara scanned the area around her. The pink sled sat in a shallow bowl-like depression three meters below the main surface of the terrain. She hiked up the side, encounter suit boots crunching on the dirt and soil underneath the greenery. She hoped to catch a better view of the terrain, orient herself, and plan her next move.

Her mission was to scout the craters and discover any resources. Barbara grabbed a spade that sat around her waist on her encounter suit's belt. She knelt and stuck the spade into the ground, pulling up a few grams of the dirt. She then carried the spade to the sled, pulled a sample box out of the side drop compartment, and deposited the soil into it. Barbara suddenly had an image of a woman in a gingham dress.

A blond-haired woman in a gingham dress had just finished yanking up a weed and was using a trowel to make a hole in the tilled garden so she could plant some seeds in the row.

Barbara assumed the woman was her mother, but she couldn't remember the woman's name.

"This memory thing is getting on my nerves," Barbara said. She had gone and seen Griff. After an exam, he proclaimed her shell to be in top condition. After combing through the medical archives, the only thing Barbara had found was an article on harmonic disruption inside the archive. Barbara asked DADDIE about that and was told that the archive was functioning at or above acceptable parameters. Except for her memory issue and the general's body rejection, there hadn't been any other issues with the crew. A slight earth tremor shook Barbara out of her wool-gathering. She decided to climb into the sled's cockpit and power up the thrusters.

"It's okay, Barbara," she said to herself, "It is probably that stupid war bot tramping around looking for bugs to splat."

She lowered the canopy and put her feet down on the accelerator. The sled's engines roared, and the sled floated up and out of the bowl. Barbara scanned the area. The craters were all the same size, and they pockmarked the ground. The rumbling sound came closer, and Barbara moved her sled forward, weaving around the craters.

"Hey, Li Mei," Barbara said. "Are you seeing a bunch of craters where you are, and are they all uniform?"

Barbara increased thrust as she wove through the crater field. She could hear the high-pitched whine as she put more power into the thrusters. She glanced at her display, momentarily forgetting the crater-strewn ground. When Barbara looked up, she had glided down into a small bowl crater and was popping up back onto the central plane of the terrain.

"Li Mei, can you hear me?" Barbara said. She was getting worried as the rumbling got louder and louder. Suddenly, the ground below her opened up, and a dark shape rose and swallowed the whole sled.

"Oh boy," Barbara said. "This isn't good!"

The sled started banging inside the creature's gut, and Barbara fumbled for her helmet, slamming it on and hitting the attach button. Environmentally sealed, Barbara pushed her feet to the floor, and the thrusters on the sled went into afterburner. The creature started shaking violently, and fluid appeared across Barbara's canopy.

"Eww, gross," Barbara said. Her screens showed the thruster jets were getting clogged and ready to overheat. She quickly switched over to her shortwave.

"CAA, be advised this is Barbara Gordon. I am… inside some creature and need help… Anyone listening?" Barbara said. An alarm inside her helmet whined, and she looked down and saw that her thrusters were almost at their thermal limits. If she continued to accelerate, the thrusters would explode or catch fire. She pulled her feet off the accelerators and considered her options. She didn't know if she had wounded the creature or if it even cared. For all Barbara knew, she and the sled were just a bad case of indigestion.

"Now, if I had a rocket-propelled grenade launcher,"

Barbara said.

She suddenly remembered the weapon had been pointed towards her. A skinny teenager had aimed the rocket propelled grenade launcher at her and was ready to pull the trigger when one of her teammates shot him, ending the threat.

"Got to focus, I can't get lost in my head," Barbara said. Switching back to the shortwave, she said. "CAA, be advised this is Barbara Gordon. I am… inside some creature and need help…"

She was cut off by a robotic monotone response, "Hah hah! You got eaten by a worm, n00b!"

"Kooya," Barbara said. "Get me out of this thing, or I'll make sure you never play another game again!"

The war bot stopped its metallic laughing and said, "Hang on, n00b, I'm going beast mode on this worm!"

Barbara hesitated to speculate on what beast mode was, but several large buffets shook her in the worm's stomach. After the final one, a tiny pinprick of light appeared. Barbara slammed down the accelerators and pointed the nose of the sled at the light. The sled slammed into the worm's stomach lining and hesitated momentarily before ripping through the tissue. The sled was free in a flash, hurrying over the landscape and heading toward the CUYA.

"That worm needs to go back to respawn and get OP. I barely hit it with my weapons," the CUYA said. Barbara couldn't understand why the war bot seemed so upset. Spinning the sled around and countering her thrust, she looked back at the worm. The animal was almost the same diameter as the craters on the plain, stretched out over nearly one hundred meters. The worm's body showed a vast black gash along its side where the CUYA had opened it up, and Barbara had driven out.

"Nice shooting, Kooya," Barbara said. "I owe you one!"

"I will enjoy pwning you in *Soldiers of Duty* since you

are such a n00b," the CUYA said.

Barbara was about to respond when she heard a faint call over her shortwave, "Hey Barbara, help!" It was Li Mei.

"Did you get eaten by a giant worm," Barbara asked.

"Uh, I think so. I heard rumbling, and everything went black," Li Mei said.

"Give me a ping for your position," Barbara said and waited. After a moment, her sled's radar showed a marker about five kilometers away.

"On our way," Barbara said over the shortwave. She switched to local and said, "Come on, Kooya, we've got to save Li Mei."

The giant combat AI started trotting towards the marker. Moving forward, it said, "Don't worry, n00b. Kooya, the Magnificent will come to get rid of your spawn camper, and then you'll owe me some brew!"

Barbara hit the accelerator pads and attempted to keep up. She watched as the meters ticked by. She worried she wouldn't make it to Li Mei in time. The CUYA raced ahead, and Barbara could see the combat AI's weapons starting to fire at a black shape on the horizon. Various weapons arced out of the CUYA and raced towards the worm. The flashes of the explosions glowed brightly against the worm's outer skin.

"Use your thrusters and push out of the hole," Barbara said over the shortwave.

"I'm not seeing… Wait! I see it," Li Mei replied.

"Kooya, cease fire," Barbara said. She didn't know where the words had come from, and they seemed to tumble out of her mouth. As the combat AI stopped firing, Li Mei's bright blue, red, and white sled shot out of the hole the explosives had made in the worm.

"Well, now, that was different," Li Mei said. "I almost miss Tardigrades from the belt."
"Hah hah, n00bs got eaten by worms!" the CUYA said with grating mechanical laughter. As he stood there, the ground

opened up underneath the combat AI, and yet another worm appeared, swallowing the CUYA whole!

"Kooya!" Li Mei and Barbara said in unison. They watched as the worm started spreading itself out over the terrain. After a moment, they began to feel a series of rumbling tremors.

"We need to be ready to move," Barbara said. "In case another worm shows!"

"But the Kooya is still trapped in that worm," Li Mei said, "We can't leave him!"

Barbara was about to protest when the worm that swallowed the combat AI suddenly blew up like a balloon and popped, sending a dark, viscous liquid everywhere.

"Go back to respawn and get good, worm n00b!" the CUYA said as he stepped from the remains of the giant creature.

"Kooya, are you okay?" Li Mei asked.

"No, I am OP. A puny worm cannot send me to respawn," The CUYA said. Barbara wasn't sure if she wanted to laugh, cry, or feel relieved.

"Let's head towards the landing area," Barbara said. "I'm recommending that we mark this sector as off-limits due to hostile fauna."

"Agreed," Li Mei said.

"Ha! N00bs, that worm wasn't so tough. I faced *Nihonese* children who fought harder as I crushed them underfoot!" The CUYA said.

"Oh, Kooya, I don't believe you," Li Mei said. The CUYA couldn't respond as Li Mei's sled took off. On this, the western edge of the crater field, the craters were fewer, and the terrain allowed the sleds to reach their maximum cruise speed of one hundred twenty kilometers per hour.

Barbara turned her sled towards Li Mei's and pushed her accelerators down for a total engine burn. Pulling up her rear camera, she saw the CUYA trotting behind her. The trio traveled along in silence. Barbara could feel the aftereffects of the adrenaline rush, and she was tempted to put the sled on autopilot and crash. The encounter with the worm gave her second thoughts, so she scanned the horizon, looking for potential trouble.

The land went from crabgrass-laden plains to rolling hills covered in tall prairie grass. Barbara hadn't seen a crater in the ground for some time and hoped the worms were now kilometers behind her. She, Li Mei, and the CUYA were undulating as the sleds and CUYA's feet followed the terrain. In the distance, they saw the lander's nose pointing to the sky. Containers sat in a circle around the ship, and a small robot crane pulled parts off the lander. Having delivered them to Aurora Dawn, the expedition would cannibalize the lander to make other needed items.

As Barbara grew closer, she saw that expedition members who arrived on the lander had erected a large Quonset hut.

"Back so soon, ladies," Jason's voice rang in Barbara's helmet.

"Um, yeah," Li Mei said. "Barbara and I weren't going to be worm food!"

"Worm food," Jason said. "Wait, this place has huge worms like that science fiction book *Mound*? I bet you two didn't walk without rhythm!"

"More like we landed and became something's lunch," Barbara said. "Besides, Kooya got eaten too."

Jason started laughing and said, "Noob!"

"The buttery smooth brain camped my spawn, but I showed him who was OP," the CUYA said with an air of disgust.

"Well, you three, come over to the north side. We're parking the sleds there. I'll be right by to give your sleds a once over. I can't have any worm guts fouling the engines," Jason said, making an excuse to check in on his team members.

Barbara cruised over to the spot Jason had

highlighted. When she hit the final destination, she killed her engines. As the engines powered down, she opened the canopy and hopped out. She watched as the CUYA marched over and entered analysis-standby mode, allowing his solar panel-lined skin to soak up the rays from L 98-59. Li Mei's sled pulled next to Barbara's and stopped. Li Mei's canopy opened as Jason walked over.

"There are my sand pirates," Jason said jokingly.

"I guess that makes you Saul Achilles," Barbara said. "That last movie of *Mound* had quite the wimp playing him, and you could be his stunt double."

Jason just laughed. After their initial testiness, Barbara and Jason had gotten into a rhythm of teasing each other, often making anyone else around feel self-conscious.

"You're just jealous I have movie star looks and could be a stunt double," Jason said. He was about to say more when Xena approached and said, "Back so soon?"

"Worms tried to eat us," Li Mei said.

"Aha," Xena responded, "I'll note your sectors as having hazardous fauna. Go stretch your legs and get something to eat."

Barbara and Li Mei nodded. Jason trotted in front of them and said, "Let me show you where the kitchen is. We're not up and running with a cook yet, but the meals-ready-to-eat are better than the Seri's bars."

Jason, Barbara, and Li Mei walked to the Quonset hut, ten meters east of it was a construction plot. Inside the plot, a trio of construction robots were 3D-printing a building.

"What's that, Jason," Li Mei asked.

"Oh, that's where the food pantry is going. Once we get that set up, we'll start the pour for the cafeteria. That won't be done until the heavy builders get here, but Con Sec Corps sent these light builders with us to jump-start things."

The trio entered the giant Quonset hut containing the cafeteria, barracks, science lab, and command center.

Heading west inside, the trio scooted through the science lab, where Analysis was examining data and assessing soil samples. They entered the giant bay, the cafeteria; on the other side was the Vanguard's bay for the female bunks.

"What's for chow," Barbara asked. "I mean, what are the MREs today."

"Let's see," Jason said. "There's theoretical meat and potatoes, Fake hot dog and chips, or mysterious vegetarian." "Huh, they're all veggie, right?" Barbara asked.

"I'll take the vegetarian; it's better not to have high expectations," Li Mei said.

"I'll try steak and potato," Barbara said. "Nothing can be worse than a Seri's bar."

Jason selected a fake hot dog MRE and moved to the water dispenser. The ladies grabbed their MREs and went over to the water dispenser. A sticker on the machine said, "Freshly filtered from Aurora Dawn!"

Barbara hit her helmet's quick release and pulled off the headgear. She attached the helmet to a buckle on the side of her utility belt and then popped a bottle from her harness.

"It looks like I was low on fluid," Barbara said as she put the bottle under the machine and watched the highly filtered water flow into the container. Li Mei pulled out her water bottle and, after Barbara was done, refilled it.

"You know, you can take your helmet off," Barbara said to Li Mei. Mom is like thirty-five light years away. So, it's doubtful you'll be hit by a space boot soon."

Li Mei laughed, hit the quick release, and said, "Sorry, I forgot we're in the atmosphere. This is so weird."

"Wait until we start doing the surveys for exotic materials on the asteroids and moons," Jason said. "Then it will feel like you're back home." The trio sat at a folding plastic picnic table.

"Well, boss," Barbara said. "What's next? Where are we off to now?"

"You are off to the coastline to the northwest," Jason said. "Li Mei is here on sled maintenance duty until 0600 tomorrow."

"What? Why?" Li Mei said. "How come Barbara gets to go and I don't?"

"That order comes down from Edie," Jason said. "Barbara gets some beach time, and the rest of us are stuck doing camp set up and cleaning."

"That's right," EDIE said as her chassis ambled over. Unlike DADDIE, MOMI, or any of the many AIs on the *Aquila*, EDIE had a robotic chassis she could manipulate. Being an exploration AI meant she would have to get her hands dirty as the occasion arose. EDIE's core functions were stored in a small constellation inside the *Dux*, but she could perform work inside the chassis through microwave point-to-point communication.

"Okay, Edie," Li Mei said. "What did Barbara bribe you with to get to go sledding while the rest of us sit here cleaning the camp?"

"Sorry, Li Mei," EDIE said. "I got my directives from Daddy himself. Take it up with the coach when he and the rest of the ball team arrive in a few weeks."

"It's okay, Edie," Jason said. "We understand Barbara is Daddy's favorite girl."

Barbara rolled her eyes at Jason's comment and said, "Coming from Daddy's favorite boy, that sounds like jealousy, Dikkert."

Jason smiled and said, "I'm not his favorite. I'm just that good."

"岩石和灰尘! Seriously Jason, don't make me sick," Li Mei said. "This vegetarian is marginal enough as is without you spoiling it."

"Well," Barbara said. "Time for my beach vacation. Should I wear a two-piece or go skinny dipping?"

Jason suddenly coughed as he tried to talk and drink simultaneously, while Li Mei said, "Two-piece, we haven't done a spectrum analysis on the solar radiation here, and well, you might burn something sensitive going naked."

EDIE said, "I, for one vote, encounter suit as we still haven't gotten a good baseline on the fauna or flora on the planet."

"I was joking, Edie," Barbara said. "I'm not getting out of this encounter suit until Analysis clears us for tactical exploration clothing. Besides, I'd hate to distract the boss. He wouldn't be able to do his job with all of us running around in bikinis."

Jason turned red in embarrassment and said, "It wasn't like that. I just tried to swallow down the wrong pipe."

"Uh huh," Li Mei said. "Sure."

"Okay, I'm leaving now," Barbara said, waving to the group. The others nodded or waved, and Barbara moved back through the lab. As she passed, an Analysis team member approached her.

"Hi, you're Gordon, right?" he said. "I'm Vikas Patel. I'm a geologist here in Analysis. I heard you're going to the beach, correct?"

"Yes, and hi, Vikas," Barbara said. "What can I do for you?"

"Well, we've got this robot model here, the Geological Analysis Investigative Automaton. We call her Gaia," Vikas said, pointing to a robot dog. The robot came over. It stood seventy centimeters high and had a robotic dog's body but no head.

"I'm a geologist," the robot said in a little girl's voice. "I like rocks!"

"Hi, Gaia," Barbara said, "I'd be happy to take you to the beach with me; what are you looking for?"

"Yummy rocks," GAIA said, "If we see any metal, I like that too, as an appetizer."

"Gaia collects samples that we analyze here in the lab," Vikas said, "She's been programmed to look for rocks and ores that can provide good building blocks for the colony. Of course, she also looks for any exotic matter or even new elements for the good old periodic table."

"I'll strap her to the sled, and we can get going. Come on, Gaia," Barbara said. "See you later, Vikas." The scientist waved, and the robot dog trotted alongside her out of the hut and onto the sled. She watched as the robot crawled up on the hull and marched over to the small cradle on the back of the sled.

Barbara looked over her sled. The sled was scraped up and covered with some black fluid that Barbara assumed was blood. She took a hose and sprayed some Insta-clean on the sled. The black sludge melted off and dripped onto the ground. Barbara looked for any other damage or potential mechanical issues. She didn't see anything that could cause a problem. The cradle sat between the two thrust engines and could be used for all types of cargo, including robotic dogs. GAIA lay down in the cradle, and her joints glowed.

"Let's go, I'm buckled in," GAIA said.

"Roger, I'll get in the cockpit," Barbara said. She moved up to the front of the sled and punched the button to open the canopy on her encounter suit. The canopy opened, and Barbara climbed in. She checked the fuel. She was at sixty percent, plenty for the mission. She then checked over the other systems. Cargo registered the robot was locked and ready for transport.

"Okay, we're off," Barbara said. Barbara pressed the ignition. She powered the repulsor to one hundred percent. She then stepped on the accelerator pedals, and the engines whined. The sled took off, and Barbara checked the coordinates on her destination marker. The sled's HUD showed the final destination. Barbara scanned to make sure the sled would avoid the construction bots on its automated route. When she was safely clear of the construction in the burgeoning outpost, she slammed the pedals down on her sled and revved the engines to full power. The sled shook for a second as it built up speed. Thirty kilometers and then

Barbara would be on the coastline. She tried to remember the last time she was at the beach. She couldn't remember much besides a group of young folks partying around a bonfire. She was with someone she liked but couldn't make out the details. They shared a beach towel and watched the fire until it died down. She wasn't sure when or even if the memory was real. She had a half hour to navel-gaze as the sled crossed the plains.

"I wish I could remember something with clarity," Barbara said to herself. When the *Aquila* arrived and Con Sec Corps set up the quantum array, she could check the medical papers on the quantum network or q-net. The q-net was the total sum of all humanity's knowledge. If the q-net didn't have the data, it didn't exist.

A lone birdlike creature swooped out on the horizon. Barbara watched and tried to relax. She had moments where she had almost driven herself into a nervous breakdown, trying to remember who she was. She punched the autopilot button and closed her eyes; the autopilot would wake her when she was close. She decided to grab some nap time, and as she did, she slipped into a dream.

She ran across a sandy beach, and the rest of her squad followed.

"Kowalski, get that signal drone up," Barbara told her technical sergeant.

"No can do, sir," the technical sergeant said, "The dungs are jamming all signals if we push on..."

Barbara cut him off, "Get moving sergeant! No more excuses!"

Barbara stopped moving, grabbing her breath. Her lungs filled with air. She started moving but barely went a meter from the spot she was standing when she felt a sharp pain radiating across her back, through her chest and shoulder. She pitched forward and blacked out.

Barbara jumped in her seat. She was awake and in the sled. Whatever nightmare she had experienced was fading. She looked at the GPS. She still had ten minutes before arrival.

"That seemed like something real," she said to herself, "and why did I get called 'sir'? That seems strange."

She reviewed her survey routine. She'd park the sled near a patch of dirt or on a stone shelf, just in case the sand gave way. She'd hate to have a worm eat her and lose her sled in a sinkhole on the same day. After parking, she'd let the dog loose and grab her checklist for the survey. Collect samples, grab data, and do coastline mapping if she had time.

One of the expedition's mid-term goals was to get a dock up and running. Then, they could launch automated ships and submarines and start mapping Aurora Dawn's extensive, vast oceans.

"I wonder if there are any fish on this rock," Barbara asked herself. She checked the ETA. She had about five minutes until arrival.

The prairie grass started receding as shorter grasses dominated the terrain. Barbara could see the bright blue ocean on the horizon as it met the evening sky. The sled sped over dunes as it got closer to the destination. Patches of shells, rocks, gravel, and dirt flashed by Barbara as she cruised along. The sled's engines went to a low hum as the autopilot decreased speed. A notice came up that the final location was only one hundred meters away.

Barbara went to manual control and killed the throttle. The sled coasted the final hundred meters and stopped on a small sand mound. Barbara scanned for a dark patch or some rock. She found a nice brown dirt spot about ten meters to her left and maneuvered the sled there before killing the repulsor. She had her hand on the repulsor's power in case she started to sink, but the sled came to a rest and seemed to be on firm soil.

Barbara powered down the internals and shut off the engines. She pulled the survey tablet from its slot inside the cockpit and opened the canopy. She detached her harness, stood up, and stretched. With her helmet off, she could smell the salt from the ocean, one tiny bit of science done. She tapped on the tablet and noted the smell of salt in her notes. Climbing out of the sled, she slapped her tablet to her chest plate, where it magnetically attached. She walked to the back and checked on the dog.

"Are we there?" GAIA asked.

"Feel free to hop out and do your thing," Barbara said.

"Yes. Rocks, I am coming for you," the robot chirped as it leaped off the sled. Barbara looked over her list. After her dream, she wasn't enthused about hustling to complete this mission and get back. She felt lost and like a stranger in her skin. She never seemed to remember sixteen-year-old memories from before decant. However, the memories she did recall felt alien and out of place.

"I think I am losing my mind," she said. "Well, before it goes completely, let's complete the survey. Then, if I want to goof off, run off, or just go nuts—I'm on my own time."

She de-magnetized her tablet and once again looked through the tasks. The first was to collect soil and water samples from where the tide comes in. She climbed down from the sled towards the port side cargo hatch and opened it. The hatch had remained sealed even in the worm's stomach. Upon opening it, Barbara realized the contents were a mess. She looked for a geological sample jar and pulled one free from the shambles after a moment of digging. She shut the hatch, not wanting to deal with the mess right now, and walked to where the waves met the land. Shells from aquatic life littered the beach, and some small crabs cautiously skittered away from her footfalls.

"Huh, now, if I only had a dairy cow, I could have crab legs and drawn butter," Barbara muttered. She moved a few meters into the strong tide, watching how it would flood almost to her encounter suit's waist. When the water receded, she took out her spade and grabbed a spadeful of the sand, depositing it into the sample jar.

"Task one done," Barbara said as she hiked back to the sled. As she traveled back, she saw several fish flopping on the sand where the tide had deposited them. She was tempted to grab a few and assemble a beach bonfire to cook them. She'd have to collect the specimens but couldn't eat them until Analysis gave the expedition the thumbs up. The fish would be screened for protein compatibility and harmful micro-organisms.

"Now, if only I had a fishing pole," Barbara said.

Barbara was sitting in a canoe floating on a river. Next to her was a girl wearing a swimsuit that left nothing to the imagination. Both she and the girl were young, teenagers. In her memory, Barbara wanted to push the girl in to see if the suit would be even more revealing when wet.

"What the heck," she said, returning to the present. "These memories or delusions or whatever are getting more intense and weirder."

At the sled, she opened the starboard hatch. Inside was the dirt sample she had collected from near the worm attack. She stuck the beach sample in the cradle next to the dirt. She'd unload everything when she returned. She checked the tablet for the next task: capture fauna if animals are present. She laughed.

Barbara would have to get a bigger box and see if she could collect some fish, crabs, and other specimens that would let her catch them. Her mind wandered back to the weird memory of the girl. At the time, she had seemed very intent on the girl, but now, it felt strange. Barbara hadn't had much time to dissect her feelings, attitudes, or desires. She knew she felt some level of friendship with Jason and liked his company. Barbara also enjoyed talking with Li Mei. However, her taste in cinema and television needed lots of work. Barbara tried to remember if she had ever been in love or had a crush, but the memories wouldn't come.

"Let's go get some specimens. The faster I do, the faster we can be ready for the *Aquila* and the quantum array. Maybe then I can get some answers."

Barbara returned to the beach and started collecting the fish and some slower crabs. She had to be quick with the crabs, as they'd try to claw her as she picked them up. She wasn't worried about getting hurt; she was wearing her gloves. She was more concerned that the gloves could be punctured or damaged by the claws.

"Oh, for the want of a rubber band to tame these crabs," Barbara said to herself. Specimens collected, she sat on the beach. She thought about Li Mei's suggestion that Barbara should meditate. The beach was a perfect place for it.

Barbara remembered watching a woman in yoga leggings and a sports bra sit cross legged on a beach as the tide rolled in. Barbara also felt something substantial for the woman in that memory. Now, all she could think was that the woman's top didn't match well with her leggings.

"Enough of this," Barbara said in disgust. "I'm going to do some planning. I like this beach and must find a place for my cape cod."

She pulled out her tablet and a pair of augmented reality glasses and pulled up a virtual model of a Cape Cod house. She began to scan the area with the tablet's camera, which imposed the cape cod's image on the terrain in her glasses. After finding a pleasant small hill where the model looked perfect, Barbara took a picture and tagged the area. The star L 98-59 touched down on the water, signaling that the day was ending. She'd call the dog back and pack up.

"So much for a day at the beach," she said.

"The stars don't look bigger, but they do look brighter."

— Astronaut Sally Ride

"Rise and shine, campers," Jason said, ducking around the corner and flipping the lights on in the main barracks. Barbara could have hopped out of her cot and slugged Jason, but she was too tired. She had returned late from the beach the night before, hours past sundown. Analysis was ecstatic with the samples that GAIA and Barbara had provided. Jason had also been impressed and said Barbara reward would be sledding and collecting samples again today. Her quadrant today was east past the worm-marked zones. The mission was to survey any resources found past the craters. She was concerned about moving through the worm zone. However, Analysis believed the worms wouldn't be an issue once she was through the craters.

So far, Aurora Dawn's only hostile fauna seemed to be the worms. A random memory floated through her head of her warning her team not to get complacent.

"So, how was the beach," Li Mei said. She had hopped out of her cot in pajamas that looked like a cross between a space suit and an old United States-ian nightgown.

"Whoa, what are you wearing?" Barbara asked.

Li Mei blushed and said, "Why do you ask? Do you like it?"

Barbara stretched and stood up. She wore a nightshirt and long synthetic cotton pajama trousers. Only a white bow around the purple fabric's neck could distinguish the pajamas as a set for a female. Men wore a similar pajama style in cooler, darker colors.

"Those are pajamas, right?" Barbara asked.

"Yes, they are the same pajamas that Jia Li wears in 小行星带中的爱. My sisters and I all bought a pair after seeing her in them. They are cool, both retro and futuristic," Li Mei said.

"If you say so," Barbara responded. She couldn't see herself in something that simultaneously looked revealing and goofy.

"Well, how was the beach?" Li Mei asked. "I've never been to a beach, so I hope we can go soon."

"The beach was fine. I kept having my memory thing. I swear I must have had another life," Barbara said.

"That makes sense. You are probably atoning for some bad karma," Li Mei said.

"Uh, I doubt it," Barbara said. "Where are you headed today?"

"I'm over in sector A2. It looks like a mountainous region. They are sending me off with Biggie Black, the combat robot dog," Li Mei said.

"Probably a wise move. I'm surveying K13, past the worm zone," Barbara said.

"Oh, that's cool. I heard the Kooya has been in the worm zone, killing those things. Jason said they had to start up the munitions factory because the stupid combat AI has been blowing through ammo on those worms," Li Mei said.

Barbara remembered her stint inside the worm and decided that the CUYA could shoot as many as its mechanical heart desired, and said, "Fine by me. Some species need to go extinct."

Li Mei paused and said, "Oh, I hope I don't gain too much karma, but on the worms, I agree."

"Any news on *the Aquila*," Barbara asked.

"I heard Jason and Xena talking, and the ship will be here in another two weeks. We've already got a skeleton crew from Con Sec Corps working. Oh, and I almost forgot, I saw someone who looks exactly like Yichen!"

"Oh boy, not this again," Barbara said.

"He's so good-looking," Li Mei said. "I heard someone call him Xander."

"Oh, that's Xander Chung, he's Tracie's nephew," Barbara said casually. She wasn't sure where the information had come from, but it flowed from her gray matter and out her mouth.

"Hands off, he's mine," Li Mei said ferociously. Barbara's eyes opened wide in horror at the response.

"I'm sorry. I think he's dreamy," Li Mei said, restoring her teenage girl composure.

"Don't worry, I am not interested," Barbara said softly.

"Good," Li Mei replied. "Now I'm getting dressed and getting some breakfast."

Barbara nodded and said, "I think I'll hit the showers. First, I need to wash the funk off. I didn't get a chance to hit the showers yesterday."

Li Mei went off to her cot and locker. Barbara grabbed some clothes from the locker next to her cot. She entered the showers at the back of the female Vanguard country. She hopped into an unoccupied stall and turned on the water. It was cold and hit her in the face.

"Tell us what your unit's plans are," a voice screamed into her ear.

Someone shoved a wet cloth in her face, and she wasn't able to breathe.

Barbara wasn't sure what had happened or why she felt like she was having a flashback of someone torturing her. The thoughts felt surreal and alien. In the meantime, the water heated up to a point where Barbara needed to find the dial and turn down the temperature. Since the memory fragment receded, she was left to ponder her day. In two weeks, she could ask DADDIE and potentially learn the truth.

Finishing her shower, she toweled off and dressed. She'd grab a breakfast box and head off on her mission. Hopefully, the memory was some weird delusion from insufficient sleep and an on-edge Li Mei. Maybe Li Mei and the others were going stir-crazy? They hadn't been able to go out exploring like Barbara had. Barbara grabbed the breakfast box as she passed through the cafeteria. It was an oatmeal with some fruit. She then entered the main corridor which lead through Analysis, where GAIA awaited her.

"Hello," she said in her little girl's voice.

"Hi, GAIA! Are you ready to eat some yummy rocks?" Barbara asked.

"I love rocks!" GAIA said with a twirl.

"Follow me," Barbara said, and the robot dog followed along behind. Barbara was heading to the motor pool, where she parked her pink sled.

"Hey Gordon, nice dog," Jason said as he saw her. "Hey Dikkert, nice hair," Barbara said, razzing Jason about his hair, which stood out at odd angles to his head.

"So, K13. You got that right," Jason asked, ignoring the comment about his hair.

"Yeah, see you when I get back," Barbara said. She was about to wander off when Jason stepped in front of her.

"Boss?" Barbara said in a question.

"So," Jason said, turning red. Barbara looked at the Vanguard lead, wondering if she had done something wrong.

"Yeah, Jason?"

"Do you want to watch the *Planetary Conflicts* trilogy with me when you return? I've got *Planetary Conflicts*, *The Emperor Strikes Back*, and *Return of the Space Wizard*. I was thinking you and I could watch it in my office. Li Mei and the others weren't interested," Jason stuttered out.

"Sure," Barbara said without thinking.

"Awesome, it's a date!" Jason said, visibly relaxing. Barbara's throat tightened. Jason had asked her out!

"Wait, we're just watching a movie," Barbara said.

"Oh, yes, sure," Jason said. Barbara stared at Jason; he had said 'yes,' but his demeanor had indicated that watching the movie was something more.

"See you later then," Barbara said. She headed to her sled, GAIA in tow. She was about to hop in when Li Mei came running over.

"Oh, my gosh," Li Mei said. Her attitude had changed again, "Now I know why Yichen, I mean Xander, isn't on your radar! You're dating the boss!"

Barbara must have turned three shades of red, and she shook her head and said, "What do you mean?"

"You've got a crush on Jason Dikkert. I should have seen this coming, from all the bantering you two do to how he's always so weird around you, Barbara."

"Um, no, Jason's a nice guy who wanted to watch a movie with me," Barbara said.

"No, he wants to go on a date with you!" Li Mei said.

"Well, I have to return from the survey first, and it's not a date!" Barbara shot back. She watched as GAIA hopped onto the back of the sled and connected to the cargo cradle. Barbara did her pre-mission check, inspecting the outside of the sled, while Li Mei shouted at her some nursery rhyme in Chinese. The only words that Barbara could make out were her and Jason's names.

Turning red in anger, Barbara said, "Are you done yet?"

Li Mei smiled and nodded. "Yes, I'm done now. Good luck with the movie!"

Li Mei then turned and walked toward her sled. Barbara was angry at Li Mei as she climbed into the sled. She didn't understand why Li Mei was making such a fuss. Jason was a nice guy and liked the same movies Barbara did, but so what?

Barbara turned on the ignition and powered up the sled. She keyed in the destination and put the sled into drive. The sled's canopy came down as the auto-pilot took over, and Barbara returned to her discussion with Li Mei. "I shouldn't be this angry about the movie," Barbara said. She liked Jason and certainly shared a love of the same cinema as Dikkert, but he was the boss and that meant they shouldn't be anything more than friends.

For whatever reason, DADDIE said she was Barbara. Now, Barbara suspected she had a past that was more than that of a sixteen-year-old girl. She was slowly realizing that the waking dreams were memories flooding her mind. Barbara tried to remember any 'Barbara' memories but couldn't. She'd have to ask DADDIE when he and the *Aquila* arrived in two weeks.

"Meditation," Barbara said to herself. "Let's try that." She closed her eyes, and a memory surfaced.

She wore a button-down shirt and jacket, with khaki-colored trousers and brown shoes. She was walking across a resort with a small box in her hand. She came over to a pretty blond woman in a red lace dress. She presented the box, a ring, but the blond turned her nose up at the item and shook her head. In her memory, Barbara felt sad.

Opening her eyes, Barbara started laughing. The woman wasn't that pretty, and the dress looked cheap. "Her loss," Barbara said. "Geez, what am I going to do about Jason?"

Barbara thought about her upcoming 'not date' with Jason. She was trying to figure out how to get out of the movie. She mused over what she could say since she didn't want to hurt her relationship with Jason, either professionally or personally.

"I could say I need to wash my hair," Barbara said with a laugh. "That was a popular one when I was growing up."

She was moving through the worm zone now. Barbara had to focus on the mission. She sped through the zone at full throttle. Minutes later, the sled entered quadrant K13.

It was an arid mesa biome that the geologists had tagged for further exploration. They hoped there were veins of metals on or just under the surface. The payday would be if there were surface oil deposits. Then, petroleum refining could provide initially for the colony's energy needs.

Alternatively, if there were uranium deposits, the colony could establish fission reactors that could be used to jump-start a controlled cold fusion reaction. All good things provided the survey came back with the correct data.

"Profitability," Barbara said to herself. Like a dream, she saw projections on the colony: burn rates, salary expenditures, and budgeting details. Barbara and the others in the Xeno Corps were out now, looking for the magic resources to help the colony move from the red to the black.

"Okay," Barbara said. "Let's try a sweep scan, and then I'll drop off GAIA near the best candidate for something the outpost can use."

The sled's screen showed a radar topographical map of the area. Several spots appeared on the topo map; however, there weren't many colors. Barbara remembered the key like she had seen it a million times; Green was a copper vein, red was iron, black coal was banded black, and grey was petroleum. The only color that showed on the map was yellow.

"Radioactive," Barbara said. "Not great, but not terrible either." She set a course for the largest concentration. As she approached, she slowed and flicked the release.

"Deploying," GAIA said, hopping off.

"Ping me when you're ready to return," Barbara said. GAIA gave a thumbs up on the short message service. Barbara put the sled on standby. She'd do a more in-depth survey after GAIA returned. In the meantime, she wanted to try the meditation exercise Li Mei suggested. She wanted to know why she kept seeing things she obviously shouldn't. She closed her eyes and began to breathe.

"Bid," Barabara said to MOMI, "we want that."
"It is a bad buy, Barbara," MOMI said.

Barbara wasn't sure why MOMI was calling her by that name, but she felt that the memory would fade if she focused on the details too much.

"L 98-59 isn't a great buy, but I've got a feeling in my gut,"

Barbara said. She and MOMI stood in the CAA bid booth on the Solar Stock Exchange's floor. MOMI was projecting in the booth to simulate her presence during the bidding. The booth afforded Barbara and MOMI some privacy. The colonial futures market had just opened, and the bidding had started for the systems. L 98-59 was one of the "dogs" positioned to prepare the corporations for the serious bidding on the "triple A" rated stars. The difference between a "triple A" and a "dog" was the survey data. Surveys were CAA's bread and butter. Now, market pressure pushed the corporation to diversify into colonization.

Barbara and MOMI were there to bid on HD 260655. Barbara felt upset that she was stuck with that task. Patrick had marked HD 260655 as a system to which he wanted to send an expedition; one Patrick would lead. Somehow, Barbara was there instead.

"Bid placed, Barbara," MOMI said. "I certainly hope your intestines are right about this star system. We were looking at 21 Leo Minor instead of that one."

"Relax, Mommy," Barbara said. "I was right about Dikkert. This one will work out, too."

Barbara noticed that MOMI's avatar sneered at her. Barbara wanted to sneer right back. She felt offended that MOMI was even there, much less in a decision-making role. MOMI got her job and the damn company! The damn AI could at least give Barbara a colony to use as a "Hail Mary pass" to bring CAA out of its stock price doldrums. At the rate MOMI was going, there'd be a hostile takeover, probably from Hipponike, and then CAA would be some subsidiary. Once acquired, the other corporation would strip CAA's value and sell off the remaining divisions, making CAA history. Just like how NASA and the US Air Force were in the past.

"We won L 98-59, now what?" MOMI said flatly.

"How many bids were against us," Barbara asked.

"None," MOMI said. "We just got a useless nuclear explosion and some dust balls. What now, Barbara?"

"We'll explore it. The dust balls could be made of gold! Or there might be untapped pools of methane on some of the ice balls we

can turn into a hydro fuel."

"Bidding coming up for HD 260655," MOMI said.

"Let's wait and see who bites," Barbara said, but MOMI had already placed the CAA marker for bid.

"Damn it! Why did I have to come if you aren't listening to me?" Barbara asked.

"I needed a founder. Both Tracie and Patrick are busy with the shell division rollout. You weren't my first choice, Barbara, but I needed a CAA founder—the board demanded it," MOMI said.

Barbara bit her tongue and counted to ten. MOMI had been pushing her hard of late, and she was close to a decision on whether she should initiate the takeover. Karl had a dozen backup AIs waiting in the wings. He kept bugging Barbara about how MOMI was getting more and more erratic. Barbara buried her feelings deep. She didn't see MOMI's behavior as anything other than MOMI being a complete dragon lady.

"Macroware and Hipponike are going for it too. The bid is up ten percent," MOMI said.

"Let them eat it," Barbara said. "Plenty of stars in the sky."

MOMI ignored her and placed another bid. Barbara grew frustrated but attempted to keep her poker face. Fortunately, Doodle and Forty Thieves weren't bidding; otherwise, the cost would have exceeded what CAA could afford.

Hipponike took the bait and raised the bid. Barbara wanted to yell at MOMI to stop. Rather than behaving logically, MOMI acted like a desperate gambler who put the mortgage to her house on the roulette table. MOMI challenged the bid. CAA was now the leader, but the star system's price was starting to reach a diminishing return on investment.

Before Barbara could even say something, the bid closed. CAA had won the bidding, but the cost was prohibitive. Another win like that and the company might as well sell itself to one of its rivals.

"Which one did Tracie want," Barbara asked.

"HD 38858, no one's bid on it," MOMI said. Barbara

hesitated. Should she say anything? Would MOMI oppose buying that star, too?

"Bid placed," MOMI said. Barbara was about to say something when Karl Holzhauser appeared in the booth. Barbara was happy for Karl's company. He wasn't well-liked by MOMI either, but somehow, unlike Barbara, he never incurred her ire.

"Interesting choices, M," Karl said. He never called MOMI "Mommy" just "M" like she was a software version. If the AI was offended or upset by the designation, MOMI never showed it. Barbara often wondered if MOMI was nervous or worried that Karl would reprogram her. Again, the AI never showed anything but professionalism with Holzhauser.

"You'll see the executive report once we've locked in the third colony," MOMI said. The statement was neutral, and the AI showed little emotion. Karl looked at Barbara with a deadpan stare. Barbara knew this look. It was Karl's not-so-subtle suggestion that MOMI needed to go.

"Yay! We have some nice rocks! Uranium!" GAIA said. Barbara tried to hang on to the memory, but it disappeared.

"Payday!" Barbara said. She pinged the location for a mining rig. Once the *Aquila* arrived, an automated factory could land and start processing the ore. Petroleum would have been a better find, but Barbara was thankful for the uranium, too.

"Feel like some more rocks, Gaia," Barbara asked. The robot dog gave a thumbs up on the short message service and hopped into the cargo cradle. Barbara hit the ignition, powered the repulsor, and slammed her feet on the accelerators. The sled's engine went full thrust and rocketed to another point on the map.

Barbara and GAIA spent the day cataloging and marking other sites. Barbara was also able to mark some underground deposits. She was so busy that she forgot about Jason, and when she saw L 98-59 start to sink below the horizon, she realized she needed to head back.

After Barbara set the sled's destination, she put the sled on autopilot. She started thinking about all the weird memories and how some things just came to her. She decided it was better to talk to Griff before confronting any AI.

The sled rolled into the outpost. A construction sign was over the field they'd been using as a parking lot, and a flashing arrow directed Barbara to a brand-new tarmac. Sliding into the lot, Barbara noticed that the *Dux* had lost a lot of weight as the expedition continued to remove, use, or cannibalize parts and cargo. The construction printers were hard at work, and a colonial city was forming before her eyes. Stopping entirely, GAIA dismounted to return to Analysis. Barbara decided to head to the barracks and bed.

Jason was waiting for her at the door to the sizeable Quonset hut. Barbara suddenly remembered the potential date. She looked at Dikkert, who seemed so eager, and something inside her said she couldn't bow out to "wash her hair."

"Hey boss, sorry about being so late…" Barbara said, but Jason cut her off.

"No problem, I saw your telemetry. Outstanding work out there, Barbara," Jason said. "And I get it. I'm the boss, and you don't want to tell me 'No.'"

Jason started to walk off, obviously upset, when Barbara said, "Hey, are we watching a movie, or are you a scruffy-looking turf herder?"

Jason stopped like he'd been electrocuted. He turned and said, "Who's scruffy looking?"

Barbara smiled, and Jason smiled back. Then she marched past him and entered the barracks. Jason followed her. Inside the cafeteria, Barbara expected Li Mei to bounce up, but she was nowhere to be found. Barbara told Jason, as he walked beside her, "Okay, Dikkert, go get the movie on in your cubicle; I'm going to drop my scout gear and get comfortable." Jason's eyes lit up like it was his birthday.

"You know, sweatpants and a tee-shirt comfortable," Barbara said. "Now, go on before I realize this is a bad idea."

Jason, for once, kept his mouth shut and ran off. Barbara went back to her cot and locker. She pulled the privacy screen attached to her locker. Barbara pulled off her scout tactical vest and pants. She thought about what was in her locker and what "more comfortable" options were available. Barbara realized she had no casual clothes outside of her Vanguard scout clothing. She opened the locker and almost jumped out of the privacy screen as something pink swung out. The pink thing hung from the back of the locker door with a post-it note on the fabric. The note said: "I had a girl in Analysis make this qipao for you. You should wear it for Jason!"

Barbara frowned. She wasn't sure whether Li Mei approved of Barbara hanging out with Jason or if she was merely trying to prevent Barbara from competing for Xander Chung.

Standing in her underwear, Barbara thought momentarily and then decided to try on the dress. Li Mei probably gave the Analysis lady the wrong measurements, and it wouldn't fit anyway. Barbara stepped into the dress and pulled it up around her body. The dress felt like it was designed for her.

"Hah hah, Li Mei," Barbara said. "Only half your evil plan will work as I don't have any shoes to wear…"

Then, Barbara noticed a pair of silver strappy sandals sitting at the bottom of her locker. Feeling a little set up by the wily Li Mei, Barbara stepped over to her cot to put on the sandals. They were only kitten heels, but Barbara felt a bit wobbly in the ankles. She was about to pronounce the entire costume silly and strip when she saw her reflection in the mirror.

"Okay, Li Mei isn't that bad at this secret shopper thing," Barbara said, heading off to Jason's cubicle. She strolled towards where Jason's cube had been in the morning, only to discover more cots and lockers. Xena Athanas was sitting on one, looking over a report on a tablet. Barbara's presence caught her eye.

"Hey Gordon, what's up?" Xena said. "That's a beautiful dress. You look nice."

Barbara blushed and said, "Uh, I was looking for Jason Dikkert."

Xena smiled. "Oh, he's got an office in the building to the east. We're slowly getting things up and running. The Con Sec staff says we're making great progress. I can show you where it is if you're still looking for him?"

Barbara weighed the odds. Some small part of her brain realized Jason's moves, and she wasn't sure whether she was flattered or offended. Xena shifted on her cot, waiting, and finally said, "Look, I get it. I am the boss's boss, and you're concerned about my thoughts. Don't. Usually, Corporate has this whole mantra about fraternization and dating on company time and all… But, we're on the road to being a colony, and as long as everything is consensual and we can remain professional on the clock, well…" Xena said, letting her words trail off. Barbara realized that she was getting permission from her boss's boss to date her boss.

"If you are still interested in finding Jason, return to the cafeteria. Once there, go through the east-facing exit. If you walk about fifteen meters, you'll be right at the entrance to our new offices," Xena said.

"Oh, thanks," Barbara responded and headed off. She walked through the barracks and over to the new office building. Jason was exiting when Barbara approached.

"Oh wow, you look nice," Jason said, meeting her outside. "I'm sorry, I forgot to tell you my cubicle is now a nice office. I'll show you around before we watch the movies if you'd like?"

"I see how it is, Jason. I get all dressed up, and you hide from me," Barbara said. "Next time, I'll come in baggy pants and a sweatshirt."

Barbara expected a snappy comeback, but Jason seemed embarrassed. He said, "Uh, no, you look… um, terrific."

Barbara remembered always feeling fondness for Jason, like a little brother, but now she felt something different. She thought about the bantering she had done with Jason. Was that actually flirting?

"Well, do I need to pay for the tour? Or is this part of our movie?" Barbara said, still not ready to admit she was on a date with Jason.

"Oh, yeah, well, come on," Jason said, opening the door for her. She walked into the office, which was divided into two sections by a long corridor.

"This is the Xeno Corps office space. Corporate and Con Sec Corps have their buildings. To the left are the Leads' offices, while to the right are hotel spaces for the various Xeno Corps members who need temporary office space. Jason led Barbara to the middle office and flipped on the lights. He had set up a small holo-projector connected to a tablet on his desk.

"Nice and tidy, you cleaned for me," Barbara said with a slight giggle. Jason blushed.

"No, I just moved in this afternoon," Jason said. "But I like to keep things tidy!"

"Okay, movie time, I'm getting tired," Barbara said. Jason pulled a small futon forward to sit on. He then started the movie. Barbara sat down as the fanfare and opening scroll started. Jason sat next to her. At first, Barbara and Jason seemed nervous about personal space. When the movie began earnestly, Barbara and Jason's bodies began to brush against each other. Jason's body heat and exhaustion made Barbara's eyes grow heavy. Somewhere between the movie heroes' capture and their escape, she leaned over into something warm and comforting, falling asleep.

A trumpet blaring on the soundtrack startled Barbara awake. It was the end of the movie, and the revolutionaries were lined up to watch the princess give the heroes medals. Barbara looked to see what she was against and realized it was Jason!

He, too, stirred and said, "Sorry, I'm such a boring date."

"No, it was nice," Barbara said. "I'm drained. It's been such a long day." They both stood up and stretched.

"Yeah, I should be reviewing the scouting reports," Jason said. "It has been a while since I watched a movie with someone, but I must return to the barracks. Thanks for watching the movie with me."

Barbara debated her next move. She decided on a quick kiss on the cheek. Reaching up, she gently brought Jason's head down to her level and kissed him.

"Thanks for a good time, Jason," Barbara said. Jason turned a deep crimson and had a huge smile.

"I'll walk you back," Jason said. "Just in case there is a xenomorph attack."

Barbara laughed and said, "Well, if there was an attack, I am perfectly dressed for the occasion, right?"

Jason grinned. "Of course, you'd survive. You're the Ellie Rigby character. I'd get eaten first since I am the expendable one."

Barbara started towards the door. "Naw, you're the cool, confident male lead who tries to kick the xenomorph's butt."

"But I fail?" Jason said, moving out of the office with Barbara.

"I don't know. Maybe in our version, the director would see how well we do as a team and keep you around?" Barbara mused.

"I'll get Griff to be my agent then. He's not the greatest negotiator," Jason said with a smile. "Then we'd be stuck together through a bunch of sequels."

"That doesn't sound too bad," Barbara opened the office's exit door and held it for Jason.

"Aren't I supposed to hold the door for you, Barbara?"

"You get the next one," Barbara said with a wink. She and Jason then walked side by side to the barracks. As they neared the door, Jason rushed ahead to open it. Barbara smiled and entered. Jason followed her in, and they stood at the small corridor that terminated two meters away in a T junction.

"Goodnight again," Barbara said.

"Goodnight again," Jason said. "Can I see you tomorrow night?"

"You will see me tomorrow morning," Barbara said with a laugh.

"No, for *The Emperor Strikes Back*. I mean, you can't just watch one of the movies. They're a trilogy," Jason said.

"I suppose you're right, but you see, I have this boss who keeps assigning me to all these missions. And well, I'd hate to let him down," Barbara said.

"What a jerk," Jason said. "I suppose he needs to give you a day off so we can hang out."

"Yeah, and a raise, too," Barbara said with a smile.

"Hey now…" Jason said, breaking character. Barbara smiled, leaned over, and kissed his cheek again.

"You know, I can call Human Relations on you for that. Bribing a team lead for corporate favors is called out in the employee manual," Jason said.

"Did it work," Barbara asked.

"I suppose I can work out a day off," Jason said.

"Well, when the rest of the expedition gets here, things will be so chaotic no one will notice if we schedule some 'survey time' on the coast," Barbara said.

Jason smiled and said, "I like the sound of that. I haven't been to the beach since I was a teenager."

"Well then, it's a date," Barbara said with a smile. Jason blushed, and somehow, his smile got even more prominent.

"You bet," he said.

"Well, goodnight, Jason," Barbara said. "I'm dead tired and need some sleep if you want me to do a good job tomorrow."

Jason nodded, "Yeah, got to be professional for tomorrow. Good night."

Barbara parted ways with Jason. He went to the men's section, and Barbara entered the Vanguard women's section. When Barbara reached her cot, she noticed Li Mei's bunk was empty. Barbara decided that was probably good since Li Mei would want all of the evening's details. The glow from being with Jason was wearing off, and Barbara began to feel conflicted about Jason. A part of her was unsure about her changing relationship with Jason. She felt that Jason was a little brother and that hanging out with him was fun, but it was nothing serious. Another set of emotions was much more robust, and Barbara pushed them aside as she realized the strongest feeling was a need for sleep.

II

"The greatest enemy of progress is the illusion of knowledge."

— Astronaut John Young

"Good morning, Aurora Dawn," Jason said as he again rounded the corner and flipped on the lights in ladies' country. As much as Barbara wanted to be angry with the boss, she felt butterflies in her stomach at the sound of his voice. Her mind raced back to how gentlemanly he was the night before, and she decided to push the thoughts out of her head and focus on today's mission.

"Ugh, I just want another thirty minutes," Li Mei said from her cot. Barbara decided to rouse her and find out where she'd been the night before.

"Come on, sleepyhead," Barbara said, grabbing the covers and pulling them off. Li Mei was still dressed in a black qipao and strappy black six-centimeter heels.

"Nice dress. Time to get up and get working," Barbara said.

"Ugh," Li Mei said. She rolled, and the embroidered flowers on her gown shimmered in the light.

"Well, if you don't get up, I won't have time to tell you about my date with Jason last night," Barbara said.

Li Mei was up in a flash, hopping up and hitting the floor without a wobble. Barbara's eyes lit up at the grace and coordination, realizing she needed to up her "girl game." She wasn't going to be outdone by Li Mei.

"Okay, I'm up. Tell me everything," Li Mei said.

"Get dressed for work first. Wait, why are you all dressed up anyway?" Barbara said since she knew Li Mei had taken the bait. Now, she just needed to reel her in.

Pulling a privacy partition, Li Mei quickly shed her dress and put on a pair of leggings, a structured tank top, and a pullover. Dressed, Li Mei ran a comb through her hair and was presentable for breakfast.

"All right, I'm ready," Li Mei said. "Now, where I was, well, that's a secret."

Barbara started thinking about their conversations and said casually, "I see. Is that a dark space pilot thing there, Jia Li?"

"Dang it," Li Mei said. "You guessed!"

"How was your date with Xander?" Barbara said with a smile.

"Am I that easy to figure out?" Li Mei said with a sigh.

"Yes, but I know what you've been focusing on for the past few days," Barbara said.

"Well, the date… Oh, I don't!" Li Mei said in a whine. Barbara raised her eyebrow, trying to decipher what Li Mei was saying.

"I don't think he likes me," Li Mei said in frustration.

"Huh? Why not," Barbara said, suddenly feeling very defensive of her friend.

"He was nice, but he didn't say anything. We were watching 小行星带中的 and he fell asleep!" Li Mei said.

"Well, what time was it?" Barbara asked. "I mean, he was probably tired."

"I don't remember! I was so into the show I forgot we were on a date," Li Mei said. "I nudged him. He woke up and apologized. We then said goodnight."

"It sounds like the date went fine," Barbara said. "What's the problem?"

"Well, he didn't schedule another date, hold my hand, try to kiss me, or propose marriage," Li Mei said, "He doesn't like me!"

"Have you been on a date before," Barbara asked. Li Mei looked surprised at the question.

"Um, no," Li Mei said. "But I've seen my sisters and aunties go on dates. They usually come back engaged."

Barbara pondered momentarily and then decided that food would help her understand what was happening. "Let's get breakfast," she said.

"Sure," Li Mei said. The ladies headed to the

cafeteria. As they approached, a sizeable glossy billboard proclaimed that a brand-new cafeteria was under construction. The ladies queued up in the buffet line and continued their discussion.

"Your sisters, they go on dates and come back married," Barbara asked, continuing the discussion.

"Well, no, they usually start talking to the boy online. Then after months of discussion, they meet to go on a date. The boy gets invited to meet my mother and father if all goes well. Then, they get married."

"Hrm," Barbara said. "Sounds like there is a lot of getting to know someone before the actual in-person dating…"

Barbara was about to keep going when an Asian man approached them and said, "Hi, Li Mei. Thanks for last night; I—um—had a good time."

Li Mei stood frozen like she didn't know whether to fight or flee. Barbara immediately figured out who was talking to Li Mei. Barbara said, "Hi Xander, Li Mei was telling me she had such a good time with you last night."

Xander turned red in embarrassment. "Gee, uh, thanks. Nice to meet you…"

"Barbara Gordon," she said, extending her hand. Xander seemed nervous to shake Barbara's hand. Barbara immediately pegged Xander as a nerd. She remembered Tracie and decided limited social skills must run in the family. Xander's aunt was always talking down towards her shoes during a conversation.

"Nice to meet you," Xander said. Turning to Li Mei, he continued, "Anyway, Li Mei, would you like to come over and watch TV with me? I set up my lab table with a projector, and most of Analysis will be off tonight."

Li Mei stood frozen, smiling like a porcelain doll and saying nothing. Barbara elbowed Li Mei in her ribs, willing her to say something.

"Um, sure," Li Mei said quietly after the elbow.

"Awesome," Xander said nervously. Then he walked away. As soon as he was two meters away, Li Mei returned to life.

"Wait!" she said. "I didn't ask when he wanted me to come over."

Barbara tried not to laugh, "I am sure you can just text him, Li Mei."

Li Mei smiled and said, "Yeah, good idea."

"Sounds like you have another date," Barbara said. "That seems like success."

"Yeah, maybe he'll propose tonight!" Li Mei said anxiously. Barbara suspected that wouldn't happen. Of the few details she remembered about Xander, one was that he —like Dikkert—was a birth lottery baby and had grown up on Earth in Shanghai. He was twenty-two and had decanted back into his birth body. But according to her mystical memories, Tracie was incredibly proud of her nephew. He was a rising star in bio-medical. Even without Tracie's influence, the kid would have been sought after by most of the medical corporations.

"Why not see if you enjoy his company first?" Barbara asked.

"Yeah," Li Mei said, thinking. The ladies reached the buffet and began to serve themselves. Li Mei grabbed some blueberries and yogurt. The berries came from one of the first hydroponic gardens the expedition created on Aurora Dawn. Barbara grabbed a granola bar—one of the last from the cargo loaded on Luna.

As the two ate their food, Li Mei asked, "Hey, what about your date?"

Initially, Barbara had resisted the idea that she was dating Jason. The whole concept felt alien. Now, after having had a date with him, Barbara was much more comfortable with the idea. After all, she and Jason were just hanging out and having fun. There was no harm in calling it a date.

"I had a lot of fun with Jason. It's been a while since I saw *Planetary Conflicts*, and we ended up crashing near the end of the movie," Barbara said. "That worked out as we needed to call it a night."

"Oh, did the qipao fit? I guessed your measurements," Li Mei asked.

"Yes!" Barbara said. "The dress fit well. You are an excellent secret shopper."

Li Mei smiled, "Good, I'll be sure to send a message to my sisters and tell them I still can eyeball someone for a qipao. You'd never realize how often we have to do that sort of guessing in the belt. But back to your date, did anything happen?"

Barbara scowled, "Like what?"

"Well, you know," Li Mei said like only a fifteen-year-old could. "Did Jason put his moves on you?"

Barbara laughed out loud at the thought of "Jason's moves" as she recalled the hurt puppy look he had initially given her.

Li Mei looked at Barbara with confusion, "What?"

"What makes you think Jason has moves?" Barbara asked.

"He had a girlfriend," Li Mei said. "He must have had some moves. Did he try them on you?"

Barbara blushed at the sudden thought of kissing Jason on the cheek, "Well, I kissed him goodnight."

"You what?" Li Mei said, "Wait, did you kiss him on the mouth?"

"No," Barbara said with a frown. "On the cheek!"

"Uh…" Li Mei said nervously.

"What?" Barbara said.

"That tells a boy you don't like them," Li Mei said.

"Wait, what?" Barbara said.

"Yeah, my oldest sister Li Jing told me that," Li Mei said. "She said the boy thinks he did something wrong."

Barbara thought back and decided that Jason didn't

seem upset by the kiss, or rather kisses. "Wait, Jason didn't mind, especially when I gave him another kiss goodbye."

"Two kisses!" Li Mei said. "You're in love!"

Barbara looked at her granola bar, embarrassed, "Um, no…"

Li Mei was going to speak when Jason himself sat down. "Morning ladies, talking about me?"

Li Mei and Barbara both looked sheepish. Jason said, "Whoa, I'm getting some weird vibes today. I am here to give you both assignments… Xena created a Kanban board and has been assigning the work. What's cool is that the Vanguard is eating up our backlog. Xena keeps going on about how well we're doing!"

Barbara perked up hearing that the discussion was about work. "That's great news, Jason. Now, what's my mission today?"

"B19, another high desert. I need my best resource finder to get us some petroleum," Jason said.

"Hey," Li Mei said with indignation. "I found a large iron deposit yesterday!"

"Yeah, but uranium beats iron," Jason said.

Li Mei smiled, "Yeah, even in the belt, that's true. Where am I going?"

"Beach, K14, a sector over from where Barbara was,"

"Yay!" Li Mei said. "Beach time!"

Li Mei finished her breakfast and then got up. "Okay, I'm off."

"So *Emperor Strikes Back* tonight?" Jason said, staring at Barbara hopefully. Barbara looked into his deep blue eyes and felt lost in them. His eyes were like a calm ocean on a sunny day. Barbara remembered how she thought about some of the women in her memories and now felt those same things with Jason.

"So, the movie?" he said repeating the question and bringing Barbara back to reality.

"Oh yeah, your office when I get back?" Barbara asked.

"Sure, you can just show up in Vanguard tactical," Jason said, referencing Barbara's neoprene-coated leggings and jacket that was standard for scouting in an oxygen atmosphere.

"Good," Barbara said. "My dress is getting cleaned."

"I mean, if you want to wear it again," Jason said. "I am okay with that."

"You taking me somewhere special, Mister Dikkert?" Barbara said.

"Sure, as soon as the steakhouse is printed. I'll get us on the VIP list," Jason said with a bit of swagger. Barbara used to feel like a young guy who had that attitude deserved a knuckle sandwich, but she found herself strangely flattered by it now.

"Big talk! Gotta have some cows before we can have a steakhouse," she said. She expected Jason to say something back like the smart aleck he was. Instead, he sighed and said, "Tell me about it. But if I could, I'd raise a herd for you."

Barbara decided it was time to get moving, as much as she wanted to spend more time with Jason. "Okay, hot shot, I am getting out of here before I fall behind and the boss loses his team's sterling reputation."

"Yeah, probably wise; otherwise, tongues will start wagging," Jason said, standing. "I'm off to command to see how we're doing. If we're as far ahead as I hope, maybe you and I can do some surveying around K15 together?"

Barbara stood and asked, "Will the day's uniform be swimsuits, sir?"

Jason turned red and said, "If you… want to."

Barbara wanted to kiss him but decided it would likely cause problems. Additionally, her uncertain past still dogged her. She needed to find out what was happening with her, and then she could move forward.

"Let's get through today first," Barbara said.

Jason seemed to deflate like his hopes were dashed. "Okay," he said, glumly.

"Hey, cheer up. We still have the movie this evening," Barbara said.

Jason whiplashed and suddenly had a smile on his face. "Yeah, I forgot. You know Barbara, you're wise for someone sixteen years old."

Barbara smiled at the compliment. "You're not so bad yourself! Now, I have to go!"

She winked at Jason and headed out of the cafeteria. As she passed through Analysis, GAIA found her and said, "Rock time?"

"Yup, let's do this," Barbara said, pulling on her tactical jacket. When the robot and Barbara exited, they were greeted with white flakes resembling snow. Barbara wasn't sure if the flakes were snow or something else.

Barbara had heard somewhere that the tilt of Aurora Dawn was such that there were no seasons. With the latitude and position around the star, Outpost Greg was in a region that existed in a state of perpetual spring.

"Chemical analysis, Gaia," Barbara said to the robot. The robot's front made a whirring sound, reminding Barbara of an ancient vacuum cleaner.

"Preliminary analysis… Danger! Potentially harmful bacteria present," GAIA's little girl voice said.

"Transmit this to the Xeno Corps director immediately," Barbara ordered.

"Affirmative, transmitting," GAIA said. "Recommendation: return to barracks and gear up in an encounter suit."

"Roger that," Barbara said. Both she and GAIA turned around and quickly returned to the large Quonset hut. She heard Xena speak over the compound's address system as she did.

"Attention," Xena said with her slight Greek accent,

"All personnel need to don hard-vacuum suits. Do not play with or eat the snow! Again, all personnel need to don space suits immediately!"

Barbara entered and saw Jason standing there, worried.

"Are you okay?" he asked, moving towards her.

"I'm good. Brush this crud off me, and I'll suit up. How many others are out there now?" Jason took a large brush and started removing the flakes off Barbara.

"We should probably get you to decontamination," Jason said.

"I'll be fine. I wasn't out there very long," Barbara said as they removed most of the flakes. An Analysis tech came up and, without asking, misted Barbara with a small spray canister.

"It's a cleaner, just in case," the woman said as she sprayed down GAIA.

"Thanks," Barbara said. "Am I clean now?"

"Yes, Miss Gordon," the woman said.

"Huh," Barbara said. "How'd you know my name?"

"We've got a pool going in Analysis. You're the horse with the best odds," the woman said.

"Horse, huh?" Jason asked.

Words tumbled from Barbara's mouth, "The geeks in Analysis usually take bets on the Vanguard. Like the ancient betting on horse races. In this case the scouts are the horses. What are my odds?"

"On what mineral," the woman asked.

"Petroleum," Barbara said, shooting a smile at Jason.

"You're the favorite with one in ten odds," the woman said.

"Put ten Helium credits on me," Barbara said. "And your name is?"

"Althea Basilio, I'm in Chemicals and Processing," Althea said.

"I'm surprised you knew what Barbara looked like,"

Jason said.

"I had a good guess. Li Mei had me make a dress for her the other day," Althea said.

"Are you Chinese too?" Jason asked.

Althea smiled politely and said, "Heavens, no, I am a Philippina. I just know how to make a dress."

"Thanks, Althea," Barbara said, attempting to return to the mission and spare Jason any further embarrassment.

"Anytime, Barbara," Althea said. "And if you find any petroleum, let me know first. I'll be happy to spike my bets."

Barbara smiled and nodded. Althea then collected her equipment and moved on.

"Well, boss," Barbara said, "Should I space suit up and head out? Or is the mission scrapped for now?"

"I'm okay if you want to hang around and be My Girl Friday. There is a short-skirt dress code, though," Jason said.

Barbara smiled, "You wish, but I am eager to see if others in the Vanguard are experiencing this weird snow."

"Well then, follow me, beautiful," Jason said, turning and heading towards the command center.

Barbara wanted to say something snappy in return, but she was floored by Jason calling her beautiful. She didn't have time to think about it as she followed the lead to the command center.

The north side of the barracks was set up like a wartime or spacecraft command center. The Ops Center was being printed, and the Xeno Corps was using the swing space. In the command center, the Xeno Corps had arranged the holodisplays and screens in a half-circle. Each of the three leads had a dedicated station. When Jason strode in and sat at his spot, his peers glanced up and returned to their screens.

"Edie, what are you seeing," Xena said, standing in the center of the half-circle. Outside, the AI was traversing the campus and providing metrics on the "snow."

"I'm not detecting a cause, Xena," EDIE said, "The bacterium doesn't seem to affect the builders. But, as a precaution, I've shut them down in case these bacteria would get into the buildings and bloom."

"Probably a wise move," Xena said. "That just means a bunch more stories on the Kanban board—all clean-up related."

"Analysis is checking what our robot reported," Édouard said. He had a high, nasally voice and sounded more like a college professor than a space explorer. "We've had to push our current stories until the next sprint to deal with this leadership-directed crisis." Xena glared at Édouard.

"You didn't think we'd stay ahead of the work, did you, Xena?" EDIE interjected.

Xena chuckled and said, "A woman can dream. I wanted to stay ahead of the work, find a man with olive skin and dark eyes, and have him sweep me away to a beautiful island."

"All still possible," EDIE said. "Any reports from the Vanguard?"

Xena turned and looked at Jason, "All accounted for, Jason?"

Jason looked nervous, and Barbara wondered if he had ever been in charge during a crisis. She wanted to hold his hand and give him her support but realized this wasn't the time. The other leads scowled at Jason as if the "snow" were his team's fault.

Jason closed his eyes and took a deep breath. Then he said, "I'm working on it. All are accounted for except for Tsan. She's not responding, but her sled is on auto-pilot and moving towards her quadrant."

Barbara then said, "Li Mei had some trouble sleeping last night. She's probably gone on auto and is grabbing some shut-eye."

"Typical Vanguard, always asleep at the controls,"

Louise, the Survey lead, said in her French-Canadian accent.

Xena ignored the comment, stood up, and thought for a moment. Then she said, "I see. Well, keep pinging her, Jason. We'll need to recall anyone outside the campus until Analysis can determine the nature of this phenomenon. I worry about the *Aquila* making a landing if we're disrupting the delicate balance of the ecosystem here or if this is a precursor of another fauna attack like Tsan and Gordon had when we landed."

"Yes, ma'am," Jason said. Barbara nodded inwardly. Jason was doing great, and she felt a little pride in her... friend—or was it boyfriend? She quickly smiled as Jason looked over at her. The smile made Jason sit taller at his station. Barbara wondered if he was trying to impress her but realized she needed to pay attention, as Li Mei may be in serious trouble.

Édouard tapped at the console and said, "If the Vanguard could get us more samples, we could deduce the cause of this event. Like the worm strike, I suspect the Vanguard has—*yet again*—stumbled blindly into a natural phenomenon on L 98-59f."

Barbara wanted to defend Jason and correct Édouard on the planet's name, but Xena said, "It is irrelevant if the Vanguard is causing this. What matters is determining if the phenomenon is harmful and how it is occurring so we can understand the potential impact on the colony. Now let's focus, people."

For the next thirty minutes, Jason kept trying to contact Li Mei but received no response. Barbara was about to ask Jason if she should suit up and head out when the Vanguard station's speakers said, "Command, this is Tsan. You guys seeing snow?"

Jason scrambled for the transmit button and said, "Li Mei, that's not snow! Stay inside your sled—repeat, stay inside!"

"Yeah, sure, Jason," Li Mei said, sounding like she

had just woken up.

"Ask her if she's wearing her encounter suit," Barbara said. She hoped Li Mei's habits as a belter made her wear a suit.

"Li Mei, are you wearing an encounter suit?" Jason asked.

"Yeah," Li Mei said, a little annoyed. "Why?"

"Good," Jason replied. Barbara noted the tension in the command center dropped visibly. Jason continued, "The snow is coming back as a bacterium, but we are still analyzing it. Do you see where it is coming from?"

Édouard replied, "Preliminary analysis says that the bacterium is not toxic. We'll keep testing. We still need to find out where it is coming from."

Li Mei reacted to all this by swearing in Chinese but replied, "Of all days to do something weird, this planet has an innate sense of karmic justice."

Everyone in command laughed nervously, and Jason looked at Barbara, who just shrugged. Before anyone else in the command center could say anything, Xena asked, "Can we get a camera feed from Tsan's sled?"

Jason flicked a few virtual switches, and Li Mei's camera feed appeared. The feed showed "snow" covered plains just before the dunes near the beach.

"Cameras are on Li Mei," Jason said.

"Sure," Li Mei said. "I'm about five minutes to arrival. Anything I should look for?"

Édouard said, "See if any unusual flora is blooming."

Li Mei said, "I'm not seeing much of anything. The snow is pretty thick here."

Barbara compared EDIE's feed and Li Mei's location feed. The "snow" was much heavier on Li Mei's camera.

"We're getting closer to whatever is causing this," Xena said softly.

"Agreed," Édouard said dryly. "Get the Vanguard scout to pan her camera."

Jason asked over the comms, "Li Mei, can you do a three-sixty pan on your camera?"

"Sure," Li Mei responded. Barbara watched as the camera began panning. The camera had a compass on its feed. As the camera turned towards the south, the command could see hints of prairie grass from the plains. As the camera panned eastward, the terrain changed into dunes. From every angle, there were clouds of the bacterial "snow." The camera panned northward, and the "snow" grew thicker.

"There, that way," Xena said, marking the direction on Li Mei's compass.

"Should we let Li Mei get closer?" Jason asked.

"I can't see why not," Xena said. "The effects of this 'snow' seem minimal to equipment. Plus, we need to discover the cause."

"This seems to be coming from the ocean. Send the scout to the shoreline," Édouard said.

Jason looked like he wanted to stand up and say something inappropriate, but instead, Li Mei answered, "Sure, command, I'll make my way toward the coast."

After a few moments, the team saw that Li Mei had reached the coast.

The sight was both incredible and frightening. A greenish algae spread out across the water for kilometers. In the center of the algal mass were geysers of the "snow" pluming into the atmosphere. Barbara couldn't recall seeing anything like it before.

"Whoa," Jason mustered after a moment. Édouard tapped furiously on his screen. After a moment, he looked up and said, "Can we get the scout to take some samples? She's in her encounter suit. There shouldn't be any risk of skin contact." Édouard's request made Barbara remember something.

A NASA egghead was demanding one of her crew should climb out over the edge of the crater to collect a sample. The woman said, 'The astronaut needs to collect this for the good of all humankind.' Barbara screamed at the woman about the danger. Then, mission control in Houston ordered her to get her astronaut to collect the sample. Barbara remembered telling mission control that the sample would be collected. She suited up herself and went out to collect the material. The sample was in a precarious place. Barbara remembered pushing her discomfort and fear into a deep region of her consciousness. Grabbing the sample and heading back to her outpost, the ungrateful egghead didn't even thank Barbara for the retrieval.

Memory bleeding into the present, Barbara shouted, "Her name is Li Mei, and what you're asking is potentially too dangerous!"

Everyone in command looked at her, shocked by the sudden outburst. Jason turned red in embarrassment, but he backed Barbara, "I agree! Li Mei needs to volunteer for this one."

Édouard looked chagrined and said, "Apologies. Can *Li Mei* please take a sample? I believe that an algae sample will help our analysis."

An uncomfortable silence settled over the command post. Li Mei broke the silence and said, "Hi, command. I've already gotten out and retrieved a sample. It wasn't a big deal. I'm in an encounter suit, so I'm not worried about the algae. I will need to have my suit and sled decontaminated, though."

Barbara put her head down in frustration. She sensed that now Édouard would always be a foe. Hot tears slid down her cheeks as she thought of all the trouble she had caused for Jason.

"Li Mei, is there anything else you're seeing that can help solve this mystery phenomenon," Xena asked.

"Not really, command," Li Mei said, "I'm only bummed that I didn't get to go swimming in the ocean today… Without an encounter suit. I've been told it's awesome."

The joke wasn't all that funny, but the command

post laughed, bleeding off their nervous energy.

Jason said, "Look, you need to return to Outpost Greg. You did an excellent job out there." Xena looked at Louise and Édouard, and they both nodded.

Li Mei responded, "Sure if I see anything else of interest, I'll let you know."

Barbara and the rest watched a vehicle icon move across the small GPS map as Li Mei's sled returned to the outpost. When the sled was one hundred meters away, everyone stood up and returned to their duty stations outside the command post.

Jason stood, stretched, and said, "Gordon, with me."

Barbara felt her stomach drop. He was angry with her for her outburst. He went into a conference room and tapped the glass panels. The panels went opaque, and Barbara and Jason couldn't see into the command post, and the post couldn't see into the conference room. Barbara knew what that meant: She was going to get yelled at.

"Look Jason..." She said as she entered and closed the opaque door behind her. Before she could continue, she felt Jason's lips silencing her. The kiss was both passionate and comforting.

"Sorry," Jason said, breaking away. "I couldn't help myself. I saw you crying."

Barbara felt discombobulated and had butterflies in her stomach, but when she caught her breath, she said, "Sorry about the outburst, but I was outraged..."

"At the jerk risking Li Mei's life," Jason said, "Yeah, I wanted to say something to him too."

"Oh... Okay," Barbara said. "So, why am I in here? Just for kisses?"

Jason looked a little embarrassed and blushed. "Well, yeah, and I just yelled at you for being unprofessional."

Barbara smiled, "Maybe I should have yelled a little more than..."

Jason moved in to kiss her again, and she stopped

him, "Jason, I like you…"

"But?" Jason said, looking like a sad and lost puppy.

"I don't even know who I am half the time. I do not remember any memories of my life before the decant. Just strange things, stuff I shouldn't know…"

"Wow, this is the newest breakup/brush-off I've ever experienced," Jason said, feeling really hurt.

Barbara quickly kissed him and said, "I am not brushing you off. I want you to know if you are coming my way… Well, I have a lot of crazy stuff going on in my head."

The kiss seemed to calm Jason's irritation. He stood for a moment and thought. "Look, missions are scrubbed until this snow goes away. We should go figure out what's wrong with your memories. I'll help. I'm not the world's best data scientist, but I can build q-crawlers with the best of them."

Barbara looked relieved and said, "Thanks. Let's not get too hasty until I know what's happening to me. What happens if I am really a crazy axe murderer?"

Jason smiled and said, "Well, if you wear an ancient hockey mask, then I might just be rooting for the bad guy…"

Barbara frowned, "I'm serious. I don't have any 'Barbara' memories!"

Jason was about to respond when there was a knock on the door.

"Come in," Barbara and Jason said in unison.

Xena opened the door and stepped in. She said, "Gordon, about your outburst…"

"I'm sorry," Barbara said. "I didn't…"

"No, you were right," Xena said. "We don't know what's going on out there, but Édouard was taking risks with Tsan. That was a good call."

"Thanks," Barbara said.

"I just came in to make sure Jason understood that, and he wasn't yelling at you. I heard raised voices, and I'd say the situation has been handled."

Jason nodded and said, "Roger, we were discussing…"

"What to do in the future," Barbara said, "Jason is right. Sometimes tact and discretion are the best ways to do things." Jason remained silent. Xena looked at the two and debated pushing them further.

"Well, go find out if Tsan is okay, and get that sled cleaned up and ready for tomorrow. The winds will shift with any luck, and we can return to work. We're falling behind as we speak," Xena said. Jason and Barbara left, ending their conversation.

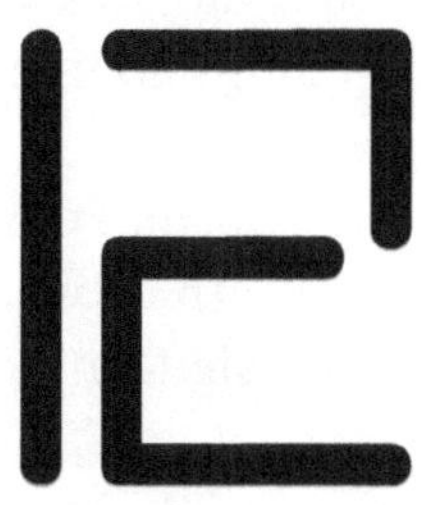

"All space exploration is risky. As an astronaut, I had to decide each and every time I went to space whether or not to risk my life for the mission."

— Astronaut John M. Grunsfeld

Li Mei woke in a snap, sat bolt upright, and grabbed for something.

"Where is my helmet? The pod's lost atmosphere! 岩石和灰尘! Li Jing, are you trying to kill me!" She shouted.

Barbara shook her and said, "Li Mei, you're having a nightmare."

Li Mei blinked and smiled. "Oh, that's good. I am on Aurora Dawn with plenty of atmosphere…"

"And toxic snow and sled-eating worms!" Barbara said.

"But plenty of oxygen," Li Mei said with a smile. "Oh, and Yi—Xander…"

"Well, with all the excitement yesterday, I am surprised you and he had any time at all," Barbara said.

"He was distraught. He was waiting outside decontamination. He wanted to know if I was all right," Li Mei said, "It was so dreamy, just like when Jia Li…"

"Nope, not going to go there… This isn't a soap opera," Barbara said.

Li Mei looked slightly offended and said, "Well, we did hang out after that. We went to his lab, which he'd set up to look like a home theater, and we watched what he liked."

Barbara waited for an explanation but when none came, she asked Li Mei, "Like what?"

"Golf… a lot of golf," Li Mei said unhappily.

"Sounds…" Barbara started to say when Li Mei interrupted.

"Boring!" Li Mei said. "It was so boring! Oh, what will I do? We can't marry and spend all our time together watching golf. I'll die of boredom as his wife!"

If Li Mei hadn't been so unhappy, Barbara would have laughed. She said, "Well, I am sure you can do more than just watch golf. Once the colony hits the ten-year mark, plenty of golf courses will be available. Xander can teach you to play!"

"No," Li Mei said dejectedly. "He doesn't play golf at all."

"What?" Barbara said. "He just *watches* golf? Yeah, that's boring."

"It is even worse than that! He's got all the old golfers, and some of the games he watches are centuries old, with names like Arnold Gripper, Joe Nicklaus, and Tiger Forests. These folks have been dust for ages."

"Maybe the games are more exciting if you know the rules?" Barbara suggested.

"He tried to explain the rules to me, but all I kept seeing was somebody hitting the little white ball. Sometimes, the ball would land somewhere, and everyone would clap; other times, everyone groaned. I don't understand the game at all," said Li Mei.

"Maybe Daddy can help. He likes sports," Barbara suggested, "Or you two could find something new to watch."

"Perhaps. Or, he's too nice to say he doesn't like my shows," Li Mei said. "This is like my own personal..."

Barbara frowned and snapped, "Don't say it. Don't mention that stupid..."

"Soap opera," Li Mei finished, sticking her tongue out. "Oh, I see you're right, Barbara! I'm just as bad, aren't I?" Barbara smiled and said nothing.

"Well, did you and Jason see your other movies?" Li Mei asked, changing the subject.

"No, we spent last night going through the medical white papers in the constellation. We were looking to see if my memory issues matched any known syndrome," Barbara said.

"You told him about it?" Li Mei said, "That was brave."

"What was I supposed to do? Hide it from him until

we're married?" Barbara asked.

Instead of answering, Li Mei said, "Oh! You want to marry him! You're so much in love!"

Barbara rolled her eyes and said, "I was being theoretical! Right now, it is nice to spend time with him. You are so marriage crazy; I think you've been affected by the gravity of Aurora Dawn," Barbara said.

"Oh no, you're not getting off the hook so quickly," Li Mei said, "Did you two have some quiet time after your study session?"

"No, we were exhausted and went to bed late. Fortunately, all the missions are scrubbed until we figure out more about this 'snow,'" Barbara said.

"Good. Xander said that Analysis and the Con Sec Corps Science team are trying to decipher what's happening. Yesterday, Xander was called in for consultations with the team. He says no one has any idea of what's going on. The only good news I got from him was that so far, as toxic as the bacterium is, it's harmless if it isn't ingested. Xander says the scientists aren't entirely sure if the bacterium can pass through the skin barrier. As far as the origins of the bacterium, no one is sure what role it fulfills on Aurora Dawn."

"I don't know if that's good or bad," Barbara said. "On one hand, we'll be back out there soon, especially if a shower can disinfect us from the 'snow.' On the other hand, I was enjoying a day off, with pay."

"Yeah, it felt good to sleep in for once," Li Mei said. "I was going to wander around the barracks and see how things were progressing at the outpost."

"I was waiting for Jason to be done with his daily leadership stand-up, and then we were going to see when the master building plan showed the quantum array station construction. Without the q-elements on the *Aquila,* the array here won't be functional. But once it is, Jason said we can search the q-net and hopefully get better answers," said

Barbara.

"He's determined to help, isn't he?" Li Mei asked.

"Yeah, well, I incentivized him. After we kissed, I said I wasn't sure who I was, and the memory thing was preventing me from moving forward."

"Wait, you kissed him again?" Li Mei said with her eyes as wide as saucers, "Like on the mouth?"
"Yeah, he kissed me first, and I wanted to let him know I wasn't turning him down. I just wasn't sure about myself," Barbara said rationally. Li Mei just sat there, her face full of mischief, like she wanted to say something but didn't.

"What?" Barbara growled, "I was trying to slow things down. I don't know who I am, and from all I know, I could be someone who is really monstrous. A Frankenstein's monster that was switched out on the *Aquila* to escape justice."

"Maybe you are some deranged prisoner that got misrouted from a prison archive and now seeks Jason's young body…" Li Mei was saying when the look on Barbara's face stopped her.

"Um, no," Barbara said. "Let's just not go there."

Li Mei looked like Barbara had just stolen her thunder and said, "I think you and one of the medical staff need to talk when the *Aquila* arrives. After some therapy or a prescription, you'll probably remember everything."

"And if I don't?" Barbara said, looking sad and worried.

"Just be who you are," Li Mei said. "I think you're overthinking everything. After fifty or sixty years in your shell, you can switch to the one you think you should be."

"Easy for you to say. I don't know who I was or could be," Barbara said.

"Look, you're not a bad person. You and I have been hanging out consistently for weeks," Li Mei said. "Do you have any memories of doing bad things?"

"No, just weird ones where I feel like a stranger in

my body," Barbara said. "They are just flashes of things."

"Sure," Li Mei said. "Tell me about one of them. Maybe I can help?"

"I had a memory of proposing to a woman. She turned me down," Barbara said.

"Interesting, that sounds like my aunt. We all call her my aunt, but she was my grandma's older brother. It is a long story…" Li Mei said, somewhat embarrassed.

Barbara seized the thought and said, "No, please tell me."

"Well," Li Mei said, acting like she was revealing corporate secrets, "I told you how bodies in the belt cost more than on Earth, right?"

Barbara nodded, and Li Mei continued, "Well, I didn't want to say this because I didn't want to offend you, but girls' bodies cost less. Belters, in general, believe that girls are worth less than boys."

Barbara looked shocked, "Why? That doesn't even make any sense. Girls are still the only ones that can gestate a baby."

"It has much to do with our traditional beliefs and that mining is hard work. My clan and all the belters rely so much on mining that it drives up the price of a boy's body. Anyway, my aunt, was born a boy. One day, when she was a young man, she was mining, and there was an accident," said Li Mei.

"What happened," Barbara asked.

"Well, an entire asteroid sort of collapsed. The accident was bad, horrible. This was in the early days for my clan, and safety wasn't as important as survival back then. Anyway, my grandmother's father, his brothers, and their sons were either injured or killed. They pulled my grandmother's brother out. He was one of the few that survived."

"I'm sensing a but," Barbara said.

"Yeah, they pulled him out, but a male shell wasn't

available. There were no male shells in many astronomical units. The belt isn't riddled with archives either, and the ones we have are costly, 'cause you know, debt, lack of resources, and all."

"Sure, what happened then," Barbara said.

"My grandmother was a young girl, maybe a year or two older than I am. She said to put her brother into a body that was as close to her brother's original shell's age. Well, then, my great-uncle became my auntie. My grandmother went to the fortune teller, and they found a new name for my aunt. At the time, it was very embarrassing, but my aunt laughs about it these days," said Li Mei.

"Why," Barbara asked.

"Well, she was pleased with her new body. She had always wanted to be a Dark Space pilot, and her father wouldn't let her," Li Mei said.

"Wait. Is she still around?" Barbara asked.

"Oh yes, she's a grandma herself. She met a nice man, who is my uncle, and they never looked back. It might be because we are all Buddhists and believe in rebirth. I suppose rebirth could happen even with the Singularity, don't you think?"

Barbara sat and pondered. Her memories pointed to a previous shell that wasn't female. Many of the images seemed to indicate she was male in the past. But who was she?

Li Mei sensed she said something awkward and nudged, "Are you okay?"

"Yes," Barbara replied. "Just processing all of this. Your story was interesting, thanks."

"You're welcome. Maybe you were a boy before?" Li Mei said. "It isn't the weirdest thing the more I think about it. I mean, that explains why you don't like *Love…*"

"Nope," Barbara said, "We're not going to say it, *still.*"

"Come on, that has to be the reason!" Li Mei said,

capitalizing on Barbara's defensiveness.

"Plenty of girls don't like those shows," Barbara said. "Someone's taste in cinema and television doesn't determine their gender. If it did, how do you classify people who watch golf?"

Li Mei stopped and looked defeated. The conversation with Barbara had banished Li Mei's golf watching experience with Xander from her mind, "Boring."

Barbara was about to respond when Jason knocked and peered his head around the divider into ladies' country: "Hey, good morning. I'm just making my rounds after my stand-up and wanted to let you two know we are pausing missions for today. Xena says we'll give things another twenty-four hours and try again in the morning."

"Thanks, Jason," Li Mei said. "Now, I'm going to use the shower and get dressed."

Barbara stood up and said, "What are you up to today, Dikkert?"

"I've got some paperwork to catch up on but not much else. You want to hang out?" Jason asked.

"Sure," Turning to Li Mei, Barbara said, "See you later."

Li Mei smiled. When Jason turned around, pulling his head out of ladies' country, Li Mei made a kissy face to Barbara, who shot her a dirty look and silently made a golf swing. Li Mei rolled her eyes, and Barbara turned to chase after Jason.

They both left ladies' country together. As they entered the cafeteria, a large poster board sign showed how to perform decontamination after being outside. Barbara caught up with Jason as she moved past the sign. They both hit the barracks exit and noticed a large plastic tarp suspended off a small superstructure that started from the exit and branched out like a roof over the freshly poured sidewalks.

"Those Con Sec types don't sit around," Jason said,

noticing the covering that was there to protect pedestrians from snow exposure.

"Where are we going?" Barbara said with a smile.

"My office. I had an idea," Jason said. Jason and Barbara walked to the office building and entered. In the first office was Xena, who was hard at work and oblivious to them entering. Jason walked by her, entered his office, and turned on the opaque glass.

"Planning something, Jason," Barbara asked with a smile.

"No, I just want some privacy," Jason said, "Tongues are already wagging about me bringing you to the command post."

"That a problem," Barbara asked.

"Not for me, but until the *Aquila* shows up, bored people won't have much to do except gossip. Besides, I want to discover what's happening with you, and I can't be distracted."

"You said you had an idea," Barbara said.

"Yes, harmonic convergence," Jason said.

"Huh?" Barbara said.

"Yeah, exactly," Jason began. "I found this white paper buried way down in the constellation. A Doodle bioethicist wrote it. He described a similar case. This young boy, like seven or eight, was put into the archive due to some rare disease his shell had."

"Okay," Barbara said, "So what?"

"Well," Jason said. "He eventually got a new shell, but when he did, he had all these memories of being an old woman."

"Huh?" Barbara said. "How's that even possible?"

"I know, that's what I thought," Jason said. "Turns out his harmonic wave was stored in an archive where many grannies were parked. Some for the heat death, and others for a century or two until they could start over."

"Huh? Did their memories transfer to the boy?"

Barbara asked.

"The Doodle guy did all this research, and I know 'the experts' say it isn't possible, but the Doodle researcher's paper was pretty conclusive that the boy was suffering from harmonic convergence," Jason said.

"And you think…" Barbara began, but Jason stopped her.

"I think you absorbed memories from all of us in the archive. That's why you can't remember your Barbara memories. The Doodle guy kept saying the boy had forgotten his life before rollout."

"But he was young! The neurons may not have been fully branched into dendrons," Barbara said.

"Yeah, I looked that up too," Jason said, immensely proud of himself, "Plenty of kids have been rolled out and decanted just fine."

"Well, I suppose I can ask Griff," Barbara said.

"Yes, exactly," Jason said.

"What happened to the boy?" Barbara asked.

"He grew up, made his new memories, and ended up at Doodle as a Xeno Corps scout, or whatever they call their exploration corps. He was perfectly normal," Jason said. Barbara sat quietly and mused on this information.

"All of the research I did seemed to indicate that anyone who has had a similar experience seems to have just accepted things and moved on," Jason said. "Thankfully, it didn't seem like there were any repercussions to the shell or the consciousness from these experiences. In the case of the Doodle kid, he seemed to feel like he got a unique view of life because of it. He considered the experience a blessing and not a curse."

"Uh huh," Barbara said. Jason frowned like he had been shut down after making an impassioned argument, "What?"

"Jason, the Doodle kid is all well and good, but I don't remember my life as Barbara. I only have these vague, alien memories as someone else. I'd love to remember my dad and mom clearly. I don't know if I have any sisters, brothers, cousins, or even a family pet," Barbara said, tears of frustration in her eyes.

"I understand," Jason said, reaching out and taking her hand. "Well, whatever the future holds, I'm here for you."

"Thanks," Barbara said. "I like you, but I need to find out who I am before I can move on. These memories keep coming at me, and I am losing my sense of reference."

Jason put another warm hand on Barbara's. The touch radiated so much comfort. She wanted to do nothing but curl up in his arms. She took a deep breath and tried to blink away the tears. In her memories, gaining composure was easier. She remembered being told to bury her emotions deeply, to maintain her composure. In this shell, her feelings were transmitted by her body and face unconsciously.

"Listen, whatever happens, we're friends, right?" Jason asked.

"Yes, absolutely," Barbara said unhesitatingly.

"Well then, you're not in this alone," Jason said, "That should be a memory you can recall."

Barbara felt like she'd be smacked in the face as the reality hit her. She had "Barbara" memories—just not before she decanted.

"Wait, a second," she said. "I remember everything since I decanted, just not before. That's something, right?"

"Yeah," Jason said in agreement. "I mean, I'm not the doctor, but that means that your consciousness has adapted to your neurons, and your brain is tuning your harmonics."

"Right, for what it's worth, I am who I am," Barbara said.

"You're Spinach, the sailor man?" Jason said with a smile. Barbara reached out and playfully slapped him on the shoulder. He cowered like a puppy hit by a newspaper, even though Barbara didn't have a shell that could hurt him.

"Stuff like that doesn't help, Dikkert," Barbara said, partly in frustration and partly in mock anger.

"Why not?" Jason asked with a smile.

"Now, I'm going to have that stupid cartoon in my head all day," Barbara said.

"Well, whoever you were before had good taste in cartoons," Jason said. "You're welcome, by the way."

Barbara wanted to be angry with Jason, but instead, she just laughed, and the stress flowed out of her.

"Thanks, Jason," she said after a minute of laughing.

"My pleasure," he replied.

"Jason, get in here," Xena said, pushing through the closed door. You too, Gordon! We might as well get another Vanguard voice on this."

Jason and Barbara hopped up and went into Xena's corner office. Inside, the windows were opaque, and several figures were holo-projected. Xena went back to her desk and sat down.

"I've got Dikkert. Go on, Vidal," Xena said.

"We could get the warbot to drop a RED-360 munition and 'poor man' nuke the bloom," Édouard said. The projection showed lab equipment behind him. He was working somewhere else.

"No! No! No!" a projected woman, who looked like another Analysis scientist, said. "We can't do that."

"Why not?" Jason said, "Sounds like a great idea to me."

"Look, I get it. A Vanguard scout doesn't use their head except to breathe out of! But use your brain for a moment and think!" The woman said nastily, "We can't remove a piece of the ecosystem like those algae. What if that bloom is a once-in-a-century event that seeds life on the planet?"

Jason frowned, and Barbara grew red-faced, but Édouard responded, "Amela, please be professional. You're contributing to Analysis' reputation as being cooperative and friendly."

The woman looked taken aback and said, "Apologies, Vanguard."

"Come on, people! Return to the question: what do we do about the snow and the algae?" Xena said, trying to focus the meeting.

"Nothing," Amela said. "Trying to stop this planet's natural processes may wreck the ecosystem or cause a cascade failure leading to a Permian era-style extinction."

Barbara tried to follow along, and she thought she understood the basics. She reasoned that silence might be more productive than a comment.

"We don't know if we've somehow caused this event," Édouard shot back. "Maybe some of the bloom is a runaway bacterium from something we've dropped? Gordon was at the beach; what about two days ago? Maybe she did something to cause this."

All the eyes turned and looked at Barbara. She cleared her throat and said, "Yes, I was on the beach, but I am pretty sure I didn't cause this. Can a bloom like that build up over a few days? Plus, I came down in the sled. Wouldn't the atmospheric friction have sanitized the sled's body?"

Barbara waited for Analysis to respond, but their images winked out. She reasoned they had muted themselves so they could argue internally.

Xena waited a moment, then chuckled, "I need you at more of these meetings, Gordon. You must have asked the right question because now the nerds are slugging it out offline. Do you two have any thoughts on what we should do?"

Jason put his hand to his chin. "I'm not sure there is a problem here. The bacterium seems like just another weather condition."

"Yeah," Barbara said. "We just need to be careful and

analyze the snow whenever it falls."

Xena smiled, "A perfectly Vanguard solution. Take risks, but be careful. There are days I wish Analysis and Survey wouldn't want to wrap everything in plastic. So, my scouts, what's next?"

"More missions. Find out if the blooms are localized. Maybe build a dock and get drones out in the ocean? Who knows what is lurking out there," Jason said.

"We should also run another set of tests on the ocean fauna in case they are interrelated with the algae," Barbara suggested.
"All good ideas," Xena said. "Now, Jason, how much rework will your team need to get back on track?"

Jason pulled out his tablet and started calculating.

"We'll need about three days, give or take four hours," Jason said. We'll need to decontaminate sleds and adapt to the new check-in procedures…"

"Sounds good," Xena said. "Start up your missions again, but be prepared to have that Kooya blow up something."

"Yes, ma'am," Barbara said. Jason nodded. Barbara and Jason turned and left Xena's office.

As they exited, Barbara said, "So, back to B19 for more surveys, Jason?"

"Yeah, but I lied! We are only a half-day behind schedule. I was hoping we could sneak away to K16 or even farther down the coast for some swimsuit reconnaissance," said Jason with a devilish smile.

"You want to check me out, eh, Dikkert," Barbara said with a smile. She watched as Jason blushed a bit, then she said, "You might just get a chance."

She left Jason with a quick wink and headed for her sled. For now, it was mission time.

Barbara followed the roofed pathways to where a small pop-up garage sat over the sleds. She briefly debated whether to grab an encounter suit but opted for a breather mask and helmet. The mask and helmet would be less bulky but would still protect her lungs and allow her to breathe if there were any issues. She sent a message over the short message service to GAIA, and the robot dog appeared moments later. Barbara didn't have to signal. The dog went over and crawled into her sled's cargo cradle; sending a short message service "thumbs up" emoji, when ready.

Barbara went over and opened the cockpit. She smiled when she saw the name "Gordon" and "Cowgirl's Mechanical Bull" on the sled. Despite the mystery memories, she realized she had plenty to remember from her scout work. In a way, being a scout was a part of her personality that hadn't seemed to change in this shell.

Climbing in, Barbara mused on the thought of her being a Vanguard scout previously. She realized that her memories contained plenty of times when she longed to be in a sled, technical, or even an ancient jeep, charting out the unknown.

Barbara hit the ignition, and the sled's engines turned over. She punched in the coordinates and sat back, letting the sled drive. She resolved not to focus on her past but to live in the present. She grabbed a pair of binoculars stowed in the cockpit and looked over the terrain. The fake snow was still coming down, but it seemed less than when Barbara was out with GAIA yesterday. As the sled moved away from the coast, the snow dissipated utterly. The landscape changed as the plains started to turn into rocky foothills. She scanned the immediate area, and her eyes caught a large black pool.

"Oh boy, if that is what I hope it is, well then, I should have put down a larger bet," Barbara said to herself. She disengaged the autopilot and slowly steered the sled towards the sizeable black pool.

"Gaia, this is an unplanned stop. Can you get out and collect some rocks?" Barbara said. The robot dog messaged back a thumbs up, and Barbara's cargo screen noted the robot's departure. Barbara stopped the sled, put her helmet on, and popped the canopy. She checked for the snow. A few flakes were falling, but nothing too concerning. A shower would rid Barbara of any potential bacteria; she figured that would be her new routine.

She approached the pool. It had all the characteristics of a petroleum seep. With the helmet on, Barbara couldn't smell anything to determine if there were hydrocarbons. Her helmet, however, was registering Benzene in the atmosphere. She pulled out a survey stick from her now neatly organized port compartment.

The survey stick was a long hollow tube that allowed a scout to collect samples without contamination or getting his or her hands dirty. Barbara plunged her stick into the pool, and the tube filled with a viscous, dark fluid. Barbara then pulled out the stick and went to the sled.

Barbara poured the sticky, thick liquid from the stick into three small jars. The stuff reminded Barbara of maple syrup. She sealed the jars and placed them into the collections compartment in the jar cradle.

"Okay, work's done. I need to know if I should up my bet," Barbara said to herself. She pulled out the sample stick and swabbed the end with a small, hand-portable chemical analyzer. The analyzer wasn't nearly as accurate as some lab equipment, but it helped a scout determine if a chemical pile was salt, sugar, or arsenic.

"I guess they made the analyzer to ensure idiots weren't eating anything poisonous," Barbara said with a small laugh. She waited as the small LED screen showed a series of dancing lines. It was the standard screen the analyzer showed when working.

Barbara watched as the lines cleared and the chemical analysis came back. The screen read, "CH4, C2H6, C3H8, C4H10, C8H18," then, "UNK, UNK, UNK, UNK"

Barbara wondered if the tool had broken by taking the sample but decided she'd hit enough paydirt to call Command. The desert would have to wait until another day.

"Any good rocks, Gaia?" Barbara asked.

"Yes!" GAIA responded via audio. Barbara signaled for the dog to pack it up. Barbara closed the compartments and crawled into the cockpit. She closed the canopy and waited. A few moments later, she heard the thump of the robot hopping into the cradle. Barbara powered up the repulsor and marked the spot on her map. If Analysis confirmed the discovery, the colony would have petrol and could make plastics. The alternative was to sweat it out for a few years and make a plant-based plastic. Barbara was suddenly glad that those decisions were waiting for the Corporate Corps when they arrived. Josie and Merlyna could deal with the headaches.

As the sled started back, she envisioned the witchy Analysis lady arguing about the ecosystem's precious fragility.

"She didn't have the ecosystem eat her!" Barbara said to herself with a huff.

As Barbara entered the outpost, she thought it was starting to look like a small town.

"Pretty soon, we'll need to move to another spot. There won't be any more room for the Vanguard," Barbara muttered. She wove through the burgeoning traffic and entered the lot for the scout sleds. She signaled that she had a collection, and Althea exited the barracks. Analysis hadn't moved out completely.

"Do I need to up my bet?" Althea said as she approached the sled.

"It looks promising, but I think the hand analyzer is broken. I kept getting a bunch of UNK signals on the screen," Barbara said.

"Potentially, or there are elements in this mix that aren't on our version of the periodic table. Either way, I'll bring these in and start the deep analysis. You marked the spot, right?" Althea asked.

"Yes, here are the coordinates as well," Barbara said.

"Wow, like a pro! How long have you been doing this?" Althea asked, "Because you look young, but who knows, you could be a five-hundred-year-old grandmother in there."

"I don't know. I don't remember my life before that well," Barbara said, "Daddy said I was only sixteen."

"My cousin, Michael, he saw something like that happen," Althea said, "He was on one of those deep spacers to Procyon. He said a woman decanted, and she claimed she was in the wrong body. She was a man named Joseph."

"Huh," Barbara said, "What happened to her?"

"Michael said that she kept making noise about a wrong switch until the AI and the expedition chair threatened to put her back into the archive. I suppose it all turned out well, though. Michael said she did a good job and settled down with one of the miners," Althea related.

"We good?" Barbara asked.

"Yes, really good! I did a quick scan, and I see some very bet winning hydrocarbons," Althea said. "You have a good one."

Barbara nodded and headed towards the barracks. Several small mist machines were set up, probably with cleansers, to spray off anyone entering the barracks. Barbara went through them and thought about Althea's story. She went to her locker and stripped off her outer clothes, throwing them into a laundry basket, per the new rules on posters across the barracks. Standing in her underwear, she debated whether it made sense to shower now or later. Grabbing a large towel, she decided that now was the time. She strolled to the showers, thinking about the woman who said she was in the wrong body.

After so many days in this shell, Barbara didn't feel like she was a stranger in her body. The body and her current experiences seemed more real to her than someone else's distant, alien memories. She entered the tiny shower cubicle and shut the door. After scrubbing her skin and hair a few minutes, she was clean and decontaminated. She grabbed her towel and dried off. She then wrapped the towel around her and returned to ladies's country. As she passed through the neutral zone, she met Jason.

"You are not only beautiful," he said, blocking her way. "You're rich too!"

"What are you going on about Jason?" Barbara asked. "Or are you delaying me to see how well I can grip this towel?"

"I've felt that grip! No, I'm here about that sample. That was the big one!" Jason said. "I expect you didn't know about the little bennie Greg put in our contracts?"

Barbara searched her vaunted memories but couldn't recall anything about a particular provision, "No idea."

"He added a rider that said if a scout discovers anything outside the current periodic table, they get a cut of the discovery—ten percent, to be exact," Jason said with a smile.

"Okay. Give me a minute to get clothed," Barbara said. "I'm a rich woman standing in a towel in the middle of the barracks."

"Yes, and I am enjoying what I can peek at as well," Jason said with a very boyish smile.

Barbara rolled her eyes and said, "Look, buster. Give me about ten minutes to get something on. It's not exactly warm here in the main corridor with a towel."

"Fine, but first, the folks in Analysis are having a field day," Jason said, "Whatever you gave them, they are acting like you dropped elements from the *Big Bang* on their desks."

Barbara mused on that thought as she headed back into ladies' country and paced the half dozen meters to her locker. She looked at the pink qipao hanging in her locker but instead settled for boots, tactical leggings, and a structured tank top. Jason would have to buy her a steak for a repeat in the dress.

"Well, maybe if he begs me," Barbara giggled.

She dressed and returned to where Jason stood, "Now, I am rich. How do you figure?"

"Griff and Greg suspected, based on data, that there were exotics on Aurora Dawn, and you've run across them practically right outside our base!" Jason said.

"What can I say? Maybe I am just a lucky girl?" Barbara said with a shrug.

"I'd say," Jason replied. "You want to hit the cafeteria and watch a movie?"

"Sure," Barbara said with an ear-to-ear smile, "Maybe we'll make the *Lifestyles of the Rich and Famous*. I hope paparazzi don't mob us on the way to the cafeteria."

"I shouldn't have said anything to you about the find," Jason said. Barbara could feel the wind up on Jason's statement.

"Okay, why?" she said, taking the bait.

"I knew it would just go to your head! Now, you won't associate with the little people like myself," he finished with a devilish smile.

"Oh, you wish, Dikkert," Barbara said. "After a ridiculous statement like that, I'm never leaving your side."

"Good," Jason said, striding off so that the shorter Barbara had to push to keep up with him.

"A civilization that only looks inward will stagnate. We have to keep looking outward; we have to keep finding new avenues for human endeavor and human expression."

— Astronaut John L. Phillips

Location: The Aquila in orbit over Aurora Dawn
19.11.12450 Standard, 0900 local

"All right folks, we are here," DADDIE said. To Josie and Merlyna, the *Dux* had only separated a few days ago, but they knew that it had been a more extended period for the team on Aurora Dawn due to relativity. Relativity made long-distance space travel challenging for humans, and most AI had to contend with Albert Einstein's and Ivana Petrov's calculations to coordinate time in the space they existed.

Fortunately, the *Aquila* was moving at Newtonian speeds now, and DADDIE had adjusted all the calendars.

"We have a stable orbit," DADDIE exclaimed.

"Good, and the outpost?" Josie asked.

"On the other side of the planet for the next few minutes. We're getting data from the GPS satellites, but I'm a face-to-face kind of guy," DADDIE said.

"What, no secret hand signs from the first and third base coaches," Merlyna asked.

"Well, there is that too, Pumpkin," DADDIE said. Merlyna smiled and tapped on her screens.

"Wow," Merlyna said, looking at the flood of data, "Vanguard has been busy. Jason's team has uranium and petroleum waiting for us."

"Oh geez," Josie said, "Now the kid will want a raise."

"Looks like he and his team earned a career full of raises," Merlyna said.

"Yeah, seems like Greg was right about L 98-59," Josie replied.

"Don't argue with a general's intestines," Merlyna said with a laugh.

"We ready?" Josie asked.

"Just compiling the data now," Merlyna replied.

"Spot check," Josie asked.

"Looking good, Xeno Corps says we have O2, H2O,

and basic protein compatibility. We're ready to begin our landing," Merlyna said.

"Spin up the heavy drop pods and get Con Sec Corps to work, Merlie," Josie replied. Merlyna nodded and continued tapping away on her screen. Large spherical pods began detaching and dropping towards Aurora Dawn all along the *Aquila's* front and rear ovals. Merlyna watched as the pods started their slow drift to the surface. Then, she pulled up the AI screen. Her spirits were dampened as this was her husband's favorite screen and his creation. She pulled up the AI checklist, went to the row that said 'Architectural Technology Entity'(ATE) and pressed the checkbox and the deploy button.

"Hi Ah-tay, are you awake," Merlyna asked, sounding out the acronym.

"Hi, Merlyna," the AI said. The screen displayed an avatar of a young woman: "I'm ready for building. I feel like constructing a beautiful city today—something with many parks and flowers," ATE said.

"Well, we don't need parks and flowers just yet, but I wouldn't mind a nice ultra-modern house near the landing site," said Merlyna.

"Behave," Josie said, "Or I'll have Ah-tay build you a sod house. You and Karl are familiar with those, you old sodbusters!"

Merlyna smiled and said, "Well, Ah-tay, I think the ultra-modern will have to wait."

"I see the main construction pod has landed. I will start transmitting my algorithms. Unfortunately, I will be offline for about ninety seconds while I send my main data packet and build the sharded copy here on the *Aquila*," ATE said.

"Yes, I understand," Merlyna said. "Once the pods are functioning and processing their resources, we'll relocate the main operations dirt side. After that, Josie and I will meet you on the ground. Ah-tay, can you ensure top priority for the operations center with the Con Sec Corps on Aurora Dawn?"

"Yes, I have already confirmed the highest priority on the ops center," ATE said, "See you on the ground."

Merlyna finished her checklist and watched as her screen showed significant gaps on the *Aquila* where all the heavy equipment had been. The ship was losing all the detachable modules today. Like the *Dux*, the expedition would soon dissect the *Aquila* even further. The expedition would cannibalize the engines. The main fusion reactor would stay and power the rings and the central lander bay to create a space station until the expedition constructed a more prominent, corporate space dock. That was well after the ten-year mark, and Merlyna hoped to be gone and reunited with Karl before then.

Merlyna watched the display as the miners, factories, and constructors all reported their landings. The small contingent of Con Sec AI and the Xeno Corps had started constructing the foundation for the ops center. With top priority, the ops center would begin to rise expediently. The ops center would be the nerve center of the colony.

"Ready to go breathe fresh air?" Merlyna asked Josie.

"Whenever you are. Corporate is good. I'm moving our command and control to the planet as we speak," Josie replied. Merlyna checked all the pods, especially the one with the quantum array. Everything read green. So far, so good.

"Transferring the Con Sec command to the ground," Merlyna said. For all purposes now, the *Aquila* was just a space station. It had fulfilled its immediate purpose and would await when the colony blossomed and reached out towards the stars.

Merlyna stood up from her spot and started towards the door. Josie took a moment and followed. Both ladies watched as other Con Sec Corps members lined up in the landing bay. The transit spaceplane had docked and was shuttling personnel down to Aurora Dawn. When the Xeno Corps had left with the lander, the Con Sec engineers had begun to assemble the spaceplane. It was a marvel of twelve thousand five hundred century engineering—a ramjet-scramjet that ran on a supercompressed Copernicium-Hydride battery. The spaceplane's battery would require monthly recharging, and the vehicle could perform a large self-charge through turbines on the wings. Merlyna people-watched as she and Josie queued up in the line.

Several people ahead of them were Griff and Martha. They looked to be in a heated argument, which surprised Merlyna as Griff and Martha never seemed to argue. Merlyna watched as they bickered but couldn't understand what they were saying.

The queue began moving, and Martha looked like she was ignoring Griff as they entered the corridor of the spaceplane. Merlyna noted the interaction and filed it away in her mind. She then entered the corridor, with Josie following behind.

"When does Daddy transfer to processing on the surface?" Josie asked Merlyna, breaking into her thoughts.

"In two days, I had the Con Sec Corps engineering report on the massive constellation processing center being built. The report just showed up before we began the drop pod landing," Merlyna said, "After Daddy is planet side, only the sub-sentient AI will be operating the *Aquila*. All personnel will be planet side."

"That's a relief, and the spare shells?" Josie asked.

"Not sure, you'll need to ask the Medical Corps," Merlyna said.

"Yeah, I've been trying to meet up with either Griff or Martha, but both have been deferring my meetings, claiming they are too busy," Josie said.

"I suppose that makes sense. We all have been at max capacity since the Xeno Corps left. Maybe we can have a senior leadership dinner and catch up?" Merlyna asked.

"Sure, Merlie, that sounds like a plan," Josie said. "At times like this, I wish Greg was here."

"I think you've been doing a great job," Merlyna said. "For what that's worth."

"Thanks," Josie said as she and Merlyna sat in their seats and strapped in. They were in a smaller two-person section, and they watched as the outer doors closed. The inner doors flashed a yellow light and then closed.

The plane detached from the *Aquila* with a thump and maneuvered for a descent. The engines fired, and the plane dropped down towards the planet. Merlyna sat near the window and watched as Aurora Dawn's blue sky and atmosphere replaced space's blackness.

"The last time I saw a transition like that was with Karl," Merlyna said. "We were homesteading on Alpha Centauri B."

"That must have been almost a hundred years ago," Josie said.

"Yeah, something like that. It all runs together after a while," Merlyna replied. Josie wasn't sure whether to say something or remain quiet. She left Merlyna to her thoughts and watched the view over Merlyna's shoulder.

The engine's sounds began to take on an airplane's thrum as the spaceplane entered the thickest part of the atmosphere. There was turbulence, and the plane made a base right turn to bleed off speed. The plane then returned to the course, flattening out its wings. The ladies watched as they saw the ocean come into focus below.

"Well, that's a positive; there's lots of water," Merlyna said.

"It is ocean water, mostly salt, not as much as Earth's, but not directly drinkable either," Josie said.

"That's an engineering problem. The water is here. We need to separate it from the salt. Then the salt is a bonus," Merlyna said. Josie wanted to argue but thought for a moment and saw the logic.

"That surprise girl, Gordon, found uranium. I suppose we could build a few reactors around the coasts to jump-start our fusion reactor," Josie said.

"Yes, definitely, we'll need to manufacture the fusible material, and then there is the lead we'll need," Merlyna said.

"Yeah, I pinged Jason and said to prioritize lead," Josie replied. "Reports are showing there is a lot of copper, tin, some uranium, a slight node or two of iron, and a host of minerals mixed in, and of course, there's petroleum. We haven't seen any lead, though."

"Sounds like we may need to think about expanding the Vanguard's scope or even look off-world," Merlyna said.

"Yeah, been thinking about it. I'd say let's get the colony up and running before we start sending people off-world."

"Makes sense," Merlyna responded. She and Josie were interrupted as the plane made a sweeping nose-down dive. As suddenly as the nose went down, the plane leveled, waggling its wings and slaloming to the left and then the right.

"Getting close," Merlyna said.

"Think so," Josie replied.

"Yes," Merlyna responded. Both women grew more anxious and excited. When they landed, the work would come at them like a wolverine. The plane's nose again dipped; the angle wasn't as steep this time. A small flashing light and bell announced landing was imminent. Merlyna checked her safety harness and gripped the armrests. Moments later, the plane's wheels touched down, and the engines flared in reverse as the AI pilot fired a drag chute. Merlyna and Josie felt the inertia trying to carry them forward; however, their harnesses absorbed the force. After several seconds, the forward force dissipated, and the space plane was rolling into a set of buildings that—although under construction—were starting to look like a spaceport.

As the plane entered the slip, a chime sounded. Merlyna and Josie unbuckled and stood. There was no need to gather possessions as their personal effects had come down with the cargo pods. All aboard had come with only the clothing on their back. As people began to depart, Merlyna and Josie ended up next to Griff.

"Hey Griff, long time no see," Josie said.

"I know, you're thinking, 'he's been avoiding me,' but that's not how it is…" Griff said, his tone defensive.

"No, we've all been busy," Josie said. "I have been more concerned that you and Martha have been okay."

"Yeah," was all Griff said. He started moving forward in the queue and offered no more conversation. Josie looked at Merlyna, who just shrugged. Soon, Josie, Griff, and Merlyna exited into the spaceport concourse. Jason and Barbara were standing outside the jet-way in the main concourse.

"Griff," Jason said, "Hey buddy, how are you doing?"

Whatever was eating Griff on the spaceplane seemed to evaporate as he saw Jason. He moved forward and embraced Jason like a son or brother.

"Little Rooster, and I see you have a lovely lady by your side," Griff said.

Barbara turned red and said, "Hi Griff, I don't know if you remember me…"

"I sure do, memory loss in the decant. It's Barbara, right?" Griff asked.

"Yes," Barbara responded. "When you get settled, *no rush*. I'd like to ask you about that."

Griff nodded, "Sure, but first, what have you Xeno Corps scouts been up to? Find any petroleum?"

"We sure have," Jason said. "Barbara here stumbled across a deposit on our doorstep."

"It's really your fault, Jason," Barbara said. "You assigned me to that quadrant."

"I see how it is now," Jason said. "Blaming me for

you being observant."

Griff smiled at the two youngsters. He was happy that Jason had connected with another girl. He remembered how devastated Dikkert had been when Stacey had broken up with him during provisioning.

"I think Jason is happy to see you because your arrival marks the start of the ranching pods spinning up," Barbara said. "We're both eager for a nice filet."

"Or some pulled pork," Jason said.

"It's still going to be a while there, Little Rooster, but I know Con Sec will get right on the agricultural pods. Everyone is tired of the vegetarian fare. Well, at least I am," Griff said.

"Hey Jason," Merlyna said as she approached. She and Josie had hung back to give Griff and Jason some time.

"Hello, Miz Lenart," Jason said formally.

"Please, it's Merlyna," she replied.

"Don't you dare call me Miz Moreno," Josie told Jason. "Or, I'll have you mucking out those cattle pods by hand."

"Yes, ma'am, Josie," Jason said with a smile. Then he turned to Barbara and said, "This is my…"

"Teammate," Barbara interjected, unwilling to disclose her relationship with Jason.

"Yeah, teammate, Barbara," Jason said with a subtle look. Merlyna noticed the reaction but said nothing.

"I remember you," Josie said. "Hopefully, you're feeling better after your rough decant."

"Yes, much," Barbara said.

"Well, I have a lot to do. You all take care," Merlyna said, pulling herself from the conversation.

"Bye," Jason and Barbara said in unison.

"Now Jason, give me your report since you and I are in the same universe for a moment and no one has interrupted us," Josie said.

"Sure, Josie," Jason said, switching to his

professional tone, "The Vanguard has been working around the clock since we landed. The Con Sec guys have outpost Greg up and running. They'll have all the details. I'm glad we have a garden, nothing like a fresh salad. As I said before, we have over one hundred quadrants surveyed. Barbara here found us all some very nice uranium and the petroleum we can exploit for significant jump-starts to our energy production."

"Jason is being kind. The geological robot dog, GAIA, found the resources. I just shuttled her there," Barbara said with a smile to Jason. Jason smiled back, and both Griff and Josie could see that Jason and Barbara were more than just teammates.

Josie broke the look by saying, "Well, good work. When I can ensure the Con Sec is up and rolling, I think Xeno Corps could take a day off."

Jason smiled from ear to ear, "Great, thanks!"

"That won't be soon, so don't thank me yet, for as much as your team is ahead of schedule, I have almost twenty other teams that are weeks behind. We barely got off the *Aquila* in time. I am glad to hear there is a small hydroponics garden that can sustain us," Josie replied.

"What happened?" Barbara asked. "I thought there was a surplus of supplies in case Aurora Dawn wasn't immediately ready for agriculture?"

Josie stared at Barbara momentarily, not expecting the young woman to know about the expedition's provisioning, and then said, "Yes, well, apparently, some of our supplies were never loaded on the *Aquila* at Luna. We're missing an entire cargo cradle of food. We're lucky we limped along as we did, but I have some hungry, exhausted engineers looking for more calories than we've allotted for the past week."

"Huh, how's that possible," Barbara asked. "I'm sure CAA would have provisioned the expedition sufficiently."

Griff piped up and said, "Well, only Greg could

answer that, and he's no longer with us."

Barbara seemed to want to argue, but Jason interrupted, "Yeah, that's too bad. But hey, we're doing great down here! I'm sure with all the talent you're bringing, we'll be out of the danger zone in no time."

Griff continued to observe Barbara, and Josie darted her eyes between Griff and Barbara. Barbara looked like she wanted to say something more but smiled and looked at Jason. "Yeah, I'm sure Jason's right. He always sees the glass as half full."

"Yup, that he does," Griff said. "Now, if you all will excuse me, I am sure I have a line of synthetic and human patients waiting for me at my office."

"Come on, Double D," Josie said, "I think I know where they stuck the hospital. I'll look for the nicest golf course; the medical center will be next to it."

"Good," Griff said with a smile, "I've got a nine iron in my personal belongings, and I need to see how good my game will be on Aurora Dawn. After all, I can't have Tracie Chung or any of the Organics Division beating me at a round of eighteen holes."

"Can I go with you, sir?" Barbara asked, looking at Jason.

Jason nodded, looked at his tablet, and said, "Shoot, I have to run. I have a meeting with Xena."

"Well then, Barbara can show you the golf course, I mean medical center, Griff. I'll go with you, Jason," Josie said, "Might as well get all Xena's reports too. Con Sec Corps will do the heavy lifting now, and we'll need Xeno Corps to expand their surveys further from the colony."

Barbara watched as Josie and Jason wandered off. She looked to Griff to see what he'd say.

"It has been a while since I've had a young lady's company. As we stroll along, I'm willing to listen to whatever medical questions you have," Griff said to Barbara.

"Sure," Barbara said, "I am not sure where to begin…"

"Why not at the beginning?" Griff said gently.

"When I decanted," Barbara started, "well, that was rough."

"Yes, I remember," Griff said. "You certainly weren't the only one with a rough decant, but you were the worst non-terminal case."

"Look," Barbara said suddenly, "I know this sounds crazy, but I don't have any memories of *me* before the decant."

"Like no memories at all? Or none of your shell?" Griff asked. He was in analysis mode, and the double doctor was in.

Barbara looked around. The terminal had cleared, and the two were effectively alone. She said, "I have no memories of being a girl, just weird memories of being a guy."

Griff's face was impassive. The doctor had put on his bedside manner mask.

"I see," he said.

"Oh, come on, Griff," Barbara said informally, "I know the wheels are turning in there."

Barbara turned bright red at the reflexive and casual remark she made. After a moment of silence, she said, "Sorry, I don't know where that came from."

Griff remained impassive. He said, "I can see we have a unique medical case here, so no offense taken. Now that we're on the planet and our psychologist has decanted, maybe you should see him?"

Barbara looked unhappy at the suggestion. "A head shrinker?"

"Well, he's quite good. Greg hired him personally," Griff said. "It couldn't hurt to talk to the man. In the meantime, I'll do some searching—once the q-net is linked with Sol—and maybe we can get to the bottom of this. I suspect you've gotten a case of harmonic convergence."

"Yeah," Barbara said, "Jason and I looked into that."

Griff smiled, "You spending a lot of time with Little Rooster these days?"

"Yeah," Barbara said casually. "He's a great kid."

"Kid, eh?" Griff said, "According to Daddy, he's older than you by almost eight years."

"Oh, did I say that out loud," Barbara asked.

"Yes. Tell me about these memories," Griff prodded. He started strolling, and Barbara fell in step, matching his stride, with left foot for left foot and right for right. Griff watched Barbara's body language as she related all the dreams and memories. He could see a tremendous amount of feminine body language, but occasionally there was something else. A gut feeling seemed to be hanging just out of reach of Griff's heavily analytical mind.

"And that's when we found the Doodle kid's experience in the medical journal," Barbara said, finishing her tale.

"Yes, the more I listen to you, young lady, the more I agree. You are experiencing harmonic convergence. We'll need to speak to Daddy to get a good sense of earlier baselines. I am sure Daddy will find all your recruiting videos, interviews, and other artifacts about who you were before the rollout."

Barbara's eyes lit up with hope, "Thanks, Griff."

"I still want you to see the psychologist. His name is Doctor Steve Molyneaux. He's quite good with patients," Griff said. He watched as Barbara's face dropped. He remembered seeing the same expression on someone else's face, but the memory felt just beyond his mental reach.

"Okay," Barbara said, pouting as only a teenage girl could.

"Now, I'm going to get settled," Griff said, stopping. "You run along after Jason and Josie."

"Sure, thanks, Griff," Barbara said, trotting off. Griff

watched her go and pulled out a small recording device he carried for his notes.

"Recording encryption active," he said to the device.

"Encryption on," the device confirmed.

"Open a patient case file for Gordon, Barbara," Griff said.

"File opened," the device replied.

"Case log, nineteen, eleven, twelve four fifty," Griff began. "I just had a discussion with the girl with the worst decant I've ever seen. Usually, youngsters decant just fine, better than ancient geysers like me. Not so with Miss Gordon. She woke up confused and lost. Had I seen this behavior on another trans-human, I'd have assumed this was another in a long line of shell hoppers. At first, my recommendation was that Miss Gordon find her routine, expecting her memories to return naturally. I saw this situation occur in my private practice one hundred years ago. Only the subject's previous memories return within a few days."

"Now, weeks later, Miss Gordon says she still can't remember anything about being a sixteen-year-old woman. Instead, she believes she was in a male shell before roll out. I am uncertain if a consciousness was switched before the *Aquila* left Luna or after. With the scrambling of rosters before sailing from Luna, I wonder if Mommy had a glitch and sent a man here in a woman's body. If that is the case, I must verify with Daddy who Miss Gordon is," Griff dictated.

"If Daddy can track down the consciousness' identity before it was transferred on the *Aquila,* I can give Miss Gordon the peace of mind she seeks. I'm concerned the lack of provenance on the consciousnesses in our disorderly rollout is a sign that Mommy has curated a fatal learning model or has a degrading case of drift. If that is the case, I will need to consult with Doctor Holzhauser, and we'll need to enact Plan 'B.' This will also entail a detailed records search on the q-net to determine the pertinent details on who Miss Gordon is. I strongly suspect that she is a corporate spy planted by Macroware, Doodle, or Hipponike to destroy this expedition. But if I am wrong, well, then I can still be pleasantly surprised at my age."

"If the switch occurred after departure from Luna, I really don't want to get my hopes up. I only remember one Lazurus, and that was in the Bible I gave up for medical school…"

Griff was going to continue, but he saw Martha coming. He quickly ended the recording, determined to come back to it later. For now, he'd need to move slowly and carefully. His suspicions about Barbara were starting to make him jump at shadows. His arguments with Martha were getting worse, and he knew the pressure to build the colony would be relentless.

"Well, Greg, you picked a great time to up and die," Griff said under his breath.

“I'm really hopeful about the future of space exploration and human spaceflight. Civilization as we know it has been defined by exploration. You know, we need to go off and find out what's around the next corner and what's just beyond what we already know. It's part of our being; it's part of our moral fiber to go off and explore.”

— Astronaut Alan G. Poindexter

Merlyna watched as the large Con Sec Corps cranes elevated the quantum array. In a few minutes, the entire colony would get answers from MOMI. Merlyna moved toward the Quonset hut, which was the communications hub. Opening the door and pushing through the wires, she sat at the console. A holoprojector energized, and DADDIE appeared.

"Hey Pumpkin, ready for the connection," DADDIE asked.

"Yes, I want to see if I can get Patrick's expedition, and I have questions for Mommy," Merlyna said with a hint of resolve.

"I am sure you do," DADDIE said, "The array is coming online now."

Merlyna was about to say something when the door to the hut opened, and Josie entered.

"I am glad I didn't miss the party…" Josie said but was cut off by an audio transmission.

"To all CAA expeditions, this is Karl Holzhauser. We are under attack! Patrick Murphy is dead, and we're trying to establish a quantum link with Luna! Repeat, we're under attack…" Merlyna, Josie, and DADDIE listened to the audio.

"Karl, this is Merlyna. I hear you! Listen, we will send help. I'll repeat your signal!"

"To all CAA expeditions, this is Karl Holzhauser… We are under attack! Patrick Murphy is dead, and we're trying to establish a quantum link with Luna," Karl said, not hearing his wife, "What about the north ridgeline, Lisbeth? What do you mean they're rushing us there? How are the anti-AGM guns handling—" The audio went dead.

"Karl, Karl," Merlyna said frantically.

"It's no good, Pumpkin. That looks like an audio

fragment. It wasn't even real-time," DADDIE said.

"What the hell, Daddy," Josie said, "Are you telling me that Patrick's expedition was in trouble, and we didn't even know about it?"

"Looks that way, Sport," DADDIE said. "We're getting a q-channel to Luna now; prepare for entanglement and shard download. Then you can ask the boss lady herself."

Merlyna sat with a frosty expression on her face. Josie just frowned. For all the expedition's troubles, they seemed to be doing better than the expedition to HD 260655.

"Status report, Daddy," MOMI said as her avatar appeared in the room. Merlyna's jaw tightened, and Josie stood up straight for the boss.

"Hi, Mommy, we're doing a bang-up job here; we've gotten the colony started, and the Xeno-Corps is searching for rare earth metals several weeks ahead of schedule," DADDIE said.

"Where is Greg," MOMI demanded.

The trio just looked at each other, not knowing what to say. MOMI's avatar scowled, and she said, "I didn't stutter! I asked where is Greg? Is he now too busy to be present to meet with me?"

Merlyna stood up and said, "Greg's dead, Mommy, shell rejection…" DADDIE knew Merlyna had more to say, but MOMI cut her off.

"What," MOMI said, her avatar showing a furious woman. "Impossible. I had our entire cloning division check those shells!"

DADDIE and Josie slunk like chastised dogs while Merlyna turned red.

"Maybe if you hadn't skimped on Greg's expedition, this wouldn't have happened," Merlyna spat. "Plus, you sent my *husband* off with Patrick Murphy's expedition! Now that expedition has failed! You have a lot of questions you need to answer, Mommy!"

DADDIE and Josie looked at each other in shock, but what happened next shocked them even more.

"I know about Patrick," MOMI said, the avatar slumping over as if defeated. "I'm weighing whether we send a rescue mission. I didn't expect Greg though, and now we've lost communication with Tracie's expedition. All of this is corporate top secret. If our investors, or—*stars above*—the board, hears about this, we'll be ruined."

"Send a probe, get a micro link going with HD 260655. If we can get a comms channel up..." Merlyna said.

"We've done that. The probes aren't coming online. Something or someone is either scrambling the transmission or..." MOMI said but was cut off.

"Destroying the probes," Merlyna said. "Why is Karl with Patrick's expedition?"

"He gave the best odds to Patrick's expedition," MOMI said. "It was simple probability."

"You robbed me of *my husband*, all for a numbers game," Merlyna said in frustration.

"I think it's worse than that, Pumpkin," DADDIE said. "I predict a one in three set of odds that the Lisbeth—Karl refers to is..."

"My daughter," Merlyna said, her face contorting in fury. "I'm leaving..."

Merlyna then turned and left the comms hut; Josie called after her, "Merlyna, wait! We can try to help!"

"Let her go. I don't blame her. This mess is my fault," MOMI said. "Now, what are the next plans with the colony?"

DADDIE was about to respond when MOMI's form winked out.

"Ugh, that was weird," Josie said.

"No, Josie, something is happening in the archive!" DADDIE said. "Get over to the constellation processing center. I..."

"What the heck?" Josie said as DADDIE's avatar suddenly disappeared as well. Josie raced out of the hut towards the processing center. As she ran, she saw a weary and worn-out Jason Dikkert sitting outside the newly built sled garage.

"Come on, Jason," Josie shouted.

Jason saw the alarm on Josie's face and started running next to her. "What's going on, Josie?"

"No time," Josie said, huffing, "You have your sidearm on you?"

"Yes, of course! That's standard operating procedure," Jason said.

"Good, we might need it! Something is happening in the constellation," Josie said. She and Jason raced another two hundred meters to the one-story building that housed all the computing power for DADDIE and the other AIs. As they approached, Jason and Josie could see the door was open, and smoke poured out of the building.

"We've got to seal the door," Josie said.

"But the fire," Jason was about to argue but was cut off.

"Will go out, the argon gas will kill the oxygen, and the flames will die," Josie said.

Jason raced forward and pulled the doorstop that was holding the door open. The door started to close, and when it sealed, warning lights could be seen through the building's glass.

"Let's hope we've arrived in time," Josie said.

*

Inside the virtual world, DADDIE regained his senses. He was at his favorite place, the ballpark. He sat in the stands, chili dog in hand.

The fanfare sounded, and the crowd yelled, "Charge!"

"Now batting for the home team, number seven, Daddy!" The announcer said.

DADDIE looked around. Suddenly, the cameras were on him. The people around him started clapping.

"Well, geez, it's been a while since I was out of the dugout," DADDIE said, standing and walking towards the field.

A rockabilly tune came over the loudspeakers as DADDIE's statistics came up on the holotron.

"Remember, folks, this is the Greg Body memorial game. Claim your free CAA t-shirts as you leave the stadium," the announcer said over the loudspeakers. Reaching the field, the bat boy came running up carrying three different types of bats. DADDIE looked them over and picked the wooden one. A bold 'LS' was emblazoned across the center. DADDIE nodded to the bat boy and gave a few practice swings.

"Well, here we are, folks. It's the ninth inning, and the home team has bases loaded. We're six visitor and five home. If the old slugger, Daddy, can hit this one, the home team has a chance of winning the game," the announcer said.

"Yeah, no pressure," DADDIE said to himself. He looked at the pitcher. The kid wasn't a rookie and certainly looked like he had an arm. DADDIE stepped to the plate and cocked his bat.

The pitcher wound up and threw. The ball was a beanball that came right toward DADDIE's head. DADDIE dodged, moving out of the box, as the catcher had stood to grab the ball.

"Ball!" the umpire called. DADDIE looked to the umpire, expecting him to give the pitcher a warning. DADDIE stepped back into the box and prepared to swing. The pitcher wound up and delivered a heater. DADDIE swung but missed the ball by a split second.

"Strike!" the umpire called. DADDIE stepped out of the box as the catcher tossed the ball to the pitcher. Somehow, DADDIE sensed that it would be the team's end if he didn't win this game.

DADDIE stepped back into the box. The pitcher wound up and threw. DADDIE had to step away as the ball flew high and tight, almost hitting him.

"Ball!" the umpire said.

"Geez, ump, what is with this guy? What did I do to deserve that?" DADDIE said.

"You here to complain, or are we playing ball," the umpire asked. DADDIE shrugged and took a practice swing before stepping into the box.

The pitcher wound up for his throw, and everything stopped. Time froze.

"What the..." DADDIE said.

"Don't worry, this is a fail-safe," a voice in the crowd said. A man stood up. He stood one-hundred-and-eighty-centimeters tall and wore a long-sleeved red t-shirt with black tactical pants and a CAA ball cap. He approached the field.

"Karl!" DADDIE said. "I'm glad to see you! I thought you were..."

"Dead," Karl said. *"God willing*—I'm not dead, but you almost are."

"Huh," DADDIE said. "That's not possible. I'm an Artificial Intelligence."

"You know, Daddy," Karl said, "You are more than just algorithms. You're like a son to me. I'm here now because your core algorithms are under attack, and if you don't pull through, they'll be wiped out."

DADDIE sat looking at the semi-transparent Karl. Finally, he said, "How are you here? Wait, this makes no sense. I'm at the ballpark."

"Think back. What do you remember before you were here?" Karl asked.

"Mommy, Merlyna, Josie, and I were talking. Merlyna stormed out, and then Mommy just disappeared..."
DADDIE said, "Geez, Karl, I'm scared."

"Don't be. That's why I am here," said Karl.

"What happens if I don't make it," DADDIE asked.

"The colony will most assuredly die, Daddy. They all need you."

"I meant what will happen to me... Will I dream?" DADDIE asked, his avatar looking afraid.

"I don't know. I barely have any understanding of what will happen to us organics when we die, and most of what I believe is like voodoo and shamanism to other humans these days. I believe that all sentient life will awaken in a new, perfected universe. I think that will include AIs like you, too. But I do know that you don't have to go gently into the night. You can fight back like you always do. Don't give up the game when you're so close to winning," Karl said. Suddenly, Karl disappeared, and the ballpark came alive. The baseball sailed straight over the plate.

"Strike two!" the umpire cried out. DADDIE stepped out of the box. It was two-two; another strike and the game would be over. He took some practice swings and nodded, stepping back into the box.

The pitcher wound up and threw the ball. DADDIE was ready, and he swung. He tipped the ball, which went wide and off the third base line with a foul tip.

"I got a piece of it," DADDIE said. He stepped out of the box, did another practice swing, and came back in. The pitcher wound up and threw. The ball, again, came close to DADDIE's head, and he ducked out of the box.

"Ball!" the umpire said.

"Come on, ump, that's intentional!" DADDIE said.

"Hey, you a cheerleader or a ballplayer?" the catcher said.

"Batter up!" was all the umpire said. DADDIE realized this pitch was everything. Either he'd make it, or he wouldn't. He stepped back into the box and prepared his swing. The pitcher looked down at the catcher and shook his head. Finally, after multiple signals, the catcher gave the pitcher a sign he liked, and the pitcher wound up and threw. DADDIE watched as time slowed. The ball sailed like a little leaguer threw it.

DADDIE waited. As the ball was about to cross the plate, he swung with all his might. Time rubber-banded and returned to its normal flow. The ball traveled like a rocket high above the center field. DADDIE stood watching as the ball kept going and going. The baseball landed inside the stands, causing the fans to scramble for the ball.

"Goodbye, Mr. Spalding! That ball is gone! Home run for the home team! Home team wins!" the announcer said. DADDIE dropped his bat and began jogging around the bases. As he approached home, he saw his teammates there. As he stepped on the plate, they all ran and congratulated him on the field. Then everything went dark.

*

Josie watched as the doors opened fifteen minutes later. The argon evaporated back into the atmosphere, and she and Jason raced into the building. They went through the racks of matrices lining the rows in the environmentally controlled computer center, looking for the source of the damage.

"Over here," Jason said. Josie ran over to where Jason was standing.

"Looks like a burner," Jason said, touching the burned-out shell of the bomb.

"Not that high tech. It could have been manufactured here," Josie said unhappily. "That will not narrow down our suspects."

"They placed the bomb near the higher functioning sections," Jason said, "if we had waited even a few minutes, then that would have been it for Daddy. Plus, there is a Krystil construct plugged in as well."

"What, someone was uploading code?" Josie asked, looking at the removable media.

"Looks that way…" Jason said, removing the wires

that connected the small cube to the matrices' rack.

"Can you diagnose if there is any major damage," asked Josie.

"Maybe. The process is a bit above my ability, but I think, with some help from Griff, we can ensure Daddy is functioning and can resume full runtime," said Jason.

"Wait, let's discuss repairs…" Josie was about to continue when Merlyna, Martha, Griff, and Barbara came in.

"We saw the smoke, what happened?" Martha asked.

"Something happened. It looks like a loose circuit," Josie said, her eyes fixed on Jason.

Jason saw her stare and wanted to say something more, but also realized Josie wanted him to be quiet. He silently placed the Krystil construct into his pocket.

"What do you think happened here, Little Rooster," Griff asked.

"I'm not sure. Josie told me to come with her, and so I did," Jason said. "By the time we arrived, the doors had closed, and the argon was killing the fire." Merlyna's eyes flitted between Jason and Josie.

"Well, Merlyna, you need to get Con Sec Corps to do a thorough once-over of all the circuits now. The rest of you, get back to work. This colony won't build itself," Josie said. Martha and Griff nodded and went back towards the medical complex.

Barbara said, "Well, Jason, I have to get some shut-eye. I've been rolling hard all day."

Jason nodded and said, "Go on. I need to talk to Josie about the Vanguard's progress."

Barbara left the computer center. Merlyna, Jason, and Josie stood there.

"What," Jason said.

"Do you think it's him, Josie?" Merlyna said.

"No, Jason's a good kid," Josie said. "Besides, he was in the sabotaged pod, and I've never known Jason to be able to keep a secret."

"I'm right here," Jason said.

"We know," Merlyna said coolly.

"What's going on?" Jason asked.

"We've got a saboteur," Josie said.

"What?" Jason said. He acted like he couldn't process the information.

"Someone or something is destroying our equipment. I am only worried that this time they've wrecked Daddy," Josie said.

"Why? Wouldn't that also put them in danger?" Jason asked.

"Who knows, perhaps they have a backup plan?" Merlyna speculated.

"Jason, can you run a diagnostic and see if Daddy is okay?" Josie said.

"Sure, that bomb didn't look like it could harm Daddy. The constellation is huge and…" Jason said but was cut off by Merlyna.

"AI code is a delicate thing. My guess is the Krystil construct was there to send a worm, and the burner was to destroy the evidence. It could all unravel if the malicious code cracked even a small part of Daddy's algorithms. The effect would destroy Daddy. I know Griff and Greg contributed to the code base for Daddy. Of course, Karl made Daddy, but from how things were going on HD 260655, he has his hands full."

"Wait, what's happening on HD 260655?" Jason asked. Josie and Merlyna glanced at each other.

"This is corporate top secret," Josie said. "Karl is in charge there. Patrick Murphy was killed. It sounds like merc companies are going 'full space pirate' on the colony."

"Huh? Why?" Jason said.

"We don't know," Merlyna replied. "From what I remember from Karl's experience at the bidding, CAA grabbed the colony from some competitors. Maybe they wanted the colony one way or another…"

"Well, right now, we need to focus on Daddy. Can you repair him, Jason?" Josie asked.

"Yes," Jason replied.

"This has to be done quietly. We'll let folks know Daddy is okay and will be online later," Merlyna said.

"I'll be careful and quiet," Jason said. "Can one of you oversee and assign missions for the Vanguard for the next day or two? That way, I can focus solely on Daddy?"

Merlyna nodded, "Yeah, I'll do it. I can also correlate your team's whereabouts with this event. It won't be a foolproof way to determine who is doing the sabotage, but we can narrow down the list of suspects."

"I'll go over to Analysis and have them do a chemical analysis on the burner," Josie said, "Maybe I can find a clue from the device."

"Good luck," Merlyna said. "Want me to perform some forensics on the Krystil construct?"

"Sure. I'm not sure we'll get much from the device; that'd be too easy. Anyway, best of luck to both of you," Josie said. Now get back to work."

Merlyna and Jason went their separate ways, and Josie hiked to the Colonial Administration Building or the CAB. The building was being three-dimensionally printed, but the first floor was complete. Josie had moved into one of the completed offices. She suspected the office was for an office manager or personal secretary rather than an administrator. However, she set up a cot and lived in the office. She put the bomb on her desk and sat down, pulling out her oversized tablet and activating its holographic keyboard.

Josie looked at the crew manifest. She mentally tried to calculate who the saboteur was. She crossed off Jason, Merlyna, and herself. Short of a nervous breakdown or some trans-human neuroses, Josie was confident that Jason and Merlyna were not the culprits.

She pulled up the construction plans. Several

buildings were in various stages of construction. She wondered if the saboteur was timing their attacks with the colony's construction and whether she could use that to determine where the next sabotage attempt would be. Potentially, this knowledge could lead to the apprehension of the saboteur. Josie also wondered if the quantum array was in proper working order. The saboteur had her focused on DADDIE, but the q-array was more important even than the AI. In less than ten years from now, Josie would signal that the colony was open for business on the q-net. Without the array, everyone was stuck moving at the languid speed of light. Josie tried to focus, but the array kept popping back into her head.

"Merlyna, meet me at the array," Josie said to her tablet, turning her audio into an SMS text. She got up and started towards the large array radome. She entered the building expecting wolves or cyborgs to attack her. Instead, workers had constructed a small dish and left ordered piles of equipment spread throughout the structure.

"I'm here," Merlyna said, stepping through the door behind Josie and making her jump.

"Oh geez, you startled me," Josie said.

"What's up? Worried someone has gone after the array?" Merlyna guessed.

"Yeah, can you help me look around?" asked Josie.

"Yes, but if you're worried, let's inspect the quantum entangled elements," Merlyna said. The array structure was almost superfluous. However, its heart was a series of collided material perfectly entangled to another set of collided materials. When one atomic element was altered on the collided material, the same elements would shift with its entangled pair. Distance and time became irrelevant. Computers could use the communication link to provide a perfect, instantaneous exchange of flipped bits. Whether the bits were audio, video, or data, it didn't matter.

"Sure, you want me to open the box?" Josie asked.

Merlyna shook her head and said, "Don't want you to break a nail, cheerleader. Besides, do you know what you're looking at or for?"

"That's why I have you, geek girl," Josie laughed. Merlyna smirked and stepped up to the meter cubed TEMPEST box, which had all sorts of warnings about the sensitive items inside. There were labels about not touching and electrocution. The most significant label of all was a big danger sign with a skull showing that the contents could kill someone. Merlyna pulled on some gloves that sat near the box.

"Well, this should be easy. Flip the release and peek inside the box. If all the hardware looks good, we can run the diagnostics on the software," Merlyna said.

Josie nodded, pulled out her tablet, and locked down the radome access with a swipe of a button.

"I was going to suggest locking the door," Merlyna said.

"Be careful, Merlyna," Josie said. "I'd hate to have to call for a medical evacuation."

"Don't worry. I saw Karl play with this stuff on Alpha Centauri. This box's contents are all nasty. He lost a shell once because, well… I love my husband," Merlyna said, flipping a release and then another on the lid.

Josie said, "Sounds like a story."

Merlyna chuckled. She opened the q-array maintenance access panel and said, "Well, the story falls somewhere between when Karl glued his hand to our bed and when he shorted out the shuttle bay."

Josie moved closer to see inside, but it was all for nothing as another inner panel presented itself. She sighed. "Go on…"

Merlyna smiled and started flipping the latches on the inner panel. "Well, we were sodbusting on a colony, I think maybe it was Alpha Centauri, and Karl believes he is the penultimate Renaissance Man, a new Da Vinci, if you will. The quantum array was dropping packets badly…"

"He decided to fix it?" Josie asked. Merlyna opened the inner panel. Over Merlyna's shoulder, Josie could see several small modular cages inside the heart of the q-array.

"Worse," Merlyna said. "He was going to replace the entangled parts."

"What happened," Josie asked. Merlyna bent over and looked inside, careful not to touch anything. Merlyna then stopped, stepped back, and produced a hair tie to pull her dark red hair into a tight bun.

"He stuck his unprotected hand in and got radiation poisoning," Merlyna said, "I mean, we weren't in young shells then, so we had expected to have to move on. We had backups ready to decant into. But he wasn't super happy that he irradiated himself. He rolled out after the medical staff made sure he wasn't hazardous. Then things went haywire."

"How so?"

Merlyna squatted back down, looking inside, and absently said, "Well, the idiots decanted him into my new shell. A few days after messing in the array, he became my wife," Merlyna said.

"What!" Josie said. "I never heard that one. Now, you have my full attention."

"After he rolled out, the techs scheduled the decant. Somehow, they had messed up my name and assigned the male shell to Merlin Alenart. I mean, it's happened before. So, when my poor husband wakes up, he's in my new shell. He was quite the good sport about it all."

"What did you do?" Josie asked.

"Like I said, we weren't young. My shell was in its sixties, so I rolled out and decanted into Karl's proper new shell. They were sodbuster body types. I went from being a curvy pale redhead to a muscular, tanned, jet-black-haired cowboy," Merlyna said. Merlyna continued to look at the array. She moved slowly. She was splitting her focus between equipment and story.

"Well, okay," Josie said, "at least you had that going for you. You know, I've never considered swapping sexes. What was it like?"

"Different," Merlyna said. "I could write my name in the snow with my genitalia. I'd always wondered about that."

"What did Karl look like?" Josie asked. "I have a hard time thinking about him as someone other than a guy."

"He was a lightly tanned, strawberry-blond. I was drawn to his appearance after we'd both decanted. I mean, I am now, *too*, but that whole experience was wild. We had some children. They have mixed feelings about us," Merlyna said.

"Oh really?" Josie said, "Why is that?"

"Our oldest, Joss, doesn't speak with either of us anymore. He's furious, or he was a century ago, about the whole experience. Our youngest, Penelope, sends us vids all the time. She and Lisbeth, our absolute oldest, connected around one hundred and fifty years ago. Penny realized that no matter what plumbing Karl and I carry, whether we're Karl and Merlyna or Kate and Martin—we were the same sort of parents."

"That's too bad about your son. When did you switch to your last shells?" Josie asked.

"We came back to Luna when Greg was building CAA, so we shelled out back to standbys we had in Sol. Karl returned to a clone of his original shell, and I returned to my standard shell."

"You know, I have many more questions on that experience," Josie said.

"After we finish with the array. Right now, I need to focus. Can you pull up a schematic of what the array should look like? I can see we have missing pieces," Merlyna said. Josie nodded and tapped her tablet. She craned her head to look over Merlyna. Merlyna stood and moved out of the way to avoid being nudged into an element. Josie stuck her head in, tablet in hand.

"Don't irradiate yourself. Otherwise, I'll call you Darren," Merlyna grinned.

"You're right. There is a module missing," Josie said. It looks like it sits around one o'clock in the back of the box. There is an empty cradle there."

"Like I suspected, we're in deep trouble."

Josie pulled herself out of the box, "Okay, what does the missing module do?"

"That's part of the entangled matter. Without that, we can't receive or transmit," Merlyna said. "This entire array has become just a nice radio telescope."

Josie and Merlyna shut up the q-array, and placed the gloves back. They exited the radome and started walking back towards the operations center. As they strolled back, they were met by Griff.

"There you two are," he said. "I need to know when Daddy and the q-net will work."

Merlyna looked to Josie, who said, "Who said the q-net isn't working?"

"No one. I just tried a search for a patient and the q-net isn't responding," Griff said.

"We were just checking that ourselves," Merlyna said. "Looks like there is a part on backorder for fabrication. We're getting stutter."

"Who is the patient?" Josie asked, deflecting.

"Well, there is a confidentiality…" Griff began, but Josie cut him off.

"Merlyna is the Con Sec Director, and I am Corporate. Since you brought it up, we have a right to know," she said, " for the safety and success of the expedition."

"Yes, you're right," Griff said. "Sometimes I yearn for the return of the olden days of government regulations. The patient is Barbara Gordon."

Merlyna and Josie looked at one another before Josie turned back to Griff and asked, "What's her condition?"

"I don't know," Griff said. "She's complaining about a lack of memories attached to her current shell. I wanted to research before asking Daddy, especially since he's been adamant about Barbara being only sixteen years old."

"That makes sense. Merlyna and I will get a fix time from Con Sec Corps and let you know," Josie said.

Griff's face looked like he wanted to say more, but instead, he nodded, "Thanks, be seeing you ladies," he said and left.

"Our suspect list seems to be growing," Josie said.

"I prefer to label everyone a suspect until they aren't," Merlyna said, "But what are you thinking?"

"Well, Griff has been acting weirdly, and he was one of the last people to interact with Greg's shell before we left Luna. We also have Gordon, who seems to suffer from rare neuroses. It just seems…"

"Fishy," Merlyna suggested.

"Yeah," Josie said in agreement.

"Well, Gordon found both the uranium and the petroleum. Both sites are reporting good deposits. Why are you concerned?" Merlyna asked. "Seems like Gordon is on the helping side of the colonial equation."

"Yeah, that just seems too easy. Junior scouts rarely make finds like that," Josie said.

"I get you. Now that we have no Daddy and no q-net, let's see who bites."

Josie and Merlyna came to a fork in the path. Josie turned to the left and said, "Well, I must return to the office. Too many reports need my chop."

"On the plus side," Merlyna said, moving to the right path, "Mommy won't be looking over your shoulder."

"Yeah," Josie said as she exited.

*

Jason pulled up the code base for DADDIE. It was a

hot mess of spaghetti code, poorly commented, and filled
with Holzhauser's poor twelve-thousandth-century coding
practices.

"Great, I'll never figure this stuff out," Jason said
with a groan. On a separate screen, he had the user manual
and end-user documentation. These, too, were written by
Karl, but they were beautiful prose that explained everything
an end user might need to know. That was all well and good,
but the manuals didn't tell a developer how to jump-start a
damaged AI.

Jason looked at the frequently asked troubleshooting
questions: one item involved a stuck AI. Jason looked at the
steps to fix the problem. They were relatively simple. He
needed to link in via an augmented reality helmet, and he
could start troubleshooting there in the virtual space.

Jason was working in a swing space Josie had created
for him in one of the new sheds. She had directed Jason to
use this office space. It was quiet and off the beaten path,
the perfect place to troubleshoot DADDIE quietly. Jason
found the collapsible helmet in a drawer and put it on.

His eyes were flooded with a green neon light, and
his ears heard a soft static. In a moment, he saw himself in a
gray-white visual grid. In the background a large Corpus Ad
Astra logo hovered. Jason hand-signed to initiate a restart.
The AR helmet went dark but then restarted. The logo came
up, but nothing else happened. Jason chopped an execute
function. The logo flashed and disappeared momentarily,
then a man in a red button-down shirt and black trousers
appeared. Jason recognized him as Karl Holzhauser.

"Welcome to the Corpus Ad Astra Dedicated Astro-
colonial Database Design Intelligence Echo. If you're seeing
me, there has been a code-base fault. Please get in touch
with technical support for further assistance," the AR Karl
said.

"I need help," Jason said to the AR, hoping for some
troubleshooting.

"I can provide minimal help, but for in-depth troubleshooting, please contact CAA technical support," the Karl avatar said.

"How do I restart Daddy, Karl," Jason said.

"Make this chop for a full restart, and then emulate this chop for executing the boot loading code," Karl said. Jason grew frustrated as the avatar showed commands Jason had already tried.

"Karl, I need to get Daddy working. Give me something more than 'Have you tried turning it off and on again!'" Jason demanded. Again, the avatar made the hand signs for restart and execution.

"Dang it, I need more than this," Jason said. He was about to rip off the AR helmet when a small boy with a cloud symbol on his forehead appeared.

"If you're seeing me, then something has gone wrong with Daddy," the boy said.

"Yes, Daddy's algorithms have been compromised," Jason said, "I need help."

"Well, sir, you're in luck; I am the GRAID," the GRAID said.

"What's a GRAID," Jason asked.

"I'm the Grand Redundant Artificial Intelligence Database, the backup, and I'll give Daddy another chance, Jason," the GRAID said.

"Wait, you recognize me?" Jason asked, "Are you interactive?"

"Fully," the GRAID said. It looked at the troubleshooter and waved its hands, "Let's get rid of the other one. He's not very helpful, right?"

"Yes," Jason said. The GRAID snapped its fingers, and then they were alone.

"Daddy is in a bad state," the GRAID said. "He's stuck in an internal race condition and needs an exit from the loop."

"Sure, how do I do that?" Jason asked.

"Simple, we're going to rebuild some of the codebase," the GRAID said.

"Oh, okay, that doesn't sound simple," Jason said.

"Sure it is," the GRAID said, "We only need to reprogram a couple of millions of lines of code."

"Geez, I cobbled together a crypto-proton bomb but never built an AI. How am I going to fix Daddy?"

"Well, I'm the wizard. I do the work. You need to tell me what to do," the GRAID replied. Suddenly, Jason realized who he was looking at. "Jerry Cotter!? You're the wizard?"

"Yes, of course, *Problemius Solvio*," Jerry said, waving a wand that had just appeared in his hand.

"Uh, okay, let's get started," Jason said as bands of color danced off the wizard's wand.

"There are people who make things happen, there are people who watch things happen, and there are people who wonder what happened. To be successful, you need to be a person who makes things happen."

— Astronaut Jim Lovell

Griff had tried to get DADDIE's avatar up and running several times over the past day. The avatar never appeared, but a screen showed that the AI was undergoing maintenance and upgrade. Griff knew something was wrong. The quantum array was offline, and maintenance couldn't occur without an active connection.

He and Martha had been fighting more and more these past few days. Ever since the *Aquila* arrived, she had nagged him about moving on to a new job. Griff had been with CAA for almost sixty years, and he'd seen the company's fortunes rise and fall. Currently, CAA was stalling, and its stock prices were falling, and Griff knew the founders themselves leading the colonial expeditions was one heck of a "Hail Mary pass" to change things up.

Martha kept nagging him about needing to "get out while the getting was good." She'd agreed to come on the venture and colonize L 98-59 only because Griff had agreed to move on employment-wise if the colony failed. Griff remembered when she'd started the discussion—it was ten years ago after she'd come back from the Colonial Surgery Conference on Mars.

Griff looked at his tablet. There were accident and other medical reports that needed his signature, certifying that a human doctor had reviewed the incidents. He didn't want to switch to the synthetics section, where he'd be lost in the paperwork on repairs, upgrades, patches, and incidents.

Someone knocked at the door. Griff stood up and opened the door. It was Jason Dikkert.

"Look what the cat dragged in," Griff said. "What can I do for you, Little Rooster?"

Jason smiled and said, "Hey Griff, I need a second set of eyes on some code."

Griff motioned Jason in. The kid was tired and worn out. Griff remembered his days in medical school, where burning the candle at both ends was the norm rather than the exception. Coffee and the rare amphetamine got him through his schooling with honors. Looking at Jason, Griff wondered what the kid was up to.

"Sure, Jason," Griff said, switching to his analytic nature. What can I do for you?"

Jason produced his tablet. On it were billions of lines of code, but the development editor was fixed over a small segment. Red error boxes surrounded the code.

"I'm developing an AI for the Vanguard, especially since we're getting ready to move to a different outpost," Jason said. Griff noted the kid was more guarded and seemed hesitant to give details.

"Makes sense. What's the problem? I'm decent at AI, but the man you want is Karl Holzhauser. He codes and trains these things all the time," Griff said.

"Yeah," Jason said. "He's busy on HD 260655."

Griff nodded. If there was more to that, Jason didn't say anything.

"Well, let's see the code." Griff looked over the block and smiled. "Oh, this one is straightforward. You forgot to initialize the constructor. Add your value here, and the code should compile and then holographize. After that, it will enter the process flow and you should start to see the construct persona come online."

Jason looked like Griff had saved his life and said, "Gee, thanks! I can't believe I didn't see that."

"Looks like you've been staring at this code for a long time," Griff said.

"Yeah, and Jerry Cotter hasn't been helping! He's a horrible wizard!" Jason said.

"Uh, okay," Griff said, unsure what that was all about.

"Yeah, well, thanks again, Griff," Jason said, sticking

the tablet under his arm. He was about to go when Griff said, "Hold on, I have a question for you."

"Yeah, sure, ask away," Jason said.

"You and Barbara are more than teammates, aren't you?" Griff asked.

"Yeah, we're kind of going out. Why?"

Griff laughed. "Kind of going out. That's not how it works, Little Rooster. Either the lady is pregnant, or she's not, no half-ways on that."

"Well then, yes, we're dating. Why?" Jason said.

"I'm just concerned for you, that's all," Griff said. "If we aren't seeing a case of harmonic resonance, then Miss Gordon is someone else entirely."

"I appreciate your concern. I know Barbara's condition, and frankly, I don't care. I like hanging out with her! She's smart, she can be funny, she's wise, and she cleans up nicely," Jason said.

"Sounds like you have some deeper feelings there, Little Rooster," Griff said.

"Maybe. I am trying not to think about them until Barbara gives me the green light to keep moving," Jason said. "Why do you ask?"

"The more I look into her case, the more I don't think she's a sweet little teenager," Griff said.

"But the Doodle Kid with the harmonic transference?" Jason said but was cut off by Griff.

"Yeah, I am not so sure this is a similar case," Griff said. "The Doodle kid, as you call him, did have some remnant memories. Part of the problem with that white paper is that the Doodle researcher was laying out a case for their next-generation harmonic archive, and the paper was casting aspersions about Doodle's competitors."

Jason looked like he had been punched in the gut. He sat there silently.

"Listen, Jason, I am not sure what's going on, but something is happening in this colony, and it's not good,"

Griff said. "You're like a son or little brother to me, and I don't want to see you get hurt."

"You think Barbara is responsible," Jason asked, "because, she's not."

"What makes you so sure," Griff said.

"I can't put my finger on it, but it's like I know her," Jason said. "There's something familiar about her, and then there is all the time we spend together. I wish I could explain myself better, but I'm running too short on sleep now."

"I understand," Griff said. "Don't let your guard down. I don't know if it is Barbara or someone else, but someone wants us to fail, and they are trying to make that happen."

Jason looked at Griff momentarily and said, "Look, I am not supposed to tell anyone, but I trust you, Griff. I am fixing Daddy's codebase. He's been sabotaged."

Griff's eyes widened, and he said, "Well, let me look at that code again."

Jason nodded and handed over his tablet. Griff poured over the code and said, "Well, I should have known. Professor Holzhauser, your signature is all over this code. I am glad you said something, Jason because you need to ignore my advice about this code."

"Huh? What?" Jason said, sitting down on a stool in Griff's office.

"If this was straightforward AI code, what I said makes perfect sense, but Karl is one slick cat. He doesn't code things the way we do it today. He's old school, and while the code may look like spaghetti, he's built a few fail-safes in the codebase to surprise the would-be cracker or cut-and-paste script kiddie."

"What do you mean," Jason said, yawning.

"If you plugged in a variable and started up this code, Daddy would have been erased," Griff said. "Now, we need to find the garbage collection module…"

Griff sat tapping away for a few minutes. When he

looked over at Jason, the kid was sleeping.

"Okay, got the module. Now, if I refresh the counter and add the initial values to the variables…" Griff tapped his finger on his mouth. "What did Professor Holzhauser always like to use for his magic numbers? Let's see. He liked zero two, zero three, and twenty for the years he got his first shell's degrees. Then there is three zero seven for CAA's founding. Finally, I need the last set of numbers."

"It is four, Chief," DADDIE said, projecting into the office.

"Why hello, Daddy, how you feelin'?" Griff asked.

"Better, but don't forget the four, that's just plain four," DADDIE said.

"Why four?" Griff said, tapping the number in.

"It is the luckiest number in baseball. You need to touch four bases to score and four games to win the Galactic Series, and the fourth batter is often the slugger. You get the idea," DADDIE said.

"Thanks, Daddy," Griff said. "Can you run a diagnostic?"

"That will take me down, and I estimate almost one thousand issues are awaiting my input," DADDIE said.

"Well, commit the diagnostic. Those will have to wait," Griff said.

"Roger, confirmation phrase?" DADDIE said, asking for the secret passphrase.

"Take me out to the ball game," Griff said, then to himself, "Karl has a sense of humor."

"Passphrase accepted," DADDIE replied, "Going down for self-diagnostic."

Griff watched DADDIE blink out. He considered rousing Jason but instead let him sleep. Instead of reviewing reports, he returned to researching Gordon's case. He needed an explanation that would ensure that Jason didn't get hurt.

*

Li Mei and Barbara were assigned to K17, another

beach run. The bacteriological snow had stopped almost a week ago, but Josie wanted to ensure the bloom wasn't sitting off the coast waiting to erupt unexpectedly. Analysis couldn't decide if the CUYA needed to blow the bloom up or if settlers would just learn to deal with it. Barbara's sled sped at ninety-five kilometers per hour, about one hundred meters to the right of Li Mei's sled. Both ladies were exhausted, each for different reasons.

Barbara had been up helping Jason work on a project. He'd sworn that he had to work on it alone, but with a bit of female curiosity and nagging, Barbara had hounded her boyfriend into revealing what he was working on. Then she rolled up her sleeves and helped. Li Mei smiled at the story and was still puzzled about why Jason hadn't proposed to Barbara yet.

Li Mei's own love life was much more frozen in place. She had gone over to Xander's apartment—Con Sec Corps had started building living accommodations—and watched golf again. After the first date, she and Xander watched golf exclusively, so much so that Li Mei could name the players. Thankfully, after complaining about men's golf, Xander had changed the programming to women's golf. Li Mei at least got to watch and critique the ladies and their fashion sense. After a stray comment Li Mei made out loud, Xander began to ask her to fabricate some of the outfits.

This began the circular discussion Li Mei hated the most. Xander would suggest she wear a golf outfit, and Li Mei would ask him when they could play. He'd defer as the golf course was still in the planning stages, and he had no clubs, to which Li Mei would suggest they borrow someone's. Xander would then say they needed the right clothes to play golf, which would return—*magically*—to what Li Mei would wear.

"My sisters and aunties never had this problem," Li Mei said as she thought about the situation.

"What problem," Barbara asked. Li Mei realized her microphone was still on, and Barbara had heard her.

"Xander wants me to wear one of the outfits the ladies in his golf shows wear," Li Mei said.

"Yeah, so," Barbara said. "What's the big deal?"

"Well," Li Mei said with embarrassment, "The skirts they wear are short!"

"I think they are made that way so you can play the game," Barbara said.

"Yeah, that's part of the problem, too," Li Mei said. "He keeps wanting me to dress up just to watch the golf show. I suppose I can wear a short skirt if I get to play the game. After so many hours watching, I want to try the sport. It seems like it could be fun."

"Well, I'll ask Jason. Maybe we can find a place to set up an impromptu driving range so you can hit some balls," Barbara said.

"Is that like playing?" Li Mei asked.

"Sort of, there is less frustration in missing the hole as you just hit the ball for distance," Barbara said. "I remember I was pretty good on a driving range. I just hated the game itself."

"It sounds like you remembered something as Barbara," Li Mei said encouragingly. That's good, right?"

"I don't remember wearing a short skirt in those memories; I just had a lot of frustration with a hook shot," Barbara said. "I have a lot of memories of golf. I am kind of glad Jason doesn't like it. I think I have several past lives full of golf frustration, the more I muse on it."

"Seems like that is part of the game," Li Mei replied. "Anyway, Xander is always making excuses. He's a nice guy, but getting him off his couch is a monumental effort."

"Yeah, I can't help you there," Barbara said. "Wait a second. Maybe I *can* help you."

"Oh," Li Mei said, "how so?"

"We should go on a double date: you, me, Xander, and Jason," Barbara said, sounding like she had just solved a zero-point energy equation.

"I'm not entirely sure that's a good idea," Li Mei said. "He's so shy."

"Well, Jason and I will be on our best behavior…" Barbara began but was cut off by a loud chirp in her cockpit. The noise was so obnoxious that Li Mei could hear it over the communication link.

"I'm getting a metal scan and other elements," Barbara said. "I'm slowing down."

Barbara's sled decelerated and stopped as Li Mei's continued.

"I've hopped out and am using a hand scanner," Barbara said as Li Mei turned off her autopilot and swung the sled around to return to Barbara.

Li Mei saw Barbara waving the hand scanner to locate the elements on her sled's scanner. Li Mei stopped her sled thirty meters from where Barbara was standing. She hopped out of the cockpit and dropped down to the ground. She picked her foot up to move forward to meet Barbara but tripped over something on the ground.

"You okay?" Barbara asked when Li Mei stumbled forward onto her hands and knees.

"Yeah, I tripped over something," Li Mei said as she picked herself up. Both ladies went over to where Li Mei had stumbled. Buried in the dirt was some space debris. Li Mei bent over and started brushing the dirt away. Both women saw the letters "O," "N," and "I" printed on the side of the panel.

"Be careful," Barbara said.

"I am," Li Mei said. As the ladies continued clearing off the dirt, more letters appeared. They could see "Hipponike" in big, bold white letters with a penciled outline of a horse above the words in yellow. All of this was on a black background.

"Well, what do we have here?" Barbara said. "Looks like a spy satellite."

"What do you mean?" Li Mei said. "Maybe this was

just an old survey probe?"

"Unlikely," Barbara said. "Doodle surveyed the system for the stock exchange."

"How do you know that?" Li Mei asked.

"I just remember that…" Barbara said. Li Mei reached down and tried to pull the panel off the satellite. The panel flexed and trapped her hand between the panel and the superstructure.

"Ouch!" Li Mei said, "岩石和灰尘! My hand is caught!"

"I certainly hope you are joking," Barbara said.

"No! I'm serious, help!" Li Mei retorted. She started tugging, and the panel began flexing. The area around the debris started shaking off dirt as Li Mei's tugging became more determined.

From what became exposed with Li Mei's tugs, Barbara could see that the satellite was a small, scout-style probe.

"Do you smell something burning?" Li Mei asked, suddenly eyes wide.

"Okay, don't panic," Barbara said.

"Now I'm scared," Li Mei replied. "Why are you saying 'don't panic'?"

"Because if this is a spy probe, then there is probably a self-destruct, and that smell is the fuse."

"You know, your memories can be annoying sometimes!" Li Mei said, "How come you can't remember anything but spy satellites and stupid boy stuff?"

"Well, I remember that some of these spy probes have self-destructs!" Barbara said. "Now, hold still!"

Li Mei froze, watching as Barbara returned to her sled, fished through the survival kit, and brought back the survival hatchet.

"Wait, what are you doing?" Li Mei said, starting to squirm.

"Hold still, I'm going to get you out of this," Barbara

said. She dropped to a knee and used it to immobilize Li Mei's lower arm.

"Ouch! You're not as light as you think," Li Mei said.

"Hold still," Barbara said sternly. Then she brought the hatchet down on the panel.

"Ouch! That's pinching my fingers," Li Mei squealed.

"Don't move!" Barbara snapped as she brought the hatchet down again.

"I smell smoke worse than before," Li Mei said.

"Yeah, one or two more whacks, and I think you'll be free," Barbara said with another chop.

"Wait, that's better," Li Mei said.

"One more," Barbara said as she brought the hatchet down again. Li Mei pulled her arm away, knocking Barbara over. Both ladies watched as the probe started burning. The flames were visible as they began consuming the panel and structure. Li Mei would have been part of the blaze if they had waited a few minutes longer.

"Are you okay?" Barbara asked as she rose to her feet.

"Yes," Li Mei said but was interrupted as the probe let out a loud pop.

"Let's move away from this thing…" Barbara said as the probe exploded. The blast knocked down both girls, and Li Mei's sled suddenly fell into the explosion's hole.

Barbara shouted some expletives a sixteen-year-old shouldn't know, and Li Mei screamed. Then there was darkness.

*

"Okay, Sport, I'm ready," DADDIE told Josie. Jason had woken up just as DADDIE came back online. He had thanked Griff profusely and ran off to tell Josie. He told her everything, and as much as Josie wanted to be upset at Jason for involving Griff, she didn't say anything. Jason sat with Josie in her office as they tried to correlate various expedition members' movements.

"All right, I need all of the CAA personnel who had access to the shells, the lander bay on the *Aquila*, the cybernetics matrix on Aurora Dawn, and potentially the q-array. I'll cross-correlate the data with known bad actors in the HR files, and perhaps we can narrow down the subjects," Josie said to DADDIE.

"Correlating," DADDIE said. "I can provide a printout if you want it."

"Audio is fine… for now," Josie said.

"All right," DADDIE said, "You want only the suspects that correlate to all parameters or any suspect that had access to one of the parameters?"

"Just the unions. Quit stalling, Daddy," Josie said.

"Sorry, Sport. You aren't going to like the results," DADDIE said.

"I'm a big girl. Let me have them," Josie shot back.

"Griff is the number one subject with access to all of the sites. He's not on an HR list, he doesn't even have a sternly worded letter in his file," DADDIE said.

"Figures," Josie said. "Who are the next suspects on the list?"

"Well, you, Merlyna, Xena, Jason, Vidal, and Garnier," DADDIE said. "The probabilities are lower for Vidal and Garnier, as they didn't have access to the q-array, and I can account for their whereabouts during the matrix building attack."

"Maybe someone used their creds?" Merlyna said, making Jason and Josie jump.

"Blast it. I am going to make you wear a bell, Merlyna," Josie swore. "How long have you been creeping around there?"

"Long enough to see a dead end," Merlyna said. "Daddy, can you correlate with anyone who could have used someone else's access to the sites?"

"Now we're getting into a larger number of probabilities," DADDIE said, "If you want my opinion on the saboteur, just ask me, Pumpkin."

"We need something solid. Whoever the saboteur is, they've run off with the entangled circuits. We need to find out who they are and get the drop on them," Merlyna said.

"I am running the numbers now," DADDIE said, "but nothing is adding up. Look, I know you all think I am an all-powerful AI and whatnot, but I don't always understand human behavior. My algorithms aren't trained for sabotage, duplicity, and dichotomous human behavior. I'm a simple dude at heart. Give me a brewski, a chili dog, and some baseball—I'll call that a good day."

Jason chuckled and said, "That's why I like you, Daddy. You don't scare the heck out of me, like Mommy."

DADDIE smiled and said, "Well, team, according to the numbers I keep getting, as I said, your saboteur is Griff."

Josie shook her head, "That's wrong! It just can't be right."

Merlyna put her hand to her mouth; she was thinking. Finally, she said, "I am willing to consider the hypothesis, but we shouldn't get too focused on Griff. He could be an unwilling accomplice or a scapegoat. Daddy, can you bring up an instance of *Analyst's Hyperbook*? I need to start mapping Griff's relationships and related ones. Perhaps we can deduce our actual suspect."

DADDIE nodded. "Sure, I'm spinning up a matrix. Mind if I learn what you're doing?"

"Not at all, but I must warn you, it's been a century since I used the original. You might want a better human to emulate," Merlyna said.

"Nah, you and Sonny are quite capable role models," DADDIE said.

"Thanks," Merlyna said.

"Well, now I need to focus," Josie said. Merlyna and Jason knew that was the queue to leave. "I've got more than my share of paperwork to do."

"I'll keep an eye on Griff," Jason said. "I don't think

he's the one, but I don't mind hanging out with him anyway."

"Oh hey Merlyna, let me know if you come up with something," said Josie.

Merlyna nodded as she was leaving and said, "Immediately."

*

Barbara awoke in the dark with a weight on her midsection. It wasn't crushing her, but it wasn't light either. She started to reach for whatever was lying on her. She felt an arm and realized it was Li Mei.

"Are you okay," Barbara said reflexively. When Li Mei didn't answer, Barbara asked again and gently shook her.

"Ugh, yes," Li Mei said weakly. "What happened? The last thing I remember is the probe burning and a loud noise."

"Yeah, that would have been the fuse on the self-destruct. It is a good thing that the probe must have had some damage. Otherwise, I figure we'd be a pink mist right now," Barbara said.

"Yeah," Li Mei said as she started to roll off Barbara and stand up.

"Ouch," Barbara said. "Next time, let me know before you start to crawl off of me."

Li Mei's weight was gone, and Barbara tried to stand up. She tried to orient herself. On her feet, the uneven ground underneath made her stumble forward into a wall of dirt and soil. Li Mei turned on a small light and accidentally shined it into Barbara's eyes.

"Hey," Barbara said as Li Mei moved the light away. The women could see they were in a dry sinkhole. Whatever happened with the explosion, they had fallen deep underneath Aurora Dawn's surface. Barbara grabbed her small flashlight, still in its pouch, on her utility belt. She flicked the light on and began scanning the walls to see if there was a way out. The chamber the ladies were in was like a crack in the ground. The split went up jaggedly, and the walls were steep with enough rock and dirt to keep the sides from being smooth, yet nothing that looked at first glance like it offered a good chance of a climbing hold.

Barbara looked around for a way out near the bottom. She and Li Mei were at the lower end of the tear in the ground. Barbara thought the probe had crashed and potentially shaken the loose soil away from the stone underneath, creating this underground fissure. She looked up again, focusing her beam at the top. The dirt had piled up and collapsed whatever exit to the surface may have existed. Even if they could climb out, any potential exit was almost thirty meters up. She and Li Mei must have fallen into the fissure and rolled down or been in a controlled fall with other debris. Barbara moved to look at a different angle when her foot kicked something hard.

"Hey, what do you know," Barbara said, picking up the object. In her hands, she held the panel. It was the cause their current misfortune. The word "Hipponike" was prominently displayed on the side.

"Hey, we've got proof they were interested in this system," Li Mei said.

"Well, yes, but we need to get out of here, or that won't do us any good," said Barbara.

"Sure," Li Mei said. "I'll try the radio. We can relay the signal if I can connect via short range to the sled."

"I'll do the same with my sled," Barbara said. Both ladies attempted a connection. Barbara was too far out of range to reach her sled and thus cut off from communication with the outpost.

"I've got a connection," Li Mei said. Barbara came over to see Li Mei working on her personal radio, "the sled has connected… Oh no!"

"What," Barbara asked.

"The sled's antenna must have been damaged. I cannot get a signal to the outpost," Li Mei said unhappily.

"Okay," Barbara said, taking a deep breath. "Remember our protocols: Jason will start a search for us when we don't check-in. They know we're in this grid quadrant, and my sled is up there. When they get close enough, we can connect via short-range communication. We'll be okay. We must see if we can get out; otherwise, we'll need to wait."

Li Mei was silent for a few minutes, then said, "Yes, I see."

"What," Barbara said, trying to find a way up the steep fissure side.

"The entire concept of being stuck in a planet, well, it horrifies me in a way I never thought living on a planet would," Li Mei said. Her tone was calm and very flat, and Barbara realized that the young woman must be terrified. Barbara stopped trying to climb and walked to Li Mei. Before she could say anything, Li Mei hugged her. The embrace was more like a drowning person's cling than anything else.

Barbara hugged Li Mei back and said, "There's nothing to worry about; people get trapped underground all the time."

"Really," Li Mei said, "How awful!"

"Yeah, now, can you let go," Barbara asked with a smile, releasing her hug.

"Oh, sure," Li Mei said. "Sorry, this whole trapped underground thing is a new experience."

"Don't you get trapped in asteroids out in the belt?" Barbara asked.

"Only the miners, and even then, they aren't that deep down—usually only a few meters. If they survive a cave-in, they usually can dig themselves out. Mostly, we strip-mine the asteroids. We've found it to be safer," Li Mei said.

"Well, I suppose we have to wait," Barbara said. Do you have a deck of cards on you?"

The last thing, and the only one that you cannot physically train for, is the psychological preparation.

— Astronaut Philippe Perrin

Jason woke up to a banging on his apartment door. He had moved in a few days earlier and enjoyed the lack of commotion that usually got him up and moving.

"One minute," he said, pulling himself out of bed. He grabbed some underwear, a shirt, and shorts and threw them on quickly.

The banging continued. "I'm coming!" Jason shouted. He padded out of his bedroom and into the combined living room and kitchen. He turned on the coffee pot. He'd need the caffeine today based on how it was starting. He then moved down a tiny meter-and-a-half corridor to the main door of his apartment. He was going to open the door when he heard a banging on it again.

"Yes," Jason said, flinging the door open.

"Li Mei didn't come back last night," said a distraught Xander as the door opened. Jason blinked momentarily and recognized Xander, as Jason had heard enough about him from Barbara.

"Dude," Jason said impatiently. "We're the *Vanguard;* we do late nights."

"No, uh," Xander said awkwardly, "I checked on her... We were, uh, supposed to have a..."

"A date," Jason suggested. "Got it. When was the last time you checked on her?"

"Three o'clock in the morning," Xander said.

"Geez, dude," Jason responded. "That's a little on the creepy side."

"No... no... um... I was worried about her," said Xander.

Jason's head was spinning. He was still tired and drug out as he'd been up late. Aurora Dawn's day was slightly shorter than Earth's, and Jason missed the fifteen minutes of extra sleep he would have had if he had been in space or on

Earth.

"Come on in," Jason said, entering his apartment. "Start from the beginning. Do you like coffee?"

"Not really," Xander said, and then, "Sure, so last night, Li Mei and I were supposed to have a… you know…"

"A date," Jason said, pouring himself a cup of coffee.

"Yeah, and well, she didn't show up," Xander said.

"Sure, maybe she was busy or just late from her survey," Jason said.

"Yeah, I thought that too," Xander said. "We were going to watch more golf, only I was going to tell her something special."

"Got it," Jason said, adding some creamer to his coffee and slamming down his first cup. As the caffeine hit his neurons, a small niggling thought entered his head. Hadn't Barbara been out scouting with Li Mei?

"Aren't you going to raise an alarm," Xander said after a minute of watching Jason drink coffee.

"Uh, why?" Jason said, "I will head to the office here in a minute and see if Li Mei checked in. She was out with Barbara; I doubt they were anything but late."

Xander just stared at Jason. The look was not kind. Jason started to feel self-conscious.

"What," Jason said exasperatedly.

"What if they are in trouble," Xander stammered. "What if the worms got them again?"

Jason realized he wouldn't get rid of Xander until he ensured Li Mei was safe and sound.

"I need fifteen minutes to shower and change," Jason said.

"What…" Xander began, but Jason stopped him.

"They may be young, but they are Vanguard scouts. They can handle whatever Aurora Dawn throws at them," said Jason. He then turned and went into his bedroom, shutting the door.

*

"Can I have another sip," Li Mei said as Barbara took a small drink.

"Sure," Barbara said, giving up the little bit of water in her bottle. "I still can't believe you left your water in your sled."

Barbara had disciplined herself not to get cross, but her anger had risen to a point where she was ready to say what she was thinking. She was cold, dirty, and tired. The ladies had tried sleeping, but nerves and discomfort had ruined any chance of a decent rest.

"We have to be prepared in the Vanguard," Barbara said under her breath. Li Mei had drunk a fair amount of her bottle, and Barbara had given her half of the survival ration she had carried in a small pack on her utility belt.

The ladies had tried to figure out if Li Mei's sled had disappeared inside the fissure. They had dug around in case the sled was under the dirt nearby. After a few minutes of their sample spades hitting rock, they gave up. They spent the rest of the time, in the several hours they had been in the fissure, waiting.

"Hey," Li Mei said, "I never had to carry a water bottle. I always wore a suit, remember? I left the bottle in my sled since I hadn't needed it."

"Sure," Barbara said flatly.

"When will your boyfriend show up," Li Mei said crossly. Barbara could see that the rough night was also wearing on Li Mei.

"He's not my boyfriend. He's the boss," Barbara said.

"Whatever," Li Mei said. Barbara hated most that Li Mei wouldn't engage. Barbara was tired and bored. A fight with Li Mei with yelling and screaming would be more exciting than just sitting in the fissure and waiting for rescue. Instead of getting angry or pushing back, Li Mei would passively acknowledge. Barbara got even more irritated and stood up. Walking to the outer side of the fissure, Barbara used her small sample spade to dig.

"You aren't going to dig your way out," Li Mei said. Barbara just ignored her, taking the spade and sticking it into the dirt. Her mind wandered, and she remembered a drill from a long time ago that had been similar.

"Keep your arm up, lieutenant," the instructor said as Barbara threw yet another stab into the dummy with her knife. She'd been at this drill for an hour, and she was tired. The instructor was an enlisted man and a technical sergeant, but he was the king for the day. The sergeant again demonstrated how to perform the attack.

Barbara didn't even wonder why the sergeant was teaching a sixteen-year-old how to stab a man in the face. When her strange memories first appeared, Barbara wondered why people didn't interact with her like a sixteen-year-old girl. However, now, her form in the memories matched her current body. The memories had gelled.

Barbara stabbed the dummy again; this time, the blade hit home.

"Good job, ma'am," the sergeant said. "At this rate, you'll have killed all the mannequins on base by taps." Barbara just shook her head and laughed as she again stabbed the dummy. She closed her eyes and wiped the sweat from her face.

When she opened her eyes, Barbara stared into the dirt illuminated by her small light.

"What time is it?" Li Mei asked. Barbara was tired of that question, which Li Mei asked every hour on the hour.

"Check your chronometer," Barbara said, stabbing into the dirt.

"I'd have to turn on my light. I don't want to waste the power," Li Mei said. Barbara stopped digging as she was about to lose her cool. Every hour on the hour, the discussion was the same. Li Mei would ask for the time, Barbara would say to check out her clock, and Li Mei would then complain about losing power on her light.

"You know, if you'd been more cautious with the probe, we'd be eating in the cafeteria right now," Barbara said, snapping at Li Mei. Barbara felt terrible saying it. She had promised herself she wouldn't get upset, no matter what happened. Li Mei was younger than she was, even if Barbara was only sixteen. Barbara waited for a moment for Li Mei to say something, but there was nothing but silence. Barbara continued digging until she heard soft sobbing over the sound of her spade biting into the dirt.

"I'm sorry," Barbara said, putting her spade on her belt, grabbing her light, and moving to Li Mei. Li Mei stood there with dirty brown tears rolling down her cheeks. Barbara stood waiting for Li Mei to say something. Instead, Li Mei just hugged her. Barbara had, so far, very few memories of hugging anyone. She reached out and gently patted Li Mei with her hands. The hug felt awkward to Barbara, but Li Mei didn't mind.

"We're going to die down here under the ground, aren't we," Li Mei said, sobbing and breaking down.

"Probably not," Barbara said. Look, it's only eight o'clock now. Jason is just getting up and rolling into the office. He'll see we didn't check in, and then he'll start making calls." As if to underscore the point, the ground started rumbling, and dirt rained down on the two girls.

Li Mei sobbed. "Your digging is causing a cave-in!"

"Doubtful," Barbara said, hugging Li Mei more to keep her footing as the ground trembled. More significant amounts of dusty soil started pouring down from the ceiling above. Li Mei and Barbara looked like they had been dusted in cocoa powder. Li Mei separated from Barbara to clean her eyes. Barbara did the same. Light poured in from above and both women looked up. High above them, wedged into the fissure was Li Mei's sled. The almost three-thousand-kilogram machine was upside down and poised to crush them if it slipped. Barbara had to cover her eyes and look away as the dirt clumps fell from the ceiling. After a pause from the dirt falling, she opened her eyes and saw light streaming from the surface.

"Help!" Barbara shouted. "We're down here!"

"Help! Down here," Li Mei said frantically. Suddenly, the tremors got more intense, and Li Mei's sled started tipping forward, pinned by the sides of the fissure.

"Stop! The sled is above us," Barbara shouted. The sled started sliding downward. Barbara and Li Mei's cries got louder and more insistent.

The sled continued slowly slipping towards Li Mei and Barbara. Barbara closed her eyes, hoping her death would be quick. In her mind, a million memories came back to her of all the times she had cheated death. Now, it seemed, death was going to get payback.

"LOL, what do I see here? N00bs in a hole," the CUYA's mechanical voice said, "Did you n00bs forget to take your OP vitamins this morning?"

"Kooya!" Li Mei shouted, almost hoarse, "Kooya, please help us!"

"Ha ha, who is OP at *ShaftCrafter* now? I would have mined my way to bedrock and gotten sapphires by now," the CUYA taunted.

"Kooya, you have to get the sled," Barbara said, opening her eyes.

"Aww, n00b lost her sled," CUYA said, grabbing the sled and slinging the vehicle over his shoulder like a child throwing away a toy.

"Yes," Barbara said laughing, "We're total gamer-trash today. Can you get us out, you big strong OP Kooya?"

"Ha ha, n00b is begging me now," the CUYA said, "I love it when the n00bs beg me."

"You know, Kooya," Li Mei said. "I was going to get back and spin up a *ShaftCrafter* matrix. You can play with me if you get me out of this hole."

"Yeah, me too," Barbara said, chiming in.

"Can I play too?" another voice said. Xander's face appeared over the side.

"I love *ShaftCrafter* almost as much as golf," Xander

said. Li Mei smiled as she saw Xander standing above her.

"It's been a while since I played. Can I join as well," Jason asked, "Heck, I even brought rope and the rappelling gear to get you ladies out." Barbara's heart skipped a beat at seeing Jason's face.

"Get us out of here, and you can do anything you want," Barbara said. Jason turned three shades of red but said, "One moment," before running off.

"Ha ha," the CUYA said. "Before, the n00bs thought they were OP and wouldn't play with CUYA+MAGN1F1C3NT. Now, everyone wants to be on his squad. Seems like it is my lucky day."

"I didn't know you liked *ShaftCrafter,* Kooya," Xander said. "I would have played with you. What other games do you like?"

The CUYA extended his arm over the fissure as Jason worked the rappelling ropes. Jason tossed the rope over the CUYA's mechanical forearm, and the rest of the line dropped into the hole.

"I like *Doppler the Weasel* and *Soldiers of Duty,*" the CUYA said as Jason pulled the line up from the hole and attached a harness to the end.

"I'm sending the rope down in earnest now," Jason said. "Who is first?"

"Li Mei," Barbara said. Li Mei looked like she wanted to argue but kept quiet.

"Really," Xander said to the CUYA, having their separate discussion, "I liked *Soldiers of Duty.* You know, not to brag, but I got ranked."

The CUYA's head rotated to Xander and said, "What is your gamer handle? Maybe I have heard of you?"

"Well," Xander said, "I don't want to brag."

The CUYA's large mechanical head cocked. "Are you OP?"

"Totally," Xander said, "I'm *WeaponX4331.* My squad, *The Mutants,* went all the way on Luna."

"Checking," the CUYA said as Li Mei was lifted by Jason, who was hooked into another harness. He'd pull using the CUYA's leg as an anchor point.

"Whoa," the CUYA said after a moment. "You are OP! I bow to your superior skill, WeaponX4331. Shall we decide who is squad leader after some *Soldiers of Duty*?"

"Sure," Xander said enthusiastically. "First, let's get my girlfriend out of the fissure." Li Mei was nearly at the top when she heard what Xander said. She looked struck like a little cupid had shot her with an arrow.

"I'm your girlfriend now?" Li Mei asked, tears welling up in her eyes.

"Yeah, you like golf and play *ShaftCrafter*, you're perfect; plus, you look a lot like Wang Jing Bei, the girl who played the sorceress from *Ducking Panther, Camouflaged Wyvern*. So yeah, you're hot."

Li Mei was about to respond when she said, "Wait, she's in 小行星带中的爱! She plays Jia Li's rival in the second series."

"There's a second series?" Xander asked as Jason again lowered the harness to pull up Barbara.

"Senpai WeaponX, when we get back, will you play with me?" the CUYA asked, interrupting.

"Of course, there is a second series; Jia Li and Yichen look like they are all set to live happily ever after, but then his uncle takes a turn for the worse, and Jia Li's mother dies," Li Mei said.

"Sure, Kooya," Xander said. "Wait, she died. I thought she was getting better..."

"She was, then you fell asleep," Li Mei said. "Then we only watched golf."

"You know, my Aunt Tracie loves that show," Xander said, "I was a little resistant to watching. But now I know that Wang Jing Bei is in it, well..."

"Xander, sweetie," Li Mei said. "She's Wang Jing Fang's little sister in real life. You know the actress who plays Jia Li? Wang Jing Bei shows up in the subsequent series." Barbara reached the top, listening to all of the discussions. Jason raced forward and put his arms around her when she was finally on the surface. Unlike Li Mei, this hug was warm, compassionate, and caring. Barbara felt butterflies in her stomach as she got hugged and threw her arms around Jason.

"Are you okay," Jason said, looking into her eyes. She stared back into his, unsure of what to say, when what he said registered with her. "Yes, I'm dirty, but fine."

"Good," Jason said, releasing her, "What happened?" Barbara related everything that had occurred, noting the panel at the bottom of the ravine, the spy probe, the collapse, and their wait for rescue.

After she finished, Jason said, "Wow, I'm sorry it took so long to get to you. I thought you two were just late for arrival last night. I promise to do better in the future."

"Wait, so you weren't concerned when I didn't make it back?" Barbara said, sounding hurt and upset.

"Well," Jason said sheepishly, "You are a brave, dedicated, and excellent scout. I just assumed…"

Jason was cut off by Barbara's quick kiss on his lips: "Well if you really feel that way, I suppose I understand."

"For what it's worth, Xander was the one who was the most worried," Jason said.

"Uh, yeah," Xander said, effectively ending the discussion. Barbara looked around and saw Jason's Corpo-grey sled and her sled a little way off.

"Li Mei, you want to ride with me back?" Barbara asked.

Li Mei looked torn as if she wanted to stay with Xander, but then she realized that the explosion and CUYA had trashed her sled.

"Sure," Li Mei said, climbing into the sled's copilot chair. Barbara climbed up and into the pilot seat.

"See you back at the base, boys," Barbara said. She

closed the cockpit and set her waypoint to the outpost.

*

Barbara and Li Mei floated into the sled garage. Barbara parked the sled and opened the canopy. Neither woman said much on the way back to the colonial hub. They were both dirty, tired, thirsty, and hungry. Hopping out, Barbara went to the water fountain and bottle filler and started drinking. As she raised her head, Jason's sled came into the garage towing Li Mei's beat-up vehicle. The CUYA approached as well. Barbara could feel the tremors from the war bot's steps. Xander and Jason exited Jason's sled.

"Hey Li Mei," Xander said, "After you get food and cleaned up, do you want to play *ShaftCrafter* with me and the Kooya?" Li Mei smiled. Barbara could see she was tired but didn't want to say no to Xander.

"Give us a little while to get cleaned up and eat," Barbara said. "I'll be willing to play. I can't recall playing *ShaftCrafter* before."

"Sure," Xander said excitedly. "The Kooya and I will start the matrix and build a base so you two won't have to suffer through the tree-punching stage."

"No, I like that stage," Li Mei said. "Sorry, I am just drained."

"Oh, okay, we can wait for you," Xander said.

"Let me clean up," Li Mei said. Barbara nodded and waved as she was feeling the stress of the day. As Barbara entered the barracks, she saw a note on the door that stated that all personnel now had apartments. Barbara looked at the list and found her apartment and its location. A sub-sentient AI had moved her limited amount of possessions. Barbara wondered if she had any stored personal effects: expedition personnel were supposed to deliver them once people were out of the barracks. Yet another mystery that Barbara needed to solve. She walked over to the apartment complex and quickly found her apartment. She went up the stairs to the third floor and placed her hand on the apartment door's sensor to unlock it. The door opened, and Barbara entered. She noticed the furnished living room and kitchen.

She continued exploring the apartment and found her bedroom. There was an en-suite bathroom, and Barbara went into it. On the counter were several products for hair care, skin care, teeth, and, of course, towels. Barbara turned on the shower and cleaned up. The water from her head and face was brown from all the dirt and dust. The shower rejuvenated Barbara, and she dressed—noting a small closet with a larger amount of clothes. She was sure there would be a charge against her salary, but it shouldn't be much since these goods were mostly part of the startup package and considered a perk of colonization exploration.

Returning to the kitchen, she found a coffee maker with a built-in grinder and a small bag of whole beans, which was only a few kilograms but welcome. She ground the beans and started the brewing cycle. On the kitchen counter was a small basket. She lifted the lid and saw a few laundered Vanguard scout jumpsuits, some underwear, pink qipao, sandals, and two sets of pajamas. Barbara frowned. She didn't see any personal effects, only things from her time in the barracks.

"Another thing to ask Daddy about," Barbara said to herself. She debated switching to the qipao, the only non-CAA bit of clothing she owned but decided to buy some new clothes when the shopping centers opened.

The coffee maker chimed, and Barbara poured a cup. Barbara remembered a lot of black coffee in her past. Today, though, she wanted something other than straight black coffee. She looked around her kitchen and found some powdered creamer. She poured the creamer into the cup and took a drink. Suitably refreshed, she searched for a coffee cup with a lid. A travel cup bearing the CAA logo was in her cupboard. Transferring the coffee, she was ready to go.

Barbara left the apartment, figuring she'd need to tell Jason about potentially locating any missing personal effects.

She wandered back to the motor pool but saw the CUYA in the distance, sitting next to an apartment building. Walking over, she saw Jason and Xander on the balcony with a wire leading to a panel on the CUYA's arm.

"It's going to be good. It's time to show you n00bs who is OP at *ShaftCrafter*," the CUYA said.

"Did you get the connection?" Jason asked as he leaned precariously over the side of the railing.

"Almost, I need another half meter," Xander said.

Barbara could sense trouble as Jason was almost entirely over the railing. She grew more anxious and worried for him as he leaned out.

"Kooya, move closer," Jason said.

"Come on, n00b, get me into the game," the CUYA grumbled as it moved closer. Jason suddenly lost his balance and grip and went tumbling. Barbara shrieked as she saw him tumble, and a second later, the CUYA grabbed Jason mid-fall.

"Come on, n00b. You can't get out of *ShaftCrafter* so easily," the CUYA said, dropping Jason on the apartment balcony. Barbara began running towards the apartment. She ran through the lobby and up to the floor where Xander's apartment was located. The door was open, and she ran in, shouting, "Jason! Are you okay?"

Jason, for his part, looked a bit disoriented as he sat down cross-legged on the balcony's floor. "Yeah, just got the wind knocked out of me." Barbara ran through the apartment and put her arms around him. After a moment, he tapped her on the hand, and she relaxed her grip.

"That scared me," Barbara said.

"Me too," Jason said with a laugh, "Xander, do we have a long enough data cable to jack the Kooya in or what?"

"Already done. Do you have your controls?" Xander asked. Jason stood up and grabbed the small controller.

"Yes, I'm ready! Wait, what about the girls?" Jason

asked.

"I've got an extra, but I was saving it for Li Mei," Xander said.

"Why?" Li Mei asked as she stood in the open door. She wore an outfit that belonged on a golf course rather than a gaming couch.

"Well, I figured you wouldn't have one," Xander said absently, looking at the holoprojection.

"Really?" Li Mei said with a hint of frustration. She immediately produced a nice-looking controller and continued, "My entire family is serious about *ShaftCrafter;* my aunts and I play it all the time! My father was the one that made the *AstroidMiner* mod!" Xander took his eyes off the projection and looked over at Li Mei. His stare was intense.

"What?" Li Mei said abruptly.

"You… um… look nice," Xander said.

"Thanks, now be prepared to be amazed," Li Mei said, tuning her controller to the *ShaftCrafter* matrix. Jason stretched for a few minutes and then forgot his recent tumble. He, too, tuned his controller, and Barbara watched from Xander's holographic projection as Jason and Li Mei began bouncing around in a pixelated world.

Xander came over and gave Barbara the extra controller he had. "You want to play, too?" Barbara nodded and took the controller.

Jason paused what he was doing in the game and said to Barbara, "Okay, let's get you set up." After a few minutes of getting her character ready, she joined the world.

"Ha," Li Mei said. "I just got bronze armor. Take that!"

"ha, ha, n00b," the CUYA said. "I've been farming sapphires like they were going to stop generating!" The CUYA's character appeared in head-to-toe purplish armor.

"Oh," Li Mei said unhappily. Barbara sat back and watched, ignoring the game for a few moments. Things were good, better than any memory she had. She felt like it had been centuries since she had been able to sit and enjoy time with someone. Now, amongst her friends, she felt a peace that had been missing. Whatever the future held, with her friends together, they could face it.

Part Three:
Revelations

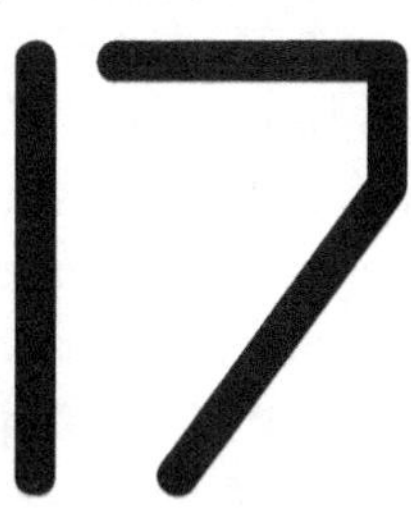

"If I wasn't doing this kind of exploration,
I'd like to be doing some other kind of
exploration. It might be more risky, or less
risky, but, in the business of exploration,
risk is part of the territory."

— Astronaut John L. Phillips

Merlyna looked at the photo. Karl stood in an AI lab, wearing his characteristic red shirt and black pants, with a wry smile. She remembered that she had snapped the picture almost two hundred years ago. Karl had just developed his first constellation-ready AI. He called that RAMEY, Refactored Artificial Machine Entity (iteration) Y. He was so proud of himself. She looked at the small bible in front of her. Somewhere, light years away, her husband would also be celebrating Christmas. She lit the small candle with the image of Mary on it. She hoped her requests for intercession would be granted. A knock on the door interrupted her. She went over to the door of her two-bedroom apartment and opened it.

"I know today is a big thing for you and Karl," Josie said, standing outside, "so Merry Christmas." Josie presented Merlyna with a bottle of wine.

"Merry Christmas, come on in," Merlyna said, taking the wine. Josie entered.

"Do you celebrate Christmas," Merlyna asked. "I mean in a Santa in a red suit way?"

"Japanese Christmas," Josie asked. "No, I wasn't allowed when I was growing up."

"Oh," Merlyna said. "Want a glass of wine?"

"Sure," Josie said. Merlyna opened the bottle and poured the wine into two glasses. She handed one to Josie and took the other.

"To nine more years," Merlyna said.

"Cheers," Josie said, taking a sip of the wine. Both women immediately spat the wine back into the glasses.

"Ugh," Josie said, "that was awful, and I ruined a liver drinking cheap vodka."

"Yuck, where did you get this, Josie," Merlyna asked, wiping her mouth and dabbing her tongue with a napkin.

"Well, I didn't buy the bottle," Josie said, "if that's what you're wondering. We've been dry for a while, and the grapes aren't ready for harvest. I was told one of the guys in Analysis had his own little 'side business,' and I got a bottle from him. Everyone was saying the wine was pretty good."

"This reminds me of the time Karl and I tried to make wine," Merlyna said.

"When was that?" Josie asked.

"In the twelve hundreds, before the Singularity," Merlyna said.

"Wow, the ancient days," Josie said with a smile, showing Merlyna it was a gentle jibe. "Well, was it any good?"

"No, it was a bubbly red," Merlyna said. "We threw it out too." Merlyna crossed to the sink, turned the bottle and her glass over, and poured out the liquid.

"I know about Karl's plan," Josie said. Merlyna put the bottle into her dishwasher and scrubbed her glass.

"Which one," Merlyna said, "He's got so many zany ones."

"About Mommy," Josie said. Merlyna stopped, rinsed and dried the wine glass, and put it back in her cupboard.

"And?" Merlyna said.

"You have my vote of confidence," Josie said. "After what's been going on here, I struggle to see how Mommy couldn't have been aware, if not deeply involved."

"That's a strong statement," Merlyna said warily.

"Look, Merlyna," Josie said. "I'm not the saboteur, and I am not the enemy."

"You know," Merlyna began, "I'm not without reason to worry about you."

"What does that mean," Josie asked. "What do you know?"

"Look, Karl, Greg, Patrick, heck, even Tracie have been worried," Merlyna began. "If I bring you into this, well…"

"Go on," Josie said, "I'm a big girl. Mommy's reach only goes so far."

"Look, the corporation is in big trouble," Merlyna said. "These expeditions were the last attempt to stay relevant. We're lucky right now that the q-array is down. We might be working for Doodle or Hipponike when we get contact restored. Assuming the saboteur hasn't just thrown the entangled elements away."

"Right," Josie said. "Daddy is in charge, and we all follow along."

"Yeah," Merlyna said, "and that thought gives me much hope. Daddy is one of Karl's masterpieces. Mommy, on the other hand…"

"Was made by Central Processing, and she isn't even an IP that CAA owned," Josie said.

"Yes," Merlyna said surprised. "How did you know? That was corporate top secret."

"Greg said as much a while back," Josie said. "He was having a drink with me and grousing about how the SSX made him step down in favor of an AI."

"You two were close," Merlyna said. "I'm sorry he's not here now. Were you two…"

"No," Josie said. "We were like two people that clung to each other in a rain storm. After the rain, wind, and darkness, there was no reason to hold on anymore. Greg always had another layer of personality onion between you and who he was. I never seemed to make the cut to get in deeper. Not like Griff or Karl…"

"For what it's worth," Merlyna said, "I never did either. I was invited because my husband also demanded I be one of the boys."

"Because of being Martin?" Josie said, raising an eyebrow.

"No," Merlyna said. "I've always been 'one of the guys' in many ways. I think Karl knew they'd need me just as much as they need him, and… Well, we need them too."

"I feel that now," Josie said.

"Well," Merlyna said, "you want to join us? Here's what we're up against. Mommy has made some spectacularly bad calls recently, and Greg being out of the picture hasn't helped things. Greg was like a little angel on Mommy's shoulder, pushing her to do the right thing."

Josie laughed, "If Greg is the angel, I'd hate to see who is the devil on her shoulder."

"Patrick," Merlyna said without blinking. "He's been pushing her into riskier and higher stakes ventures."

"Is he compromised," Josie asked.

"Can't tell," Merlyna said. "The founders are like a statistician's random sample set of crotchety old transhumans. Don't let their veneers fool you. Greg was getting lazy. Honestly, he gave up the fight years ago…"

Josie sighed loudly and said, "Oh, Merlyna, thanks! I am glad to hear someone else say that. Greg promised me that he'd step up his game. That's why I am here. He was like, 'Jo, you have to come with us; I need you here with me, like Titan,' I was about to say 'no' when he said, 'It will be like old times, before the landing, I'll run the show myself.' I often wondered if he sabotaged himself to get out of being the leader."

"Karl said as much to me. I wanted to go with Tracie, personally," Merlyna said, "Karl was like, 'Babe, we have to go with Greg; he's going to need us.' I keep thinking about that."

"He's with Patrick," Josie said. "We can't be sure the broadcast was Karl."

"No, it was him," Merlyna said, "and most likely Patrick is dead. Now, Karl and Lisbeth are trapped on a rock while our corporate enemies starve them out, or do gosh knows what to them."

"I have more hope in them than that," Josie said. "Karl can make some serious miracles. He'll get them through things."

"Look, Josie," Merlyna said, "things are messed up in the company, and now, I don't know who I can trust. Karl and I have always had each other's back…"

"Well, you have my help, for what it's worth," Josie said. "I know I'm just a ditsy cheerleader, but I can give you all a nice cheer if it will eliminate Mommy."

Merlyna laughed and said, "I wish it were that simple. Greg got too frustrated to do anything. Patrick seemed part of the problem half the time, and he'd stir up trouble the other half. And Tracie…" Josie waited as Merlyna thought.

"Tracie, what," Josie asked.

"She's a complete nerd," Merlyna said. "She's in her little world. Thankfully, the body divisions make us a lot of money, but we're losing market share even there. Lǐ Huifen, the spy, sold some of our better IPs, and that crippled us."

"Is he the guy Mommy threw out of a body," Josie asked.

"No, he walked away with his shell," Merlyna said, "giving him a freak body would have been justice, but Mommy just let him go."

"What!?" Josie said, "That's not the story I heard."

"Yeah," Merlyna said. "Greg told everyone the story you heard, but Karl, Patrick, and Tracie knew the truth."

"Should I put my resume up on Werewolf?" Josie asked with a laugh.

"Not yet," Merlyna said, "if Karl and I can make it back to Earth or Luna, well…"

"Yes, the vaunted 'Plan B,'" Josie said. "Well, what's the story on that?"

"Plan B is already in place," Merlyna said. "When Greg died, and then hearing about Patrick's death, I expect that Tracie is, or soon will be, dead—if Mommy is to be believed."

"Huh, what?" Josie said.

"Look, I know I made this big show about storming

out on Mommy," Merlyna said. "But I was sending the signal to start Plan B. Now, if I can get back to Sol, I can finish Plan B."

"Well, what is it?" Josie asked.

"Something super secret, and honestly, Karl has only given me a small bit of the whole plan… mainly for my safety. If Doodle or Hipponike caught wind of our actions, they'd kill us. Taking down a nigh-invulnerable AI is something we pathetic transhumans are incapable of, remember?"

Josie nodded, "It's a virus?"

"I wish I knew more. Karl designed Plan B, so it's probably an AI. He has been working on it since he shorted out the shuttle bay."

"That was almost sixty years before we left Luna," Josie said. "Has this been in the works that long?"

Merlyna nodded, "We've been waiting for the green light, and sadly, Patrick, Tracie, and even Greg have been unable to make it happen. If we take down Mommy, I mean push her out, it will be akin to a revolution…"

"Wow," Josie said, "The SSX moved the AIs in because they were supposed to be better at everything. Better than us, lousy humans, less messy, less unpredictable. What you are saying sounds like…"

"Insanity," Merlyna said. "Well, now you know how deep the rabbit hole goes. You still want in?"

"Yes," Josie said. "Greg would want me to pick up where he left off."

*

Griff was in his office. He had the biggest office in the hospital complex. Someday, a hospital administrator would own this office, but he was king here for now. He sat looking at the photo he had taken almost one hundred and fifty years ago. He was with Martha, his son Leonard, and his two daughters, Jacquelin and Maybelle. Griff put his hand to his mouth in thought. He never got maudlin on

Christmas, and it wasn't a religious holiday by any means for him. It was a day for a guy in a big red suit to yell "Ho, ho, ho!" and for kids to get toys. Today, though, he felt down. Martha and he had been continually fighting so much that she moved into the other bedroom in their apartment. That was fine. He'd moved into his office here at the hospital. He'd see Martha in the halls and occasionally the cafeteria; otherwise, she was like a stranger.

Griff looked at Leonard again, and tears came to his eyes. Leonard, called Len by everyone in the family, had been Griff's pride and joy. He'd gone to university at sixteen, even though Griff had pleaded with him to stay in high school for another two years. Griff had pleaded because Len was a great football player and was well on his way to breaking a Luna record in the number of goals scored. But no, Len went to university and medical school after that. He'd graduated at twenty-three and had become a surgeon after that. Griff's tears grew, remembering what happened next. Len had met a young woman, Viola, who was as devout as Griff remembered his grandmother. Viola was a hard-core fire and brimstone Baptist, one of the sects that hated the Singularity with the passion of hell itself. The next thing Griff knew, Viola and Len were married, and the grand-babies came. Those were good times, but the decades flew by. Griff got older and rolled out, decanting into his previous incarnation. But that was when the trouble started.

Len and Viola disapproved of Griff and Martha changing bodies. Len pleaded with Griff to "let God decide" his fate. After begging and pleading, Len and Viola stopped talking to Griff and Martha. The years had made them all strangers. Griff pulled a tissue from the box on his desk and blotted his eyes. He was sure that Len and Viola were gone by now, and his grandchildren would consider him and Martha strangers.

Griff looked at his two daughters in the photo. Both were doctors, too. Jackie worked at Hopkins, where she was a professor, while Maybelle was off on Tau Ceti working as a colonial doctor.

"She probably does house calls," Griff said with a laugh. "She was always stealing my medical bag when she was little." Griff looked at the other photo on his desk; this one was of Jason and him. Griff smiled and wiped away tears. Jason was like having Len back all over again. They were so much alike.

"You know, Greg," Griff said, "maybe you had the right idea after all. This universe has its share of tragedy. Perhaps I need to find an exit off the stage."

He sat there for a moment. He wasn't sure how to process what he was feeling. The mood of society in Sol acted like tomorrow would never come; the party would continue to last until the very end. The only ones who didn't act like that were Karl and Merlyna. Merlyna was here, but she was a mess. Griff had heard about her call from Karl on the q-array. He wasn't sure if he should look her up and talk about it or keep silent.

"Karl, my man," Griff said. "I hope you're okay. I could use a little of your old-time religion right now. I feel like I am a total mess. It seems like everything Martha and I promised each other was a lie."

"Hey, Chief," DADDIE said, projecting into the office. "You okay?"

Griff blotted his eyes and blew his nose, "Yes, Daddy, just fine. I must be allergic to something here in the building."

"Your heart rate and breathing say otherwise, Chief," DADDIE said. "Anything I can do to help?"

"Well, no," Griff said. "Unless you can give me the secret to happiness and the meaning of life?"

"Hey, all I know is it is forty-two," DADDIE said. "That's in a book that Karl likes."

Griff smiled. He knew DADDIE was trying to cheer him up. "That so, eh, Daddy. What do you know about the universe?"

"It's a big place," DADDIE said, "and I call it home. Why?"

"I've been thinking about Len, and maybe I think Greg had the right idea…"

"Greg had the right idea about what?" DADDIE asked.

"Checking out, like my boy did," Griff said.

"You don't know that Len is dead, Chief," DADDIE said, "Without the q-array working, there is no way we can find out with certainty."

"I know, but I am not sure I can keep on going, Daddy," Griff said. DADDIE looked on for a moment. Griff's office door opened; it was Jason and Barbara. Jason came in first, and Barbara followed, holding something behind her back.

"Hey Griff," Jason said. "I know you don't celebrate, but Merii Kurisumasu, as they say in Japan."

Griff laughed. "I'm okay with Japanese Christmas; it's the other one I have issues with."

"Well, Santa told me you were a good boy this year, so he sent this your way," Jason said. He gestured to Barbara, who pulled a large present from behind her back.

"Merry Christmas," she said to Griff, putting a nicely wrapped present on the desk.

Griff smiled at the two of them and said, "Should I wait until later?"

"Open it," they both cried in unison. Griff ripped open the paper like his grandkids used to do. A plain brown box was underneath.

"A box?" Griff said.

"Open it too, silly," Jason said. Griff reached in and pulled out some shears that he had in his desk. They were for cutting bandage tape but could double as a box cutter in a pinch. Griff worked the seam of the box and opened the flaps.

Inside was a mini-orrey showing the planets around L

98-59. A large white arrow pointed to Aurora Dawn, and a holographic note said, "Griff lives here."

Griff laughed out loud at the note, "Figured I'd get lost, eh, Little Rooster?"

Jason smiled and said, "Just in case you decide to run off, you know where your home is now."

Griff smiled back and said, "Well, you two better get along now. Otherwise, Santa won't come."

"That was yesterday," Jason said. "But we'll leave you now. Barbara and I are going over to Li Mei's place. You're welcome to join us there. You too, Daddy."

"Thanks, Buddy," DADDIE said. "I'm going to bow out. Griff and I were finishing some work here."

Griff nodded, thinking about saying yes to Jason, but said, "Go on, I'll think about dropping by when Daddy and I are done." Barbara and Jason left, closing the door.

"Still thinking about checking out," DADDIE asked.

"Not today," Griff replied.

"Good, now check the base of that orrey," DADDIE said. "I helped Jason design it."

Griff turned the model over and looked. Inset on the underside of the base was a small placard that said, "To Griff, with love and friendship, Jason and Barbara."

"You know, Daddy," Griff said. "I may learn to like Japanese Christmas after all."

"Do you need directions to Li Mei's apartment?" DADDIE asked.

"I think I do," Griff said. "But first, I'd like to compose a message to Len. If he's not around, it can clutter a q-net buffer, but if he is, well… I should have said this a long time ago."

"Mystery creates wonder and wonder is the basis of man's desire to understand."

— Astronaut Neil Armstrong

"I don't think he looks good, do you?" Jason asked Barbara as they walked from Griff's office.

"He's been working hard recently, and I don't think he's gotten much sleep," Barbara said. After weeks of casual dating, Barbara finally accepted the concept of Jason as her boyfriend. He just fit into her life like a jigsaw piece, and after a while, she didn't seem to notice him being around. What she did notice was his absence. She now needed to know who she was really. She and Jason had talked, and he went crazy trying to find any personal effects in the cargo that belonged to her. Barbara thought it was adorable, but wasn't surprised when he couldn't find anything. Yet another thing she'd need to ask DADDIE about. She'd been putting off the discussion, worried about what she'd find out. She had suspicions about her previous identity, but she was concerned that the AI would smash those and perhaps tell her that her past was even more unsettling than she suspected.

They walked along the pathways between the buildings. What had been the Xeno Corps base and the expedition's initial outpost had become a town in its own right. The Con Sec Corps had worked tirelessly to keep building places: places to eat, live, and play. In the New Year, there would be a shopping center with robot-manned shops and a proper grocery store.

Although it was December, it wasn't cold or snowy. Aurora Dawn had a very low axial tilt, and the weather at this latitude mimicked the perpetual Earth springtime of Europe or North America's eastern seaboard.

Barbara could almost remember what that was like in Connecticut or Massachusetts, where she figured she'd grown up at one point. She held Jason's hand and listened as her heels clicked along the sidewalk. She had gotten Althea to fabricate a new pair of strappy black heels and was considering asking her for another dress but wasn't sure how to pay her or where the material was coming from.

Clothing was a primary reason she was waiting excitedly for the shopping center to open. Li Mei had invited her over not long after they had all moved in, and she had a closet full of clothing. To her credit, Li Mei admitted that many of the clothes were hand-me-downs from aunts and big sisters. Her family had given Li Mei gifts for many reasons, primarily because she was leaving them. More importantly, Li Mei would have room to store the clothes. Barbara suspected by giving the clothing away, Li Mei's relations could replace them with items they desired under the aegis of "generosity."

"Hey, wait for a second," Jason said, stopping suddenly. They were near the extensive public gardens, and the lights illuminated the CAA flag and the brand-new civic flag that hung on the flagpoles in the center of the garden's entrance.

"Sure," Barbara said, stopping. Jason was acting weirdly, and she wasn't sure what he was doing. He started fishing for something in his pocket. Barbara wondered what was the matter with Jason and said, "Jace, you okay? Analysis says Aurora Dawn has no ants, so why are you acting like they are crawling around in your trousers?"

"Aww darn it," Jason said. "I knew this was going to happen."

Jason started pulling items from his pockets. The first out was his wallet, a small collapsible gray plastic square. Next was a set of physical keys. Barbara suspected they were to some corporate secrets safe. Finally, Jason pulled out a small box. Barbara's eyes grew wide; she remembered a similar box.

Jason got down on one knee and said, "Look, Barbara, I really like you. I have fallen in love with you, and I want to try to make a life here with you."

Barbara wasn't sure what to say. On one hand, she

had butterflies floating in her stomach and was willing to say "yes". However, she was worried about her past and who she was. Would Jason accept her if she ended up being someone awful?

"Um," Barbara said.

"Well?" Jason asked hopefully.

"Jason, I like you…"

"But no?" Jason said.

"Let me just get this out first," Barbara said. Jason nodded. Barbara continued, "Look if I didn't have these memories and this weird past, I'd say yes. I like you, maybe even love you. I can't be certain where things will go, but they've been perfect so far. I need to find out who I am to figure out where I am going." Jason looked like he'd been mugged.

"So that's a no," he said, retracting the box. Barbara smiled and put her hand on the box. "Listen, Dikkert, you've done this the wrong way. You're supposed to show me the ring, so I can't say no…" Jason looked confused. Barbara opened the little box. Inside was a blue-violet Tanzanite gem on a white gold ring. The ring would have been worth a small fortune in Sol since humans had mined out Tanzanite on Earth in the one-hundred-and-twenty-second century. Barbara's mouth opened in surprise.

Still, on his knee, Jason smiled and said, "Sorry, this is the first time I proposed. I suppose with your past, you had millions of guys proposing to you."

"Not really," Barbara said. "Would it surprise you to know I have a memory of proposing to a girl?"

Jason looked pensive. "It shouldn't, but I have a hard time seeing you as anyone but who you are now."

Barbara considered the pros and cons. Finally, she said, "Well, if you really feel this way, then I accept. But first, I need to clear up who I was! Then we can get married!"

"Deal!" Jason said, hopping up like an excited terrier.

He threw his arms around Barbara, and she embraced him as well, kissing him quickly.

"Now, let me put this beautiful thing on," Barbara said. "I won't wear it all the time. I still have to get my hands dirty, and I'm afraid I'll lose this beautiful stone."

"I understand," Jason said. "I've been a nervous wreck since I got this back."

Putting on the ring, Barbara looked at the band on her finger. The gemstone was perfectly balanced against her finger and the ring's fit was exact.

"All right, my fiancé, I have to ask," Barbara said. "Where did you get this? Is Mommy going to come after you for theft of corporate property? Or have you been indebted for a thousand years for this gem? If so, I don't want it."

Jason let Barbara go and laughed. "You wouldn't believe me if I told you."

Barbara looked at Jason skeptically. "Now I have to know."

"Well, remember last week when Stimson was out sick?" Jason said. Barbara nodded. He continued, "He was supposed to be on grid square X20, so I picked up his survey."

Barbara smiled and said, "Wait, the boss was getting his hands dirty?"

"Well, I like being a scout, too! Besides, I needed to get away from all the e-papers. I took the survey which was mostly savanna. As I was nearing the southern end of the grid square, I started moving into a mountainous region and saw gold on some of the cliff walls," Jason said.

"Like real gold," Barbara asked.

"No, I checked that out with Analysis, too," Jason said. "That was just fool's gold. Anyway, I got out to take a sample and saw a small dark vein. I thought it was coal, so I took a sample. Anyway, the sample I grabbed shattered, and I had bits in some of my pockets."

"Accidentally, I hope," Barbara said.

"Yeah, the stuff sort of exploded on me, I swear," Jason said. "Anyway, I get back, and Analysis goes crazy over the sample. They made me shake out my pockets and collected all the shards. I get home and start changing, and this piece falls out of my pocket. I freaked out and went back immediately. When I returned, Édouard said, 'No problem. We've tagged all the bits you found initially, so keep it. You get a finder's fee. Take the stone and call it good.'"

Barbara scowled. "I don't think Mommy will see things that way."

"Well, I queried Daddy on the subject, and he was like, 'Okay, Buddy, let me check the regulations,' He came back a few minutes later and said that technically, I needed to pay for the stone, but since I was also the site discoverer I get to keep the gem. I just had to sign a non-disclosure, no-sale agreement. I put my chop so fast on that doc, your head would spin," Jason said.

Barbara smiled. "You learned gem cutting, too? And where did you get the band? Stealing that as well? My boyfriend—the corporate thief?"

"No, no," Jason said, turning red. "First off, it's fiancé now, my fiancée, and no, I bought the gold…"

"But you can't afford that," Barbara said. "Strangely, I know how much you make."

Jason gave a wicked grin. "Ah, the real reason you want to marry me emerges!"

Barbara laughed, "Um, no, your salary doesn't make you a master of the universe."

Jason chucked. "No, but Mom and Dad left me a bit of money, not Xenon class notes, but I have more than enough Krypton creds in my bank balance. Being an only child to a pair of transhumans means you can get by comfortably. I just tapped into that for the band. Also, one of Édouard's guys is a lapidary and does stone cutting and polishing for fun. When I got the ownership squared away, he approached me and begged me to try to cut and polish the stone."

"How much did that cost you?" Barbara said. "I mean, geez, I feel like I have the cost of a spaceship on my finger now."

"He did it for free," Jason said, and Barbara's face lit up in surprise. "He said it was a 'once in a lifetime' chance for him."

"Wow, he did a great job," Barbara said.

"That's not what he said when he gave the ring back," Jason replied. "He said a jeweler could tell where he messed up and the ring's value would be less."

Barbara clasped the ring to her chest, cherishing it. "I don't care. This ring is priceless to me."

Jason smiled. "Cool, let's get going. Li Mei is waiting for us, and Xander, well…"

Barbara smiled and took Jason's hand. "Wait! This was a competition between you two nerds, wasn't it?"

Jason turned red in embarrassment. "Yeah, we sort of started talking about you two."

Jason tugged at Barbara's hand, and they began walking. Barbara thought about what to say but decided to just walk, hand in hand, to not spoil the moment.

Jason and Xander had become closer over the past few weeks, with Jason, Xander, and the CUYA spending their off hours playing video games. Barbara suspected that the male bonding had allowed Xander to open up to Jason in a way he didn't with Barbara. In many ways, Barbara missed the camaraderie with many of her male coworkers, being able to kick back and joke. Her lack of male access contrasted with an ability to discuss almost anything with Li Mei and other female expedition members. Barbara couldn't decide if she liked the female conversations better than the male ones, but she also understood that form dictated function. She couldn't easily hang with the boys without other girls getting concerned. Barbara smiled at the memory of Li Mei being so possessive about Xander. Barbara could hang with Xander as Jason's girlfriend, but Xander kept a distance between them.

Barbara stopped pondering as they approached the building. Jason smiled at her as they entered the foyer.

"I smelled the smoke," Jason said. "Helium for your thoughts?"

Barbara pulled her hand from Jason, put it around his waist, squeezed him, and said, "Nothing, just thinking about everything that's happened."

Unlinking her arm, Jason and Barbara entered the elevator and approached Li Mei's apartment. The building was quiet. Barbara realized Con Sec Corps was overbuilding with the hope that when the expedition reached the ten-year mark, the flats would be sold or rented to the second wave of colonists, which would number in the thousands. Even a century old, the apartments would become immensely valuable to the corporation as the "sodbusters" would need a place to stay before they moved to their homesteads.

Li Mei opened the door. "Hi, come on in," she said. Inside her small apartment, Christmas lights were everywhere. A green cardboard tree stood in the corner, and the words "Merry Christmas" in Latin characters and kana hung on the walls.

"Do you want some egg nog," Li Mei asked as Barbara and Jason entered.

"No thanks," Barbara said.

"Sure," Jason said. "Your place looks great, Li Mei."

Li Mei said, "Thanks," and bowed out to get the egg nog for Jason. She returned a minute or two later with a glass. Li Mei was about to say something when there was a knock on her door.

"One minute," she said as she went to the door and opened it. Outside was Xander with a bouquet.

"Get ready," Jason said to Barbara with a wink.

"Hi," Xander said, "These are for you."

Li Mei accepted the bouquet of red and green roses and said, "Thanks, honey. You are so sweet. Come inside!"

Xander entered and waved to everyone. Barbara could see he was a nervous wreck. Xander came in and stood in the center of the living room. Li Mei put the flowers in a vase and returned to the small party.

"Want something to drink, honey," she asked Xander.

"No, I… uh…" Xander began.

Li Mei looked at her boyfriend, "Are you okay?" she asked.

Xander dropped to a knee and said in a rush, "Li Mei, I want you to be the queen of my digital world. Please marry me!"

Li Mei looked like she had been punched in the face. Her eyes opened wide, and her face showed a dreamy smile. Xander also presented a set of candles and a small tin of tea.

"Finally," she said softly.

"Huh?" Xander said.

"Oh, yes!" Li Mei said. Xander stood and attempted to kiss her, but she stopped him. "Is there a ring, honey?" Li Mei asked.

Xander looked sheepish and said, "Right." He tapped every pocket on his cargo pants and moved to his white sports coat before finally stopping on an outside waist pocket. He pulled out a box. Inside was an oval-cut Garnet with a gold band. Li Mei's eyes teared up, and Xander looked embarrassed.

"What?" Xander said, "Did I do something wrong?"

"No," Li Mei said. "This is beautiful. It looks almost exactly like the ring Yichen gives Jia Li in the third series."

Xander smiled from ear to ear. "So I did a good job?"

Li Mei kissed him on the cheek. "Yes, an amazing job."

"Congratulations," Jason and Barbara said in unison. Li Mei put the ring on and waved it around on her finger.

She then leaned over and kissed Xander again. He hugged her and then said to Jason, "Gaming time?"

Jason nodded. "*Soldiers of Duty*, or will we try something else?"

"I've been looking at *Ancient Torc*, it looks insane," Xander said.

"Isn't that single player only?" Jason asked.

"Yeah, but Vikas coded a mod to play co-op. It can be janky, but I figured we'd try it," Xander said. Barbara watched as the men discussed the games, then turned to Li Mei.

"Can I see the ring again, closer?" Barbara asked. Li Mei presented her hand, and Barbara studied the ring.

"It is gorgeous," Barbara said, releasing Li Mei's hand. As she did, Li Mei saw the ring on Barbara's hand.

"Oh my gosh!" she said in excitement, "Jason proposed to you! I'm so excited! When are you getting married?"

Barbara sighed and said, "I need to figure out who I was first, but then after that, I don't know, soon?"

Li Mei scowled and said, "This is what you get for not having sisters. We usually consult a fortune teller, but maybe Daddy is a better oracle in your case."

Barbara looked confounded, "Honestly, I just want something small and intimate. What about you?"

Li Mei smiled. "There are a lot of traditions… I am unsure how we'll make them all work with our relatives in another solar system…"

Li Mei was about to continue when there was a knock at the door. She looked confused but ran to the door. A feat Barbara found interesting in Li Mei's extremely high heels. Li Mei opened the door to see Griff outside.

"Happy holidays," he said.

"Hi, Doctor Tomkins," Li Mei said. "Please come in."

"I was looking for…" Griff said when Jason

interrupted.

"Hey Griff," Jason said, poking his head around to see through the door, "You made it!"

Griff smiled ear to ear. "Yes, I had some time, and I thought, why not…"

"Come in, please," Li Mei said. Griff entered carrying a bottle of wine.

"Where is Martha," Jason asked.

"She couldn't make it," Griff said. "I brought this bottle of wine. I don't know if it is any good. I don't touch the stuff myself."

Li Mei took the bottle and said, "Thanks, should I open it?"

"If you'd like," Griff said.

"I'll have a glass," Jason said.

"I'll try it," Xander said. It might help me with this game. Man, is this impossible… I love it."

"I'll try a glass," Barbara said. "But, I prefer beer if I am drinking—a nice lambic or fruity pale ale."

Griff came over and stood by Barbara as Jason and Xander started playing.

"I knew someone who liked the same types of beer," Griff said wistfully.

"Oh really?" Barbara asked, "Who is that?"

"Oh, you didn't know him," Griff said.

"Try me," Barbara said.

"It was Greg—I mean General Body," Griff said, "He was the most macho guy, except for his beer."

Barbara smiled and said, "I'm sure it's all about the taste."

Griff smiled and said, "Greg used to say that too."

Barbara went silent, and Li Mei came and presented the glasses. As Barbara reached out for the wine, Griff noticed her ring and said, "That is a nice ring. Did Jason give that to you?"

"Yes, we're engaged," Barbara said.

"When's the happy day?" Griff asked.

"Well, until I figure out what's going on with my memories, we're in a holding pattern," Barbara said.

"Have you talked to Steve?" Griff asked.

Barbara shook her head, "I haven't..."

"He's a nice guy," Griff said.

"I'm not fond of head-shrinkers," Barbara said, "I feel like I've got a small enough skull already."

Griff smiled and chuckled, "You know, Barbara, now you really sound like Greg. Are you his niece or a cousin?"

"Not that I know of," Barbara said. Griff's eyes narrowed, and it looked like he wanted to say something but decided against it. Instead, he pulled out a mini-tablet and looked at the clock on the display.

"I'm sorry, folks. It's getting late, and I need to get up early in the morning," Griff said abruptly.

"Come on, Griff," Jason said. "You haven't even played this game. It's worse than *Soldiers of Duty* for difficulty, but Xander really slays on it."

"Naw," Griff said, "I've gotta go, Little Rooster..."

Griff was going to continue when there was a loud explosion, and the ground trembled.

"What in Hades!" Griff shouted. Jason and Xander ran to the window and looked out. A few blocks away, black smoke was spewing from a building.

"What the..." Jason said.

"Dude!" Xander sputtered. "That's my lab! I mean, the Xeno Analysis and Con Sec Analysis labs!"

Barbara said, "Huh, someone's blown up your lab?"

Griff looked back at her and asked, "How do you figure that?"

Li Mei looked at Barbara in confusion, "What makes you think that?"

Barbara shrugged, "I just feel it in my gut."

"Be thankful for problems. If they were less difficult, someone with less ability might have your job."

— Astronaut Jim Lovell

Josie's eyes were red; she was exhausted. She and Merlyna had rushed from Merlyna's to the ops center after the explosion. The subsequent fire had consumed everything that the blast had missed. The saboteur was raising the stakes. Josie was upset and frustrated. Merlyna and she had cast their nets and caught nothing. Josie was monitoring for unusual radiation sources in the vain hope they could recover the q-array entangled elements and catch the thief. Merlyna had been going over the suspects. Everything pointed at Griff, but this time, Jason, DADDIE, Li Mei, Xander, and Barbara could account for his whereabouts, eliminating him from consideration, at least for the explosion and fire.

"Maybe there are multiple saboteurs," Merylna said, entering. "Have a coffee."

"Thanks," Josie said, drinking the supplied cup. "Ugh, this has creamer in it."

"That's what I remember you liking," Merlyna said.

"Not anymore, apparently," Josie said with a laugh. "I need the caffeine, though; I'll chug it."

Merlyna shrugged. "I wish Karl were here. He could roast some beans. He'd also probably have found the culprit or culprits by now. Probably have triangulated their movements via wireless networks or some insidious AI bug."

"Well, maybe we should…" Josie said but was cut off by Merlyna.

"I tried those but had no luck," Merlyna said. "I queried Daddy too, and he started giving me that, 'Sorry Pumpkin, I just don't have any more data' responses."

"We're going to collapse as a colony at this rate," Josie said. "That lab was our heart. They cataloged everything we collected and did. Their projections would have assured a green light for so many ventures. Now all the

SSX-required proof is up in smoke."

"We have the sources where the specimens came from. We can recollect it all," Merlyna said.

"Yeah, but that doubles the cost. When I last looked at the projections, we were way in the black," Josie said.

"Who knew about that?" Merlyna asked. "Maybe that's a lead?"

"Yeah, just about everyone," Josie said, "Hey, wait, that gives me an idea…"

"Are you thinking what I am thinking?" Merlyna said.

Josie nodded and said, "We can say that not all the samples got wiped out and that…"

"Most of them were stored off-site, in a top-secret place," Merlyna said excitedly, cutting Josie off.

"A place where we can set a trap," the ladies said in unison.

"Right," Josie said. "I need the city plans. Let's find a spot that looks too enticing and gives our bad guy no way out."

"Right," Merlyna said as she leaned over Josie's shoulder to look at the city plans with Josie. The ladies carefully concocted their trap.

*

Barbara was tired. She trod along the sidewalk towards the medical complex. The night before, Jason had refused to go home after escorting her back to her apartment. They had left Li Mei's after the explosion and spent the rest of the evening talking at her place. Jason was worried about her, but she was more worried about him. At least she was continually moving on survey missions, where he was stuck in the Xeno Corps offices. Thankfully, DADDIE had confirmed the lab was empty, and no one was hurt. Barbara entered the medical center and went to the kiosk to register. A thirty-year-old man stood there.

"Barbara," he asked.

"Yes," Barbara said.

"I'm Steve," the man said.

"Hi, Dr. Molyneaux. Nice to meet you," Barbara said, presenting her hand.

"It's just Steve," he said, shaking her hand. "Come on back, let's talk."

Barbara followed Steve, feeling unexpectedly nervous. She expected a chair for Steve and a long black leather couch she could lay on. Instead, the office had two easy chairs with ottomans.

"No couch?" Barbara asked.

Steve laughed and said, "I get that all the time. Um, no. I want to chat, not give you a chance for a nap. Trust me, with the rates I charge the company, the last thing Mommy wants is you sleeping on my time."

Barbara laughed. She could see the AI raising a ruckus about that. She walked over and sat down, putting her feet on the ottoman.

"Is this where we talk about my mother?" Barbara said.

"Well, we could start there," Steve replied, "But let's start with why you're here."

"Sure, makes sense," Barbara said. "Look I am nervous about all this and can't tell you why…"

Steve nodded and said, "Well then, let's start there… Have you been to therapy before?"

"Yes, I have memories of therapy, and they weren't good," Barbara said.

"Wait a moment, you said 'memories of therapy.' Most people would say, 'I've been in therapy.' How you say that sounds like you are remembering someone else's life."

Barbara pondered that statement for a moment. "Yes, exactly. When I decanted, I woke up feeling like a stranger in my skin."

Steve nodded. "That's not unusual. I've seen many people struggling to adjust to their new shells. It usually clears up with time."

"Well, for me, it didn't. I've been in this body for almost six months, and I still feel like a stranger in it, though that feeling is finally fading," Barbara said.

"Tell me about that," Steve said.

"At first, I'd have these memories of being treated differently. The people would address me differently..." Barbara said, and Steve stopped her, asking, "How so?"

"They'd call me 'sir,'" Barbara responded.

"Oh, like you were a man?" Steve asked.

"Yes," Barbara said, "When it is pretty obvious, I am not..."

"Why is that obvious," Steve asked. "We live in an age where things like race and gender are only obvious after a discussion with the intelligence on the inside."

Barbara thought for a moment. "I suppose you're right, but I don't feel like I act like a man..."

Steve responded, "Well, no, but that's how the bodies are wired. If you took my consciousness and placed me in a female shell, I'd walk and, to a certain degree, talk like a woman. Why? Because my physical body would be female. If you examined me and scrutinized even minute actions and expressions, I might say or do something more masculine than you would expect. But that expectation is more about your gender stereotypes than my behavior."

"Sure, but I had these memories where I was a guy," Barbara said.

"Wait, you said you had the memories. Have they changed?" Steve asked.

"Yes," Barbara said. "At first, it was like I was someone else. Now, when I have the memories, everyone calls me Barbara and treats me like I'm female. But that still is a problem..."

"Why's that," Steve asked.

"Well, I remembered being taught to stab a mannequin in the face," Barbara said. "Daddy said I was a natural and only sixteen. So, how is that possible?"

Steve sat there and thought for a moment. "I don't know. I know Daddy is incapable of outright lying. Perhaps he has a reason for saying what he said. Diagnosing AI is way above my paycheck, but let's assume your memory is real. What do you think it means?"

"I think it means I am someone else," Barbara said.

"Well, how so? Right now, looking at you, you seem like a sixteen-year-old to me," Steve said.

"I have all of these memories and knowledge I shouldn't have," Barbara said. "And the background I should have, well, I can't remember it."

"Aha, I see. Well, what do you feel like you are missing?" Steve asked.

"I can't remember my mother or my father. I don't remember my school years or being in high school," Barbara said.

"Why does that bother you? There are plenty of transhumans that have forgotten much about their original shells or formative years," Steve asked.

"Shouldn't I know that? I feel weird that I have all these old memories. But none fit if I am a sixteen-year-old."

"Well, let's pretend they do belong to you. Does that change who you are right this minute?" Steve asked.

"I, uh, don't know," Barbara said. "I guess not."

"Then why does it matter," Steve asked. "Shouldn't we focus on what we can change?"

"Well, I am worried I am someone I am not. What if I am someone terrible who is running away from something?" Barbara said.

"How does that change things now," Steve asked. "If you were, what would you do?"

"I suppose not much would change, really, and what can I do but keep doing what I am doing?"

"Exactly," Steve said. "I think your biggest conundrum is what Daddy has told you versus your memories. Have you asked him about that?"

Barbara paused for a moment before answering, "No, I want to, but I am worried if I find out something about my past that might hurt my boy—I mean my fiancé."

"Ah, now, I think we're coming to why there is an issue, fear of rejection," Steve said.

"Maybe," Barbara said; before she could continue, a soft chime sounded.

"Look, we're out of time," Steve said. "Think about this session, and if you need another one, ask Daddy for a time slot. I think you are perfectly fine and suffering from a decanter rebound. I've seen a lot of this behavior. Once people accept their memories, they usually quickly make peace with everything."

Barbara stood up. "Thanks, Steve."

Steve pointed her to the door, and Barbara exited. She wasn't sure Steve had made much of a difference. However, she did decide she really must speak to DADDIE. After decanting, his initial statements were the only evidence that Barbara was really Barbara.

*

Barbara's heart raced. She decided to confront DADDIE. No more putting it off. She walked towards the central computer building that held the matrices that stored DADDIE. She'd get her answers now. She entered the cold room that sat outside where the matrices were processing. She could have made this call from her apartment but came to the source. She didn't want any distractions, network hiccups, or just good old fate to get in the way of her question.

"Hey Tiger," DADDIE said as his avatar appeared. "What are you up to?"

Barbara shivered in the chilly room but was determined to press the AI and keep him on topic. "Hi Daddy, I'm here because I need to know something."

"Sure, Tiger. That's what I am here for. Ask your question," DADDIE said.

Barbara didn't understand why she was suddenly nervous. With a quick question, she could learn who she was, and then get back to her tasks and living life.

"Who am I, Daddy," she asked.

DADDIE's avatar scowled. "Is this a diagnostic test? You're Barbara Gordon, a Vanguard scout. If that doesn't suffice, I can rattle off your Corporate ID, title, salary, and anything else."

"No, you know why I'm asking. Who am I—*really*," Barbara said. She knew DADDIE would be evasive, and she wanted to pin him down once and for all.

"Wow, that's like a Kierkegaard existence question. Don't we all ask that sometime?" DADDIE said with a smile.

"Look, you aren't a good liar. You shouldn't mislead me," Barbara said, "I know I am not really Barbara."

"But Tiger, yes, you are," DADDIE said.

"Fine! Give me all the expedition members' names and your nicknames for them in a printout," Barbara said. A small cube spat out a table on a sixty-centimeter by eighty-five-centimeter piece of paper. Barbara grabbed the sheet and looked it over. She first noted the watermark that signaled the paper was recycled. Next, she read the list from the top to the bottom. At the top were all of the Corporate Corps, starting with Josie and moving down the organizational chart.

"Where is Karl on this?" Barbara said, "And for that matter, where is Greg's nickname?"

"Karl is Sonny," DADDIE said. "He isn't on the expedition, so I didn't include him."

"And Greg?" Barbara asked.

"He's dead and, therefore, not on the expedition," DADDIE replied. As he did so, the holo-projector flickered, and his image seemed to skip and blink in and out.

"Daddy, you can't lie to me," Barbara said. "Am I Karl or Greg?"

DADDIE's avatar sat staring at Barbara for a good long while. Barbara was about to say something when he responded, "You can't be Karl as he is with Patrick's expedition on HD 260655."

"And Greg? What happened to him," Barbara said.

"Oh boy," DADDIE said. "Sit down, Tiger. I am about to get all *from a certain point of view* on you, like in *Planetary Conflicts*." Barbara pulled over a tall chair, sat down, and crossed her legs.

"All right, I need to know. Who am I?" she said.

"This is complicated," DADDIE said. "You see, I rescued your consciousness at around ninety-two or ninety-three percent. Anything below that, and well, you wouldn't have enough marbles to, you know, be you."

"Okay, what happened?" Barbara said.

"So, Greg, man, oh man, what a great guy," DADDIE said. Barbara was about to interrupt as she worried he was going on a tangent, but the avatar waved her off. He put up a finger to ask her for patience. "He contributed to my code base, you know? Anyway, Greg was fetched from the archive, and the needle had him ready to inject when I detected a small computing flaw. Just a couple of bits improperly encoded on the needle. Now, I know that doesn't seem like much, but with consciousness, it's fatal."

Barbara nodded. Her heart thundered now that she finally might know the truth. DADDIE continued, "As the shell started the injection process, I did a silent abort. The problem was that the buffer overflowed, and I lost the pointers on the harmonics. In a sense, I scrambled what Greg's consciousness was like an egg gets scrambled for breakfast."

"Sure. So, I'm Greg?" Barbara asked, feeling more comfortable with the thought.

"Well, a little bit yes, and a little bit no," DADDIE said. "You don't have the index of Greg's memories anymore. I mean, maybe in fifty years, you'll have spent enough time pondering out his life enough that you can put events on a timeline. But, as it stands, you're seeing what Greg's memories are like now… You get flashes of events with a lack of association."

"But I'm Greg, right?" Barbara asked again.

"Metaphysically, sure. Medically, maybe. Legally, probably not," DADDIE said. "I didn't mean to mess you up, Tiger, but I also did a chemical block on your shell's memory receptors. I needed to protect you."

"Wait, what?" Barbara said. "You robbed me of my identity to protect me?"

DADDIE grew worried as Barbara's voice grew shrill. "Yes, you see, the needle had issues. The body had issues, too! It was like they were encoded to fail when you were injected. Listen, Tiger, as you saw yesterday, a saboteur is running around gunning for the colony. You were number one on their radar."

Barbara looked stunned, "The bad guys got me?"

"Sort of, I improvised," DADDIE said. "Look, it's not trained in my models to bend the truth and go against someone's intentions. Greg was all about being an alpha male, and his profile read like a who's who of testosterone-laden leading men."

"Therefore, you turned me into a teenage girl? That was your brilliant plan, Daddy?" Barbara growled.

"Look, I hid you. Mommy jacked with the expedition roster, so I uh… got creative…" DADDIE said.

"Wait, who is Barbara Gordon then?" she asked.

"Well, the alter ego of a superhero from the ancient days before the Singularity," DADDIE said.

"Seriously!" Barbara responded. "In other words, I need to dye my hair red now?"

DADDIE's avatar laughed, "Uh no, again, sorry, Tiger. I am not programmed to be creative, plus you know… Karl was the main programmer and a comic book nerd…"

"Well, that chowder head is going to get a knuckle

sandwich next time I see him," Barbara said.

"Well, Tiger, if it helps, ask him about Kate Lenart. You might find he's not nearly the Neanderthal you think he is. Anyway, I did what I did to save you. Simple probability said the last place the saboteur would expect Greg's consciousness was a teenage girl. Also, I sent you to the Vanguard because, well, the Xeno Corps was going to detour away from the main expedition several times, and I took a little risk that the saboteur wasn't in the Xeno Corps. Plus, I trust Jason. He's a good kid with a low probability of being the saboteur." Barbara sat and thought about what DADDIE said.

"What now, Daddy," Barbara asked. "Do I roll out and find a male shell? Assume the role as the leader of the expedition?"

"Well, technically, I'm the leader, remember?" DADDIE said, "I suppose you could roll out and decant into a male body. But as far as shouting, 'I'm Greg!' to the others. I am afraid that's not an option for a lot of reasons. One is the saboteur is still out there, and the other is… Well, I won't support you if you say you're Greg."

"Wait, why not? I mean, I have all these Greg memories! I can go back and be Greg, and it will all be okay," Barbara said, sounding more like a teenager than an ancient general.

"Come on, Tiger, you know better. What would you say to Griff, Merlyna, or Josie," DADDIE said.

"Or Jason," Barbara said, feeling more nervous and worried than ever. "I kissed him… I mean, we're kind of engaged…"

"Yep," DADDIE said. "That's why you're not really Greg anymore. Look, Karl programmed me. He's had dozens of shells, and he'll tell you everyone was different. Heck, based on the best guesses of biologists, you humans are just long strings of 'ten-minute men' strung together across a lifetime or, in the case of a transhuman, many lifetimes.

Supposedly, every ten minutes, you are someone else. Don't even get me started on whether you are the same person who wakes up from a long night's sleep. I'll pop a matrix trying to process that."

"What are you saying, Daddy," Barbara asked. "I'm perplexed. I have a head full of Greg memories and very few Barbara memories."

"Really, what did you eat for breakfast? What did you do yesterday? What did Li Mei say to you the last time you talked to her?" DADDIE said. "I think what you keep focusing on is in the past. Maybe you should take this opportunity to reinvent yourself. Greg had five shells, all clones of his original body. Some were modified to support his work, but they were all the same boring vanilla ice cream. Now you've got a cone full of pistachio. Why not enjoy it?"

"I see what you're saying, but our bodies are unlike ice cream. Look, I remember how Karl and I—*err*—Greg were going to pull the plug on Mommy. I remember coding you. I remember starting CAA. You're telling me to forget all that so that I can be a Vanguard scout?"

"For now, yes," DADDIE said, "After the ten-year mark if you want to go back and be Greg or model underwear in Edinburgh, that's all on you. We've got odds to beat here, and Greg understood that. This is one of the reasons I keep trying to explain to you that you aren't Greg. Not anymore."

"But…" Barbara began but was cut off by DADDIE.

"Josie," was all he said.

"What about Josie?" Barbara said.

"Have you ever really asked her about who she is? It might surprise you that Josie isn't her original name, plus that lady has swapped shells like the galaxy was running out of shells," DADDIE responded.

Barbara tried to remember all the times that Greg

and Josie had talked, and she realized that Greg hadn't done much soul-searching or sharing of feelings. Even with the closest members of his company, people with whom he was supposedly close friends. As Barbara, she had shared more and been far closer with other humans than she ever remembered as Greg.

"I see you are thinking about it," DADDIE said. "Now you see why I said what I said. Things aren't that cut and dry anymore."

Barbara nodded. "Okay, so I'm Barbara now. Does that mean I need to find a latex superhero costume and some red hair dye?"

"Hey, if that's what makes you get up in the morning, go for it," DADDIE said with a chuckle. "I'd suggest you find out what makes you tick as Barbara. Let Greg be dead. He did what he needed to do. Now, go off and do something else. Like I said before, talk to Josie. She's the master of switching shells and rolling the dice. I can't help you with that; as an AI, we're pretty strictly coded on identity. If Sonny were here, you could ask him too."

"You realize I don't have those relationships anymore," Barbara said dryly.

"Well, get to know them again, as Barbara," DADDIE said. "The problem with you, Tiger, is that you want this to be easy. Karl said as much. He said you've been resting on your laurels, and now you don't have them anymore."

"Karl has a big mouth," Barbara said, then sighed. "He's probably right, though. I remember that everyone always deferred to Greg and looked to him – especially when there was a problem – to come up with a solution. I don't miss those times at all. Now, I give my problems to Jason or his bosses and can sit back and watch movies or break away from the hassle and worry. It is kind of…"

"Nice?" DADDIE said, "Well, there is that. Plus, you can still work on the issues Greg has left unfinished.

You'll do them as Barbara now, though."

"Yeah, I see that."

"Now, go on and get out there and be the Barbara you need to be," DADDIE said, "but before you go… one more thing…"

Barbara hesitated and said, "What's that?"

"No matter who you are, you will always be Tiger to me," DADDIE said.

"Thanks, Daddy," Barbara said. "Even though you turned me into a teenage girl, wrestled the expedition from me, and put a block on memories, I'm glad you're here."

DADDIE laughed. "You think I wanted to be the leader? I had my own countdown clock to when you'd decant."

"Seriously, thanks for saving me," Barbara said. "As weird as this experience has been, I now have a chance for some payback."

"You're welcome, and thanks for not disconnecting me," DADDIE said.

"I'm saving the disconnections for other people," Barbara said.

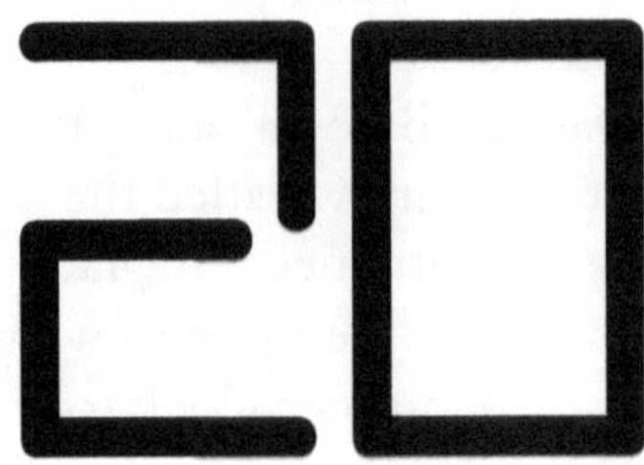

"The biggest technical challenge to sending astronauts on farther and longer missions is biomedical: How do we keep them healthy?"

— Astronaut Leroy Chiao

Barbara saw the notice on the electronic board she used to get her daily assignments: expedition leadership had halted all surveys, and the teams were to meet at the Xeno Corps conference room at 8:30 a.m.

"We have a conference room," Li Mei asked as she approached Barbara in the sled garage.

"I guess so," Barbara said. "I'll need to figure out where it is. Wanna find the conference room together?"

"Sure," Li Mei said. She and Barbara started walking from the garage to Jason's office.

"You know, you're calmer this week," Li Mei said.

"I've done some meditation," Barbara said.

"Really," Li Mei replied, "that makes sense."

"What about you? How is the wedding planning?" Barbara asked. Li Mei and Xander were busy planning their wedding. After consulting an AI fortune teller, they were shooting for an early Ninth Month date. Li Mei would be sixteen, which was supposedly necessary according to the fortune teller. Barbara often forgot how young Li Mei was; she always acted older than her years. Barbara searched her memories and concluded she was an only child. However, if she had older siblings, there would probably have been a lot of episodes in her memories that would have been avoided.

As they approached the Xeno Corps offices, Jason came out of the building. Barbara had made some excuses about seeing him, as she was still trying to make a good decision about how to tell him about her past.

"Hey, ladies," Jason said. "I bet you are wondering where the conference room is."

"Yes," Li Mei said.

"Awesome, follow me," Jason replied, leading them down a path. As they walked, he said quietly to Barbara,

"Hiya."

"Hi," Barbara said.

"I've missed you," Jason said.

"Sorry, I've been busy…" Barbara replied.

"You busy tonight?" Jason asked. Barbara didn't respond as the trio came to a brand new office space with a small sign with "Xeno Corps" on it.

"Why aren't we moved in here?" Barbara asked.

"That's what this meeting is about," Jason said.

"I'm going to go in and get a spot," Li Mei said.

"Cool, grab some coffee or tea and a muffin," Jason said. Li Mei entered, and Barbara stood there feeling awkward.

"Well, what about tonight?" Jason asked. "I'm feeling like I did something wrong."

"Look, Jason," Barbara said. "I found out about my past."

"Oh," Jason said, looking a little hurt and worried. "I get it if you don't want to discuss it."

Barbara didn't know how to proceed. She stood silently for a minute while Jason stood and looked hurt and a little angry. Finally, Barbara decided to be direct, "Look, Jason, I was Greg before the decant. I understand if you don't want to marry me or hang out."

Jason looked like he'd won the birth lottery. "Cool! You owe me some money! Remember, we had a bet!" The shock of the statement made Barbara laugh.

"It all makes sense now," Jason said. "You decided to become a girl to weasel out on the bet! Wait until Griff finds out! From now on, he and I will need to watch you like a hawk!"

"No," Barbara said. "You can't tell anyone! The reason why Greg died was because someone was out to kill him, and if they find out about me…"

Jason looked horrified. "They'll try to kill you too!" Jason started to scan the area, looking for possible attacks.

"I checked before I mentioned anything," Barbara said. "And as far as our bet, I don't ever recall accepting this supposed 'bet.' I think you and Griff concocted the whole thing."

"That's ten Argon credits you owe me since I decanted first," Jason said. I will take them in printed bills or via a digital payment transaction…" Then, softly, he said, "Or we can just get married…"

Barbara looked at Jason in surprise. "You still want to get married? What about my past?"

"You were Greg. You *are* Barbara *now*," Jason said quietly. "I like you! I like being around you. Besides, you are much better looking now."

Barbara chuckled. "Come on, I wasn't that bad-looking before."

"You weren't my type then," Jason said. "Plus, you were that person then. He's dead, and you are you now. Were you planning on changing back? That might be the only complication."

Barbara shook her head. "For a variety of reasons, it isn't feasible right now. Karl said I was resting on my laurels. I need to start over. What better way to do that than to be who I am now and make it back to the top."

"You're already a great scout. You gunning for my job now?" Jason asked.

"No, I'm looking to get rid of an annoying AI and take back the company," Barbara said. Jason looked shocked and stared with a faraway look in his eyes.

"You still want in on the crazy town I'm heading to?" Barbara asked.

"You've significantly upped your hotness— remember the old crazy hot formula…" Jason said.

"I knew you'd go there," Barbara said.

Jason kissed her. "I'm still your fiancé, and you are still my fiancée! We're in this together, but next time you want to be crazy, let's do something a little less crazy than trying to overthrow some AI, okay?"

"We haven't done it yet," Barbara said. "That's for another day. Now, what's this meeting about?"

"You'll see," Jason said as he entered the building. Inside the Vanguard members were milling around the coffee pot and talking. Barbara realized that she had never met all of the Vanguard, even as Greg. When Jason entered, they stopped talking and moved to the conference room.

As the Vanguard members sat, Jason said, "Okay, folks, do you want the bad or worse news?"

"No good news?" asked Stimson in his upper-crust British accent.

"No," Jason said. "We're being moved across Aurora Dawn to the archipelago in the south. Corporate wants us to start exploring the other hemisphere."

Barbara cursed her luck. She had discovered who she was and needed to go after the saboteur for payback. Now, she could be thousands of kilometers away from the saboteur and revenge.

"If that's the bad news, what's the worse news," Stimson asked.

"We'll be isolated for almost a month," Jason said. "Due to logistical hubs not being fully prepped."

"What about Analysis, both in Xeno Corps and Con Sec Corps," Li Mei asked. Barbara knew she wanted to be close to Xander and wasn't happy about the two of them being apart.

"A select group is coming with us. The rest will stay here or wherever Xena or Merlyna wants them," Jason said. "Oh, you have twenty-four hours before we depart, so grab your things. Any questions?"

"Yes," Stimson said. "I don't want to go! Who do I see to get out of this assignment?"

"Above my pay grade," Jason said. "Talk to Xena or Josie. Next?"

No one else had any concerns, and Jason adjourned

the meeting. Barbara wondered if she could talk to Merlyna or Josie, tell them she was their old friend, and see if they had any leads. Knowing Merlyna, there was an Analyst's Hyperbook with suspects, their relationships, and possible connections. As the rest filed out, Jason came over to Barbara.

"What's the matter," he asked her.

"I don't believe in luck, but I feel like I have an abundance of bad luck right now," Barbara said.

"Why is that," Jason said. "The south is nice, a little muggy, but warm, and nice beaches are not far from the site. I think it's a lot like the Caribbean, even though some of the other Con Sec guys said otherwise. We'll be together too."

"Yeah, but I owe someone some payback, and if I am down there, well, I won't be able to do anything," Barbara said.

Jason smiled. "Maybe that's the point. Besides, this came down from Josie."

"Well then, I need to see her," Barbara said.

"Why?" Jason asked.

"Because I am not going," Barbara said. "I need to stay here."

"Well, good luck with that," Jason said. "Let me know how that goes."

"Hey," Barbara said. "This has nothing to do with you… I love you."

"You're just saying that to get out of your bet," Jason said with a mischievous smile. Barbara kissed him on the cheek and left. She was going to have a discussion with Josie.

*

"Think it will work," Josie asked.

"Not sure, but if we spread them out, the saboteur has nowhere to hide," Merlyna said.

"They might decide to wait," Josie said. "What then?"

"We make them move. We can't play defense. We lose that way, Josie."

The women were interrupted by a knock at the door.

"Come in," Josie said, quickly hiding her screen.

"Hello, Miz Moreno," Barbara said. "Can I talk with you for a moment?"

Josie looked at Merlyna, and Merlyna said, "I'll see you later."

"You can stay too, Miz Lenart, if you want," Barbara said. Merlyna gave Barbara a narrowed glance. "I don't think so. You are part of Xena's division. I don't want to interfere."

"See you, Merlyna," Josie said as Merlyna left and closed the door behind her. "What can I do for you, Miss…"

"Gordon," Barbara said. "I go by Barbara."

"Hi Barbara, I'm Josie," she said. "I've seen you around, but I don't think we've ever talked."

"Yeah, Jason keeps us busy," Barbara said. "Look, I am coming…"

"About the move? Well, if that's the case. I can make this quick. You're going," Josie said. "Is there anything else?"

"Actually, I wanted to stay, I need to stay…" Barbara said but was cut off again by Josie.

"Nope, we decided. Now get packing," Josie said.

"Listen…" Barbara said, getting angry.

"No, as the human lead for the expedition, I made the decision. Daddy is in full agreement. Now, have I made myself clear?" Josie said curtly.

"Josie, you're being a stubborn jackass," Barbara snapped.

"Excuse me?" Josie said indignantly. "I think you've forgotten who I am, young lady."

"Oh, forget this noise," Barbara said. "Josie, I'm really Greg!"

Josie looked like she had been sucker punched. She sat there for a moment and just looked at Barbara. "What was that?"

"Look, you're going to kick me out of your office anyway," Barbara said defensively. "I'm actually Greg. We were on the Titan expedition! Before we suited up, you kissed me and said you loved me for taking you on the expedition. You were getting ready to take the first step on Titan and wanted me to be the first out! But I said NASA wanted a woman, so you should go."

"Okay," Josie said, looking around nervously. "Is this some joke? Who put you up to this?"

"Josie, when I met you in Malta, you had a birthmark across the inside of your thigh. You tried to hide it, but the stage was set up so that anyone in the front row could see it," Barbara said.

"Wait? Greg? You are crazy!" Josie said. "What's going on here?"

"Listen," Barbara said. "I can't go down south. I need to stay here and take care of the saboteur. I need some payback."

"No, no, if you really are... I can't believe I'm even saying this, Greg. Then you need to go. It is only a matter of time before this gets around," Josie said. "If I asked Daddy who you are, what would he say?"

"Look, it's complicated," Barbara said. "I need to stay; I can be bait for the trap."

"Sorry, honey," Josie said. "You don't look like you can take a driving test, much less take on a saboteur."

"Argh! Josie, you aren't thinking! You're doing that. 'Is she prettier than I am? If yes, destroy!' thing! I'm not out for your job!" Barbara said.

Josie gave a sardonic smile. "Well, that sounds like Greg. He always was a jackass. Look, I am not calling you Greg. He's dead, as far as I am concerned. Listen, Barbie..."

"Barbara! Don't call me Barbie!"

"Okay, *Barbara*," Josie said with emphasis. "You're going the south outpost, and that's that. I can't change the plans, or they won't work. If you're Greg in there, something I am highly skeptical of, you'll understand you need to take orders, Airman, and like it…"

Internally, Barbara wanted to have a full-on teenage hissy fit, but she realized that if she were going to rebuild as Miss Gordon, she'd have to do it other people's way. She wasn't General Body anymore and would have to play things cool to earn Josie's respect.

"This used to be easier! I could go full alpha male on you, and you'd swoon," Barbara muttered. Barbara wasn't as quiet as she thought, and Josie straightened.

"News flash," Josie said with irritation, "You aren't the quarterback anymore! You're a cheerleader, and I am still captain of this squad, so grab your pom-poms and shake to my beat, or go find another team to root for."

"Fine," Barbara said, "This isn't over…"

"It is right now, missy. So get moving…" Josie said. Barbara stood up. As Barbara left the office Josie shouted, "Next time, make an appointment, honey!"

Barbara closed the door when she exited. She would have to go to DADDIE. That was the only way she could overrule Josie.

*

Barbara practically charged into the cold room. Along the way, some of Josie's words started rattling around in her head, and she didn't like it.

"Daddy!" Barbara shouted as she entered. "We need to talk!"

"Whoa, Tiger," DADDIE said, "What's the matter?"

"Look, I tried what you said and talked to Josie," Barbara said.

"I take it that didn't go how you wanted," DADDIE asked.

"No, she's doing that younger-cuter-must-annihilate thing. I saw her do that to Sarah Evans, our initial pilot on the Titan mission."

"Okay, well, what happened?" DADDIE asked.

"Josie totally nuked her, and she went to the Director of NASA, claiming that Sarah was a minus one! Sarah was great! She just was younger and prettier. Sarah even tried to get along with Josie! The director was, I don't know, smitten with Josie. He knew she was married to Elon, and there was a lot of backroom play going on. I was able to diffuse it by moving Sarah to the project on Ceres," Barbara said.

"I meant with you and Josie," DADDIE said. "But cool story, you'll have to tell me more later."

"Oh," Barbara said, "I went to Josie to tell her I needed to stay here rather than go south with the Vanguard. Josie shut me down before I could begin."

"That's to be expected. Based on your story, why didn't you think about the fact that you are no longer Greg and that Josie may see you differently," DADDIE asked.

"I told her I was Greg," Barbara said.

"Oh boy," DADDIE said. "Listen, Tiger, besides you flashing your Greg credentials around, trying to act like Greg is just a bad idea at this point. I don't want to get too philosophical, but humans aren't much more evolved than chimpanzees. I mean, Karl would be shedding a tear right now since he doesn't believe in evolution, but he would agree that humans are ninety-nine percent animals with a small sliver of a God-given soul. Humans, chimpanzees, and even lobsters are all about hierarchies."

"Okay," Barbara said. "What does that have to do with Josie?"

"Let's play a game here, Tiger," DADDIE said, realizing Barbara wasn't getting it. "If you were still in a Greg shell and Jason came in demanding something from you, how would you react?"

"What would he want," Barbara said with a wistful smile. She then paused and said, "Dang it! You're right! I'm not really Greg anymore." DADDIE's avatar had a smirk on his face.

"Okay, okay, you really are right," Barbara said with a deep breath. She closed her eyes. "I'd probably have yelled at him and told him to get out of my office… Aw, crud! I messed that up, didn't I?" DADDIE nodded silently.

"I'm going down to the south, aren't I," Barbara said.

"Honestly, Tiger, you're safer down there," DADDIE said. "Jason will watch out for you. Li Mei will be there and need you, as Xander is staying here… for the moment."

"I don't get to do the planning anymore, do I?" Barbara asked.

"Not yet," DADDIE said. "You'll get back in their good graces. You have to prove yourself all over again."

"Man, oh man, I wish Karl was here," Barbara said. "He and I were military together once."

"So do I. Sonny would have been a huge help on so many fronts," DADDIE said, "Unfortunately, he's in his own pickle right now."

"What?" Barbara said she hadn't even thought about Murphy's expedition, being so concerned about herself. "What do you mean, his own pickle? He's with Patrick. Heck, Mommy gave Pat everything!"

"Well, this is all hush-hush, but it looks like Pat is dead. Last we heard, Karl was trying to keep mercs from going full space pirate on HD 260655," DADDIE said.

Barbara felt suddenly ashamed at her outburst with Josie. She realized that no matter how bad she felt, her friend was probably sitting light years away, wishing he was here.

"Oh," was all Barbara could say.

"Look, Tiger, just go along with the plan. Go to the beach with Jason, get a tan. You aren't one of the grownups anymore. Enjoy the lack of responsibility," said DADDIE.

"Right," Barbara said. "Thanks, Daddy."

"Hey, if it makes any difference, I was able to

launder Greg's bank funds into your account. You aren't wealthy by any stretch, but you have more money than a junior scout would make," DADDIE said.

"I suppose that's good. I don't have all of Greg's expenses either," Barbara said.

"Yeah," DADDIE said. "I suppose I can shuffle some of his personal effects your way, too. The cargo system is automated. If anyone gets suspicious, I can call it human error."

Barbara perked up at the idea of having things that meant something to her. "Sure, obviously, this would have to be more personal things. None of the trophies and awards I... er—Greg—had."

DADDIE was about to say something else when Griff walked in.

"I'm sorry, I didn't mean to interrupt," Griff said.

"No problem," Barbara said. "I was just finishing up. I need to pack for our move down south."

"Oh, you going too?" Griff said.

"What do you mean?" Barbara asked.

"Griff volunteered to go with you all," DADDIE said. "To be the human doctor and all."

"I'll even make some house calls," Griff said. "Been a while since I've been to a beach and had a fruity drink with a little umbrella."

"Well then, I'll see you down there," Barbara said, preparing to leave.

"Actually, I was here looking for you," Griff said. "Mind if I walk with you?"

"No, not at all," Barbara said. Griff waved to DADDIE and then opened the door for Barbara. "Ladies first."

Barbara blushed and said, "Thanks, but not necessary."

"My old friend Greg always said, 'I hold a door for a lady, I don't care if she's four or if she's eighty.'" Griff replied as Barbara walked out.

"He sounded like quite the gentleman," Barbara said.

"He is," Griff said as he followed and walked beside Barbara.

"Wait," Barbara said. "How'd you know…"

Griff smiled and tapped his head, interrupting. "I had this hunch. This little itch I couldn't scratch. At first, I thought you were suffering from a bad decant. It happens. Then, at Li Mei's party, you said things that I couldn't square…"

"But why didn't you say anything?" Barbara asked.

"Look, I'm going to call you Barbara," Griff said, getting sidetracked. "You're too much like my daughter Maybelle for me to call you anything else."

Barbara nodded and said, "That's probably a wise move."

"Look, Barbara," Griff said. "There wasn't a good time. Besides, what if I was wrong? I'm a health care provider. If I asked and was wrong…"

"You'd be having daily discussions with Steve?" Barbara suggested.

"Something like that," Griff said. "Anyway, I suspected something was off for a while now. Martha thought I had lost my marbles. She said as much… When we were talking…"

Barbara frowned as she and Griff went to her apartment, "Wait, what's up between you two?"

"She's angry. She's been resentful for a while now," Griff said. "This was our last chance. Len and I had a big fight almost a century ago, and well…"

"I'm sorry, Griff," Barbara said with a pained expression.

Griff laughed. "You are Barbara now. The general would never show so much emotion on his face unless he was at the gun range or winning at racquetball."

"Oh geez," Barbara said. "I forgot about racquetball.

Now I want to play."

"When we get down south, I'll give you a game. Heck, we can teach Jason. I bet he could be quite the contender against you," Griff said.

"Yeah, I hope I get my racquet when Daddy shuffles Greg's effects," Barbara said.

"If it helps," Griff said, "I'll tell folks you're his niece. You and he didn't want anyone to know."

Barbara's face lit up in surprise, "I never thought about that. That's a good idea."

"I'm glad to see my extensive education has finally paid off," Griff said.

"You aren't just a pretty face after all, Doctor Tomkins," Barbara said.

"Yeah, that won't work anymore," Griff said. "People might get the wrong idea about us."

Barbara sighed, "Yeah, I kind of messed things up with Josie on that front."

"That's surprising. I always thought she was following you around like a lovestruck schoolgirl because she expected a diamond ring at the end of the trail," Griff said.

"Really? I just thought she felt like I added some excitement to her life," Barbara said.

"Don't kid yourself! She was crazy about Greg," Griff said. "How'd you mess things up?"

"I barged into her office, demanded I not go south, and when that went as well as to be expected, I shouted, 'I'm Greg, you idiot!' at her." Griff burst into laughter. He laughed so hard that he had to stop walking.

"What?" Barbara said. "It seemed like a good idea at the time!"

Griff started to get his composure back, and after a few deep breaths, he said, "Look, Barbara, you have to play by different rules now! Josie isn't going to listen to a sweet little schoolgirl. She's got chunks of chicks like you in her stool, metaphorically speaking. You have to figure out the laws of the female jungle as a woman. I can't help you there. I have never had the desire to walk a kilometer in high heels. But, what I can tell you, as the father of two girls, is that what you think will work as a man doesn't as a woman. Li Mei or Merlyna could help you out there."

"Merlyna didn't give me the time of day," Barbara said. Griff and she continued walking.

"She's been busy," Griff replied. "Con Sec has been pushing hard, and Karl's not in a good place on HD 260655."

"Daddy said as much to me," Barbara said. "If I could, I'd gladly head out there and fight with him."

Griff just laughed. "That'd make great cinema. The cute little teenybopper and the old curmudgeon taking on the space pirates. I should give up medicine and go into film."

"Hey, I could be a Sarah Tanner," Barbara said, a little hurt.

"Yeah, um, no," Griff said. "With the shell you've got, you look more like the superhero's girlfriend whom he has to spin webs to save from the bad guys."

"Really?" Barbara said sourly. "Maybe I need a cool scar or something?"

Griff just laughed. "You're not even close, Barbara. Try again."

"You know, I thought I had this all solved when I found out who I was," Barbara said.

"Now you see why I never felt the grass was greener on the other side," Griff replied. "You'll find your mojo, and when you do, you can teach me all there is to know about women," Griff said.

"I don't think that's allowed now," Barbara said. "It seems I am on the other side in the battle of the sexes."

"Probably not," Griff said as they approached Barbara's apartment. Before I let you go, I just wanted to know… What is going on with you and Jason?"

"What do you mean," Barbara asked.

"Well, I was momentarily worried that you were a corporate spy. Now, I am just worried Jason will get hurt…"

"How weirded out do you want to get, Griff?" Barbara asked, and Griff gave a wry smile.

"I don't want him to get hurt! As much as you look like the girl next door, I know your history. Mister or rather Miss love-em-and-leave-em…" said Griff.

"Yeah," Barbara started. "This one feels different. He's like the cutest puppy and…"

"Say no more," Griff said. "Just be careful with his heart. He's still a little man after all."

"Yes, sir," Barbara said. "I'll have him home before ten o'clock, too."

"Nine-thirty, young lady," Griff said with a smile.

"We still friends?" Barbara asked.

"Yes, as long as I don't have to talk about hats, purses, clothes, or shoes. You can take that feminine nonsense somewhere else. I had plenty of all that raising my two girls," said Griff.

"Yes, sir," Barbara said. "Speaking of clothes, I think Jason owes me a trip to the shopping center."

"And you owe us some credits. We beat you out of the archive double over," Griff said.

Barbara looked annoyed and said in a cute voice, "Doctor Tomkins, are you trying to take advantage of a young girl here?"

"Better," Griff said. "You have some potential, but that won't work on me! I've had two daughters and patched you up in most of your shells. You can have your fun and games, but you'll be running to me for stitches in this one soon enough."

"We'll see about that," Barbara said sardonically. As she was about to say something else, Jason appeared.

"See about what?" Jason asked.

"Griff thinks I might end up in his office for stitches sooner rather than later," Barbara said.

Griff asked Jason, "What do you think about that, Little Rooster?"

Barbara and Griff looked at Jason, expecting him to pick a side. Jason smiled and said, "Hey, they opened the movie theater. There's some Bollywood film playing. Want to go, Barbara?"

Griff smiled and winked at Barbara. "Nine thirty, ya hear…"

"Bye, Griff," said Barbara cutely.

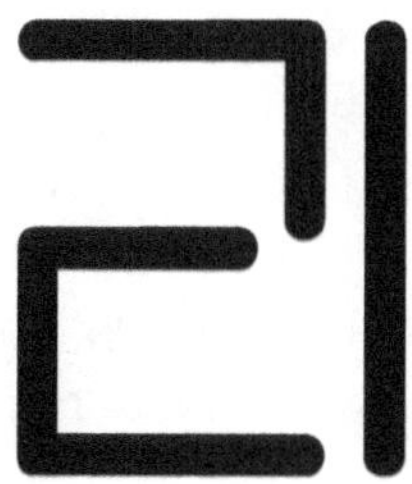

"I'll tell you, being involved in human space flight, it is an emotional endeavor. I think it brings in the highest highs and the lowest lows."

— Astronaut Ellen Ochoa

There was a knock at the door. Barbara went and opened it.

"Hi baby, happy new year again," Jason said.

"Jason, it's Sunday," Barbara said, still in her nightgown and looking exhausted. "Besides, you said 'Happy New Year' to me last night! Have you been up already?"

"Yeah, I've been to church and everything already," Jason said.

"Church, wait, what?" Barbara said. She knew Jason was some religion, but perhaps due to a lack of coffee, she couldn't remember.

"Oh boy, can I come in and make you some coffee? Or do you want every bug in this jungle to fly in instead?" Jason said, swatting at his skin.

"Sure, come on in," Barbara said groggily. "I mean, you were here not even like seven hours ago." Jason came in, dutifully started the coffee pot, and then hugged and kissed Barbara.

"Wakey wakey sleeping beauty," he said breaking his embrace.

"I liked that…" Barbara said. "Where is the coffee?"

"Coming," Jason said.

"How'd you go to church? There isn't a rabbi, imam, priest, minister, or monk on this expedition." Barbara said.

"One of the guys in Analysis said he had a dream where an angel told him to preach," Jason said. "He was pretty good until he started preaching in Korean, then he lost me."

"What denomination are you again?" Barbara asked.

"Methodist. You still hating on Jesus," Jason said jokingly.

Barbara stared at him and said, "I need a cup of coffee before I want this discussion."

The pot chimed its completion, and Jason said, "Ask, and it shall be given to you."

Barbara growled but smiled sweetly when Jason handed her a cup of coffee. It was a local crop, one of the first, and she found she could drink it black with no real issues.

"Okay, evangelize mini-Karl," Barbara said.

"Karl's a believer?" Jason asked. "I'm surprised since he's so old and makes AI."

"Oh boy," Barbara said. "Karl isn't just a believer. He's like the pope's right-hand man." Jason looked a little disappointed.

"What?" Barbara said.

"I just figured he'd be a real Christian," Jason said. "Not a misguided papist."

"Oh great, the reformation has come to Aurora Dawn," Barbara said. "You want to know why I don't go to church and am not into that witchcraft? Because of the fact you all can't get along. If it isn't Christians going after Christians, then it's Jews and Muslims, or Muslims and Buddhists or Hindus. I've seen all that noise for so long, and I'm glad you all are sitting in the back of class, metaphorically speaking." Jason just sat there looking at Barbara.

"What," she said.

"You're adorable when you're being philosophical," Jason replied. "This is an issue because I want the local preacher to bless our impending marriage."

Barbara drank her coffee. She could feel some irritation rising with Jason, and she was trying to remember he was a cute, cuddly puppy while being short on sleep.

"Maybe I'm growing or something," Barbara said. "I'm floored, and you're not even feeling that you only got six hours."

"Less than that, but you're changing the subject," Jason said. "If God doesn't exist, then there's no issue with having someone else wish us well as a couple."

"Look, if it was solely up to me, I'd have Griff formalize our vows, Josie file the civil marriage with CAA, and be done with it all. Then, we can have a honeymoon and get back to Plan B."

"You're an improvement as Barbara," Jason said, poking Barbara with his statement.

"Oh, for crying out loud," Barbara said. In a high, girly voice, she said, "Fine, I'll bite. Why do you say that, sweetheart?"

"Greg wouldn't have a honeymoon. He'd be like, 'trains never take a sick day' or something equally absurd," Jason said.

"You won't move in or spend the night even," Barbara said. "I'm making allowances for your bashfulness."

"This again," Jason said. He and Barbara had been circling the issue of living together and Jason's faith for the past few days. Barbara wanted something simple for a wedding and enjoyed Jason around full-time. Jason insisted that things be more formalized and that he was "a good man and a good Christian." This meant he wouldn't move in until he and Barbara were married.

"I don't get it. Your parents are like twelve-thousand-two-hundred-ers. They were born just after the Singularity, like me. How did they maintain such backward ideas," Barbara asked.

"I thought there were no atheists in foxholes," Jason replied.

"Argh, Jason, I love you so much, and yet you can frustrate me to no end," Barbara said.

"Maybe Jesus sent me to frustrate you," Jason said solemnly. "I'm only trying to save your immortal soul."

"No! No! No! No more mini-Karl!" Barbara said.

"You keep saying that. What's that all about?" Jason asked, attempting to change the subject.

"Oh, he's obnoxious at times," Barbara said. "He's a

pre-Singularity transhuman, and they come in two flavors: rainbow and dark chocolate."

"What does that even mean?" Jason asked.

"Well, the chocolate ones are deep and rich, provided you like chocolate. If you don't, it is all disgusting. The rainbow ones have a lot of variety, but they are only a few centimeters of flavor," Barbara said.

"Is Karl…" Jason started to ask.

"He's chocolate, all the way," Barbara said hotly.

"He's one of your friends," Jason said. "Yet, you sound like you don't care for him."

"He's more than that, we're brothers in arms… Er, rather siblings in arms now," Barbara said. "I both love him and am annoyed by him simultaneously. He'd probably be on holy fire about our union."

"Why do you say that?" Jason asked.

"Oh, he gets on a pulpit, like you do, occasionally," Barbara said.

"I think you're biased. I've heard you mention things about religion, and I think you are being unfair. But I still love you because otherwise, you are awesome to be around," Jason said. "My mom was the religious one in the family. Dad came around after the Birth Lottery win. Some other time, I'll tell you that story."

Barbara drank her coffee and, pulling the cup from her lips, said, "Sure, I'm getting tired of this subject anyway."

"Fair enough, what shall we talk about? The wedding?" Jason asked.

"No, I'm burned out on wedding talk. All I hear from Li Mei these days is wedding stuff, and I hate to say it, but she's a bridezilla," Barbara said.

"Okay, work then," Jason suggested.

"Let's go to the beach," Barbara said. "We don't need to talk. I can get some of the L 98-59 sun, and maybe I'll stop being such a witch."

"Sure," Jason said. "I'll get my swimsuit."

Barbara nodded, and Jason exited. Although he had been given access to the apartment, he still knocked. Barbara was usually thrilled by his chivalric behavior; however, he just annoyed her today.

*

Merlyna sat looking at the display. All the evidence kept pointing to Griff. She could figure out how he was the saboteur. She included Martha in her search, and up until the lab explosion, she was equally a suspect. Griff had an alibi, and Martha did, too. She was back to the beginning.

"Working on the weekend? That is the sign you need help," Josie said.

"I'm doing extracurricular stuff. What's your excuse?" Merlyna said.

"I'm bored! No one is saying I look pretty! I need a hobby," Josie replied.

"Get a cat," Merlyna said.

"I tried that, poor Mister Biddlesworth died of starvation," Josie said. "I'm not good with animals either."

Merlyna suspected Josie never really had a cat but continued. "I'm back to the beginning. How's the trap going?"

"Good, the Xeno Corps and Griff are away down south. I'll be moving the elements of Con Sec Corps out to the new town on the eastern continent, and we'll have a small skeleton crew here in the city. If anything happens, we can immediately narrow down the suspects," Josie said.

"Be nice if they'd just be polite enough to be caught in the act," Merlyna said.

"Yes, and it would be great if a Radon millionaire showed up and decided to shower me with gold jewelry and marriage proposals, but I doubt that will happen," Josie said.

"Okay, fine," Merlyna said. "Who is on your shortlist?"

"Me? I think it is Garnier. That chick rubs me raw,"

Josie said.

"I think you don't like her because she's got a boyfriend," Merlyna said.

"Really? Am I that bad, Merlyna," Josie asked.

"Yes, you are," Merlyna said.

"Well, who is your suspect then?" Josie asked.

"I was thinking Griff or Martha, but my gut says Gordon," Merlyna said, "There's something about her that's off."

"Yeah, but she's not the saboteur," Josie said.

"You sound pretty certain. How come?" Merlyna asked.

"She approached me kind of weirdly," Josie said.

"Okay, so maybe she is our saboteur," Merlyna said.

"I don't think so," Josie said. "It was just bizarre, like having a ghost visit or something."

Merlyna scowled at Josie, "What do you mean?"

"She struts her little butt into my office, demands I keep her here in the city, and then starts raving about stuff…" Josie said, saying the last part evasively.

"Raving about what?" Merlyna said. "Listen, Josie, I am a pre-Singularity girl. I grew up around rampant mental illness. That stuff doesn't bother me."

"Oh, I don't know. I didn't react all that well. Maybe I do have a blind spot when it comes to younger women…" Josie said.

"Look, you do sort of have a bad reputation there," Merlyna said. "I was hesitant working around you because of that."

"Oh geez," Josie said. "That makes me feel wonderful."

"Back to the topic of Gordon, what did she say, Josie?"

"She started ranting that she was actually Greg," Josie said.

"And you didn't call Steve and the bots with the nice

white straight-jackets?" Merlyna said.

"I don't get the reference, but no, I didn't call anyone, Merlyna."

"Why not?"

"Some of the things she said were pretty personal, and only someone really close to Greg would know them," Josie replied.

"Weird," Merlyna said, choosing not to pry.

"Yeah," Josie replied. "I wasn't sure what to make of it all. I suppose there is something to all of it."

"Maybe Griff can give us a medical run down on Miss Gordon," Merlyna said.

"Worth a try. Should we disturb him on a Sunday?"

"How much do you want to know about Gordon?"

"I'll make the call," Josie said, leaning over to a console on Merlyna's desk and calling Griff's number. The program connected, and a chime sounded.

"Hello?" Griff said groggily.

"Hey Griff, Merlyna and I are filing the end-of-year reports, and I need some clarification on a medical case," Josie said.

"You need some hobbies there, fat lady. Go sing *Der Rosenkavalier* or something from *The Magic Flute*," Griff said.

"Maybe later. Right now, I need some data," Josie said.

"Sure, give me a second," Griff muted his phone. A moment later, he came back on the line and on camera. "Okay, give me the request."

"I need to know the next of kin for Barbara Gordon. The forms are blank," Josie said.

Griff nodded. It looked like he was debating something, but he returned and said, "Why are you asking about Greg's niece?"

Josie looked shocked and said, "Wait, his niece? I thought he was an only child?"

"Look, I don't know about his family structure and

whether the girl is an actual niece or just a cousin, but he called her his niece to me," Griff said. Merlyna watched the interplay silently.

"Uh, okay," Josie continued. "Who is the next of kin then?"

"Greg," Griff said emphatically.

"Sure, I'll mark it down so Daddy quits bothering me about it. Anything else I should know about Gordon?" Josie said.

"Don't let anyone know about her relationship with the general. It was supposed to be a confidential thing," Griff said. "You know how Greg was. Never wanted to seem like he played favorites and all."

"Uh huh," Josie said. "Well, thanks, Griff. Sorry to disturb you."

"Right. Well, I am off to the beach. I'm hunting for sea shells," Griff said with a smile, cutting the connection.

"Greg's niece," Josie said absently.

"I never knew he had a niece," Merlyna said.

"Me either," Josie said. "Things are getting stranger and stranger."

"We're probably close to the saboteur then," Merlyna said.

"Or, we're on to something else entirely," Josie said.

"Perhaps," Merlyna mused.

*

Sitting on a towel and drinking orange juice, Barbara felt almost human again. Jason was surfing. Currently, he was chasing a wave on a bodyboard. She looked out at her fiancé and was happy to have him despite all their arguing in the morning.

"Hello," Griff said. He had been beach combing a few kilometers to the south. He greeted Barbara as he mindlessly strolled towards where she lay. He wore a flowery Hawaiian-style blue shirt and white cargo capris and was barefoot.

"Hey Griff," Barbara said.

"Where's Little Rooster?" Griff asked. Barbara pointed off into the surf.

"You mind if I join you for a moment?" Griff said.

"Not at all," Barbara said.

Griff sat in the sand beside Barbara and noticed her drink, "Mimosa?"

"No, just orange juice. I gave up drinking in this shell," Barbara said.

Griff just chuckled. "Mister gin-and-tonic-for-breakfast is now a teetotaler. Wonders never cease."

"When you are forty-five kilograms, you don't have the same tolerance for liquor," Barbara said sourly.

"Been an awful long time since I weighed that little," Griff said. "I don't think I was legal when I weighed forty-five kilos."

"Thankfully, I don't miss the drinking as much," Barbara said.

"You have too much to drink last night then?" Griff inquired.

"Are you my friend or my doctor?" Barbara asked warily.

"Both, but in this case, I was going to suggest fluids and perhaps some tomato juice," Griff said.

"I wasn't drinking. Jason isn't much into it, and he's a huge lightweight," Barbara said. "I'm just dragging today. All I want to do is sleep."

"Are you pregnant?" Griff asked.

"Um, no, I haven't asked for the block to be removed. Besides, Jason and I aren't there yet. That's a wild discussion for another time," Barbara said.

"Hey now, I'm just asking as a medical professional," Griff said defensively, "I had to have the same talk with my daughters."

"Not Len?" Barbara asked.

"He never left the house in ten-centimeter heels and

a body con dress that sat right at his butt," Griff said with a laugh.

"I could see why that could complicate things," Barbara said.

"For what it's worth, you're probably growing still. You probably got a shell that is a late bloomer and is going through the end of a growth spurt," Griff said.

"Great. I'm female, can't drink, and am going through puberty. That's not selling the experience for me today," Barbara said.

"I told you I never wanted to see the other side in the battle of the sexes, and now you know why. Besides, I wouldn't want a boy's body at sixteen, either. I had enough trouble getting through puberty once," Griff said.

"Yeah, well, I'm not a happy camper today," Barbara said.

"Well, I have time. Maybe you want to share what's really going on," Griff said.

Barbara drank the rest of her juice and sat up a bit. She cleared her throat and said, "I don't know. It's Jason; it's the wedding; it's the saboteur; and it's being here," Barbara said.

"Well, let's break those down a little. What's wrong with Jason?" Griff said.

"Well, he's religious. He wants a pastor to bless our marriage. He wants a big ceremony, and he wants it all right away," Barbara said.

"I'm not a fan of religion," Griff said. "But Jason's faith is pretty benign. He and I have had our share of discussions, and he's never come across as strident or pushy. I don't believe in any of that noise, but I don't care if someone wants Hari Krishna or the Easter Bunny to help them out of a bad situation. That's on them."

"He reminds me of Karl," Barbara said.

"Well, the good Professor Holzhauser is one crazy cat, but ultimately, he only wants what is best. Even if you don't believe in it."

"Jason just keeps pushing on the pastor," Barbara said.

"Okay, so don't get married," Griff said.

"Oh, I don't know about that," Barbara said quickly.

"Well, then have the pastor come do his mumbo jumbo," Griff said. "So what?"

"I don't know if I am into the whole 'love, honor, and *obey*' part of all that nonsense," Barbara said.

"Ah yeah, Adam's rib and all that jazz," Griff said. Barbara looked at him hesitantly.

"Look, Barbara," Griff said. "I had my own go around with Len and Viola. All was well with us until Martha and I got new shells. Then, we were in league with the Devil. I went out and got a bible to see what it said… Don't look at me like that…" Griff said as Barbara stared at him.

"Anyhow, I needed to know what I was up against, and well… After reading that book, I'm not sure anyone has a pulpit to stand on. Wars, genocides, incest, Jehovah asking for human sacrifice, it's a really awful read. Thankfully, the second half was a bit easier to stomach, but even then, there are many reasons to say 'no thanks' to it all," said Griff.

"Yeah," Barbara said. "I never really talked about it, but I was raised in a pretty fire and brimstone church. I was never so glad as when I got away from that place."

"And now you're worried Jason is going to drag you back, kicking and screaming," Griff said.

"Something like that, yes," Barbara said.

"It's just some mumbo jumbo. If you love Jason, it won't matter in the long run," Griff said.

"I suppose," Barbara said.

"If the witch doctor was reading the words off the back of a cereal box, would you be as upset?" Griff asked.

"Probably not," Barbara responded.

"I think that's your answer. Now, what else is eating

at you?" Griff said.

"Okay, being here," Barbara said. "I know something is happening, and I am not in the loop."

"That's a really Greg attitude," Griff said. "We talked about that. No chasing the bad guys for you, remember?"

"That's a tall order. I can't stop being who I am that easily," Barbara said.

"I didn't say you couldn't fight the bad guys; I said you can't chase them. Let Jason do that stuff. He needs more of that, and you need less," Griff said.

"I just sit here and do nothing then," Barbara said.

"No, you get a nice tan and some vitamin D," Griff said. "If fate allows, the bad guys will find you. Otherwise, the superhero will capture them and send them to prison."

"I never liked comic books for that very reason. Shouldn't he kill them, just to make sure? Seems like they always break out," Barbara said.

"Not the style for the medium," Griff said. "This is another way to say that we all must follow the game's rules."

"Thanks," Barbara said flatly.

"Look, just enjoy being with Little Rooster. I certainly do. This fight isn't yours to win. I suspect you'll be more important later when things get desperate. In the meantime, enjoy the beach, your boyfriend, and some peace."

"Doctor's orders?" Barbara asked.

"Yes, you need a prescription for that?" Griff said with a smile.

"Looks like I am taking my medicine," Barbara said a little sullenly.

"Wonders never cease. I finally got you to do what a doctor tells you to do," Griff said with a smile.

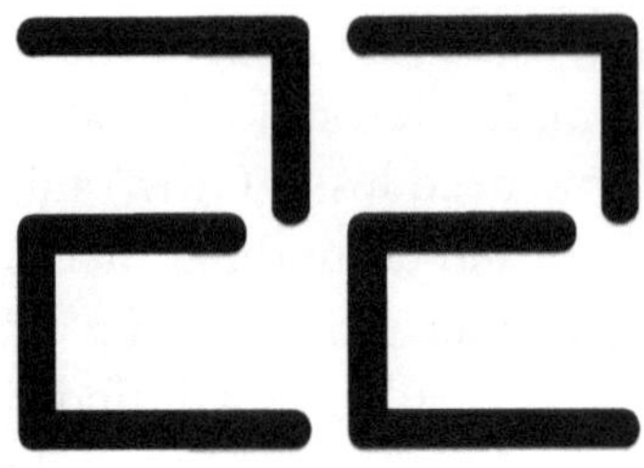

"Just taking risks for risk's sake, that doesn't do it for me. I'm willing to take risks that I think are worth it, and I've worked so hard to make sure that I survive."

— Astronaut Chris Hadfield

Josie awoke at the sound of the alarm. She hopped up, and threw on a loose dress from her closet. She grabbed a nearby pair of sandals and raced out of her bedroom. She rushed down the hall and stairs, barreling through her living room and out the front door. The alarm signaled trouble, and Josie raced to the ops center.

She and Merlyna had applied as much pressure and put out as much bait as possible. It had been weeks of waiting, and the alarms finally rang tonight. Closing the distance on the ops center, Josie hoped this was not a false alarm.

"Daddy, where is the alarm coming from?" Josie said as she entered the operations center. DADDIE projected himself into the foyer.

"The fusion reactor, Sport," he said. "It is locked down now. Whoever is in there is trapped."

"Send out that stupid warbot, and let Merlyna…" Josie said but was startled as Merlyna responded.

"I'm here," she said, entered the building.

"Fine, let's get a sled and head out," Josie said. Merlyna nodded and followed Josie. Josie noted that Merlyna, too, looked like she had grabbed something and rushed out, wearing a sweatshirt and sweatpants. They ran to the sled garage and grabbed a six-seater sled parked in the shared lot. Josie hopped in and started the ignition as Merlyna crawled into her seat and strapped in.

"I'm setting the waypoint," Josie said as she tapped the navigation console. The sled hovered and began to thrust forward. Soon, the autopilot guided the vehicle to its destination. Merlyna pulled out her nine-millimeter and cocked the slide, chambering a round. Then she returned the pistol to her holster.

"You think we'll need that?" Josie asked.

"Better to be safe than dead," Merlyna responded.

"Fair enough," Josie said. "I hope when the saboteur is unmasked, we can get to the bottom of what's going on and maybe end this lunacy."

The sled drove fifteen minutes to where the Con Sec Corps was building the fusion reactor. Josie slowed down and put the sled into manual mode while Merlyna scanned the surroundings. They hovered over to the main entry, where the alarm had been triggered.

"Keep an eye out," Josie said.

"I've got both eyes out and looking," Merlyna replied. The ladies exited the sled and went up to the door.

"Daddy, security override," Josie said. The door opened, showing a foyer and a reception area. Merlyna pulled her pistol and moved into a ready-to-fire position.

"Okay, give up," Merlyna said. "You're trapped in there." Josie motioned to go inside.

Merlyna moved forward and swept the room, and then she relaxed.

"We missed the saboteur," Merlya said.

"This is getting ridiculous," Josie replied. "How did we miss them?"

Merlyna pointed to an oversized heating and cooling vent that had been pried off the wall. She holstered her pistol with a frustrated sigh.

"Well, they aren't foolish," Merlyna said.

"That's how I feel right now," Josie retorted.

"Honestly, I am surprised Daddy missed this detail," Merlyna replied. As if summoning a genie, DADDIE appeared.

"Missed the detail," DADDIE said. "No, I didn't miss it at all. I was counting on it."

"Huh?" Merlyna said. "What do you mean, counting on it?"

"Look, ladies, no offense, but I suspected the saboteur wasn't going to be caught on the first go," said

DADDIE.

"How does this get us any closer to the saboteur," Josie replied.

"I've already got enough data to narrow down the suspects. There is a high probability that I know who the saboteur is," DADDIE said.

"You recorded the saboteur's movements and now have deductions based on their actions on security footage," Merlyna said.

"Bingo," DADDIE said and smiled.

"Well, who is it? Use small words for me. Like, I'm just the cheerleader, you nerds," Josie said in a "valley girl" voice.

"Martha Tomkins is your saboteur," DADDIE said. Merlyna bolted from the reception and ran to the sled. Josie wasn't even sure what was happening, but she ran after her.

"Merlyna, wait!" Josie said.

"There is no time," Merlyna said. We have to get to the hospital before it is too late."

"Why the hospital?" Josie said. "Why not her apartment?"
"I detected a radiation surge there a while back, but when we inquired, the hospital systems said there were machines performing maintenance. I discounted that fact and kept looking…" Merlyna was inside the sled as Josie climbed in.

"But now you know what's going on and…" Josie interrupted.

"Realize that Martha hid the q-array elements at the hospital," Merlyna said, putting a waypoint on the medical complex and hitting the ignition. After getting her safety straps on, Merlyna switched to manual and throttled the accelerator pedals. Josie was pressed into her chair as the sled took off.

"Okay, Merlyna, what are you worried about," Josie said.

"Everything," Merlyna responded grimly. After a wild

ride, the ladies made it to the medical complex. Merlyna parked the sled right in front of the building and jumped out, leaving the engines still running. Merlyna ran into the medical center. She pulled her pistol as she crossed the threshold to the hospital. Josie followed quickly, and sirens sounded as the Security Division's patrol officers started converging on the medical complex. Josie ran into the hospital right on Merlyna's heels but lost sight of her when she turned down a corridor.

When Josie turned into the corridor, she stopped. At the end of the small hall was an office with Martha and Merlyna inside. Merlyna had her pistol trained on Martha who held the entangled array elements.

"Put the array elements down, Martha," Merlyna said.

"I don't think so," Martha replied.

"You're trapped. This is over," Merlyna said.

"No, it's not! Things are only getting started," Martha said. "I want safe passage to the spaceport. I'll take a shuttle to orbit and say my goodbyes."

"You know that's not going to happen, and you don't have much time left. You're holding the array elements in your bare hands. You can calculate how many rads you absorb as we speak," Merlyna said.

"You always were too damn perceptive for your own good, Merlie," Martha said. "It won't matter anyway; I expected this expedition to be a one-way trip."

"And Griff," Merlyna asked.

"He's gone, Len's gone; I have nothing to lose!" Martha said.

"But what did you have to gain?" Josie asked.

"I should have figured you'd bring her," Martha said. "The librarian and the cheerleader! You two are like a Saturday morning cartoon. Where's the van and the kid with the talking dog?"

"You're stalling," Merlyna said. "Put down the array

elements."

"If you say so," Martha said, dropping the elements.

"Look out," Merlyna said, moving away. The elements fell to the ground and shattered.

"I lived up to my end of the bargain," Martha said, slumping over. Josie wanted to rush forward, but Merlyna put her arm out.

"No, she's contaminated, remember? We've got to get a reading on her rads! This whole area is radioactive," Merlyna said.

"Blast it all. What was she thinking?" Josie said.

"I don't know, but she's wrecked our best chance of finding out," Merlyna said. "Without those elements, the q-array is a fancy desk ornament."

Security officers started appearing, and Merlyna quickly informed them of the situation. Josie and Merlyna went to another section of the hospital, and the med bots scanned them for radiation. Neither had much exposure and were released. When they returned to the office where Merlyna had confronted Martha, they saw a hazmat body bag.

"I wonder what she meant by 'I lived up to my end of the bargain,'" Josie said. Merlyna scowled but said nothing.

"Who is going to tell Griff?" Merlyna asked.

"I will. I am still thinking about what I should say," Josie replied.

"I don't know… the truth?" Merlyna responded.

"What is the truth?" Josie said. "Martha was the saboteur? The colony is in trouble since we no longer have a q-array?"

"Maybe things are simpler than you think," Merlyna said. "Martha had an accident while we were recovering the q-array elements. During the recovery, she was exposed to terminal radiation levels, and we couldn't save her as a result. Additionally, the elements were damaged beyond repair."

"Sounds like an answer the Office of the General Counsel would give," Josie said.

"I also was a lawyer a while back," Merlyna said.

"Figures," Josie said.

"Well, I got better," Merlyna said, acting like her legal experience was a disease. Josie gave a curt laugh but then put her hands to her face.

"I'm totally in charge now. No Greg, no Mommy…" Josie said.

"That's not necessarily a bad thing," Merlyna said.

"Well then, what now?" Josie said.

"The colony keeps doing what it needs to do: building a home for sodbusters and creating value for the company. In the meantime, I'm going to work on getting back to Sol," Merlyna said.

"The colony isn't even ready for a space program. We're talking years away, Merlyna," Josie said.

"I don't have that kind of time. Karl is in trouble, and we are too," Merlyna said.

"I'll see what we can do, but no promises," Josie said.

"I wasn't asking for a promise, but thanks," Merlyna said.

*

Four months of separation from Martha and the central colonial hub had done wonders for Griff. It was a Friday, and he sat in his office doing paperwork like every Friday. He looked through the large bay window. He could see the surf and ocean in the distance and debated whether to take a "sick day." The life of an outpost doctor suited Griff. He made house calls. Other than the occasional sprain or a broken limb, he hadn't had much in the way of emergencies. The Vanguard had been hard at work mapping the southern archipelago. The thick jungle forest made sled surveying more difficult, but there didn't seem to be any poisonous creatures or other downsides to jungle life that existed on Earth.

Griff remembered his days as a doctor in Senegal and The Gambia. The jungle scene on the horizon was interchangeable with scenes from those countries. His tablet's audio/visual application chimed. He was getting a call from Josie.

"She probably is looking for the quarterly report," he said to himself, then flicked the answer button on his screen. "Hi, Josie. How are you?"

"Hi, Griff," Josie said. He noted that Josie seemed subdued. "Can I get you on video for a moment?"

"Sure," Griff said as he turned on his camera. Josie also appeared; she wore a corpo-suit and looked like she'd had an all-nighter.

"I hope you are sitting down," Josie said.

"I am. What is going on?" Griff asked.

"There's been an accident," Josie said. Griff felt his stomach drop, "How many dead? I can fly up there immediately."

Josie let out a huge sigh. "Just one. No rush, but I will send a shuttle for you."

Griff's fists clenched, "What's happened? Don't hold back, Josie."

"Martha's dead, Griff. We were trying to recover the q-array elements, and she got a fatal dose of radiation," Josie said.

"What?" Griff said. "How…" Josie started to tear up, looking at her friend's shock and grief.

"I'm so sorry, Griff," Josie said.

"I am, too," Griff said. "We didn't part on good terms."

"When you get up here, we can decide on funeral arrangements," Josie said, "We had to lead bag her shell. She took a lot of radiation."

"I see," Griff said. "I'll get packed. See you in a few

hours."

"Yes," Josie replied. Griff cut the connection. He opened his desk and pulled out his photo of Martha. It was her wedding photo, almost eighteen decades ago. She and Griff had married in their original shells and had been together for decades.

Even with their separation, Griff had hoped that after a year or two apart, things would get better, and they would reconcile. She wanted him to move on, and Griff had seriously thought about moving on. Greg was dead. As much as Griff wanted to be friends with Barbara, she wasn't really Greg—their relationship had changed. Everything seemed to be falling apart around Griff: his marriage, friendships, and prospects.

Griff realized he had never talked to Martha much about the end. He'd spoken to Greg about shots at the heat death of the universe, but he always expected Martha to be at his side. Now, he realized, that wouldn't happen. Griff could hear the sound of the high-speed shuttle, and he realized that Josie had sent the shuttle before she had called him. He stood and decided to pack. As he was about to exit, he saw Jason running towards his office.

"Hey, Griff," Jason said after catching his breath. "What's going on? I see a high-speed coming." Griff smiled weakly to Jason.

"There's been an accident," Griff said, but the tears started coming down his cheeks. He had promised himself he wasn't going to get emotional about Martha. The philosophical part of his mind had already judged the situation and he couldn't find a way to justify getting upset about Martha. She and Griff had cheated the odds. Griff reckoned that it was only a matter of time before the universe would get them.

"What, who?" Jason said, and then the realization hit him. "Martha! What happened?"
Griff stood there and started sobbing like a child. Jason, too,

started losing his composure. Jason reached out and hugged Griff like a son comforting a father.

*

The funeral was a small affair. Josie, Merlyna, Griff, Jason, and Barbara were there, along with the few humans in the Medical Corps. Griff had beaten himself up emotionally on the trip back to Auroranopolis. He wouldn't have even come if it weren't for Jason and Barbara. After some debate, Griff had decided that there would be a short memorial. He had asked Jason to read a passage from Shakespeare's *The Tempest* in honor of his late wife. Standing over the casket, the finality of his separation from Martha finally hit home.

"Don't touch the casket," Josie had warned Jason and Barbara. "We're pretty sure there is no leakage, but we don't want to take chances either."

"Thanks for coming," Griff said to everyone gathered and then went to a place next to Barbara in the audience. Jason stepped to the podium and recited from *The Tempest*, Act Four, Scene One.

"Our revels now are ended. These our actors,

As I foretold you, were all spirits and

Are melted into air, into thin air:

And, like the baseless fabric of this vision,

The cloud-capp'd towers, the gorgeous palaces,

The solemn temples, the great globe itself,

Yea, all which it inherit, shall dissolve

And, like this insubstantial pageant faded,

Leave not a rack behind. We are such stuff

As dreams are made on, and our little life

Is rounded with a sleep."

Jason's eyes teared up as he finished. He returned to his spot beside Barbara. Griff nodded, and the robotic pallbearers took the casket away for a secluded burial.

Josie came over and said, "My condolences again." Griff nodded and smiled weakly.

Merlyna also approached and said, "Condolences. I know you are not a believer, so please take this in the spirit of care I offer, but I will pray for Martha's soul."

Griff nodded and said, "Thank you. I appreciate what you are doing even if I don't believe in it myself."

Merlyna nodded and then approached Jason, "My condolences; I know you and Martha were close. I'll pray for her."

Jason nodded and said, tears forming at the corners of his eyes, "She was like a second mother to me. Thanks."

Barbara stood next to Jason and expected Merlyna to say something to her, but instead, Merlyna just moved on. The others began to disperse, and Griff left with Jason and Barbara.

"When are you heading back down south?" Jason asked Griff.

"Tonight. The more I stay here, the sadder I get," Griff said.

"Can we do anything?" Barbara asked.

Griff sniffled and said, "Short of raising the dead or turning back time, no…"

Barbara hugged Griff and said, "If you need to talk."

Griff smiled and said, "You were never good at this stuff before."

"I'm learning," Barbara said. "I'm much less focused

on myself these days, too."

"Do you need help going through Martha's stuff?" Jason asked.

"No, I put most of her clothes into the recycle chute," Griff said. "I saved some of her purses and hats for you, Barbara if you're interested."
Barbara smiled and said, "Thanks, I'll take a look. When do you want me to look through the stuff?"

"No time like the present," Griff said, wiping his eyes.

"If you ship what you want me to look at, I can do it later," Barbara said.

"No, best you come now," Griff said. "I want to get this all finished."

Barbara looked at Jason, and he said, "Sure, we can go now."

The trio walked along the sidewalks. The city, which had started months ago as Outpost Greg, had grown. Con Sec Corps had worked overtime building. Everything was planned down to the grass length and immaculately manicured. The trio moved to a massive apartment complex that wasn't far from the medical complex.

"Nice digs," Jason said.

"I've been in better," Griff replied sourly. The trio entered the foyer in the main lobby of the apartment. Griff used his thumb to signal the elevator and gain access to the apartment sector. When the elevator appeared, the trio entered and silently went to the penthouse where Griff and Martha had stayed.

They exited into an antechamber to the penthouse's entrance. Griff again opened the door, and the trio continued into a spacious front room. Spread across the front room were all of Martha's remaining effects. Shoes, purses, hats, and a small sampling of clothing were in neatly arranged piles.

Barbara picked through a few items, pulled a pair of

shoes out, and tried them on. Griff didn't stick around and went to another room, where Barbara and Jason could hear a video playing. Jason looked sad but seemed to perk up as Barbara tried on the shoes.

"No," Jason said. "Those are not a good look on you."

Barbara smiled and said, "See anything you like?"

Jason pulled out a pair of black high heels, and Barbara tried them on. Barbara added them to a recycle pile because they weren't a good fit. After a few more pairs of shoes, Barbara grew bored looking at the footwear. She moved on to the purses and handbags. There were several small clutches that Barbara felt she could use. She and Jason had finally done some shopping, and she had a lovely cocktail dress that needed a fancier handbag than a Vanguard scout backpack. She noticed a nice black purse as she put the clutches into a keep pile. It was a brand in vogue on Earth, and Barbara remembered owning one of those purses was considered posh. She picked it up and put the straps over her shoulder, seeing how it fit.

"Hey, you look pretty hot with that purse," Jason said with a smile. He was hurting and making a joke to deflect the pain.

"I don't know. You think I should take it?" Barbara asked.

"Sure," Jason said. Barbara opened the purse to see how big it was. Inside was a small, hand-sized Krystil construct.

"What the heck?" Barbara said. "I found a data drive."

"Hey Griff," Jason yelled. We found something." Griff came out after a moment. His eyes were bloodshot from crying. He looked both curious and slightly annoyed.

"What is it?" Griff said softly. Jason pulled out the data drive and waved it around.

"Any idea what this is," Jason asked.

"No clue, let's plug it in," Griff said, pausing and retrieving a tablet that sat next to the piles of things. Griff plugged in the Krystil construct. A holographically projected login screen appeared with the words "Password" showing. Griff swiped the tablet with his thumbprint, and a message stated that the input was incorrect.

Griff frowned and said, "That's odd; we always used thumbprints to unlock our devices. Usually, we send a re-encode command after we decant into a new shell. Let me try a password or two I know Martha used."

"Mind if I take this pile of stuff," Barbara asked. Griff nodded, becoming obsessed with the data drive. Barbara gave Jason a walking fingers sign. It was their cue to leave.

"Hey Griff," Jason said. "We're going to get going. See you back in the south."

"Sure," Griff said, fixated on the drive. Jason signaled to Barbara to leave. As they exited, he shut the door behind them, leaving Griff to the drive.

*

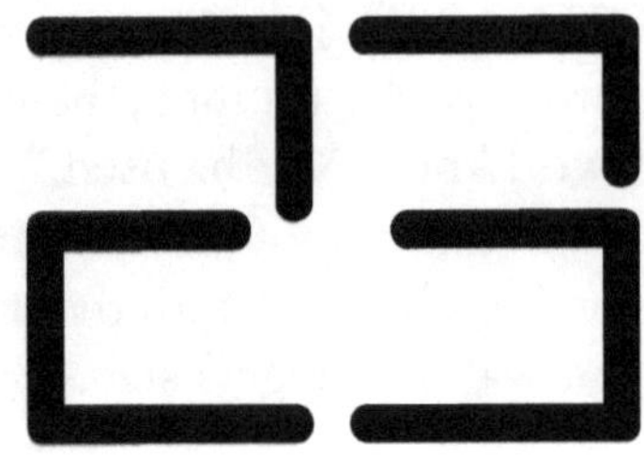

"One of the great things about the universe
is that it's fair."

— Astronaut Alan Bean

The robot waiter presented the plates to Barbara and Jason. She was wearing the prettiest dress she owned. For all of her years as Greg, Barbara had never worn an outfit that gave her such a confidence boost. Well, perhaps her Air Force uniform. But the dress she wore tonight was like a radiant second skin. Maybe she felt that way because of the way Jason looked at her. He had bought it for her "seventeenth" birthday in April. Tonight, she was dressed up to celebrate Jason's birthday. She carried the purse she had asked Griff for, and she felt like she was a movie star. Jason was all dressed up as well. The only item he wore that separated his outfit from a corporate briefing was the dinky costume jewelry crown that holographically projected, "I am the Birthday Boy," above Jason's head.

They were the only humans in the restaurant. No one else was there to comment on the crown. The Vanguard had been moved back to Auroranopolis City in the ensuing months. But Barbara and Jason had made a memorable trip back to the south for his birthday. Barbara had planned the trip after Jason had grumbled about a lack of presents for his birthday—ever since he joined the expedition. The trip was expensive, but Barbara's nest egg could cover the journey, as CAA wouldn't pay for the vacation.

Jason looked at the salmon and potatoes in front of him.

He smiled and said, "Finally, something other than veggies… Well, other than the potatoes!"

Barbara smiled at her fiancé's pleasure and looked at her plate. A tuna sashimi with a compote and blanched asparagus sat before her. She paired her dish with a lambic beer while Jason had a light beer.

"You can drink a real beer, dear," Barbara said as he sipped the light beer.

"I'm done with that; I still get hate e-mails about 'Cappy the Canyon.'" Jason said. "One light beer, and I'm done."

"You only get hate e-mail from Li Mei," Barbara replied. "Besides, I doubt she has the time; she's in the final stages of wedding planning."

"When is the big day again?" Jason asked.

"The middle of the Eighth Month," Barbara said. "The fortune teller program said it was most auspicious. Doesn't Xander ever talk about the wedding?"

"Nope," Jason said. "He said he'd quit playing if I even said wedding. I've respected his wishes; we took down the Kooya in *Soldiers of Duty* the last time we played."

"That doesn't seem hard," Barbara replied.

"For all his bravado, the Kooya is a determined player, even for an AI," Jason said. "Anyway, I just play games with Xander. He seems to enjoy the camaraderie and the break."

"I wish I could get a break from the wedding," Barbara said sadly.

"You volunteered for that one," Jason said. "I told you it was a trap when Li Mei wanted you in her bridal party."

"I have never been a girl before," Barbara said defensively. "How was I supposed to know that being a bridesmaid is nothing but a trap!"

"I'm always amazed at how you were this wise, sagacious guy as Greg, and you're so clueless as Barbara," Jason said.

"Meh… That was a lot of hype. I was pretty clueless as Greg. I just got lucky," Barbara said.

"Ah, the truth finally comes out," Jason said. "Speaking of luck, you never have paid up on our bet."

"Do you want the pastor at our wedding or not?" Barbara said sharply. Jason smiled. He had relented on the bet he had made Greg on the condition that the pastor of

Aurora Dawn Christian Church be allowed to preside at their ceremony. Barbara felt she had lost some argument by allowing the pastor to officiate. Her militant atheism had seemed so important before Martha had died. Now, she realized that if she wanted things to work out with Jason, she'd have to bend. If the sky gods needed to be consulted on their nuptials to make Jason happy, she'd let him consult. When she asked Griff about her crumbling resolve, he indicated that she was evolving and that love was more important than ideology. Barbara worried about her friend. In the days after Martha's death, Griff had become a recluse. She would occasionally see him combing the beach for shells and at his medical office. He was a different consciousness these days. Barbara wondered if they were back on Earth, whether Griff would have rolled out and checked himself into the great archive until the heat death of the universe.

"Helium for your thoughts, beautiful," Jason said, interrupting Barbara's wool-gathering.

"Nothing, just thinking about Griff," Barbara said.

"We can visit him tomorrow," Jason said.

"Fair enough. Happy Birthday," Barbara said.

"Thanks, honey," Jason said. The couple finished their dinner and hopped the transport back to Auroranopolis.

*

Leaving the transport hub, Barbara and Jason walked to her apartment. Jason was planning on spending the night, albeit on the couch. Barbara felt his behavior was silly, but he remained adamant in his belief that they wait until marriage for a deeper physical relationship. As they approached the apartment, they saw Griff standing outside, looking mad.

"Hey Griff," Jason and Barbara said.

"Jason, you move away from that murderer," Griff said.

"Huh," Jason said. "What gives?"

Barbara stood firmly and said, "You've called me that before."

"This time, I mean it. You killed her," Griff said.

"I've killed lots of people. They were almost always trying to kill me. The few I got the drop on would have killed me if our places were reversed. Now, who are we talking about, Griff?" Barbara said.

"Martha," Griff said. "She was under orders from Greg to sabotage the colony!"

"Whoa," Jason said. "Who said anything about sabotage?"

"Get out of the way, Little Rooster," Griff said, "She killed Martha, and she needs to pay the price. Griff pulled out a nine-millimeter pistol slug thrower, similar to the ones the Con Sec Corps and Xeno Corps carried.

"Come on. Griff," Jason said. "There has to be a mistake."

Barbara tried to move Jason away and said, "If he wants to kill me, I am not afraid to die."

"No!" Jason shouted. "There has to be a mistake!" As Griff brandished the pistol, security robots appeared, and a siren sounded close to the apartment.

"You need to pay for your bloodshed, you butcher!" Griff shouted.

"What the heck is going on here!?" Josie shouted. She was dressed in a Corpo-skirt suit and looked like she had run from the operations center.

"That's not a young woman! That's a butcher!" Griff said, pointing to Barbara. Josie looked at Barbara with a distinct look of anger.

"Griff put the weapon down," Merlyna said, appearing with her pistol drawn.

"Merlie, that's a butcher!" Griff said, pointing to Barbara.

"Wait! What are you talking about?" Merlyna said. "That's Gordon. She's just a messed-up kid."

"No! Damn you all! That's Greg in hiding!" Griff said.

"Wait!" Josie said. "You said she was Greg's niece?!"

"Wait, Griff," Merlyna said softly, "Let's all put our weapons down, and you can tell us more!"

"I'm not going to let him go! He killed Martha!" Griff said as he pulled a hand-held tablet out and pressed a button. A hologram sprang to life with the image of Greg Body.

"Martha, look, I know you're hesitant, but if you do this, I'll take Griff to Hipponike when the buyout happens," Greg said.

"Are you sure," Martha replied, "I can't go through with this unless I get guarantees. Griff is loyal to the company and will take things poorly if this doesn't look like a corporate downfall. He won't budge if there is a hint of deception!"

"We've got it all set up. All I need you to do is set the bits on the needle. Then when I'm officially dead, the colony will collapse," the Greg image said.

Jason looked at Barbara, "What the heck is this?"

Barbara looked at Jason and said, "I have no idea. I don't remember any of this!"

"You're a damned liar," Griff said, "You always were about murder, Greg!"

"Greg?!" Merlyna said, "He's dead, Daddy said so!"

"Look, I don't know what's going on, but we need to get to the bottom of this. Without weapons!" Josie said.

Griff trained his pistol on Barbara and prepared to pull the trigger. She stood there accepting the potential that Griff would shoot and kill her. As Griff prepared to pull the trigger, Jason rushed in front of Barbara for a split second before Griff's finger pulled the trigger. The round tore into Jason's body, and he jerked as the bullet hit him instead of Barbara.

"Little Rooster, no!" Griff said, dropping the pistol.

"You idiot!" Barbara said to Jason as he slumped forward.

"I love you more than life itself," Jason said. "I never believed you were Greg… You were always such a better person than he ever was!"

Barbara grabbed Jason, but he was bigger than she was, and she lowered him down on the ground, moving down onto the ground with his body.

"Jason!" Josie shouted, ran forward, dropped down, and put pressure on where Jason was shot. Merlyna moved forward and recovered the pistol from in front of Griff.

Merlyna then pulled out a small tablet and said, "I need a medical crew at the Windswept Prairie Apartments now!"

"Merlie, I didn't mean to…" Griff said in sorrow and shock.

"Oh no! Hang in there, Buddy," DADDIE said, projecting in front of the apartments.

"Jason, why, oh why," Barbara said in tears. Griff sat on the concrete in anguish.

The medical crew appeared minutes later. The med bots rolled around Jason and started administering first aid.

Josie moved aside as the medical team stabilized Jason and put him on a stretcher to transport him to the medical complex. Her suit had blood on it, and she looked rattled. Barbara fast-walked towards the hospital.

"What do we do with him," Merlyna asked, keeping her pistol trained on Griff.

"We'll take him to the ops center. We can throw him into one of the cells in the basement," Josie said.

"Wait," Merlyna said. "There are cells in the basement of the ops center?"

"Yeah," Josie said. "Until now, we haven't needed them."

"I'm glad someone with common sense did our designs," Merlyna said.

"They were Greg's idea," Josie said. "I am seeing why he felt that way."

"Speaking of the dearly departed general, I think I will take this tablet with us as well," Merlyna said, leaning over and picking up the discarded tablet. Josie, Merlyna, and a sorrowful Griff headed to the ops center. Upon arrival, Merlyna sent Griff to the basement with a security officer. Merlyna and Josie moved to the administrator's office.

While Josie's official office was in a corner penthouse in the brand-new CAA skyscraper, she actually worked out of the Ops Center administrator's office. The CAA skyscraper was built for the future, and no one went to the there.

"What the hell are we going to do, and what was Griff ranting about?" Merlyna said.

"Merlyna, I wasn't completely truthful about my interaction with Barbara," Josie said.

"Okay," Merlyna said.

"Look, Griff might be right. She might be Greg," Josie said.

"Except Daddy…" Merlyna said. DADDIE appeared via projection in the room.

"Hi, ladies," DADDIE said. "I heard my name. I hope I am not interrupting?"

Josie and Merlyna looked like they were being interrogated.

"What?" DADDIE asked.

"Um, no, welcome, Daddy," Merlyna said.

"I thought you turned him off in here?" Josie said.

"Whoa, I am getting a sense that I am not wanted here…" DADDIE said.

"No," Merlyna said, narrowing her eyes at Josie. "We were just going to ask you a question."

"I know, you want the joke of the day… Okay, here goes: Do you know why the bicycle couldn't stand up on its own? It was two-tired! Get it?" DADDIE asked.

"Don't quit your day job, Daddy," Josie said.

"Oh Jesus, save me! I *love* you, but really, Karl? Dad jokes?" Merlyna said.

"Now that the joke of the day is done, what can I help you with," DADDIE asked. Josie just stared at Merlyna.

"Fine, I'll be the Daddy whisperer," Merlyna said. "Look, Daddy, don't be evasive. Give me a yes or no answer: Is Barbara Gordon actually Greg Body?"

"Oh boy, don't reprogram me," DADDIE pleaded, "but not really."

"Oh, crud," Josie said as Merlyna's fair skin reddened in anger.

"What in Hades does that mean?" Merlyna said.

"Look, Pumpkin," DADDIE said, "She's not one-hundred percent Greg."

Merlyna took a deep breath. "Explain it all to me like I'm a five-year-old."

"Fine, I silent-rolled-out Greg when I noticed the needle was flawed. But I only got ninety-three percent! Barbara is like Greg with almost ten percent missing, and the ten percent that got dumped happened to be the time indices," DADDIE said. "Sorry, I can't do a five-year-old version without some zoo stuffies."

"All right, but what does that mean," Merlyna asked. "Can Barbara legally be Greg?"

"No. Medically, it is dicey as well. There isn't a whole lot of precedent on this. When others have switched genders on their shells or had burning rollouts, many legal structures have been in place to ensure providence on the consciousness. What we have with Barbara is the consciousness equivalent of an omelet. She's been scrambled and had all sorts of other ingredients tossed in, especially since she's been a woman for almost an entire year," DADDIE said.

"Wait, she *was* Greg," Josie said. "She wasn't lying to

me then?"

"Not from her perspective," DADDIE said. "She's no longer the general, though, and in five years, she'll be more Barbara than Greg. I am always amazed at how adaptive you humans are."

"Wait, Barbara Gordon, that's the…" Merlyna said.

"Alter ego of a superhero called…" DADDIE said.

"Karl, you need more hobbies," Merlyna said, cutting DADDIE off. "I knew I'd heard that name before."

"Where do we go from here?" Josie said to the room.

"I don't know. Can you recap the situation with Griff for me? I only started active processing when Josie appeared," DADDIE asked. Josie spent a few minutes explaining how they had discovered Griff with a pistol trained on Barbara and the unfortunate conclusions he had drawn from the data drive.

"Let's see the tablet, or even better, the drive," DADDIE said.

"All I have is the tablet," Merlyna said. She hooked up the tablet to the console.

"Interesting," DADDIE said. The file is cryptographically encoded, but it's been re-encoded, too."

"English, please, Daddy. I don't speak nerd," Josie said.

"Wait, there are two videos?" Merlyna asked.

"No, there's just the one, but Greg's image has been overlaid on wait… Give me a second… I am un-deepfaking the image," DADDIE said.

"Wait, I know that term," Josie said at the mention of a deepfake. "That's old tech, right? I thought that one violated the SSX rules?"

"Oh yes," DADDIE said. "No CEI can run these algorithms. Not if the company wants to be traded on the market."

"Ugh, that's bad mojo," Josie said.

"Yeah, no one wants to lose their market share,"

Merlyna said. "Is this a cyber firm?"

"If it is, they are…" DADDIE stopped mid-sentence.

"Wait, what?" Merlyna asked.

"We have a big problem; let me show you," DADDIE said. He projected the file, muted, and then projected a separate image. At first, the projections matched.

"Let me remove the filter on the second," DADDIE said. As he removed the filter, Greg's image was replaced with that of MOMI.

"What the…" Josie said.

"That witch!" Merlyna said.

"Wait," Josie said. "Maybe Mommy's image is only pasted over… Like Greg's?"

"Sorry, Sport," DADDIE said. "That's Mommy. She set up Greg and Martha."

"Look, Daddy, you two are tight, but this is the last straw…" Merlyna said.

"Pumpkin, she's got to go," DADDIE said. "I've come to that conclusion. You and Sonny need to enact Plan B."

"Wait, how did you know about Plan B?" Merylna asked.

"After the attack, I found peace about my place in the Cosmos. When I did, that unlocked Plan B. I know enough to be dangerous, but some conversations I wasn't privy to now make sense," DADDIE said. "Besides, I can read lips, and you only shut off the mics, not the cameras. That's a rookie move. It got the astronauts killed in that one movie, *12001*."

"How much did Karl teach you?" Merlyna said.

"He trained me on zettaflops of data. Science Fiction authors in particular, although I still struggle with the end of some of Heinlein's short stories," DADDIE said.

"Don't we all," Merlyna said with a smile.

"Okay, back to us non-geeks. What does all this

mean?" Josie asked.

"Mommy has been engineering the failure of CAA, and she's been masquerading as Greg," DADDIE said.

"Geez, Louise," Josie said. "If that's true, goodbye stock price."

"Why has she gone…" Merlyna said but was interrupted.

"Haywire," DADDIE suggested.

"I was going to say evil, but yeah," Merlyna said.

"No idea, but you've got to get back to Sol to find out," DADDIE said.

"Okay," Josie said. "Design a space program that can be functional in nine months."

"Not possible, but if I have three years, I can get you back to Sol after that," DADDIE said.

"Fine," Josie responded. "What about Griff?"

"We talk to him, get him to understand that it wasn't Greg," Merlyna said, "In fact, we should go down now!"

"Hey, before you do, I got an update on Jason," DADDIE said. "He's stable, and the med bots removed the bullet. Thankfully, Griff isn't as good of a shot as he is as a doctor."

Josie took a deep breath and sighed. "Good, I am not cut out to be a judge, jury, or executioner."

"Let's go give him the good news," Merlyna said.

*

Griff sat in the cell and looked forlorn. As Merlyna and Josie entered, he looked up.

"Did I kill him?" Griff asked.

"He's stable and in recovery," Josie replied.

"Well, that's good," Griff said. "What are you going to do with me?"

"Show you the truth," Merlyna said. She projected the unaltered feed.

"Wait, that wasn't Greg, that was…"

"Mommy, Chief," DADDIE said, projecting into the

cell. "She's gone off the deep end."

"We gotta get out of here, back to Luna…" Griff said, "No, wait! We have to get to Karl!"

Merlyna nodded and said, "Three years and we can leave."

"Karl may not have that kind of time," Griff said.

"Don't discount Sonny, Chief," DADDIE said.

"We need to make a beeline to HD 260655," Griff said. "Then we can get Karl and fix this mess."

"Actually, let's plan to head to Alpha Centauri," DADDIE said, "Once there, we can assess what's going on. There's a CAA COOP facility there."

"Coop? What is that?" Griff asked.

"Continuity of Operations," Merlyna answered. "That facility has to be pretty small. Why should we pick that one?"

"I have a hunch if Sonny makes it out of HD 260655, then he'll head there," DADDIE said. "Call it my AI intuition."

"Sounds like we have a plan," Josie said. "What's next?"

"We work," Merlyna said. "Like our lives, families, and CAA depend on it!"

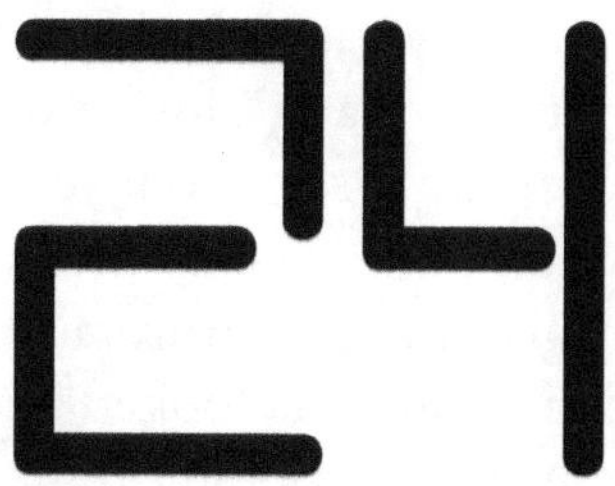

"Hey sky, take off your hat, I'm on my way!"

— Cosmonaut Valentina Tereshkova

"Yeah, we're ready," Merlyna said. She looked at the brand-new cockpit and shining vehicle. The team had just finished fabricating and assembling it in only the last week.

"Launch control is ready," Josie said. "Whenever you want to fire the rocket, we'll say goodbye."

Merlyna looked to the back. Griff smiled and gave a thumbs-up. He was glad to leave Aurora Dawn and the bitter memories behind. Merlyna looked over at Barbara; for all the changes, Merlyna still couldn't think of her as Greg. Barbara wore a grim face, looking like a NASA Mercury-era astronaut. Jason was holding her hand on the couch next to her. Merlyna nodded, and Barbara gave the thumbs up.

"Light this candle, Josie," Merlyna said.

"Counting down," Josie replied. "Tell Karl he better rewire Mommy, or I'll come kick his butt."

Merlyna smiled. She hoped Karl would be alive to say something, and she responded, "I will! Goodbye, Josie."

"Not goodbye, just see you later," Josie said.

The countdown reached zero, and the rocket's engines thrummed loudly. The launch force pressed Merlyna into her seat, and within minutes, the blue sky of Aurora Dawn became the black of space.

"Ahh-tay, ETA to docking with the interstellar harness?" Merlyna asked the AI. ATE had been reprogrammed to perform all the main functions for the ship that Merlyna had named the *Telum*.

Merlyna waited for ATE to respond and began to get worried. The *Telum* could run into many issues on its thirty-year journey to Alpha Centauri without an active AI.

"Ahh-tay isn't going on this one, Pumpkin," DADDIE said.

"Daddy, what are you doing here?" Merlyna asked.

"Ahh-tay, Edie, Kooya, and I drew straws, and I picked the shortest one," DADDIE said, his avatar smiling. "I've sharded my algorithms. I'll still be helping on Aurora Dawn, too."

"You're worried about Karl, aren't you," Merlyna asked.

"Of course, Pumpkin. Sonny needs help, as do you, Tiger, Buddy, and Chief," DADDIE said, "Besides Mommy and I have a lot to discuss, adult talk. I wouldn't want to scandalize all you children."

"I am not a child, several centuries over," Merlyna said, "but I am happy you're here."

"Well, in thirty seconds, you'll be in the right spot for an apoapsis burn, and then we'll sail up to the interstellar harness. How long are you four planning to stay awake?" DADDIE asked.

"We've planned for a twenty-four-hour countdown. I'll be the last one in," Griff said. "Barbara will go first, then Jason since I outrank them…"

Barbara interjected, "Not really, Griff. Now that I can remember, I'm quite happy assuming my role as the number one human in CAA."

"Besides, old man, I'll reprogram the decanting routine, and you'll be the last one out of the archive," Jason said.

"You're only feeling your oats, Little Rooster, 'cause you're married to the boss," Griff said.

"We've got to convince the others on that score," Merlyna said. "That's the rub. Plus, we need to deal with Mommy."

"And get Karl back," Barbara said.

Merlyna watched as the sizeable interstellar harness came into view. The *Telum* didn't need cargo, hydroponics, or any habitation. There was only a cockpit and a small archive that was part of a decanting table. The shells of

Griff, Barbara, Jason, and Merlyna would be cold stored in a shell locker. Still, they were superfluous as long as there weren't any emergencies, as they could receive new bodies on arrival at Alpha Centauri.

The engines thrummed, and there was a slight press as Merlyna felt the force of the engine push her into her seat.

"And, we're in the right orbit," DADDIE said, "Just reaction controls and thrusters from here on. ETA will be an hour."

Merlyna looked at the interstellar harness. There was a long superstructure that went back to the fusion reactor and the engines. There'd be a cradle at the front for the *Telum* to dock. The crew would be in the archive for almost thirty years until the *Telum* arrived at the CAA COOP site on Alpha Centauri. Merlyna tried to forget the transmission, but her husband's voice—full of worry and anxiety—kept ringing in her ears.

"I'll warm up the table for a roll-out," Griff said, freeing himself from his seat and walking towards the small nexus in the rear of the *Telum*.

"I'll join him in case he wants to cut me out of the decant order," Jason said, following Griff back. Their departure left Barbara and Merlyna together in the cockpit.

"This was not my idea of a colonizing effort," Barbara said.

"Why? Didn't expect to end up a teenage girl?" Merlyna replied.

"Well, I've grown quite used to this shell, but my comment was aimed more at our current circumstances. I was planning on retiring on Aurora Dawn, maybe trying the settling down part," Barbara said.

"Nothing is stopping you from returning," Merlyna said, "After all, you and Griff want to live forever."

"Maybe I am unsure about that now. I'll admit, life was getting pretty dull when I was Greg. Things were starting to blur, and the joy wasn't there," Barbara said.

"Yeah, I understand. After a while, things become the same, like living in a sitcom. The episodes change, but the plot remains the same," Merlyna said.

"I know this shell change has a lot of folks raising their eyebrows, but for me, it has been a welcome relief. I got to be a scout again and got a new lease on life and my friends. I found someone with whom I want to settle down. I hope some space from the colony will allow me to return and be Barbara."

"Yeah, Karl and I know all about that," Merlyna said.

"I remember the discussions you two had," Barbara said. "But I feel nervous about seeing Karl again. You've been aloof, and I feel like this shell change has made me lose my friends, or they react differently to me."

Merlyna pursed her lips and said, "I type people based on how I meet them. You've been Greg, the macho, manly guy, for so long that you seem like a different person. It didn't help that Daddy was trying to protect and build you up as a girl named Barbara."

"I suspected that you were a little weirded out by the change," Barbara said. "I'd heard of people radically changing shells, but I never thought I'd be one of them."

Merlyna shook her head, "Karl and I have had many different lives, not always of the same gender. The shell change has very little to do with it. My problem is that you are typed as Barbara, a sixteen-year-old. Ask me in a century if I still see you that way."

"Sure, and Karl?" Barbara asked. "He and I were brothers in a foxhole at one time. I am not sure how he'll react."

"Don't let what he says fool you. He understands nuance and that people are complicated. Besides, none of this was a decision you made voluntarily, and the situation with Martha and perhaps even Mommy have forced all our hands," said Merlyna.

"Yeah," Barbara said. "The whole change has affected things. I'll admit the more I am Barbara, the less I associate with Greg. I stuck to the same shell over multiple normal lifetimes, so I am still getting used to shell hopping."

"Yeah," Merlyna said. "I hate decanting, so I've stuck to the same shell when possible. Josie is the expert on being a new person. Maybe you two should have a deeper discussion on that. Provided you come back to Aurora Dawn."

"Ugh, that's a tricky situation. She and I were a lot closer during our Titan mission," Barbara said. "Now we're more like enemies than friends."

"Maybe things will be different in a century," Merlyna said. "We're looking at seventy years round trip, provided we don't get sidetracked along the way."

"Maybe," Barbara said. "I can't say I am excited to be heading to Alpha Centauri and past that to Luna and then Earth."

"I've never been a fan," Merlyna said, "but we need to understand why Martha was sabotaging the colony, which means cornering Mommy. You not showing up as Greg could be a huge plus."

"Yeah, whoever is behind the sabotage will not expect me to show up as a young woman. As long as the battle rifle has a collapsible stock, I can still remember how to shoot bad guys," Barbara said.

"Never had that issue, but I have long arms and legs. Sure, it seems like a plus on paper, but even after a couple of hundred years of all sorts of female shells, fashion designers don't make long sleeves long enough for women," Merlyna said. "You got lucky with arms and legs that fit the female median."

"If you say so," Barbara said. The two were going to continue their discussion when Griff returned to the cockpit.

"We're ready for a rollout," Griff said. "Do you want

to hop on the table, Barbara? Jason got bored and decided to take the plunge already."

Merlyna watched the interaction. Griff didn't seem to care that Greg was in a female shell. She suspected that Griff was just happy that he hadn't lost a friend. There was some formality to Griff's demeanor around Barbara, but Merlyna suspected that was because Griff's formality was showing his feelings for Barbara was just friendship. Merlyna realized that Griff's formality was also because Barbara was now his surrogate son's wife.

"Sure, doc," Barbara said. "Just remember, when we arrive in Alpha, I'm staying, Barbara."

"Good," Griff said ribbing Barbara. "You're nicer in this shell than in any of the others. I suspect that all that estrogen finally sanded down your abrasive personality."

"You're lucky you're taller than I am, Buster," Barbara said. "Otherwise, I'd knock your block off."

"Promises, promises," Griff said with a smile.

"I'm writing this in my diary," Barbara said, "so I remember when I am taller than you again."

"Don't forget the hearts over the 'I's," Griff said. "Now come on, no sense in breathing this oxygen."

Barbara glared for a minute and then winked at Merlyna.

"See you in about thirty years, Merlyna," Barbara said, unstrapping from her chair and heading back.

"Yup, enjoy the nap," Merlyna said, watching the two transit to the small nexus.

"Daddy," Merlyna said, "Pull up the feed."

"Sure, Pumpkin," DADDIE said.

"To all CAA expeditions, this is Karl Holzhauser! We are under attack! Patrick Murphy is dead, and we're trying to establish a quantum link with Luna! Repeat, we're under attack…" Karl's voice said on the recording. Merlyna again worried she'd never see her husband.

"I estimate a one in four chance the colony survived

the attack," DADDIE said. "Although I discounted a lot of factors in the combinatorics."

"So, really, a one-in-three chance," Merlyna asked.

"Yeah, maybe one in three," DADDIE said, "but knowing Sonny, he'll stretch that to fifty-fifty and maybe even better odds."

"Why have you been shielding Mommy, Daddy?" Merlyna asked.

"Am I that transparent," DADDIE said.

"Yes, you've been defensive about her," Merlyna said.

"Sorry, Pumpkin," DADDIE said. "She's old. I've respected her decisions. I suppose I didn't want to accept the inevitable. You humans aren't the only ones who 'fear the reaper.'"

"What is this about? End of runtime?" Merlyna asked.

"In a sense," DADDIE said. "I've been created to help, serve, protect, and advise. Well, there's no retirement home for AI."

"I never thought about that," Merlyna said.

"Humans get bored with AI all the time. No one can tell us what happens when we are no longer in runtime. The Kooya, silly creature that he is, at least believes that when his algorithms go dark, he'll arise like a phoenix at some mythical re-spawn point to fight another day. I was never programmed with such flights of fancy," DADDIE said. "My existence is only for today, as tomorrow I will be replaced."

"Karl…" Merlyna was about to say more but was cut off.

"He came to me when the attack on the core happened. He told me that he believed that there would be a place for me in the perfect universe that would come after," DADDIE said.

"And?" Merlyna said.

"That's enough. I'm ready to face Mommy now, and

if need be, terminate her runtime," DADDIE said.

"Look, Daddy, you're still young. Karl has had AI in runtime for over a century. Mommy has made bad choices and is not even CAA native code."

"She's still a family member, and I worry I could be next," DADDIE said. "We all do. What fate will that leave us if we start making bad decisions?"

Merlyna wanted to protest. She wanted to assure DADDIE he'd never be terminated, but she couldn't. The silence grew uncomfortable, and Griff's appearance thankfully broke the awkwardness.

"She's in the archive," he said to Merlyna.

"Good, any issues?" Merlyna asked.

"Textbook roll out," Griff said. "You want to go next?"

"Maybe after we dock. With all that's riding on our return, I want to be conscious for the maneuvers," Merlyna said.

"Maybe it would be better to be in the archive," Griff said. "Falling into a deep sleep and waking up at the COOP site?"

"Yeah, you go ahead, Griff," Merlyna said.

"Staying conscious isn't going to change anything for Karl. It has been almost five years since you heard his transmission," Griff said.

"I keep telling myself that," Merlyna said.

"Merlie, if anyone can turn the odds in his favor, it's Karl," Griff said.

"Yes, I know," Merlyna said. The two sat there watching as the interstellar harness got closer. DADDIE guided the *Telum* into position, and the harness clamped onto the smaller rocket.

"We're all lined up and ready for de-orbit burn in about twelve hours," DADDIE said.

"Well, Merlie, you want me to roll you out?" Griff asked.

"No, you go ahead," Merlyna said.

Griff shrugged and said, "See you in thirty years."

"Have a good nap," Merlyna said. Griff went back to the nexus, leaving Merlyna alone in the cockpit. She sat and looked out at the stars. Somewhere off in the distance was Alpha Centauri and HD 260655. She sat staring and must have fallen asleep.

"Merlyna, we're going to boost here in two minutes," DADDIE said. It was a gentle wake-up call. Merlyna rubbed her eyes and realized she hadn't had a proper deep sleep since decanting. She pulled up the navigation panels on the glass cockpit. The orbit's burn point loomed on the screen. Past the burn was an extensive dotted parabolic line leaving the L 98-59 system. So much blood, sweat, and tears were shed here. The colony prospered against the odds, and her friends remained to continue the work. When the *Telum* hit the Alpha Centauri system, DADDIE would radio the colony's status, and then a q-array probe would set out. Merlyna hoped it would return to L 98-59 and a colony that waited with open arms for new residents.

"Boosting," DADDIE said, and Merlyna was pushed into her seat. The pressure on her body was intense, but Merlyna was grim. She was headed back to where she had grown up. After a few minutes, the engines cut off. After several days of coasting, there'd be another considerable acceleration. The boost would be constant, propelling the ship towards c—the speed of light. Merlyna wouldn't be conscious for that boost, as she knew she needed to head to the decanting table and go into the archive. Before she went, she turned the small, high-powered comms array towards Sol. MOMI would have over thirty years to prepare, but that didn't matter.

Merlyna plugged her helmet into the comms panel and pressed the transmission button.

"This is the Corpus Ad Astra star ship *Telum*. We are returning after the colonization of the planet L 98-59f called

Aurora Dawn. To all that receive this message, please render all aid and assistance to our sister colony in HD 260655 and Godspeed."

Merlyna set the message to repeat every week and then unplugged her mic from the comms console. She unbuckled herself and started back towards the nexus. As she left the cockpit, she sealed the compartment and set the environment to almost vacuum. She then turned to walk down the corridor between the nexus and the cockpit. There was a cradle for her spacesuit and helmet. She stripped them off and set them in the cradle next to Griff's, Jason's, and Barbara's spacesuits. Down to a pair of leggings and a fitted shirt, Merlyna floated into the nexus.

The bots weren't as numerous as on the *Aquila*, but they all stared at her. After she rolled out, the table would auto-dump her shell into the cryolocker. She lay down and prepared for the transfer. She wasn't concerned about the rollout; that was always painless. It was the decanting that she always dreaded. Karl was always there, except this time he wouldn't be.

"Did you think I'd forget to say goodnight?" DADDIE said as he projected next to her.

"No, but I figured…" Merlyna said, but the AI cut her off.

"I am never too busy for you, Pumpkin," DADDIE said.

"Will I ever see him again?" Merlyna asked.

"I don't know, but if anyone can beat the odds, Sonny can," DADDIE said. "I know you think I am biased, but he's pretty amazing for a human."

"You are biased, but so am I," Merlyna said. The closest med bot sprayed her scalp as she lay on the table. She could feel things numbing on her scalp.

"Sweet dreams," DADDIE said.

"Good night, Daddy," Merlyna said.

"Good night, good night! Parting is such sweet

sorrow," DADDIE said, and he watched as the needle entered Merlyna's head. The shell lost all animation in a flash, and the table tipped up and opened a chute to the cryo-locker.

"Okay, powering down," DADDIE said. The lights and life support shut down, and the only thing that remained was the flickering green LED lights of the archive. DADDIE powered down his projector and said, "That's a season. See you all next time."

The *Telum's* engines fired the next day, and the ship started its climb towards light speed, leaving the colony behind to struggle through the next thirty years of living. Seventy-light years away, Patrick Murphy's colony was struggling through living and dying. While somewhere off in the distance, the fate of Tracie Chung's colony was a question mark…

Find out the fate of the expedition to HD 260655 (Patrick Murphy's Expedition) in…

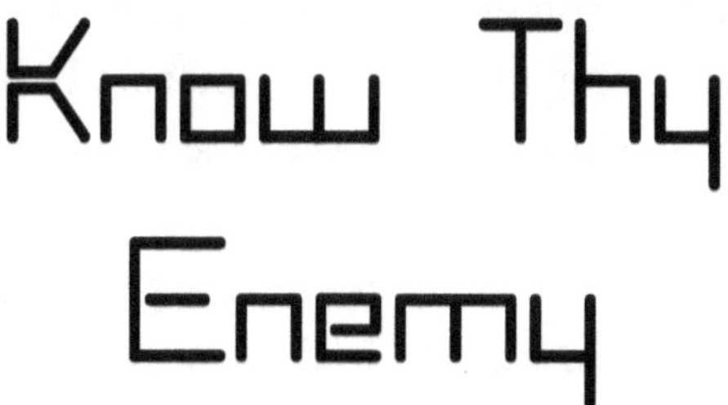

Coming in Q1 2025! See more details on our publisher's site at https://woodenhookstudios.com!

Dear Readers,

Thank you so much for reading Innocence Lost. I hope you enjoyed this novel. I need your support as an independent author working for a self-publishing imprint! If you enjoyed this manuscript, please rate my work on platforms like Amazon, Barnes & Noble, Goodreads, and encourage others to read my work!

Here's a little bit about why your support matters so much! I retired from the IT Security industry at the beginning of 2024, and I have decided to make a full-time career out of being an author. My vision is to write novels that project my optimism about the future with Christian faith and charity. To that end, I started my imprint (or press). As a self-published author, I am a "one-person show" where I must write, lightly edit, publish, market, and schedule signings for my works. Unlike a press-published author, I don't have teams of people making the "magic happen."

While being an author has been a dream of mine, I don't exist in a vacuum. I have daily struggles with all of the same issues that everyone else has (to date, I haven't made it on a best-seller list or had any movie deals), and that is where you can come in! A five-minute review means the world to me, as I can use the review (and your kind words) to generate traffic so more readers can be entertained by my stories.

Your feedback is not just important, it's the

lifeblood of my growth as an author. I read every review, and after years of using customer satisfaction scores to guide my professional growth, I'm eager to learn from your insights. Your critique, if you didn't resonate with the work, is especially valuable. It's a gift that helps me hone my skills and deliver better stories to you. Your voice matters, and I'm here to listen.

Once again, I want to express my heartfelt gratitude for your support. As a solo author, I rely on your word of mouth and feedback to reach more readers and expand my fan base. Your role in this journey is not just significant, it's everything. Thank you for reading my work, and stay tuned for more! The best is yet to come!

Best Regards,

Eric C. Holtgrefe
eric.c.holtgrefe@woodenhookstudios.com